PRAISE FOR ANDREA J. STEIN

PRAISE FOR *DEAR ELIZA*

"Touching and deeply romantic, *Dear Eliza* is a tender love story about a heroine whose bravery in the face of grief leads to discovery and the possibility of romance."
—Abbi Waxman, bestselling author of *The Bookish Life of Nina Hill* and *Adult Assembly Required*

"The beautiful and heartfelt tale of a woman who goes looking for her biological father and ends up finding herself. Andrea Stein deftly dances on the line between grief and love—keeping the story upbeat without shying away from the depths of emotion. I loved it!"
—Colleen Oakley, *USA Today* bestselling author of *The Mostly True Story of Tanner & Louise*

"A wonderful journey of resilience, grief, and love told in Andrea J. Stein's beautiful, breezy prose. *Dear Eliza* grabbed me from page one and did not let go!"
—Jane L. Rosen, author of *Seven Summer Weekends*

"Written with humor and hope, *Dear Eliza* is the story of a young woman navigating the complexities of loss, love, and family. I couldn't put it down! Perfect for fans of Katherine Center and Mhairi McFarlane."
—Elyssa Friedland, author of *Jackpot Summer*

"*Dear Eliza* is a deeply felt exploration of grief, mothers and daughters, and the secrets we keep from others and ourselves."
—Laura Hankin, author of *One-Star Romance*

"*Dear Eliza* is an engaging and heartfelt look at grief, the consequences of long-held secrets, and the true meaning of family. Stein's writing is thoughtful and well crafted with splashes of humor in all the right places. I was Team Eliza from page one!"
—Lisa Roe, author of *Welcome to the Neighborhood*

"*Dear Eliza* skillfully examines how family ties unravel when the loss of a parent exposes a shocking secret that sends a young woman reeling. Timely and relatable, this novel is a perfectly paced exploration of loss, love, and learning how to carry on when your world is turned upside down. Brimming with just the right mix of humor and heart, *Dear Eliza* is sure to be a book-club favorite."
—Liz Alterman, author of *The House on Cold Creek Lane*

"*Dear Eliza* is an emotionally compelling story filled with tension and drama that hooked me from the start, with vivid characters so real that they jump off the page. Stein has crafted a compulsive narrative that examines the complications of uncovered family secrets while exploring the question, Where do we go from here? A juicy, heart-tugging read."
—Annie Cathryn, award-winning autho
of *The Friendship Breaku*

"Andrea J. Stein's stunning sophomore novel, *Dear Eliza*, i
must-read! As Eliza navigated her complicated feelings of gr
while simultaneously learning that her parents weren't wh
she thought they were, I couldn't put this heartfelt, engag
and ultimately hopeful book down. I loved everything ab

it—especially its relatable, funny, honest heroine, who will stay with you long after you turn the last page. Perfect for fans of Josie Silver and Jennifer Weiner."

—Angela Terry, award-winning author of *The Palace at Dusk*

PRAISE FOR *TYPECAST*

"Callie is wise, knows what she wants, and has a sense of humor you can't help but love; however, the most remarkable thing readers get to witness about this main character is her journey of coming to terms with herself to make amends with the past."

—BuzzFeed

"Filled with many great supporting characters, Stein's writing is sharp and her character development for Callie is strong . . . Perfect for fans of Josie Silver."

—*Booklist*

"Stein's novel presents a charming tale of first love and second chances that's likely to entertain fans of the works of Emily Giffin . . . A heartwarming modern romance for movie mavens."

—*Kirkus Reviews*

"Jumping between past and present, you will get sucked into both versions of Callie's world."

—*Her Campus* magazine

"A clever mix of ingredients: a strong and intelligent heroine (although she might not realize it), a messy plot, and . . . a healthy dose of 90s nostalgia."

—*Literary Mama*

DEAR ELIZA

DEAR ELIZA

a novel

Andrea J. Stein

FLASH POINT

Published by Flashpoint Books™, Seattle
www.flashpointbooks.com

Produced by Girl Friday Productions

Cover design: Bailey McGinn
Production editorial: Laura Dailey
Project management: Kristin Duran

ISBN (paperback): 978-1-959411-70-3
ISBN (ebook): 978-1-959411-71-0

Library of Congress Control Number: 2024902021

First edition

For my mother, who was my most ardent champion and who I miss more than words can say

CHAPTER ONE

Eliza surveyed the dining room table, which was groaning beneath the array of shiva platters, wondering if the dish of pickles in her hand would be the straw that broke the camel's back. She found a spot for it between a pyramid of bakery cookies adorned with multicolored sprinkles and a plate of overstuffed sandwiches. At the last minute, she plucked a half-sour wedge from the plate and sank her teeth into it.

"Eliza, dear, I'm so sorry!" A hand came down on her shoulder, and she turned, quickly trying to swallow the pickle without choking.

"Thanks, Mrs. Kazinsky," she mumbled as the older woman pulled her into an awkward hug. She smelled of lavender and mothballs.

Mrs. Kazinsky released her, and Eliza pushed wisps of hair from around her own eyes. They had escaped the messy bun on the top of her head. She hadn't intended it to be a messy bun, but it had become one as the endless day wore on.

"How are you doing, dear?" Mrs. Kazinsky had been her parents' next-door neighbor for ages. *When did she get so wrinkled?*

"I'm okay." Eliza shrugged. "You know."

Mrs. Kazinsky nodded. "I keep thinking about when your mother passed away. Poor, poor Laura. It feels like yesterday. Funny how ten years can go by just like that. How old were you then? Seventeen?"

The back of Eliza's throat burned. "Sixteen."

"Sixteen!" Mrs. Kazinsky shook her head sadly. "And now you've lost both your parents."

"Yes, Mrs. Kazinsky. I know."

The older woman patted her arm, but Eliza interrupted quickly before she could speak again. "I'm sorry, I need to see if Carol needs help."

"Oh, yes, of course."

Eliza left the dining room, her eyes trained on the floor. But instead of the shiny wood planks, she saw herself as a five-year-old, sitting on her mother's lap watching TV past her bedtime. She was utterly convinced that, if she didn't turn around, her mother wouldn't know she was there. Now her twenty-six-year-old self hoped the same magic would work—cloaking her in invisibility as she made her way through the house. Despite the excuse she'd given to Mrs. Kazinsky, Carol was the last person she wanted to see. She slipped down the hall to the back door and stepped outside, sucking in a deep breath of the crisp fall air—early this year—before flattening herself against the back wall of the Levinger house.

The small backyard was usually neatly kept, but no one had raked the leaves that had just begun to litter the lawn. Inside the house, there was a framed photograph of Eliza and her brother, Scott, nearly buried in a pile of leaves they had jumped into moments earlier. Scott was laughing, his mouth wide open, and Eliza was gazing at him adoringly, the way only a younger sister could look at her beloved older brother. She wasn't sure if she actually remembered that day or if it was just the picture that had fixed the image so firmly in her mind.

The door next to her creaked, and she jumped. *Please let it not be Carol.*

"Hiding out, huh?" Scott stepped outside. "I figured I'd find you here."

Eliza had no response, so she didn't make any. She still couldn't get used to seeing her brother in a suit, even though he surely wore one to work every day. And he'd worn one when he'd gotten married. Nonetheless, it always made her think of another framed photo in the house—of Scott standing on the bimah the day of his bar mitzvah. It used to hang next to another photo, of all four of them that same day—their mother wearing a dark green crepe dress, with sleeves that ended at her elbows. That photo had disappeared from the wall shortly after Carol moved in.

"It's times like these I wish I smoked," Scott quipped, shoving his hands into his pockets.

"You could always start," offered Eliza.

"Yeah, no, I think I have enough vices."

Eliza snorted. The idea of Scott having vices was beyond ridiculous. Not Scott, the golden child.

He raised his eyebrows. "Oh, you may think I'm perfect, but go talk to Maren. She could give you a long list of my faults."

"Where is she anyway?"

"Sitting with Carol."

No wonder she hadn't seen her sister-in-law.

"You've got to work on that poker face of yours, sis." Scott shook his head. "You know, she really did make Dad happy. And she's totally devastated."

Carol hadn't been able to speak at the funeral. She couldn't stop crying. Her eyes had been puffy even before the service started. Eliza wanted to be a better person. The kind of person who could be a comfort to her stepmother. But given their history, it was hard for her to think kindly toward Carol, even now. Perhaps especially now that time had run out for Eliza to fix her broken relationship with her dad—a relationship Carol had done nothing but widen the cracks in.

Leaning against the back wall of the house, she smoothed the nonexistent wrinkles in her knee-length black skirt, which she wore with black tights and tall black boots. Her black sweater was making her itch. She wished she'd been able to find something else in her closet that would have been appropriate to wear, but there hadn't been much time.

When her mom died, Aunt Claude had taken her to buy a dress. She dragged her through Macy's, Eliza's eyes trained on her own red Chuck Taylors instead of on the dresses Claude was trying to show her. What difference did it make what she wore to her mother's funeral? It wouldn't bring her back, and why would anyone care what she looked like?

Claude pulled her to a mirror and pointed her face at it, holding a dress in front of her. Eliza dragged her eyes up from her Chucks to look at the dress. It had long sleeves and a boatneck. Decorative buttons adorned the shoulders. On any other day, she would have announced that she wasn't forty years old and that the dress was hideous. On that day, however, she was silent, waiting for her aunt to say something. When she didn't, Eliza raised her eyes higher to meet Claude's in the mirror. Her aunt was crying.

Claude quickly swiped at her tears and sniffed. "Oh, Liza, I'm so sorry. I just look at you and think, *No girl your age should be shopping for a dress to wear at her own mother's funeral.*"

Eliza looked back down at her Chucks. Who could have imagined they'd be so interesting?

Claude cleared her throat and patted Eliza's shoulders. "Anyway. Let's try this on. If it fits, let's get out of here."

It did fit, and on the way home, they stopped for ice cream. Eliza managed to eat half her small cup of chocolate before it melted into soup. By the time her appetite came back, she'd lost twelve pounds.

"Liza? Yoo-hoo?" Scott was waving his hand in front of her face. "Where'd you go?"

Eliza blinked. "Sorry. What did you say?"

Scott exhaled loudly. "Nothing. Doesn't matter." He looked away, staring unseeing across the yard before turning back to her. "How are you doing, anyway?"

She shrugged. "You?"

Scott closed his eyes and pinched the bridge of his nose. "I just can't believe it, you know? Dad was never sick a day in his life."

Eliza raised her eyebrows. "Or maybe he just didn't want to admit it. Always the tough guy."

"Maybe." Scott pressed his lips together—a childhood habit he hadn't broken. Eliza knew he was trying not to cry, and she reached out to touch his arm. It was Scott who had called her on Monday with the news. Carol had come home to find their dad, Jack, on the kitchen floor. He was already dead. Eliza couldn't count how many times people had asked her in the past three days if her dad had heart problems. No one knew the answer because he never went to the doctor. Perhaps he'd had enough of doctors during his first wife's two-year-long death march.

Scott squeezed Eliza's hand. "I'm okay," he said, and Eliza wondered if he was speaking to her or to himself. "We should probably go back inside."

Leave it to Scott to "should" her into doing the right thing.

He opened the back door and stepped aside, allowing her to go first.

More people had arrived, and a loud burst of laughter erupted from the dining room, where there was now a dent in the cookie pyramid. Eliza had a sudden memory of screaming at Aunt Claude ten years earlier. "I'm not going back downstairs. Everyone is acting like it's a party. And Mom is *dead*!" Eliza slipped into the powder room. Before she even realized she was going to do it, she ran her wrists under the cold water, a trick her mom had taught her when she felt anxiety bubbling up inside her. *When your heart starts beating so fast that the blood is pounding in your ears, the cold water will slow it down. Just keep your wrists under until you can breathe again.* Adult Eliza wasn't sure if Laura's explanation made any medical sense, but somehow the trick still worked for her.

She took a deep breath and looked at herself in the mirror. With the tip of her pinky finger, she repaired her eyeliner. Her honey-blond hair was barely contained in its bun, so she pulled it down and twisted it into a long braid over her right shoulder. It still looked messy, but it was the best it was going to be.

As soon as she left the bathroom, one of her dad's golf buddies spotted her. And then she was back running the gauntlet of neighbors, friends of her dad's, cousins, and some old friends of hers and Scott's who still lived in Westchester—or near enough to drop in for the Jack Levinger shiva. Maren convinced her to have something to eat, and when she returned to the living room after managing to swallow a few bites of corned beef, Aunt Claude had arrived. Claude's hair was still dark thanks to the wonders of chemistry, but golden highlights helped conceal the gray as the roots grew out. She was wearing the trim black suit she'd worn at the funeral, even though she'd gone home after the cemetery service to drop off Uncle Mitch.

Claude's hand was on Carol's arm, and Carol was introducing her to someone Eliza didn't recognize. "This is Claudia, Jack's sister-in-law. I mean, she was Laura's sister."

Eliza hovered on the periphery, waiting to catch her aunt's eye. It didn't take long—it was as if Claude had special Eliza radar—and before she knew it, she was enveloped by the firm hug she knew so well.

"Oh, Liza, so sorry I couldn't get here sooner," Aunt Claude whispered into her hair.

And for the first time, Eliza allowed the tears to fall.

Later that evening, after the rabbi had come and gone and the prayers had been said and only a few stragglers remained, Eliza granted herself permission to leave. She gave Carol a hug—which her stepmother accepted without returning—and followed Claude out the door so her aunt could drive her to the train station. Scott and Maren had headed back to the city a little earlier.

Claude put her arm around her as they headed toward the street. "I'm not going to ask how you're doing," she said with a little laugh.

Eliza smiled wryly back. "And I'm not going to tell you," she replied.

Then Claude's face changed. "Actually, I need to give you something. I'm not sure if now is the time, but I don't know when the right time is."

Eliza looked at her, puzzled, and wrapped her arms around herself. It was chilly, even now that she was wearing her jacket.

"Let's get into the car."

Eliza nodded and followed Claude, sliding into the front seat. It had been a long time since she'd been in her aunt's car. Then, Claude still had the minivan, but now that her two kids had left for college, she'd downsized to a sedan. Teddy and Nora were both plane rides away and, not surprisingly, hadn't flown in for their uncle's funeral. Though Claude had remained snugly rooted in Eliza's and Scott's lives, the rest of Laura's family had drifted away after Jack married Carol less than a year after Laura's death.

Claude sat behind the steering wheel, her large purse in her lap. "Okay, so," she started, and then paused.

Eliza's eyebrows drew together as she waited.

"So," Claude started again. "I have this letter."

Something in her aunt's voice made Eliza's heart beat a little faster, and her body temperature dropped another degree.

Claude reached into her purse and pulled out a standard white business envelope with something written on it. She held it for a moment before speaking again, as if she were considering stuffing it back into the bag and pretending it didn't exist.

Finally, she took a deep breath. "Your mom wrote this before . . . before she died. She asked me to hold it for you."

Eliza's hands went cold, and she clasped them together to keep them from shaking. Her aunt looked at her as if she were trying to see into her mind. Or her heart.

"I didn't give it to you before because she specifically wanted you to have it only after your dad was gone." Claude continued to hold the letter tightly in both hands.

Eliza's mouth was dry, and it took two tries before she could speak. "What does it say?"

Claude shook her head slowly. "I don't know." She passed the envelope to Eliza, who reached for it with one trembling hand.

On the front, in blue ink and in her mother's script, it said *For Eliza*. Underneath, in Claude's careful print, it said *Give to Eliza only after Jack's death.*

As if she could read her niece's mind, Claude quickly explained, "I wrote the instructions in case something happened to me. I wanted to make sure Mitch and Nora and Teddy would know what to do."

Eliza bit her lip. Somehow, she was no longer twenty-six. She was sixteen again, and when she looked down at her feet she expected to see her red Chucks in place of her high-heeled black boots. Why would her mother have written a letter for her that she wouldn't see for . . . how many years? Jack was fifty-nine when he dropped dead. No one could have expected this. Maybe her mother had thought she'd be getting this letter twenty years from now. Thirty years from now. She smoothed it out on her lap.

"I don't know what to do," she whispered.

"Do you want to open it here, with me?" Claude reached out, putting her hand on Eliza's knee. Her fingernails were perfect plum-colored ovals.

Eliza's breathing was shallow, and she felt a little light-headed. Part of her wanted to rip open the envelope immediately. But another part wanted to just hold it for a while. She had never thought she'd have any other words from her mother. This wasn't ever going to happen again.

"Are you okay?" Claude rubbed her knee, and Eliza looked up.

She shrugged helplessly and then had a sudden thought. "Do you have any other letters?" Maybe Laura had written one for her wedding day. Or the birth of her first child.

Claude shook her head sadly. "No, this is it."

"Is there one for Scott?"

Her aunt shook her head again.

"And you have no idea what's in it?"

Another shake of the head. Eliza nodded slowly. "I think I want to read it alone, if you don't mind."

"Are you sure?"

Claude's concern wasn't surprising. Or unreasonable, given Eliza's history. But she needed to have this final moment with her mother alone.

Claude nodded. "You know I'm here for you, right?"

She did. Sometimes she wondered if her cousins resented

how much attention their mother had paid her when Laura was dying and after she was gone. Claude had spread herself so thin being both a mom to her own kids and a substitute mom to her niece, especially once Scott left for college and Carol entered the picture.

"Don't worry. I'll be okay." Even as Eliza said the words, she wondered if they were true.

CHAPTER TWO

Eliza was in a fog as she rode the train to Grand Central Station. She'd tucked the envelope into her purse and kept checking that it was still there—the same way she did when she went to the airport and needed constant reassurance that she'd brought her ID with her. She almost wished she'd read the letter sitting in the car next to Aunt Claude—if only so she wouldn't be so afraid she'd lose it before knowing what her mother had written.

Clutching her handbag under her arm as she made her way to the subway uptown, she began the final leg home, finally emerging at her stop on the Upper East Side. She was practically shaking by the time she got into her apartment and slid the deadbolt shut.

After forcing herself to hang up her jacket and pull off her boots, she sat down on the sage green loveseat that served as the sofa in her tiny apartment. Then she jumped up again to find a knife in the kitchen to use as a letter opener. She carefully slit the envelope and slid out a single folded sheet of paper, which she brought back to the sofa. The letter was handwritten in her mother's script.

Dear Eliza,

I'm sure you're surprised to get this letter from me. Your whole life, this has weighed on me, especially once I knew I wouldn't be here with you as you become an adult. I suppose my deciding to do this this way is the coward's way out. I should have looked into your eyes when I told you. Given you a chance to yell at me, or ask me questions, or . . . honestly, I don't know how you will react. Especially since you will probably be much, much older when you read this than you are today. But knowing that Dad will be the only parent you have left very soon, I don't want to do anything that will hurt your relationship with him. And, if I'm honest, I guess I just don't want him to know the truth. But you deserve to know it.

Eliza felt like she'd stopped breathing. Part of her wanted to put the letter back into the envelope. Wait until she felt stronger to keep reading. But the irony was she didn't have the strength to set the letter aside. She had to keep going.

Your biological father is a man named Ross Sawyer. He was my high school boy-friend. I'm sure you've been in love by now—and know how powerful first love is. Ross always had a part of my heart, and I always wondered how things would have turned out if we hadn't gone to college on opposite coasts. Anyway, when I went

to my ten-year high school reunion, he
was there. Things with your dad and me
weren't great. You probably know we had
our ups and downs. Well, it was a time of
a pretty big down.

I'm not proud of myself. I could blame
it on drinking too much, but I know that
I'm responsible for the choice I made that
night.

Unconsciously, Eliza clenched the letter in her hand, crumpling the paper. It was incomprehensible. She tried to reach back into her memory for the name Ross Sawyer. Had she heard it before? Had she ever met him? She didn't think so, but she also knew her synapses weren't firing correctly. Her brain was muddled, and her memories were jumbled and out of order.

Ross doesn't know. He reached out to
me a few times after, but I told him what
we did was a mistake. But YOU are not a
mistake. I love you so much, my beautiful
girl. And I'm sorry for not having the cour-
age to tell you this sooner. Please know I
never regretted having you—and I tried
to make the best decision I could when
I found out I was pregnant and did the
math. I knew for sure when I saw your
eyes. They're Ross's eyes.

I'm not perfect. But I did the best
I could. I wish I could be there with you
now, but I'm sure you've turned into an
amazing woman—even more beautiful,
kind, and strong than you were as a girl.

I hope you're happy and have found love.
You deserve the best.
    I love you,

Mom

Eliza read the letter again. And then a third time. Absently, she realized she was shivering and reached for the throw next to her and pulled it around herself.

How did you wrap your head around news like this? Her father wasn't really her father? A stranger out there somewhere had contributed half her DNA? And her mother . . . ? Her mother had slept with another man? And kept it a secret for all those years? Did anyone else know? Aunt Claude? Had Aunt Claude hidden this from her?

But wait. Maybe it wasn't true. Had Laura known for sure? There had been no DNA test. Eliza bit her lip. *No.* Her mom wouldn't have written this letter had she not felt one hundred percent positive.

All these years that she and Jack had grown more distant, and now it turned out he wasn't even her father. Had Jack known? Had he guessed? And Laura—how could she drop this bomb on her like this? Give her this earth-shattering news knowing she'd be long gone and unable to help her work through it? And while she was mourning the only father she'd ever known?

Eliza huddled over herself, having never felt so alone. With no warning, her stomach clenched, and she ran for the bathroom, bringing back up everything she'd nibbled at the shiva. And then she curled up on the cold tile floor, not even able to pull herself up to the sink to wash out her mouth.

When Eliza woke up, she was still on the floor. Her mouth was sticky and tasted like manky socks, and her throat and eyes felt raw. It was dark, and she had no idea what time it was. She rolled onto her back and stared at the invisible ceiling. How had she come to this place in just four days?

On Monday afternoon, she had been sitting at her desk at Nourish Our Youth, the nonprofit where she'd worked since graduating from college four years earlier, going over a spreadsheet for their annual gala. All she had on her mind was whether they could beat last year's numbers; whether the board members who had lost the battle for the evening's theme (Roaring Twenties beat out Wild Wild West by a single vote) would put their disappointment aside and serve on the decorations committee; and what she was going to get for lunch. And then Scott had called with the news.

It wasn't surprising that Carol had called Scott rather than her. Eliza had done everything she could to avoid that house since it had become Carol's home. How Jack could have gotten married so soon after Laura died—it was an insult to her mother's memory. But now, as Eliza stared at the ceiling, she had to ask herself whether she really knew anything about her parents' marriage. Had Jack suspected what Laura had done?

She rose slowly, her bones aching from the hours on the tile floor, and brushed her teeth vigorously. Then she went out to the kitchen to put up hot water for tea. *Kitchen* was really a misnomer—if you expected a kitchen to have four walls and space to prepare food. This one had only two and a half walls, with a small refrigerator and a tiny wedge of counter space. But it was New York City, and it was all hers.

According to the clock on the microwave, it was 4:32. If not for the darkness outside, Eliza wouldn't have known whether it was a.m. or p.m. She wasn't sure why she was making tea, but it was something to do. While the water heated up, she went into her bedroom to change out of her funeral clothes. A few minutes later, she was back on the couch, wearing a pair of fleece pajama pants and a T-shirt, her hands cupped around the mug of tea. Her mom's letter lay on the floor where she'd dropped it when she went running for the bathroom.

She found her phone and checked her messages. There was a text from Mo asking how she was doing and telling her she would see her at the shiva at Scott's tomorrow—which, Eliza realized, was actually today. Mo felt terrible that she hadn't been able to come to the funeral, but she had a huge new business pitch at work that her team had been preparing for weeks.

There was also a text from Aunt Claude, checking in. Eliza was sure she was eager to know the contents of the letter. *Unless she already does?*

And there was a text from Carter. It had come in around nine in the evening; he was wondering if he could come over. Typical. Eliza hadn't even told him that Jack had died. If that didn't show her what kind of relationship the two of them had, nothing would. But no matter how often Mo—Eliza sometimes wished she'd never gotten into the habit of shortening her friend's name, because Mohini was so much prettier—lectured her about wasting her time with Carter, Eliza was okay with the way things were. She wasn't looking for anything more.

It was now 4:54 a.m., and Eliza was wide awake. Before she could think too hard about it, she retrieved her laptop and Googled "Ross Sawyer." It turned out to be a not-uncommon name. She found a Ross Sawyer who ran a landscaping company, one who was a stockbroker, and one who'd placed first in his age group, twenty-one to thirty-five, in a half-marathon in Jersey City. And that was just in a few minutes of searching. She shut her laptop. She couldn't handle this yet. She clicked the remote control for the TV, found a couple looking to buy a beachfront vacation home, and curled up under the throw.

Late that afternoon, showered and wearing a loose gray silk blouse with wide-legged black trousers, her hair wound into a braid over her shoulder, Eliza was knocking on the door of her brother's Kips Bay apartment. Maren opened the door and enveloped her in a hug, her wild red curls a cloud around her head.

"How are you doing? Stupid question, I know." Maren answered her own inquiry as she put her arm around Eliza's shoulder and steered her into the apartment.

Eliza shrugged. "How's Scott?"

"Not great. Can I get you something? I was going to open a bottle of wine."

"Perfect."

The dining table at one end of Scott and Maren's open living space was already laid out with food. You simply couldn't go hungry at a shiva. Eliza looked at the plateful of mini black-and-white cookies and wished she had an appetite. She'd managed a slice of toast around midday, but that was all she remembered eating.

The day had passed in something of a blur. She'd texted Aunt Claude saying she'd read the letter but wasn't ready to talk about it. She'd texted Mo that she was doing okay—Mo knew her well enough to know that was a big fat lie—and that she'd see her at Scott and Maren's. And after some hesitation, she'd texted Carter that her dad had passed away.

Shockingly, her phone had immediately rung.

"Babe! I'm so sorry! Why didn't you tell me?"

How could she explain that, despite the fact that she regularly shared her body with him, she wasn't sure how much else she wanted to share?

"I don't know."

"What can I do? Do you want me to come over? I mean, I can't right now, but . . ."

Of course he can't. "It's okay. I'll be going to my brother's soon. He's hosting the shiva tonight." As soon as it was out of her mouth, she was sorry she'd said it. She tended to keep her sex life and her family separate. She knew they never liked anyone she dated. Of course, neither did Mo. And sometimes, neither did she. *He won't offer to come anyway.*

"Well, I'll meet you there, then. What's the address?"

She opened her mouth and closed it again before anything came out. But then she figured, *Why not?* She gave him the address, and he said he'd get there by six thirty.

Now, Maren put a glass of white wine in her hand. "Come sit," she said.

Eliza followed her sister-in-law to the big sectional sofa. The dining chairs had been pulled over and placed around the perimeter of the room.

Sitting down with her legs tucked under her, Eliza took a sip of her wine. "Are you expecting a lot of people?" she asked, indicating the chairs.

"Probably. A lot of Scott's friends are coming. I assume yours, too, right?"

"Some, I guess. Mo was letting people know. And some people from work might come." Eliza decided not to mention Carter. He might not actually show up anyway.

Scott came in from the bedroom, wearing a dark green V-neck sweater and khakis. He was blotting his cheek with a bit of tissue.

"Still haven't learned to shave?" Eliza smirked at her brother.

"My only shortcoming," he quipped before heading into the kitchen.

"So, Maren, is that true?" Eliza asked—loudly, to ensure Scott would hear.

Maren's eyes twinkled. "Well, he's got a few others," she replied as Scott came in with a bottle of Rolling Rock. "Like drinking beer from the bottle when we've got wine open and glasses."

Scott sat down heavily beside his wife, and Maren put her

hand on his knee. Eliza looked at her brother's face. His skin looked drawn around his eyes, and shadows smudged beneath them. She could read his pain so easily—could he see that she was keeping a secret?

Scott took a long swallow from his beer. "Sorry we didn't wait for you last night," he said, wiping his mouth with the back of his hand. "I just needed to get out of there. Claudia said she'd give you a ride to the train."

When had Scott dropped the honorific? Eliza couldn't remember. But at the same time, he'd also stopped calling her Claude.

"It's fine. Actually, she wanted to . . ." Eliza trailed off, realizing she was about to talk about Laura's letter.

"Wanted to what?"

Eliza hesitated. She still couldn't wrap her head around the fact that no one else knew. She knew this wasn't the right time to blurt out that they didn't have the same father. She couldn't do to Scott what that letter had done to her, not now, not as they were about to be inundated with people coming to pay their respects. But even as she told herself she needed to wait, she couldn't keep the words from leaving her mouth. "Did you know Mom had left a letter for me?"

Two pairs of eyes drilled into her.

"A letter?"

"What letter?"

"I guess that answers that." Eliza tried to laugh and took a sip from her wine.

"Lize?"

And just then, the doorbell rang. Eliza jumped up. "I'll get it." She quickly crossed to the front door and flung it open. Immediately, she was in Mo's arms.

"You okay?" Mo whispered. "I mean . . ."

"I know what you mean. I'm okay."

Eliza and Mo had met in college, two and a half years after

Laura died. They lived in the same hall and connected right away. But their friendship was sealed the night Mo steered a drunk Eliza home from a party. Mo sat outside the bathroom door while Eliza puked and then came inside and wiped her face with a damp washcloth.

"You remind me of my mom," Eliza had said, swaying slightly.

"Whoa there!" Mo steadied her, remarkably strong considering her petite frame. "Let's get you sitting down." Mo guided her to her room and straight to her bed. "Where are your PJs?"

Eliza indicated vaguely toward the institutional bureau, and Mo quickly found sweatpants and a T-shirt.

With only a little assistance, Eliza got changed, and Mo found her hairbrush. "If you leave your hair like this, you'll be sorry in the morning. Believe me, I know." Mo pointed at her own thick dark locks.

Eliza's hair was loose and tangled, and Mo sat next to her, patiently pulling the brush through it.

"You really are just like my mom," Eliza sighed, her eyes closed.

"Well, I'm sure she might react differently to the drunken puking than I did."

Eliza shrugged. "Dunno. She's dead."

The hairbrush stopped midway. "I'm so sorry. I didn't know."

Eliza hadn't talked about her mother's death since she'd gotten to college. Laura's illness and her passing had defined her in high school. Eliza was the girl whose mom was sick. Then the girl whose mom died. And then the girl who was crying in the girls' bathroom when she was supposed to be in class learning trigonometry. Eliza was tired of being that girl.

She hadn't meant for those words to slip out of her mouth. And once they were out, she thought maybe she could play it off as if it weren't such a big deal. But it was exhausting to pretend she didn't have a hole that nothing could fill—not even the copious amounts of alcohol that had seemed to be doing the trick, at least for a little while.

Mo turned out to be a good listener. And good at keeping her friend's secrets. Meanwhile, Eliza proved good at talking Mohini off the ledge when she was stressed about schoolwork and getting her to laugh when she needed it most.

Now, Mo peered at Eliza's face, trying to read the truth in her eyes. "Really, Mo, I'm okay," Eliza assured her. It took everything she had to tamp down the truth. Keeping secrets from Mo wasn't usually in her repertoire.

Mo pointed at her own right eye, dark brown and neatly lined with eyeliner. "I've got my eye on you."

"I know."

Maren appeared in the vestibule. "Mohini! Eliza said you were coming."

"Of course. I'm so sorry for your loss. I wasn't sure what to bring." Mo held out a bottle of wine.

"Looks perfect to me!" Maren took the bottle, and the three of them moved deeper into the apartment.

Within minutes, the doorbell rang again. This time Scott got it, then left it slightly ajar—in keeping with shiva tradition if not the norms of Manhattan living—and Eliza saw a thirtyish couple step inside. The woman was unfamiliar, but she recognized the man.

"Isn't that Carol's nephew? Adam?" she asked Maren.

Her sister-in-law nodded. "He and Scott are still friendly. He was at the funeral yesterday, but couldn't come back to the house."

Eliza's eyes rested for a moment on Adam before she turned back to Maren, assuming her sister-in-law knew the pivotal role he'd played in their family. Scott and Adam had been high school tennis teammates, and Adam's family had thrown an over-the-top backyard graduation party for his classmates and their families—all that was missing was a pig roasting on a spit. But what the party—held only a couple of months after Laura's death—did have was Adam's single aunt Carol, wearing a bright yellow sundress and offering a listening ear to Scott and Eliza's widower father.

The apartment became increasingly crowded, and Eliza was on her second glass of wine while talking with Mo and two other friends from college, explaining again how sudden her father's death was, when she found herself wishing it was over. Everyone talked about the beauty of the shiva tradition—being surrounded by family and friends in the early days of mourning—but something about it made Eliza feel like her oxygen was slowly being cut off. Maybe because her mother's letter was a huge weight on her chest.

"Sorry—I just need to use the bathroom," she said suddenly, noting Mo's sharp look at her and willing her friend to just let her go.

She wove through the clusters of people, catching snippets of conversation. "I realized a few years ago that the only skiing I truly love is in Utah. So unless I can go there, I don't bother." "Did you hear that Julie and Todd split up? I have to say I wasn't *totally* surprised." "Can you imagine walking into your kitchen and finding your husband *dead on the floor*?" (This last uttered in a loud whisper.)

"Eliza?"

She'd nearly made it to the hall en route to the bathroom when she heard her name and looked up. Her already rapid pulse increased. It was Josh, Scott's best friend from high school. She blinked at him, still in escape mode.

"I'm so sorry," he said quietly.

She remembered that sorrowful expression from when he'd worn it after Laura's death, whenever he looked at her—which wasn't very often. Somehow, Josh never seemed to be at the house after that. Scott was always out meeting him somewhere instead. Eliza figured Josh thought hanging around the death house was a buzzkill.

The rest of him looked the same, too—if anything, only better with time. His brown hair was thick and just the right amount of unruly. His shoulders seemed a little broader under his suit jacket than she remembered. Not that she remembered him all that well, she reminded herself.

Josh reached toward her, and she let him hug her, trying not to notice the scent of his aftershave.

"I couldn't believe it when Scott told me. Your dad looked great at the wedding."

Josh had been Scott's best man a few years earlier, and had come to the wedding with an attractive brunette. If high cheekbones and big green eyes were your thing. Eliza had coveted her silky emerald green dress that draped just right across her hips. That day, Eliza wore a strapless bridesmaid dress that was inexplicably brown. She hadn't asked the guy she was seeing at the time to be her plus-one. The thought of all the assumptions that would spark had given her dry heaves.

Eliza shrugged. "I know. He seemed totally fine." She hoped he didn't notice the clog in her throat, but he touched her arm.

"You hanging in there?" he asked softly.

She glanced at the worried expression in his eyes.

"You know. What can you do?" She tried to be flippant, but treacherous tears forced her to blink rapidly.

Josh's hand on her arm tightened. "Come on. Let's go sit somewhere."

Unable to come up with a plausible excuse to extricate herself, she let him guide her back into the belly of the beast and pour her another glass of wine. She hadn't drunk this much in a long time. She pushed aside the thought that it was probably not the best idea.

CHAPTER THREE

Sometime later—it could have been five minutes or five hours—Josh had left Eliza in the company of her coworkers. They'd all come—Vanessa, Nourish Our Youth's director; her assistant, Bridget; Davin, the communications director; Patrice, the vice president of operations, and their admin, Amber. Eliza found herself thinking it was a good thing none of the youth needed to be nourished at that moment, since no one was minding the store. The fact that this thought amused her probably had a lot to do with the wine she had drunk and the food she'd failed to consume.

"I don't want to bother you with work, but where do we stand on securing lunch with the mayor for the silent auction? I'm working on the press release and . . ." Davin was all about issuing press releases.

"Leave the poor girl alone," Vanessa interrupted, her immaculately plucked eyebrows raised. "Eliza. You take the time you need. But I'm sure you'll be back next week, yes?"

Bridget rolled her eyes at Eliza, and she only just stopped herself from rolling hers back.

"Yes, next week. Sure. Next week." Or that was what Eliza

thought she'd said. But maybe it came out "wext neek"? So she repeated it again. "Next week."

Vanessa looked at her oddly, and Eliza realized she was still nodding. She stopped.

Patrice, whose ubiquitous cardigan was black today, probably in deference to the shiva, interjected. "What can we do for you, Eliza?"

Amber replied before Eliza could. "I know—I'll bring you some bread. My sourdough starter is perfect now." Eliza wasn't sure how Amber managed living in Queens when her hobbies were much more suited to the great outdoors. She was forever bringing herbs into the office for everyone to use in their cooking, not seeming to realize that most of them ordered their meals in, already cooked.

"Bread. Great." Eliza looked over toward the table, now crowded with all the offerings everyone had brought. Food. Maybe she should have some. That side of the room just felt so far away. As she pondered, a voice she recognized separated itself from the others.

"Hey—I'm looking for Eliza?"

And there was Carter—his navy button-down tucked into jeans, his nearly black hair flopping into his face. He was exquisitely beautiful. And he knew it. He'd spotted her and was heading in her direction. She realized in that moment that she'd never actually expected him to show up.

"Babe!" He put his arms around her. "I'm so sorry."

"You came!" she said.

He drew back. "Of course I came, babe."

"I didn't think you would." *Did I say that out loud?* Eliza's eyes slid across the room and caught on Josh's own narrowed ones. She reached up to Carter's face, feeling the stubble on his jaw. "But I'm glad you did." And then she was kissing him, right in the middle of the room.

She heard throat-clearing. Scott was standing next to them, his hand outstretched. "Scott. Eliza's brother."

Carter flashed his disarming smile. "Carter."

"My . . ." Eliza trailed off. "Right. Carter."

And then Mo was there, too. "Hi. I'm Mohini. Eliza's best friend." Clearly that relationship status was defined.

"Mohini. Nice to meet you." Carter shook her hand as well. "And, Scott—I'm sorry for your loss, man."

Scott acknowledged Carter's words with a nod.

"Do you think I could grab something to eat, babe? I'm starving."

"Oh, right, sure." Eliza felt a little off-kilter. Having all these people together in one room was wrong. Like kung pao chicken served with potatoes au gratin and baklava for dessert. Her coworkers, Scott, and Mo watched Carter head off toward the food.

Davin spoke a moment later. "Well. I guess I should be going." The rest of the Nourish Our Youth group murmured assent.

Amber gave her a quick hug. "I'll bring you some bread this weekend."

Vanessa patted her shoulder. "Let us know when you'll be back in the office."

As soon as they'd moved away, Mo sidled up to her. "So this is the famous Carter."

"You haven't met him before?"

"No, Eliza, I haven't met him before," Mo replied with exaggerated patience.

Scott watched the two women's back-and-forth. "Is this another one of your winners, Eliza?"

Eliza rolled her eyes at her brother and walked away, leaning up against Carter as he piled pastrami onto rye bread.

"How long have we been together?" she asked.

He glanced at her and then back at the array on the table, reaching for a pickle. "Together?"

"You know." She pointed from him to herself and back to him. "You and me. Together."

He shrugged. "I dunno."

It was suddenly very important to Eliza to know the answer. It had been a while, but Mo hadn't met him? How was that possible? Maybe because they spent most of their time alone in her apartment?

"We met that weekend I was out in the Hamptons, right? So it was July . . . ?"

"I guess so, babe. Does it matter?"

Easier to puzzle about how long they'd been bumping uglies than about the fact that her dead father wasn't her father.

As they turned from the table, Scott appeared again. "Eliza. Can we talk?"

"Sure. Talk."

Scott looked pointedly at Carter. "In private?"

Eliza gave a deep sigh. She was so very tired.

"Go ahead, babe, I'll be fine."

From the look on Scott's face, it appeared he didn't appreciate Carter giving them permission to step away.

Eliza followed Scott into the bedroom. He switched on the bedside lamp. The bedspread was striped in muted gray and taupe, and a collection of pillows—some round, some square, and some cylindrical—were artistically heaped against the padded headboard. Next to the lamp on the nightstand was a copy of the latest Fredrik Backman release. *Must be Maren's side of the bed.*

"So can we go back to that little bomb you dropped earlier?" Scott asked.

Eliza blinked. Her head was full of cotton.

"Eliza! You said Mom left a letter for you. What are you talking about?"

Oh, that *little bomb. Scott, you don't even know what a bomb is.* She thought hazily about the group of people in the other room. Josh. Carter. Adam. Mo. It was all such a blur. "Can we do this another time, please?"

"Seriously? You can't just say something like that and not expect me to ask questions." Scott pushed his hand through his hair.

"I know. You're right. But it's too much. It's too big. I can't."

Would Scott look at her differently when he knew they were only half siblings? Would he think of Laura differently? How could she tell him Laura's secret when their mother wasn't even here to defend herself? To explain herself? *But she created this mess of a situation, didn't she?* Was it up to Eliza to protect her? If not her, then who?

"Eliza. Come on. She was my mom, too. And you and me—we're all we've got now." Scott's voice caught, and tears sprang to Eliza's eyes.

"Seriously, Scott. I just can't right now. I'm sorry I said anything." She turned to leave, and the room spun around her. She closed her eyes to get her bearings and then made her way back out. She found Carter with Maren, Maren laughing at something Carter must have said.

"There you are!" Carter reached for her, and she let him pull her in to his side.

"Eliza! You can't walk away like that!" Scott was right behind her, his voice quietly loud—expressing his frustration while trying not to draw attention to them. Quite a feat.

"What's going on?" Maren's eyebrows drew together, lines bunching between them.

"I just want Eliza to tell me about my mom's letter."

Since when did she become his mom and not our mom?

Eliza looked at Maren, who was clearly torn between wanting to take Scott's side and feeling uncomfortable interjecting.

"Scott . . ." Eliza's voice trailed off.

Carter took a half step forward. "Look, if she doesn't want to talk about it, just let it go." Eliza appreciated his gamely entering the fray for her, even as she wished he'd stay out of it. More cooks weren't going to turn down the heat in this kitchen.

Scott's face hardened. "I'm sorry, *Carter*, but I don't think this has anything to do with you." His voice was quiet, but still angry.

Eliza noticed people drifting toward them. Mo. Josh. They'd clearly been keeping a watchful eye. She put her hand on Carter's arm, silently asking him to let it go. She knew her brother was hanging by a thread. Carter glanced at her and raised his eyebrows.

"Do you want to get out of here?" he asked.

Did she? What she wanted was to turn the clock back twenty-four hours to when she didn't know what she knew. She closed her eyes for a long moment, and when she opened them, it seemed like everyone was staring at her. Just like everyone stared at her when she went back to school after Laura died. She felt like an animal in a zoo—if it were the kind of zoo where visitors were allowed to get close enough to poke at the animals.

She nodded. She needed air.

"Eliza . . ." Scott's tone was pleading, and Maren stepped to his side, gripping his hand.

Eliza's heart was pounding, and her hands went cold. Josh's eyes didn't leave her face. She opened her mouth to say she needed a minute. To repeat that she couldn't talk about it. And everyone was looking at her. And the walls were closing in.

"Fine!" Her voice was loud to her own ears. Was she

shouting? "You want to know? I'll tell you. Dad wasn't my dad. Mom slept with her high school boyfriend at her reunion. And got pregnant. With me. That's the big secret. That's what was in the letter."

CHAPTER FOUR

Eliza's eyelids felt like lead, and her head pounded. She shifted to find a cool spot on the pillow, but the movement made the pounding worse. Her mind reached back to the night before to figure out why she felt so awful.

Ah, yes, there was a lot of wine. And sympathy. And her outburst.

Wait, back up.

Had she really announced to a roomful of people—including complete strangers, probably Scott's coworkers or racquetball buddies *(Does he play racquetball?)*—that her mother had slept with someone other than her father, and that that mystery man was her father?

Yes, it seemed she had.

Eliza squeezed her eyes shut even more tightly and flipped onto her stomach to bury her face in the pillow, pounding head be damned.

"Oh, good, you're up." Carter's voice reached her from somewhere above her. Right, he'd taken her home. Sliding herself around on the sheets, she confirmed what she suspected—she wasn't wearing any pajamas.

The side of the bed sank as he sat down. "How are you feeling?"

She mumbled something incoherent.

"Sounds about right." He chuckled. "Can I get you some coffee? I can run down to the corner."

She didn't have a coffee maker because she didn't drink coffee. In fact, she couldn't stand it. The taste or the smell. But of course he could never seem to remember that. No matter how many times she told him. She shook her head.

"Is that a yes or a no?"

"No," she croaked. "I hate coffee."

"Really?"

She rolled her eyes into the pillow. Even that made her headache worse.

There really wasn't anything wrong with Carter. He was certainly easy on the eyes. He was good in bed. Enthusiastic, anyway. And he could be charming. At least, he was charming the night they met. And he seemed to charm Maren last night. But mostly he was good in bed.

Eliza wasn't entirely sure what he did when they weren't together. They rarely went out. He'd text her—or she'd text him—and they'd hook up at her place or his. He claimed he wasn't sleeping with anyone else—but it was quite possible he dated other women. They never said they were exclusive except for the sex. It was clear he wasn't looking for anything more. But neither was she. Despite the fact that Mo kept telling her that this wasn't a mature relationship. And she was a little shaken to realize her friend had never even met him. She'd tried to get them together for a drink . . . and then Carter had canceled.

But what they had suited her just fine. She didn't have to consider him when she was making plans. If she had to work late, no one was waiting for her. And what was the point of trying to build a partnership with someone when life was so fragile anyway? *Carpe diem.*

But last night when Scott was clearly hurting, and Maren sidled up next to him to take his hand . . . There was something nice about that. Too bad she didn't believe it could exist for her.

Now she needed Tylenol and a cup of hot tea. And her bathrobe.

"Can you grab me my robe?" She pointed toward the bathroom.

Carter crossed the room in two strides and was back with her fluffy blue robe. Eliza scooched out from under the covers to push her arms through the sleeves. She felt his eyes on her.

"Or you could just stay in bed . . ." His voice was low. Needy.

"Are you kidding me?" She quickly pulled the robe around her and swung her legs to the floor. He followed her to the stove, where she put up the teapot, and watched while she grabbed the bottle of Tylenol and downed two caplets with a swig of water from the tap. Carter sat on the sofa while she puttered around, and when she couldn't avoid it any longer, she went and sat next to him with her cup of tea. All she really wanted was to be alone. And the beauty of him was that he didn't tend to hang around in the morning.

She took a long sip of the steaming tea. Ambrosia.

Carter cleared his throat. "So, seems like you got some big news."

She looked at him and nodded, waiting for him to ask something. Anything. But as the silence grew, she realized that Carter wasn't the person she wanted to talk to about this. The person she really wanted was Laura. But she had watched her lowered into the ground ten years before.

It was one of those moments that was crystallized in her memory. It had been unseasonably hot for the middle of May.

So hot that she could feel beads of sweat rolling down her back under the dress Aunt Claude had picked out for her.

The coffin sat in the apparatus that would lower it into the freshly dug grave. She looked at it, hoping that some sort of machinery had been used to dig that grave and that it hadn't been done the old-fashioned way, by a hunched man bearing a shovel, sweating in the unusual heat. It was a strange thing to think about—but easier to contemplate than the casket, awaiting its final descent.

The crowd was large, though not as large as it had been at the funeral home. She wondered where the others had gone. Maybe they had something better to do. Maybe it was one thing to mark the passage of life and death in an air-conditioned chapel, where you could sit in a pew and read and reread the program that summarized the life of the person lying in the coffin at the head of the aisle. A summary that couldn't possibly capture anything at all. Couldn't capture the songs she hummed under her breath when she was packing lunches. Couldn't capture the way her toes looked in flip-flops in the summer. Couldn't capture the neat way she tucked the sheets in so you could slide in like a hot dog, snug in a bun, safe and cozy and protected.

Then the rabbi was speaking again. Eliza's dress was sticking to her back, and she wanted to pluck it away from her skin. But it felt like everyone was looking at her, and somehow, she had to stay still. Unmoving. Unmoved. Because otherwise she would collapse into a puddle of flesh and tears.

She wished for a butterfly. Or a bird. Or something that could be interpreted as a sign. Even though she didn't believe in signs. But the air was still. Clearly, no living thing, other than the people standing by this grave, wanted to be out in the still, humid air of the cemetery. The only spots of brightness were the flowers left on some nearby headstones. They looked like roses, mostly. She thought that she would bring daisies. Her mother would like those.

Her face was wet, but she wasn't sure if it was sweat or tears. Scott was passing the shovel to her. How could she shovel earth on top of her mother's coffin?

Her memory stopped there. She couldn't let herself go back. To what happened when she'd refused the shovel.

Carter kissed her neck, drawing her back into the present.

She moved away and rubbed her forehead. "What I want right now is to go back to bed and try to get rid of this hangover."

He moved his leg against hers. How had she not focused on the fact that he was wearing only his boxers? "I could go back to bed with you . . ."

Seriously?

"I'm really not feeling well. And this is a lot to process."

"I get it. No worries. I'll get out of your hair." He stood and put on his pants. They were on the living room floor. Apparently, the disrobing the night before had begun as soon as they'd come inside. "You know, you've got a lot going on. You probably need your family now. I don't want to get in the way. Call me. You know, when you're feeling better."

Feeling better? Like she had a sore throat? Or maybe was bummed because she'd lost her favorite gloves? She knew that Carter wasn't someone she relied on. That she didn't want to rely on him. It wasn't what their relationship was about. But how could he be this oblivious?

Within minutes, Carter was fully dressed and out the door, dropping such a quick kiss on her forehead that she might have mistaken it for a gnat.

Finally alone, she nursed her tea and carefully let her memory reach back to last night. Like tentatively poking at the edges of a wound.

Her announcement had been met with deafening silence. Then Mo had grabbed her arm. "Oh my God, Eliza! Is that true?"

"Looks like it." She shrugged as if it were no big deal, when actually she felt like throwing up. *Again.* Her eyes shifted to her brother, who looked stunned.

"No. It can't be," he said slowly.

"I don't know what to tell you. I can't believe it either. But it must be."

Eliza's heart rattled inside her chest. What was this going to do to her relationship with Scott?

Mo's hand on her arm tightened. "Eliza! Are you okay? You look white."

She was able to smile weakly at her friend. "That's kind of my natural color."

But Mo didn't smile back. "Not like this. I think you need to sit down. Can I get you some water?"

The prospect of everyone fluttering around her made it all worse. "I just have to get out of here."

She expected to hear Scott protest, but he was ominously silent.

Mo's voice adopted its "take charge" tone. "Okay, let's get you some air."

Eliza was vaguely aware of Mo saying quick goodbyes. She felt Maren's and Josh's eyes on her—while Scott looked at his shoes. And then she was being steered out of the apartment and down to the street by Mo, with Carter immediately behind. And then Mo was flagging a cab and they were headed uptown to Eliza's apartment.

She was conscious of being squeezed between them as the TV screen in the back of the cab played a commercial for *Wicked.* The cab hit a pothole and swung into the next lane, the motion pushing Mo into Eliza and Eliza into Carter.

Eliza had closed her eyes against Carter's shoulder, and

there was some conversation going on above her head. It reminded her of being asleep in the back seat as a little kid. Their voices got louder.

"Shh. Don't fight," she whispered, her eyes still shut.

There was more murmuring, and she caught a few words, but it was too hard to make any sense of them. Next thing she knew, they were at Eliza's building, and Carter was easing her out of the car.

"Are you sure?" Mo was asking, but Eliza wasn't sure who she was talking to. She was just so tired. And then the cab was gone and Carter was guiding her to the front door and then to the elevator and up to her apartment.

Now alone again, Eliza knew she should call Mo soon—before her friend showed up banging down her door. Instead, she texted to suggest that they meet at their favorite coffee place. The last thing she felt like doing was getting dressed and going out. But she knew the kinds of bad things that happened when she gave in to the desire to glue herself to the couch. So off she went to the shower.

CHAPTER FIVE

Like so many other cafés throughout the city, Grinders was rustic and cozy. The wooden floor was scuffed, and the small round tables were surrounded by mismatched chairs. In one corner, two overstuffed orange armchairs observed the rest of the room. A large blackboard hung behind the register, listing coffee and tea flavors.

Grinders was Eliza and Mo's favorite meeting spot because, despite the name, the tea brand they stocked was one of the best, and the aroma of coffee was moderated by the scented candles that were always lit, emitting the fragrance of vanilla and maple.

Eliza arrived first and ordered her Darjeeling, which was served in a large, bright yellow mug. About half the tables were occupied, mostly by people alone with their drinks and their electronic devices, but she was able to snag a spot near the window. She was just sitting down when Mo swept through the front door. A few minutes later, they were both seated, Mo's hands cupped around her own bright green mug.

Eliza bit her lip. "Before you say anything, I have to apologize for last night. I was out of control."

"Just a little." Mo held up her thumb and forefinger, about an inch apart, and then widened them. But quickly her face grew more somber. "But, seriously, Eliza, how are you doing? I can't even imagine what this week has been like for you."

Eliza snorted. "Yeah, I can't imagine what it's like for me either!" Sober, caffeinated, freshly showered, and having slept a decent number of hours, she was feeling more clearheaded than she had in days, despite the lingering hangover.

Mo pushed her shiny hair—cropped chin-length and razor sharp, much different from the long sheets she'd had in college—behind her ear. "So, what's the story about your dad?"

Eliza told her about the letter Claude had given her, and then passed her phone across to her friend so she could read it for herself. She'd taken a photograph to make sure she wouldn't lose it.

Mo's eyes widened as she read, and then she silently passed the phone back. "What are you going to do? Are you going to look for this guy?"

"Honestly, I don't know. It's crazy. One minute, my dad is dead, and then the next minute, I have a different dad. I mean—obviously my dad is my dad. The dad who raised me. This other guy doesn't even know I exist."

Mo nodded and sipped her tea. "For what it's worth, I think you should wait. I mean, once you contact him, you can't take it back. And you don't have any way of knowing what he's like. If you even *want* him in your life."

This was one of the things she loved about Mo. She didn't hesitate to speak her mind and offer advice—but somehow it never came out bossy. It was clearly from a place of caring—and almost always made sense.

"I did Google him already," she admitted.

Mo raised her eyebrows. "And did you find him?"

She shook her head. "Ross Sawyer isn't a super uncommon name. And I was sort of afraid to dive too deep, I guess."

Mo nodded. "It's got to feel weird. Aside from everything else, you just lost your dad. It must feel like you're . . . I don't know . . . looking for his replacement."

"Yeah, especially since I wasn't always his biggest fan." She was aiming for a quip, but her throat clogged at the end of her words. Mo reached across the table and squeezed her arm.

"Was I too hard on him, Mo?"

Her friend drew her hand back and pinched her own bottom lip. "You felt what you felt. He couldn't be anyone other than who he was, and you couldn't be anyone other than who you are."

"Yeah, a bratty daughter."

"Don't do that. That's not you talking. That's Carol. You were grieving. You handled it the best you could. And your dad was grieving. He handled it the best he could."

By finding a new wife. The thought was one that she'd had many times before. But now it was followed by *Perhaps to replace the one who cheated on him?*

"Anyway, the first thing I need to do is talk to Scott. If he'll even talk to me."

Mo grimaced. "Of course he'll talk to you."

Eliza raised her eyebrows. "Would you be eager to talk to *your* sister if she lost it in the middle of your living room and announced that your mother cheated on your father? And then ran out?"

Mo's eyes searched her face. "Okay, true. It wasn't one of your finer moments. But Scott's a good guy. He'll accept your apology."

Eliza wasn't so sure. Scott was always the steady one. She was always the screwup. He had to be getting tired of picking up the pieces. And that display of hers had been . . . *bad.*

"What about your aunt? Have you talked to her?"

Eliza shook her head. "I don't even know how to start." She

laughed ruefully. "I guess that was the advantage of getting drunk. It gave me a place to start."

"Yeah, I wouldn't advise that again." Mo's voice was solemn, but her eyes twinkled.

"Thanks for the tip." Eliza's smile faded. "But it's so weird. Aunt Claude was my mom's little sister. The way she's always talked about her—you'd think my mom walked on water. How do I tell her what she did?"

"Maybe she already knows. Maybe your mom told her."

Eliza rearranged the sprig of flowers in the small bud vase in the center of the table, her hands looking for something to do. "Maybe. It's all so . . . hard. My mom was always the one who did the right thing, you know? Bringing brownies to new neighbors. Writing thank-you notes. Making me invite all the girls in my class to my birthday parties—even the ones I didn't like." She sighed. "And I always thought that if she hadn't . . . if she were still alive . . . we'd have this happy family. But now . . ." Her voice trailed off.

Mo sighed. "It's hard for us to think of our parents as people, right? They're our parents. The idea of them . . . I don't know, having a crush on someone . . . it's hard to wrap your head around. God knows I can't imagine *my* parents being anything other than my mom and dad, wanting me to do well in school, get a good job, get married . . ." Mo waved her hand around to indicate all the many things her parents asked of her. "And now you're having to face your mom being *human*."

Mo was right, but it was also so much more than that. Suddenly she had to face the fact that everything she thought she knew about who she was was a lie. How could she expect Mo to understand that? Instead of trying to explain, Eliza just nodded. "And making the kind of bad decision she tried to raise me *not* to make. Not that that worked out so well."

Mo was already shaking her head before Eliza stopped

speaking. "You have to stop being so hard on yourself. You're not the disaster you seem to think you are."

Eliza shrugged, picking up her mug to take a sip before realizing it was empty.

"Seriously," her friend continued. "Look at you! You're only five years out of college and you're director of development at a respected nonprofit. You own your own apartment. You've got an amazing best friend . . ." Mo grinned.

"Agreed on the best-friend part. But I wouldn't be a director if Johanna hadn't crashed and burned." Eliza wished she'd felt ready for the job, but she was promoted from her assistant position when Johanna—the prior director—had suddenly left. She didn't know all the details, just that it had something to do with Johanna having a torrid affair (as described by their colleague Davin, *sotto voce*, with his characteristic gift for linguistic flourish) with the corporate giving manager at one of the financial institutions she had been "courting." After Johanna's departure, it became clear that Eliza was the only one who understood her prior supervisor's systems. "Systems" being a word that could be applied only very loosely to the chaos in which Johanna had operated.

"However you got the job, you're kicking ass at it. And if they didn't think you could handle it, you wouldn't be running this year's gala, would you?"

"I suppose," she said grudgingly.

"No supposing. You've told me yourself that this is their biggest fundraiser. And you're going to knock it out of the park. You want another tea?" Mo nodded at Eliza's empty cup.

"Darjeeling."

"*Obviously.*"

She watched Mo go up to the counter, where the barista with spiky hair and an eyebrow ring gave her a big smile. When she returned, she had two cups of tea and a croissant. "On the house," she announced.

"And does that mean you have a date, too?" Eliza raised her eyebrows.

"Ha. Can you imagine what my parents would say if I brought home a barista?"

"Since when do you care what your parents say?"

Mo laughed. "True. But speaking of men . . ."

Eliza blew on her tea before taking a sip. "Don't you mean inappropriate men?" she asked over the rim.

Mo rolled her eyes. "Well, it was nice to finally meet Carter," she said dryly.

"He's not so bad . . ."

"Exactly. Don't you think you deserve better than 'not so bad'?"

"Come on, Mo, we've been through this before. I'm not looking for anything serious. He's hot. He's fun. It's fine." But even as she repeated the words she'd said so many times before, Eliza wondered if they were still true. The hot part definitely was. The fun part—well, maybe. But fine? Was "fine" really enough?

Shortly before Laura died, Eliza's heart had been bruised by a boy she thought she could trust. Then, in the wake of her mother's death, boys weren't really on her radar. High school became a matter of survival—getting out of bed in the morning was sometimes an insurmountable challenge, especially once Carol was on the scene. But ultimately, it was Carol's presence that compelled her to pull herself sufficiently together to get into college—a way for her to escape a home that had become too painful.

In college, she discovered sex. It wasn't that she slept around—not that there would have been anything wrong with that, she would insist in a post-feminist, control-your-own-orgasm, woman-power way—but the boys she pursued (or who pursued her) weren't, as 1950s movies might have called them, "the marrying kind." Well, except for Pete.

Mo had loved Pete. He was kind, and smart, and funny. He joined them in the cafeteria for lunch, and he fit in well with their friends. When he discovered Eliza's weakness for dark-chocolate-pecan clusters, he started surprising her with a bag of them "just because." Once before a sociology exam she was worried about, once on the five-week anniversary of their first date, once on a random Tuesday afternoon.

Pete was from Oregon, and as spring break approached at their Connecticut college, they planned that he would go home with her for a few days. It was just about ten days before they were due to make the trip, while they were studying together for midterms—a public-sector economics class for her, biology for him—that Eliza suddenly felt like she couldn't breathe. She was struggling to get some theoretical constructs straight in her head, and Pete offered to help. She started to pass her notes to him and then pulled them back. "I think I really need to get this myself," she said.

"It's no problem," he replied amiably. "I can take a break from my stuff."

"I know, I just have to figure it out on my own. I'm going to head back to my room."

He looked at her quizzically. "See you later, then?"

"Maybe. Let me see how this goes." She couldn't even look at him as she scrambled to push her books and papers into her backpack. All she could think about was getting air into her tight lungs.

After that, without consciously deciding to do so, she started to avoid him. After a few days, Mo—who by then was her roommate—stormed into the 144 square feet they shared demanding to know what was going on. "He's like a lost puppy. What happened?" Her long hair was tangled in her scarf, her hands on her hips.

Eliza, cross-legged on her bed, pressed her hands into her

eye sockets. "Nothing. Nothing at all. I just—I don't know. I can't do this anymore."

"Do what? Be with a nice, predictable guy who cares about you?"

She knew it made no sense. She had what most of her friends were looking for. And Pete truly was lovely. That day in the library when he'd offered to help, she felt such an overwhelming sense of relief, riding on top of a wave of what might actually have been the beginning of something big. Something like love. And then a minute later it was like someone had squeezed a fist around her heart, all the good feelings oozing out. Suddenly there was a solid lump in her throat, blocking her words.

Mo sat down beside her on her green-and-blue-striped comforter, still wearing her parka. "Eliza?" She took her hands between her own tiny ones, her darker skin contrasting with Eliza's paleness. "Did something happen?"

Eliza shook her head wordlessly and shrugged her shoulders.

"You know, sometimes even when you're not looking for something, it sneaks up on you. And that's okay."

She knew Mo was trying to understand. Eliza had certainly told her often enough that she wasn't looking for a serious boyfriend—particularly after she'd hooked up with someone new. But the truth was, she didn't understand it herself. She just knew that being with Pete wasn't working for her anymore. If she didn't know better, she would have characterized the feeling that rose in her gut when she thought of him as terror. But what could be terrifying about kind, sweet Pete?

And here she was, some six years later, having the same conversation, yet again, with Mo. "What about you?" she asked, changing the subject. "Anyone interesting in the online sea?"

Mo shook her head, her shiny hair swishing. "Sometimes

I think I should tell my parents I want an arranged marriage after all. Except I don't want to be married to anyone who wants an arranged marriage."

Eliza laughed. "That *would* be a problem."

"Anyway, work is nuts right now. We won that new business pitch, so you're looking at the project manager for the most innovative, integrated marketing campaign the next-level smartphone has ever seen." Mo grinned, a single dimple appearing in her right cheek. It only made an appearance when she was especially proud of herself.

"Mo, that's fantastic! Congratulations! Why didn't you tell me?"

"Um, your week was a little busy, I think."

"True," Eliza acknowledged before they dissected Mo's news as they shared the complimentary croissant.

"Hey—maybe you can throw some social responsibility into the marketing mix. Provide those next-level smartphones for the swag bags at the gala."

Mo pursed her lips. "I know you're kidding—but it's actually not a bad idea. Not phones, but maybe something else." She pulled out a fabric-bound notebook and pen from her bag and jotted a note. "Anyway, what's your plan for the rest of the day?" she asked as she slipped her notebook back into her bag.

Eliza looked at her phone to see the time, noticing a text from Claude. But none from Scott. Somehow, they had whiled away more than two hours. "Not sure. I may go back to bed."

Mo's eyebrows drew together. "I don't think that's a good idea."

She wasn't wrong, but Eliza suddenly felt tired. As if someone had dropped a weighted blanket around her shoulders. Focusing on the bombshell news and on work had pulled her out of her grief, but now it was back. An old friend she knew too well. Despite whatever had been lacking in her relationship with her dad, he *was* her dad. Biology be damned. And for the first time, she realized the word *orphan* applied to her. *Or does it?*

CHAPTER SIX

When Monday morning rolled around, Eliza got out of bed and headed for the shower. She hadn't really planned to go back to work yet, but what else was she going to do? Sit at home and scroll through Instagram? Start researching Ross Sawyer? Eat the rest of the sourdough bread Amber had brought her the day before? She wasn't sure why Amber thought she needed three loaves, but it was a sweet thought. And apparently, they could be frozen!

She tried to slip into her office unnoticed but should have known that was impossible in an organization whose culture was all about being in everyone's business, all the time. It was entirely possible they had all known Patrice was pregnant before her wife had.

As she sat at her desk powering up her computer, she could almost hear the whispers. *Should we all go in? Maybe just one of us? Who should go?*

Davin clearly pulled the short straw, appearing at her door in a checked blue shirt and red pants.

"So, how are you doing?" he asked, his sleek blond hair flopping in his face. "We didn't think we'd see you today."

She shrugged. "Better to be busy. Besides"—she pointed at the big calendar on the wall, counting down days to the gala—"time's a-ticking." *Time's a-ticking? Where did that expression come from?*

Davin picked up a stack of folders from the extra chair and dumped them unceremoniously onto her desk before sitting down. "How are the numbers looking?"

"Okay. Not great. I'd like to finagle a few more sponsorships. Vanessa certainly expects me to, anyway."

Since joining Nourish Our Youth (or NOY, as it was affectionately, or disparagingly, known, depending on who was speaking) as director, Vanessa had been scratching and clawing to expand the organization's coffers. She refused to accept the conventional wisdom that they were never going to be a major player in foundation circles.

Founded by the daughter of a wealthy upstate New York family, NOY had long been content to bump along fairly steadily. The initial board of directors was composed of the founder's friends from her prestigious northeastern women's college, and they spent many hours disagreeing on what children so unlike themselves needed. Some wanted to focus on physical needs (food, clothing, and shelter) while others wanted to focus on education (schools, books, and scholarships). In the end, NOY sought to do it all, making it difficult to compete with more single-minded organizations for donors.

Vanessa was trying to correct this lack of direction by pushing them toward education while simultaneously raising NOY's profile—hence her decision to bring Davin in as communications director. One of his biggest brainchilds thus far had been the Empty Library. The prior summer, they'd set up a symbolic "library" in Washington Square Park. It consisted of two walls of bookshelves, enough to accommodate at least three hundred books. But only a dozen tomes were displayed underneath a banner that said *Our Children Deserve More.*

The idea was to demonstrate the unmet educational needs of underprivileged students and to invite the community to contribute. Unfortunately, it was a bit of a debacle to keep the display in working order for the full week. Several pornographic magazines appeared on the shelves overnight, and some words parents wouldn't want their children to learn were graffitied on the back of the shelves. (Cleverly, they were carefully printed as rhymes: *LUCK, DUCK, SUCK,* etc.) Nonetheless, Davin secured NOY's first blurb in *New York Magazine.*

Now Amber appeared in the doorway of her office. "I brought you a cup of tea," she announced, holding a mug emblazoned with the logo of a line of educational toys. Eliza recognized it as a leftover from the swag bags at last year's gala.

She reached for the mug. "The bread was delicious, by the way."

Amber smiled broadly, her dangly earrings jingling. "Isn't it yummy?"

"Hey, why don't you bring us all some bread?" Davin asked.

Patrice stepped in before Amber could reply. "Because she's not a baker. She's our admin. Eliza! Why are you even here?" Her face creased with worry.

"I need to keep busy. Besides, there's lots to be done." Eliza found herself pointing again at the calendar.

"You also need to give yourself space to grieve," Patrice said gently.

"I'm sure Eliza knows what she needs," Vanessa said briskly, squeezing into the office herself. Her entrance had the same effect as a light being flicked on in the kitchen in the middle of the night, sending the mice scurrying.

Moments later, Vanessa was seated in the chair Davin had vacated, one leg neatly crossed over the other, her high-heeled pump dangling off one toe. "You're okay?" she asked in a tone that suggested there was only one correct answer to her question.

Eliza nodded.

"Good. And you're absolutely right. It's important to keep busy. Now. Where are we on our numbers?"

Eliza clicked through a few screens on her computer to scan the back end of the online invitation. There had been little movement since she'd been gazing at these figures when Scott called her with the news the prior week. As she tried to quickly analyze what she was seeing, the data began to swim in front of her. She blinked rapidly, realizing her eyes had inexplicably filled with tears.

She cleared her throat. "Slow but steady," she offered.

"Steady is good. Slow not so much." Vanessa uncrossed her leg and put both feet on the floor, leaning toward Eliza. "You know we've upped our marketing budget. I really need to see ticket sales and sponsorships go up commensurately. The board will be expecting that."

Eliza knew how this worked. Vanessa made budget decisions that didn't pan out, and then it was up to everyone else to repair the damage so the board didn't string her up.

"Of course," she replied, willing calm into her voice. "I have a few irons in the fire that I can try to nudge along this week." Nothing like a well-placed cliché to fill the silence. Then she had a sudden thought. "And just the other day I was talking with the marketing team at Swishtech. We're trying to figure out a way for us to partner." *No need to elaborate that this was a chat over tea with Mo.*

"Excellent. I have every confidence you'll bring this home. But I need you to think big." Vanessa picked up the snow globe sitting on Eliza's desk—a gag gift from Mo, after they'd spent years marveling at how many souvenir shops flourished in Times Square. As Vanessa absentmindedly jiggled it in her hand, silver sparkles swirled around the Empire State Building. "Maybe we should have a team brainstorming session."

Eliza nodded. "And I'll follow up with the board. Make

sure they're nudging all their personal contacts." A few weeks earlier, when the physical invitations went out—cream card stock with the NOY logo embossed in rose gold—board members had sat in the conference room, handwriting notes on the invitations and scrawling their own names on the envelopes above the NOY return address. That afternoon now felt like it had been a year ago. In another lifetime.

Vanessa stood, brushing a piece of nonexistent lint off her pencil skirt. "Sounds good. I'll shoot around an email to set up the team brainstorm." She sometimes seemed to forget that she no longer worked at an international conglomerate.

After work, Eliza found herself veering away from the subway station that would take her home, heading down Third Avenue instead. She consciously slowed her pace, feeling like a slug alongside everyone else moving at New York speed. She didn't realize she had a destination until she found herself in Kips Bay, a few blocks from Scott and Maren's. Maren had texted her over the weekend—a check-in to make sure she hadn't gone completely off the deep end, Eliza surmised. But she hadn't heard from Scott. Sitting on the shelf next to that conversation she needed to have was the conversation she needed to have with Aunt Claude. Her aunt had texted her every day but was respecting her privacy by not asking about the letter. The truth sat like a stone in her stomach, filling her up so that she could barely swallow anything else. She knew she needed to share it—as the keeper of the letter for so many years, Claude deserved to know. But when she thought about saying the words aloud again, her throat closed up.

As she turned the corner onto Scott and Maren's street, the distinctive sweetness of roasted chestnuts wafted by. As New York smells went, it was one of the pleasant ones—although Eliza had never met anyone who actually ate roasted chestnuts. On a whim, she stopped to buy a bag from the vendor, who wore a canvas apron over his clothes and a Sikh turban.

"Here, take two," he said, raising his hands in protest when she tried to give the extra one back. "You're my last sale for the day. I always give a bonus on my last sale." He smiled, his eyes crinkling. "Especially when it's to a pretty girl," he added.

She felt her face flush and wished she had learned how to gracefully accept a compliment. "Have a good night," she called to him over her shoulder.

A few moments later, she stood in front of Scott and Maren's apartment door, clutching her bags of chestnuts, suddenly afraid to knock. They probably weren't even home yet from work, she reasoned. She paused and heard a burst of male laughter from behind the door. Quickly pulling her phone out of her purse, she texted her brother. **Hey. Can I come over? I'm in the neighborhood.**

She waited, watching the three dots dance on the screen.

Finally four letters appeared: **Sure.** Impossible to tell from that single word what he was feeling. If he was still angry with her. She knocked.

When the door opened, Eliza was peering into one of the paper bags, moist with steam. "I brought chestnuts," she said.

"I can't say I've ever tried them." Josh's voice was amused, and Eliza stepped back, annoyed by the stutter his voice activated in her chest.

"Oh! Josh. I didn't know you were here."

He shrugged. "I stopped by to check on Scott. I guess you did, too."

She cleared her throat. "Something like that."

He moved aside to let her in. He wore a dark blue half-zip sweater that looked like it had at least some cashmere in the weave. She didn't think she could reach out and touch his sleeve without it seeming really odd. Even if she said she just wanted to feel the fabric.

Scott stepped out of the kitchen in jeans and a plaid button-down over a T-shirt. "Eliza—you weren't kidding when you said you were in the neighborhood. You must have been in the elevator when you texted."

"Well, I didn't know if you'd want to see me." She glanced at Josh, hating that she was doing this with an audience. "After the other night."

Scott scrubbed his face with his hand and exhaled a deep sigh. "What the hell were you thinking, Eliza?"

A part of her rose up at his words—true, she had behaved badly, but hadn't her whole world been turned upside down? But she tamped her emotions down. "I wasn't thinking. I hadn't eaten. And it just came out."

Scott raised his eyebrows. "And you were drunk."

Would she ever reach an age at which her older brother wouldn't scold her?

"And I was drunk," she repeated heavily, digging the fingernails of her empty left hand into her palm, very conscious of Josh standing beside her. "I shouldn't have told you about the letter until I was ready to talk about it. You pushed me—and it just came out."

Scott was quiet, his lips pressed together. "Well, I guess it made for a more exciting shiva than most."

Something eased inside Eliza.

"I brought roasted chestnuts," she said, extending the bag in her hand.

"Does anyone actually eat those things?" Scott's eyebrows drew together.

"We could try them . . . ?"

A few minutes later, they were sitting around the dining table, the roasted chestnuts dumped into a cereal bowl Scott had grabbed from the kitchen. They all studied the dark brown spheres, split open to reveal the almond-colored flesh inside.

Odd to think of the insides as almond colored. Aren't they—by definition—chestnut colored?

"Okay, well, one of us has to go first," Josh announced, reaching for one and popping it into his mouth. Scott and Eliza both watched his face as he began to chew. And chew. And then swallow. He looked from one to the other before announcing, "Yeah, no, I won't be having one of those again."

Scott snorted, and Eliza was happy to hear him laugh. Without a word he went back to the kitchen and returned with a plate of cookies covered with cling wrap. "Shiva spoils," he said, putting them on the table. "Maren and I were talking about ordering Chinese food. You guys should stay."

Josh glanced at Eliza. "Well—if E doesn't mind. You guys might have family stuff to talk about."

She had forgotten that Josh used to call her E. It had been a long time.

"It's all good," Scott replied before popping a shortbread cookie into his mouth.

Later that evening, the four of them sat around the dining table, the plates in front of them marked with streaks of soy sauce and grains of fried rice that had escaped their chopsticks. Eliza had served herself a small portion of moo shu and an even smaller one of rice.

"That's all you're eating?" Josh had asked.

"I filled up on cookies," she replied, looking at her plate. When she glanced up at him, she could tell from his expression that he knew she'd eaten only one cookie, but he dropped the subject.

"Ugh. I ate too much," Maren moaned, pressing a hand to her stomach. "But it was so good."

"I told you not to have that third helping. You're going to

be up all night," Scott said, but his smile belied the scolding in his words.

"Eh—it's worth it." Maren moved her plate farther away from herself. Then she glanced at Scott briefly before turning to Eliza. "So—can we talk about your mom's letter?"

The little bit of food she'd managed to consume churned. "I guess. I don't know what to say about it."

Scott shook his head. "I just can't believe it. I can't believe Mom would . . ." His voice trailed off. "Jesus. I wonder if Dad knew."

"I guess we'll never know," Eliza replied, the words getting a little stuck in her throat.

"Unless Carol knows."

The thought of Jack confiding in Carol that Laura had cheated made Eliza's scalp tingle. Could that be why Carol had been so cold when she spoke about her husband's first wife? Had been so prickly with Eliza?

"Do you really think he would have told her?" she asked, in a small voice.

"She was his wife, Eliza." Scott's tone suggested that the honesty and openness between husband and wife were complete and total. *But are they?*

"But what are *you* going to do, Eliza? I mean, your biological dad is out there somewhere." Maren leaned forward and looked at her intently.

Eliza couldn't pretend that this question hadn't been bobbing on the horizon of her mind ever since she'd read Laura's letter. Sometimes the clouds scudded past, obscuring it, but it was always there, taunting her.

Before she could reply, Scott interrupted. "No matter what, Eliza, Dad was your dad. This other guy—what do we know about him? That he slept with another man's wife."

It was all so black and white for Scott. But this "other guy" wasn't his birth father. He was Eliza's father. And in her mind, she kept coming back to Laura's letter and her confession that she and Jack had "ups and downs" in their marriage. The more Eliza thought about it, the more she knew it was true. The times that her parents barely spoke. Or spoke through Scott. *Tell your mother that I'm going out to take care of some things. I'm not sure when I'll be back.*

And this "other guy" had been Laura's high school boyfriend. She'd loved him. At least once upon a time.

Eliza was very aware of Josh sitting opposite her at the table. "I know he's basically a stranger. But the truth is—he's my father. And Mom wanted me to know. How do I ignore that?"

"I don't know, Eliza. I have no idea what I'd do if I were in your shoes. But it's not like you can just replace Dad. Ooh—instant dad!"

"Scott—come on."

Eliza appreciated Maren's interjection. And didn't appreciate Scott's tone.

"Look—I don't know what's going to happen. I don't even know how I'd find him. But there's definitely a part of me that wants to."

Scott abruptly pushed his chair back from the table, picked up his plate, and went into the kitchen.

Eliza shrugged. "I guess the conversation is over?"

The roasted-chestnut vendor was long gone when Eliza and Josh passed his corner on their way to the subway. When she'd announced she was heading home, Josh stood up, too.

"You don't have to go—I'm just tired," she'd said immediately, not sure how she felt about the prospect of having to make polite conversation with him alone in the elevator.

"No, it's getting late. I should go, too."

So now they were walking side by side toward Park Avenue South. It was the first time they'd been alone together in a very long time. Since the afternoon Eliza tried not to think about.

"Sorry I ended up intruding on a family conversation," Josh said, hitching his messenger bag higher on his shoulder.

"S'okay. I probably gave up my right to privacy when I announced the news to a roomful of people."

"Still." Josh stopped, and Eliza drew to a halt beside him. "I was worried about you the other night."

She felt a flash of annoyance—and something else she couldn't name. What right did he have to *worry* about her? "I'm fine. I mean, not fine. But you don't have to worry about me."

Josh looked at the sky and sighed. "I didn't mean it like that. I just . . ." His voice trailed away.

"Yeah." Eliza started walking again, and he followed a moment later, his long legs easily carrying him alongside her again.

"Look—if you want to try to find your dad—I mean, your biological dad—I might be able to help. I have access to lots of databases and records at my firm."

"Not sure Scott would want you helping me. Doesn't seem like he wants me to look at all."

"Scott doesn't always know what's best." Josh's tone was sharper than she would have expected, and this time she stopped walking.

She pushed the strands of hair that had come loose from her braid behind her ear. "So are you saying you think I should look for him?"

Josh shrugged. "Obviously, it's your choice. But I can understand why you'd want to. I mean, you've got to have a lot of questions, and no one else can answer them."

She swallowed hard and nodded, blinking rapidly. Somehow, Josh had struck right to the heart of what she was feeling. *How is he still able to do that after all these years?*

"Shit, E. I'm sorry. I didn't mean . . ."

"No, no. It's okay. I'm just a mess."

"No, you're not. You're grieving. Your dad's only been gone a week."

She sniffled and flapped her hands in front of her face. She hated how she looked when she cried. And hated that she cared how she looked in front of Josh.

"Look. We don't have to talk about this now. Or ever. But I just wanted you to know that whatever I can do to help, I'll do."

Is this his way of trying to make amends?

Before she could reply, her phone pinged in her pocket. "Sorry, just a sec." She pulled it out and swiped, glancing down at the text. "My friend Mo with her nightly check-in," she explained, smiling. "She worries if she doesn't hear from me." As she said it, she realized the irony of her words—she so hated to be worried about, but guessed it was okay to have one "authorized worrier."

Josh nodded. "That's nice. What about this Carson guy?"

"Who?" Her eyebrows knitted together before she realized who he meant. "Carter," she corrected.

He made a face like it really made no difference if his name was Carson, Carter, or Cowabunga.

"What about him?" she prompted.

"Just . . . I hope he's looking out for you, too."

She actually hadn't heard from Carter since he'd left her place Saturday morning, but that was hardly something she wanted to share with Josh. Why was he asking all these questions anyway? It had been years since the two of them had really talked.

She sidestepped his question. "How's what's-her-name? The woman you were with at Scott's wedding." She resumed walking, and he fell into step beside her.

"Susannah? She's okay as far as I know. We broke up nearly a year ago."

"Oh—sorry. I didn't know."

"It's fine. It was mutual."

They reached the subway station at Park Avenue South and Thirty-Third Street.

Josh pushed his hand through his unruly dark hair. "Let me give you my number. If you want to reach out about finding your dad . . . or anything . . . give me a call."

"Sure, thanks." She tapped his number into her contacts, even as she doubted she'd ever use it, then headed down the steps to the uptown train.

CHAPTER SEVEN

Eliza huddled under her quilt in a long-sleeved T-shirt and sweatpants. She was exhausted, but every time she closed her eyes they popped open again, staring at the shadowy ceiling. When Laura died, Eliza's brain had forgotten how to regulate her sleep-wake cycle. She'd longed to curl up under the covers and seize unconsciousness, but no matter when she went to bed, she'd be wide awake at 4:00 a.m. Ever since, the fear of losing the ability to sleep again had buzzed beneath the surface whenever she went to bed. Having someone in bed with her was an effective way of turning the volume down on that fear, but when Carter had texted her **You up?** a few minutes earlier, she'd ignored him.

There was no doubt he could provide pleasant distraction, so she wasn't sure why she didn't even consider texting back. Well, for more than three seconds, anyway. Or why she'd had the urge to fling her phone across the room when the text came in.

She'd spent more time Googling Ross Sawyer, but there were too many in the right age bracket to know which one was her mom's ex-boyfriend. *Her father.* She suspected he wasn't the minister in Iowa. But there was a vice president at a Manhattan-based bank who was the right age. And a blogger on Medium who had written a single post about sticking to your New Year's resolutions. And a Boston College alumnus who had donated at the "Friend" level to the school's endowment fund. And a few others whose age she couldn't figure out. But nothing included information either confirming or denying that he'd grown up in the Albany suburb Laura hailed from.

Mo continued to advise caution since this man was, obviously, a complete stranger, whoever he was. But it was more complicated than that. Jack—the man she'd called Dad all her life—had just died. Suddenly. Without warning.

When Laura had passed away (Eliza hated that phrase—there was nothing gentle about the demarcation between life and death), they'd known it was coming. Eliza had come straight home from school every day, doing her homework at the coffee table while her mom rested in the recliner. And, later, at a snack table in her bedroom when Laura could barely get out of bed. They talked about school, and Eliza's friends, and even what college might be like—knowing it was too soon for her to have any idea where she'd go, but that Laura would be gone long before the decision was made.

Eliza knew how Laura's skin changed, and how she could feel the bones in her mother's fingers when she held her hand. When hospice nurses came and the morphine dose was raised, she started to stay home from school, so that when her mom's eyes fluttered open in a moment of alertness, she'd be there to tell her that she loved her.

Jack and Scott were there, too, but were hazy in Eliza's memories. Scott was a senior and playing varsity tennis. Jack went to work, and when he came home, he immediately flipped on the TV. She couldn't understand why they didn't want to hold on to every Laura-minute while they could.

And then Laura was gone. And Eliza forgot how to sleep.

But when Jack died, it was a lightning bolt. Eliza couldn't remember the last time they'd spoken. Probably nearly a month before. And the last time she'd seen him? She'd been talked into attending the Fourth of July barbecue he and Carol hosted every year. Which, whether it was intentional or not, always felt like an ode to the graduation party at which they'd met, only a month after Laura's death.

The truth was, Eliza might as well have lost Jack at the same time she lost Laura. And now she'd lost any chance of ever getting him back—even as she had a new potential father dangling in front of her. A part of her felt guilty for even considering displacing the dad she'd lost, the dad who hadn't been there for her as she wanted him to be, but who—she had to admit—she'd probably helped push away. But another part of her wondered if, as unlikely as it seemed, maybe Ross was the dad who could actually understand her. Could give her something she'd been missing since Laura died. Something that felt like unconditional love.

By the time Eliza finally fell asleep, she'd decided she couldn't put off talking to Aunt Claude any longer. When her eyes popped open at 4:26 a.m., before she could change her mind, she shot off a quick text that Claude answered at 7:03. It must have been the first thing she did before she got out of bed. Eliza could picture her, pushing her dark hair behind her ear and reaching for her reading glasses to look at her phone. And then immediately typing a response.

Mere hours later, Claude was at the door of her apartment, carrying a white bakery box. *Why does food play such a big role in grief?*

"Eliza . . ." Claude's voice trailed off, her lips pressed together.

Eliza smiled sadly in response.

"I brought pastries." Claude held the box aloft. "Are you eating?"

"Sort of."

The expression on her aunt's face suggested that she could recognize a lie when she saw one.

"Well, you're not going to be able to resist these." She opened the lid and tilted the box toward Eliza, simultaneously flipping back the wax paper to reveal the crowded collection of mini cannoli, sfogliatelle, madeleines, cream puffs, and napoleons.

"I'll get some plates." She went into her matchbox kitchen and pulled a couple of square white dishes from the cabinet alongside the refrigerator. "Do you want anything to drink? I can make tea."

"Sure, if you're getting it for yourself."

Eliza busied herself with the teapot while Claude took off her quilted jacket. When Eliza turned back toward her, Claude was gazing around the apartment, seemingly looking for something.

"Just put your jacket wherever. No coat closet. No coatrack."

Claude laughed softly. "Right. New York City apartments." Once she'd arranged it on one of the two chairs that hunched around the small table alongside the refrigerator, she moved toward Eliza, who was dropping tea bags into two mugs. One had the NOY logo on it; the other was white with blue block lettering: *Life's a bitch, and then you die.* Eliza picked that one up and held it toward Claude.

"Kinda perfect, right?" she asked.

Claude sighed. "Eliza. I don't even know what to say."

Eliza shrugged in response. "There's nothing *to* say. Anyway, sit. Sofa is comfier than the table."

A few minutes later, they were seated on the couch, the box of pastries open on the coffee table next to the envelope with Laura's and Claude's handwriting on it. Eliza had spent a long time turning her apartment into a home. She'd scoured thrift shops and boutiques choosing furniture and accent pieces, supplementing with Wayfair and Joss & Main. She especially loved the round distressed-wood coffee table and the plush area rug that was cozy under bare feet. Eclectic art, mostly purchased from street artists, decorated the soft gray walls.

Snuggled into the sofa with her feet tucked under her, Eliza took a small sip of her tea and then put the mug down. "So," she started. "Here's the letter." She passed the envelope to Claude.

"You want me to read it?"

Eliza nodded, and watched her aunt slip the paper out of the envelope. She'd read it herself so many times that she almost thought she could recite it by heart as Claude read it silently. Her aunt's eyes widened and she brought her hand to her mouth, glancing at Eliza before refocusing on the letter. When she finished reading, she carefully refolded the piece of paper and slid it back into the envelope. It was as if she'd been struck mute.

"So I guess you didn't know?"

Claude shook her head slowly. "I'm speechless. I . . . I can't believe Laura didn't tell me. I can't believe Laura . . ." Her voice trailed off.

Eliza bit the inside of her lip. Her aunt was her only hope when it came to getting information about her father. "Do you remember him? Ross Sawyer?"

Claude stared at her for a moment before seeming to realize that she was expected to answer. "Sure. Of course. He and your mom were together for a long time. A couple of years at least. They started dating sophomore year in high school, I think."

"What was he like?" Eliza reached for a cream puff from the box and brought it to her mouth before realizing she didn't think she could swallow a single bite. She dropped it onto one of the plates instead.

Her aunt made a sound like a laugh. "It's funny. I kinda had a crush on him myself. I mean, I was twelve when he started coming around . . . Cool older guy . . ." She made air quotes around the word *older.*

"He was cool?" Eliza had a sudden, ridiculous image of someone resembling the Fonz—or James Dean in *Rebel Without a Cause*—sauntering through her grandparents' living room.

"Oh, I don't know what I meant by that." Claude stared off into the middle distance for a moment. "I remember when he got his license—he'd saved up for a car. It was blue. God. I know that's not telling you anything."

Eliza shook her head, clasping her hands together to keep them from shaking.

"Let's see. He was tall. At least, he seemed tall to me. Taller than your mom. Sandy hair, kind of curly. Our dad—Grandpa—used to say he should get a haircut. He was lanky." She paused. "There have to be photos somewhere. I know your mom had some up in her room. I doubt she would have thrown them away. Or at least the yearbook. For sure that's still around."

"Where?"

Claude shrugged. "I don't know. It could be in the attic at your parents' house . . . I mean . . ." Claude suddenly stopped, clearly hung up on the word *parents.*

"I know what you mean. I mean—my dad is my dad. Jack, I mean. He raised me."

Claude nodded. "Jack and Ross were pretty different, actually," she said thoughtfully.

Eliza pushed her cold hands under her thighs. "In what way?"

"This is going to sound woo-woo . . ." She fluttered her

fingers in the air. "But they had a different energy. Jack was always steady. Ross bounced in different directions. He had trouble sitting still. He'd jump up from his chair a lot. Fiddle with things. Wow. I hadn't thought of that in—well—forever. It drove Grandma insane. After he left our house, there'd always be a ballpoint pen taken apart. He talked about doing stuff like taking time off after high school and going cross-country on a motorcycle."

Eliza had that flash of James Dean again. Maybe it wasn't so far off.

"He wanted to change the world. I remember Grandma saying he could get his college degree and *then* change the world."

"Why did they break up?"

Claude bit her lower lip. "I'm trying to remember. They stayed together for a while after they left for college. Ross went to . . . it was Hamilton or Haverford . . . I can't remember. Small school kinda around here. You know this was all before cell phones and email. They talked on the phone, but it was hard because of the time difference with Laura in California. There was a big fight, though. I think Ross met someone else . . . ? Laura was *really* upset—but she didn't want to talk about it."

"And then she met Dad? Jack?"

Claude nodded. "You know this part. He was in business school. Your mom was working in the library, and he started going there to study when she was at the circulation desk."

This was the family lore. When Eliza had seen *The Music Man*, she'd pictured her dad as Harold Hill, romancing Marian in the Gary, Indiana, library—though Jack was hardly someone who would dance around among the stacks. At least not the Jack she knew.

"It's funny," Claude continued, "they really were different— in what they cared about, and how they carried themselves— but they were both pretty . . . I don't know. Strong-minded?

What was right and what was wrong was pretty clear for both of them."

"Dad certainly never hesitated to share his opinions."

"Nope. And neither did Ross. Funny. Never thought about that before . . ."

"Why would you? You probably forgot Ross existed."

"True." Claude took a sip of her tea and put the cup down on the table. "Sorry, Lize. I just don't know what to say. I can't believe it."

"Me either." She twisted her fingers together. "Did Mom talk about him at all? Was he 'the one who got away'?"

Claude shook her head. "I don't remember her ever saying anything. But when you kids were little she was always so busy and overwhelmed—and then I had my kids. We were close, but we didn't talk all the time. I can barely even remember her *going* to that reunion."

"What about Dad? Jack? The letter said that their marriage wasn't great."

Claude sighed. "What marriage doesn't have its ups and downs? Look—I wasn't ever super close to your dad. I think you know that. So if your mom was going to complain about him, it wouldn't have been to me. If that makes sense."

"So who would she have talked to?"

"Good question. Maybe no one."

One dead end after another.

Poor choice of words.

Claude picked up the envelope again and ran her finger along the words on the outside. "All the years she kept this secret. I can't even imagine what that was like for her. I wish . . ." Her voice faded away, and she blinked rapidly before clearing her throat to begin again. "So, what are you going to do now?"

"Honestly? I have no clue. Do you have any idea what happened to him? Ross Sawyer?"

Her aunt shook her head.

"Scott doesn't think I should look for him. That Dad is Dad and that's that."

"Well, all due respect to Scott—it's not his decision." Claude put her mug down on the coffee table and reached for Eliza's hands. "Only you can decide what to do about this. But if you want my advice . . . give yourself some time. You just lost your second parent. This is huge news. Don't rush into anything."

Eliza knew that was sound advice. But she wasn't sure she was going to be able to take it.

CHAPTER EIGHT

For a week, Eliza tried to push it all out of her mind. She went to work and pinned down two more sponsors for the dinner—a maker of educational toys and a publishing house. Her predecessor had opened a lot of doors, and Eliza had discovered she had a gift for keeping them open and even parlaying them into finding other doors. Vanessa was delighted with her progress and with the fact that she was still sitting at her desk when everyone else had gone for the day.

Despite the chill in the air, she walked home—the full thirty-two blocks north—rather than take the subway, willing her mind to be blank as she people-watched and window-shopped. She'd get takeout somewhere along the way and hope that she'd get home exhausted enough to finally fall asleep. But every night she found herself staring at something streaming on her laptop and ignoring Carter's texts. She was tempted to let him come over, just for the distraction. But as much as she didn't want to talk about what was really on her mind, she also didn't want to spend time with someone who would let her get away with that.

As the weekend approached, she decided to go up to her

dad's house—*Carol's house?*—to look for her mom's old year-books and photos. She considered asking Scott to go along with her—he'd always gotten along better with Carol than she had—but she knew he wouldn't approve of her mission.

With the benefit of distance, she sometimes wondered if she would like Carol if she weren't her stepmother. If she hadn't moved into her home less than a year after Laura died. If she hadn't taken down the photos that included her predecessor. If she hadn't reorganized the kitchen. If she hadn't intimated that Eliza was using her grief to manipulate everyone around her.

Eliza took the train up to Westchester and Ubered to the house. She had an empty tote bag over her shoulder ready to fill with anything she found. The front yard was pristine; the landscaper must have been there recently with the leaf blower. The windows, framed with shiny black shutters, looked out at her blankly from the brick facade. At the front door, she rang the bell. Once she'd graduated from college and moved to the city, Carol had asked that she no longer use her key to let herself in. "I think it would be better if you rang the doorbell," she'd said, careful not to even glance in her direction from where she stood at the kitchen counter, pouring creamer into her coffee.

Now, Eliza stood on the front step, wondering if she should ring again. She was about to when the front door opened. Carol wore a neat pin-striped shirt, unbuttoned to reveal a scoop-neck tank that showed her cleavage, along with slim-fit dark-wash jeans and a smile that didn't reach her eyes.

Eliza automatically stepped forward to hug her step-mother, who allowed it. Jack had insisted upon these hugs for years—despite the fact that Carol didn't reciprocate. She was plenty affectionate with Jack, always perching on the arm of whatever chair he sat in, her hand on his shoulder. But Eliza had never received a proper hug from her, not even on Carol and Jack's wedding day, when Eliza and Scott had served as maid of honor and best man at the simple ceremony at the country club Carol had wanted them to join.

"How are you doing?" Eliza asked, reminding herself that, whatever her own feelings about her, Carol *had* just lost her husband.

"All right, considering," she said evenly.

Eliza took off her olive green utility jacket and stood holding it—unsure if she should put it down somewhere, go to the closet and hang it, or wait for Carol to take it. The woman had a way of making Eliza feel completely unsettled in what was once her own home.

Carol took it and hung it in the closet. "Can I get you something?" she asked. The signals were clear. Eliza was the guest.

"No, thanks, I'm fine."

Carol nodded and turned toward the kitchen. Eliza followed, conscious of how strange it was to be in the house with Jack gone. For the first time she wondered if Carol would continue living there. Before she could stop herself, the words were out of her mouth. "So, do you plan to stay here?"

Her stepmother glanced over her shoulder, her eyebrows raised. "It *is* my home. It has been for nine years."

"I know. I just meant. Well." Eliza's voice disappeared. By now they were in the kitchen, and Carol topped off her ever-present cup of coffee before sitting down at the round kitchen table. The rectangular one at which Laura had served meals, along with the padded banquette seating that ran along one wall, had been removed many years earlier. Eliza sat opposite her.

"And you? How are you doing?" Carol asked, gazing at her over the rim of her cup.

"Fine. I mean, sad. But fine."

It was a knee-jerk response. In truth, Eliza wasn't sure how she was. But even if she were, it was unlikely she'd share it with Carol. Carol, who had seen her at her worst—pale and drawn and sometimes unable to drag herself out of bed to go to school. There had been conferences with Jack and the high school guidance department. Schoolwork sent home. Scott was away at college, seeming better able to move past—or at least compartmentalize—his grief. When he'd come home for a weekend during October of her junior year, he'd been shocked by her appearance. She could hear him talking to Jack about her. "What's going on with Eliza?" he'd asked. "I'm worried about her." And Jack's gruff response: "I'm doing the best I can." Which meant going to work and spending more and more time with his new girlfriend. Carol had brought her treats for a while, store-bought cookies and brownies that only made Eliza think about the homemade ones Laura used to bake.

And then, suddenly, they were engaged. Jack announced it to Scott and Eliza over holiday break. Carol came over to cook them all dinner. Somewhat gluey lasagna. Eliza picked at it and considered announcing she was becoming a vegan. Meanwhile, Jack and Carol kept exchanging glances until finally, Jack cleared his throat. "Carol and I have an announcement to make." He reached to take her hand; she was sitting in the chair that used to be Eliza's. Scott was in his usual seat, with Eliza next to him. Laura's chair was conspicuously empty. "I know it may seem sudden. But when it's right, it's right. I couldn't have gotten through the past seven months without her. We're engaged. We'll get married in the spring, but Carol is moving in immediately."

The lasagna congealed in Eliza's stomach. Scott recovered first. "Wow. Dad. Carol. Congratulations."

Eliza looked up at Carol and was sure she saw triumph in her eyes. "Wait. Married? Already? And this is how you tell us?" Her face grew hot and her hands shook. She could see herself, predictably stepping into the bratty-daughter role that Carol had already cast her in. But she couldn't help herself.

"Mom hasn't even been gone a year. How could you?" She pushed back her chair so abruptly that it would have crashed onto the floor if Scott hadn't caught it.

"Eliza!" Jack's voice followed her as Eliza bolted toward the stairs. She heard Carol's voice murmur something as she headed up to her room, expecting her father's bellow to follow. But there was nothing but the sound of her bedroom door slamming.

It was much later that Scott knocked softly and then let himself in when Eliza didn't respond.

"Shove over," he said, plopping down on her bed as she quickly slid toward the wall to avoid being sat on.

"Congratulations," Eliza said in a simultaneously gruff and singsong voice, mimicking her brother's response to Jack's announcement.

"Cut it out, Eliza. Getting pissed off doesn't change anything."

"Whatever." She wanted to be the kind of kid who could be happy for her dad. But she didn't know how to be that kid without also being the kid who was betraying her dead mom.

"Look. I know it's hard. And I know it's easier for me because I'm gone most of the time. But you only have another year and a half to get through. If you can pull yourself together and actually graduate from high school, you can leave for college. Start fresh. Mom would . . ."

Eliza sat up. "Don't tell me what Mom would want!" she hissed.

Scott heaved a deep sigh. "Fine. I won't. But think about it yourself. What would she say if she were here?"

She balled up her fists as her eyes stung, and she found herself thinking, *You get what you get and you don't get upset.* She almost choked on the strangled laugh that started to bubble up out of her.

Scott suddenly swiped at his own eyes, and Eliza looked at him. "You okay?"

"Jesus, Eliza. Of course I'm not okay. I'm just trying to keep it together here."

She pressed her lips together. She could hear the unspoken *And having to referee between you and Dad doesn't help.* She put her head on his shoulder. "Hey. Wanna play some *Legend of Zelda*?"

Scott pulled away and looked at her. "Wow. You must really think I'm a mess if you're offering."

She had shrugged. "Hey. I have my moments. Grab them while you can."

Now, sitting across the table from Carol, she wished she had brought Scott with her. At least he knew how to make small talk with their stepmother.

"So, do you still have food left over from shiva?" she asked. "Are you hungry?"

"No, I just . . ." Words once again failed her.

"I've had neighbors and friends dropping off meals. They seem to think I have the appetite of a family of four."

Eliza nodded, remembering the endless meal train that started before Laura died and continued for months. So much food that she couldn't eat.

Carol drummed her fingers on the table. "So. Are you going to tell me your news?"

"My news?" Eliza was bewildered.

"Your mother's letter."

"Wait. What? How did you . . . ?"

"My nephew Adam was at Scott's for your . . . outburst."

Eliza ticked back through that hazy evening. Yes, Carol was right. Adam had been there. She could imagine him picking up the phone immediately to call his mom, Carol's sister. Among Scott's high school friends, he was definitely not her favorite.

"Quite the turn of events," Carol observed, rising to refill her coffee. Again.

"Yes. I really don't know what to say about it."

"I can't imagine you do." Carol turned and watched her.

Eliza's mouth felt like cotton. She wanted something to drink but was a little afraid to ask for water. Or to go to the cabinet for a glass herself. *Is now the time to ask if Dad knew? If he suspected?* She didn't think she could. Not now. Maybe not ever.

"Actually," she began, "I wanted to go through my mom's things. Yearbooks. Photo albums . . ."

"Of course. They're in the attic. Help yourself." Eliza rose from the table, eager to leave the kitchen, and then Carol continued. "Feel free to take those sorts of items. But I'd prefer you not take anything else. The will does need to go through probate. I'm sure you understand."

CHAPTER NINE

Later that afternoon, Eliza was again on the train headed to Grand Central, her tote bag crammed full of yearbooks, photo albums, and a few envelopes containing random pictures and memorabilia. She'd probably looked through the yearbooks before but didn't think she'd ever seen the other items. Perhaps Laura had boxed them away from curious children's eyes.

She was grateful that Carol hadn't chucked it all, even as she was simmering about her stepmother's remark that she shouldn't "take anything else." What did she think she was going to take? She already had the pieces of her mom's jewelry that were important to her—a locket with Eliza's and Scott's photos inside, a delicate gold watch, a pretty silver bangle, and a few other items. Scott might want some things of Jack's—perhaps his well-worn wallet, or his heavy, multifunction watch. Would Carol keep those items from him? What did she mean the will had to go through probate? Eliza had never thought about what would happen when Jack died. Who had he left everything to? She suspected Scott knew—it was the kind of thing he would have paid attention to. That Jack would have discussed with him. Not much of anything was discussed with Eliza.

She'd wanted to get out of the house as fast as possible. Carol's eerie calm made her uncomfortable. And she didn't want to answer any other questions about her biological father. So when she found the photo of Ross Sawyer in the yearbook, she hadn't pored over it. Hadn't examined it—yet—for any resemblance between her features and his. She was hoping she'd find more photos of him, and maybe even other things— did teenagers in the seventies write letters to each other? But all she'd done was cram everything she could find into her bag so she could head back into the city.

When she got to her apartment, she immediately emptied the tote onto the kitchen table and stood staring at the detritus of a life. Or at least the teenage portion of it. Her lips were pressed tightly together, and she could feel the telltale burning of rising tears in her sinuses. Whether it was grief over her mother, or over her father, or over the death of her origin story—or a mixture of all three, along with a dash, or more, of anger—she couldn't tell. Whatever it was, she wasn't sure she could face it alone. She quickly texted an SOS to Mo, who appeared at her door within the hour, wearing leggings and a windbreaker, not her usual pressed-and-dressed tailored garb.

"I know, I know. But I just got out of yoga, and it didn't sound like you could wait for me to shower. So apologies in advance if I stink."

Whatever she smelled like, Eliza was grateful to see her.

"What did you find?" Mo asked, heading straight into the kitchen for a tall glass of cold water.

Eliza gestured toward the table. "Haven't looked at it yet. To be honest, I'm a little freaked out by what might be there."

Mo took a long swallow. "Got it. Okay. So let's take it one step at a time. How about yearbooks first? Probably the least radioactive."

Soon they were poring over the black-and-white photos. Eliza resisted turning directly to the *S*'s.

"Why in the world did people in the seventies think that feathered hair was a good look?" Mo marveled. "It's not even just the girls. Some of the boys have it, too."

"And is anyone *not* wearing a collared shirt?" Eliza concentrated on keeping her breathing even and slow as she turned the pages. "There's my mom. Laura Saperstein."

"I always knew I'd have liked your mom. No feathered hair."

Laura's hair was smooth and straight, with a center part. "She's got some Marcia Brady going on, though."

"But it suits her."

Eliza had never known her mother with long hair—it was bobbed by the time she was born—but she always loved seeing her long tresses in old photos. Without thinking, she reached up to touch her own long braid. And then her eyes moved across to the opposite page of the yearbook.

Ross Sawyer. She pointed to him without speaking.

"Oh wow. Is that him?" Mo peered closer.

As Aunt Claude had described, his hair was light in color—at least it was a light shade of gray in the black-and-white photo—and looked thick. It was tousled—the kind of hair that probably looked worse when you brushed it. He was barely smiling and had an intense look in his eyes.

"He reminds me of that actor—the one in the movie about Watergate."

"*All the President's Men*? You mean Robert Redford?" Eliza didn't see the resemblance—but she was more focused on finding a resemblance between this man and herself.

"No—the other one. Although his coloring is more like Robert Redford's."

"Dustin Hoffman," Eliza replied absently, picking up the yearbook to look more closely at the photo. "Do you think I look like him?"

"Maybe—hard to tell in that little black-and-white picture. Your hair might be similar. And your eyes have the same shape."

"That's what my mom said in the letter. That we have the same eyes."

Mo peered at her. "Are you okay, Lize?"

She took a shuddery breath. "I guess. It's just the oddest feeling. To look at a picture of a man I never met—that I never heard of until, what, ten days ago? And know he's my biological father. That half my DNA comes from him."

Mo touched Eliza's hand. "Do you want to stop?"

She shook her head, blinking. "No, let's just tear off the Band-Aid."

They learned that Ross had been the opinion page editor at the school newspaper—*The Ludlow High Observer*—and that he was a cross-country runner. Most of the other items Eliza had found were clearly Laura's—photos of her at dance competitions (Eliza felt renewed guilt at having been a ballet dropout in first grade), birthday cards from her parents and Claude, ticket stubs from movies that she might or might not have seen with Ross. In the graduation program, they found that Ross had been awarded the social-studies prize.

Eliza sat back in her chair. "I guess I was hoping for some photos. Or letters. Or something personal." She sighed as Mo continued to shuffle through the papers.

"Wait! What's this?" Mo held out a color photo of a group of people in graduation gowns, their caps either in their hands or gone entirely.

Eliza grabbed it and scanned the faces. Right in the center was Laura, her gown open to show a pale green minidress, her hair piled on the top of her head. Next to her was Ross. He was a little taller than she, and his hair was dirty blond. Unlike in his yearbook photo, here he was smiling, his eyes crinkled at the corners. Their heads were inclined a little bit toward each other. The only possible indication that they were a couple. But obviously she knew they were.

Mo had gotten out of her chair and was standing behind Eliza, looking at the photo herself. "He was cute," she said.

"Ew."

"You know what I mean. Just looking at him as a male specimen. Not as your father."

Eliza again felt the wind knocked out of her. "My father. That's my father," she breathed.

Mo rubbed her shoulders like a coach might to buck up a player in the locker room.

"I wonder what he looks like now . . ." Eliza tried to imagine the same face with thinning hair. The body with a gut. He'd be the same age that Laura would be—fifty-five. A few years younger than Jack. Jack was broader and beefier—even in his youth. Would age have treated Ross better?

"Well, there's one way to find out. There's this thing called the World Wide Web . . ." Mo teased.

Now that she had a face to go with the name, maybe she'd be able to figure out which of the many Ross Sawyers was the right one. They moved to the sofa and sat hunched over Eliza's laptop.

"Do you think this is him?" Mo pointed to a Ross Sawyer who was an endocrinologist in Boston.

"Don't think so." She scrolled down. BS from Boston College. Aunt Claude seemed to think Laura's Ross went to a college that started with H. She clicked back to the Google search results. The next one was a stockbroker with dark hair and bushy dark eyebrows. Definitely not a match. And then, suddenly, there he was. Professor of education at New York University. BA from Hampshire College. PhD from Teachers College, Columbia University. No question that the face in the photo was his. A little older, sure, but same eyes. Same smile. Hair shorter but still thick.

They clicked through to read his bio, which talked about his research interests and included a long list of publications with links. But nothing personal. His LinkedIn page was similar, and his Twitter was largely retweets of colleagues in the field. No Facebook.

"Professors probably don't want to get friend requests from their students," observed Mo.

Eliza rose and headed for the kitchen to put up hot water for tea. She needed to do something with her hands.

"Lize?" Mo followed her like an anxious puppy.

"I'm okay. I mean, I'm not okay. But I'm still breathing, so that's a plus." Eliza forced a laugh that sounded a bit like someone being strangled. She didn't know how to explain how *real* this had suddenly become. Ross Sawyer wasn't just a name in her mother's letter. Or even an old photo in a yearbook. He was a living, breathing man who taught at a university in the very same city in which she and Mo were standing right now. What was she supposed to do now? There was no handbook to check. *No mother to ask for advice.*

"Do we know anyone who went to NYU and studied education?" Mo reached for the box of assorted teas and rifled through it, selecting peppermint, apparently unaware of the knots in Eliza's intestines.

"I don't think so." Eliza poured hot water over the tea bags and bit her lip, seeking to be as nonchalant as her friend. "Do you think I should just email him? It feels so—impersonal. And what if he's a big jerk? What if he's an axe murderer?"

"I sort of doubt he's an axe murderer." Mo dunked her tea bag up and down. "But he could be a jerk. Is there any way you can find out more about him? I mean, it would be good to know if he's married, right? If he has kids. I mean, other kids."

Eliza carried her own mug of tea over to the sofa, and Mo followed her. "My brother's friend Josh might be able to help," she said hesitantly. She didn't want to admit, even to herself, how often Josh had popped into her head over the past few days. Nor did she necessarily want to ask him for assistance.

"Was he at the shiva?"

"Yeah. He's Scott's best friend from high school."

Despite how close they were, and how much they'd shared, Eliza had never told Mo—or anyone—about Josh. Whatever had happened between them—or hadn't happened—was her secret. One that she kept folded up in a box in the back corner of her mind and tried not to look at very often. All these years later, there was no reason that it should still hurt so much, but she supposed it was all tied up with everything else she had gone through back then.

Josh had been a fixture in the Levinger house for all of Scott's time in high school. His family had moved to town the summer before their freshman year, when Eliza was about to start seventh grade, and the two boys became fast friends. Before Laura got sick, she had made their home an easy place to hang out. There were always snacks, and the basement's squishy sectional and big-screen TV were a huge draw. Eliza knew that some of her friends opted to be at her house rather than their own because they had a thing for Scott or for one of his buddies. For her, orbiting Scott and his friends was less appealing. Her brother typically either ignored her or asked her to fetch more drinks or chips. And his friends tended to take up a lot of space—sprawling on furniture, leaving trails of crumbs, and laughing loudly at things that made no sense.

From the beginning, though, Josh was different. Even though he was new and presumably trying to find his place in the group, he didn't pile on to whatever they were doing and didn't try to one-up everyone else. And he made it a point to say hello to Eliza. He even acknowledged her in public if they bumped into each other at the supermarket or the drugstore. Scott liked to joke that if Josh—an only child himself—wanted a little sister, he'd be willing to trade. Especially if it involved

Josh's gaming system, which was the newer model of the one the Levingers had. The joke had made Eliza seethe. Not because Scott wanted to trade her in for a game console but because she didn't like encouraging Josh to think of her as a *sister.*

"So what does he do?" Mo pushed her hair behind her ear.

Eliza had to rewind their conversation in her mind to remember what they'd been talking about. "He's a lawyer. He told me he could maybe help get background information."

"No-brainer, then! Maybe he has a PI on retainer."

Eliza laughed. "This isn't a TV show. I'm not sending someone out to follow him."

"Well, whatever—you should ask him."

She nodded, not wanting to open up the can of worms that was her feelings about Josh. At least not right now. Besides, it suddenly occurred to her that she had other news to share. "Hey—did I tell you that Carol knows about my mom's letter?"

Mo's eyes grew wide. "What the hell? How?"

"Her nephew was at the shiva at Scott's. He reported back, apparently."

"What an asshole."

Eliza shrugged. "Can you blame him? How often do people get to experience a Maury Povich moment in real life? And at a shiva no less. *Jack—you are* not *the father!*"

"Ugh. Did Carol say anything to you? When you went to the house?"

"Not really. Just told me she knew."

Eliza had spent the train ride back to the city kicking herself that she hadn't questioned her stepmom. Asked if it was news to her. Asked if Jack had known—or suspected. But how did you start that conversation? Especially with a woman who hated you? She could still hear Jack telling her that Carol didn't hate her. *It's not easy for her. Stepping into another woman's house. Another woman's family.* Why didn't he care that it wasn't easy for Eliza? Having another woman sleep in Laura's bed? Put her hands all over Laura's husband? Take what was left of Eliza's family away from her? Which reminded her . . .

"You know what Carol *did* say to me? She was very clear that she didn't want me to take anything out of the house except my mom's personal stuff. Said that the will had to go through probate."

Mo cocked her head to one side. "Who did your dad leave everything to?"

"Honestly, I don't know. I would think he left it to her."

CHAPTER TEN

Later that evening, Eliza was again on her own, trawling the internet for more information about Professor Sawyer. Mo had left to shower and change for a dinner date with a guy she'd met online and had a drink with earlier in the week. She'd offered to postpone, but Eliza insisted that she go. "Anyone you're willing to see a second time definitely should *not* be put off."

"It's not a big deal," Mo protested.

"Hey—how would you feel if, because you postponed, he met someone else instead and she ended up marrying *your* husband?"

Mo rolled her eyes at the *When Harry Met Sally* reference. "I don't think I'd lose any sleep over it."

"Still. Go. I'll be fine."

So Mo did, and Eliza was scrolling through a site aptly called ProfessorReviews.com.

"If you want to learn about education, take a class with Professor Sawyer. He knows everything. Just listen to him for five minutes and he'll tell you so," wrote one disgruntled student.

"I took one class with Prof. Sawyer. I'd heard he was a hard grader—but then I realized that as long as you feed his opinions back to him, you'll do just fine."

Moving her cursor down the page, she read more of the same. *Is this the right Ross?* She looked back at his photo on the NYU website and compared it to the yearbook image. *Yep.* Hard to deny that he was sounding a bit like a jerk. On the other hand, she'd been scanning the names of his courses and the abstracts of his recent research papers, and they were all about closing the achievement gap and how to help kids of less advantaged backgrounds make up lost ground and attain educational success. Just the kind of thing NOY was trying to achieve. So could he be all bad?

No one is all bad or all good.

Hadn't Laura said those exact words to her? She'd always been the one reminding her that no one was perfect—and that even people you didn't like sometimes did the right thing. *People are people. We all do our best. And sometimes it's not good enough. But we try.*

Those words took on such a different meaning now. Was Laura doing her best when she was unfaithful? When she decided to give birth to another man's child without telling anyone?

Jack had always been the less-than-perfect parent. As far as Eliza was concerned, the far-from-perfect parent. The one who didn't understand her. Who was quick to anger. And now he was gone, and everything Eliza thought she knew had been turned on its head.

Her phone chirped and she picked it up, expecting that it might be Carter again. But it wasn't.

**Hey. It's Josh. Just thought I'd see
how you're doing.**

She paused with her thumbs hovering over the screen,

not sure what to say, noting that he was alone on a Saturday night.

Thx. I'm ok. She hesitated and then continued. **I found my dad.**

That's big!

She closed her laptop and pulled her knees up to her chest as she typed. **I mean, I haven't contacted him. But he's here in the city. He's a professor at NYU.**

Wow! What are you going to do?

The million $ question! ☺ I was reading his reviews online. His students think he's a jerk.

College kids! What do they know?

She smiled. **Oh, right. I forgot you're an old man.**

HAHA. Srsly—jerk how? Hard grader? Or creepy?

Love that you're trying to show your youth cred by writing srsly. But instead of HAHA you should try "LOL." It stands for "Laugh Out Loud." But as far as jerkiness goes, basically sounds like he's a know-it-all.

Eh. Not so bad. And thanks for the tip. It's hard to keep up with all the lingo from you young'uns.

Any time. She paused before continuing. **What I can't figure out is anything about his personal life. Wife. Kids.**

> You want me to dig around?

> I can't ask you to do that.

> Sure you can. And btw, you didn't. I
> offered.

> If you're sure it's not a big deal.

> It's fine. Give me a few days.

> Thx. And do you mind not telling
> Scott?

> 😬

> Impressive emoji use! 😌

> LOL. (see, I'm a fast learner)

She smiled. She'd forgotten his sense of humor. And how
they had this natural rhythm with each other. Then her smile
faded as she reminded herself that he was just being nice to
his friend's little sister. She wasn't going to misinterpret his
intentions. Not again.

When she got out of the shower on Monday morning, Eliza
peered at herself in the foggy bathroom mirror. There were
dark smudges under her eyes. She stretched her neck from side
to side. Even when she slept, the sleep wasn't restful.

She padded into her bedroom with her towel wrapped

around her and pulled panties and a bra out of her dresser. Knowing no one was going to see them, she didn't worry about finding a matching pair. She'd let Carter know she wasn't up for seeing him and suspected she wouldn't hear from him again.

She zipped up her pants, which slipped down onto her hip bones. How little had she been eating? In the kitchen, she dug in the freezer for the box of pastries Aunt Claude had brought. She hadn't been able to stomach eating them, but hated to throw them away. But now the thought of a (microwaved) napoleon for breakfast seemed appealing.

Those had always been Jack's choice. Cream puffs for her. Éclairs for Scott. And cannoli for Laura. Whenever Scott had a tennis tournament in Rockland County, Jack would stop at a French pastry shop on the way home and pick up a box of goodies for them all.

She sat heavily in one of her kitchen chairs. She hadn't thought about that in so long. She couldn't remember the last time she'd felt the desire to pick up the phone and talk to Jack—and now here it was. She wished she could call him and ask if he remembered those pastries. Something else that changed with Carol, who was anti refined sugar. *What did refined sugar ever do to her?*

On some level, she always thought things between her and Jack would change. That there was plenty of time. She had just enough memories of family game nights back when she and Scott were in elementary school, and of Jack taking her for ice cream during Scott's soccer practices, to hang hope on— despite their having grown so distant.

And if she was honest, the distance hadn't begun when Carol arrived on the scene. Perhaps it started with Laura's diagnosis. Aunt Claude was around a lot then, taking Laura for treatment and picking up the slack with carpooling when Laura was too sick or too weak to drive. Jack didn't deal well with illness. He never had. Laura was the one who sat with Eliza and Scott in the bathroom when they had stomach flu. Jack's go-to was to tell them to go to bed when they were sick. *Out of sight, out of mind,* she'd always thought. Or was it more than that? Did he find it hard to see the people he loved in pain?

She felt the familiar burn of tears in her sinuses. No wonder she never managed to eat anything. She forced herself to take another bite of the napoleon, feeling the pastry dissolve on her tongue as she went to her bookshelf to find her family photo albums.

Laura had been meticulous about documenting their family outings and events, and Scott and Eliza had split the albums up between them. Flipping through, she found the photo from Scott's bar mitzvah—a copy of the one that used to hang on the hallway wall in the Levinger house. She slipped it out of the album and looked at it. The smiles on their faces before the diagnosis that would change their lives forever. Jack and Laura bracketing their children—Scott before his growth spurt, Eliza with her hair loose down her back. When they posed like that, did Laura ever think about the fact that on the DNA level, they weren't actually all family? Or did she push that knowledge down into a part of herself that she kept hidden, even from herself?

It was getting late, and she needed to get to work. She picked up the photo and put it in her purse. It deserved a frame.

CHAPTER ELEVEN

When Eliza got to work, she peeled off her jacket and hung it up, putting her handbag on the filing cabinet that stood along the wall, perpendicular to her desk. As she dug inside looking for a pack of Life Savers—though she was having trouble eating and swallowing these days, sucking on the candies with their fruity flavors was soothing—she pulled out the sixteen-year-old family photo. It was a little bent around the edges, so she propped it up on the file cabinet, leaning it against the sad African violet Amber had given her on her last birthday.

Just as she sat down at her desk, Vanessa appeared in her doorway.

"Bad news," she said.

What can Vanessa possibly say to someone who just lost her second parent that would qualify as "bad news"?

"Peggy Devlin has cancer."

Okay, that is bad news.

"She won't be able to keynote the gala."

As far as Vanessa is concerned, is the bad news the cancer or the disruption to her carefully planned program?

Eliza nodded. "Okay. So we need a plan B."

"Let's all convene in my office to discuss. Peggy will be hard to replace. Ten minutes."

Peggy was a remarkable "get" for NOY. A former Miss America, she'd gone on to become a teacher on the South Side of Chicago while getting her graduate degree in education. She then developed a primary school curriculum used in hundreds of districts across the country—districts that had seen remarkable improvements in reading and math scores. But beyond that, she was a dynamic speaker. Her TED Talk had been seen by millions. Vanessa had gotten to her through a friend of a friend of a friend, and she'd agreed to come to New York and speak at the gala. Eliza sighed as she headed down the hall.

Vanessa's office was all sleek blond wood. Her desk was a simple table with Scandinavian lines. All that sat on it was a slim computer monitor and a telephone. The cordless keyboard lived in the pull-out drawer. It looked like an office in a magazine, not a place where someone actually worked.

Vanessa was seated in her ergonomic chair behind the desk when Eliza arrived. The two simple chairs that typically faced the desk were turned ninety degrees to face one another. With the small sofa on the far wall, this created a makeshift circle for staff meetings. Davin was already in one of the chairs, one leg crossed over the other, his tablet in his hand, ready for note-taking. Eliza took the chair opposite him, and Patrice and Bridget immediately followed.

"Does anyone want coffee?" Vanessa asked, her manicured finger poised over the intercom button on her phone.

"I'll take some," Davin replied as the others shook their heads.

"Amber, could you bring us two coffees? One for me and one for Davin? So." Vanessa switched gears, her hands forming a pyramid. "We've lost our keynote speaker."

Eliza glanced around; no one looked surprised. Clearly, their director had already informed everyone else.

"We need an alternate plan," she continued.

"What about people who've already purchased tickets expecting Peggy?" Patrice asked.

"We'll have to notify them—but we need to have our solution in place beforehand. Most people are coming because they believe in NOY. But for those who were just coming for Peggy—if we give them something equally compelling, we shouldn't lose them."

"It's pretty bad form to withdraw a charitable contribution," observed Davin.

"Why should that stop them?" Bridget rolled her eyes. "I'm still getting complaints about the tote bags. The *free* tote bags."

At the prior year's gala, each guest had received a swag bag of items, packed in a NOY tote bag. Unfortunately, the bags were from a defective run, with only one row of stitching on the handles. More than a few calls had come in purely to complain about the shoddy quality of the bags—and they came up in conversation with donors and board members at least once a week. *We just need to be sure to double-check the quality of anything we distribute. Do you remember those* awful *tote bags?*

"Oh my God. We're not doing tote bags again, are we?" Amber stopped just inside the doorway with the two cups of coffee. "Those were the *worst!*"

Bridget pointed at Amber as if to say *Exhibit A of complainers.*

Vanessa sighed as she took her cup of coffee from Amber. "Let's not get distracted. This is not a meeting about tote bags. So. Ideas?"

"Well, if we're thinking someone with star power, we could ask Senator Whatshisname—the one who lives on Long Island. He's on the education committee," Davin suggested.

Vanessa raised her eyebrows. "And what about our Republican donors?"

"Fair enough. No politics."

"I'd love to bring in some young people who have been helped by NOY funding . . ." began Patrice.

Vanessa shook her head. "That's what the video presentation is for."

Eliza suspected that their director already had the "right" answer in mind and that this entire meeting was performative.

Davin drummed his finger on his tablet. "I was reading about this amazing principal out in Queens who has really turned her school around. She was written up in *Metro News*."

Vanessa cocked her head to one side. "Hmm. We could look into whether there's specific overlap in the programs we've funded and what she's done."

Davin tapped a few words into his notes app. "I'll get on that."

"So, this is what I was thinking." Vanessa leaned forward, her hands flat on her desk.

Why couldn't we have just started here?

"I've said before that we don't do enough to build partnerships with the universities right here in the city. Teachers College, NYU, CUNY . . . There's great work being done in education. I think NOY needs to be on the cutting edge of that research."

Eliza's heart rate sped up.

"I want us to launch an award."

Davin was already shaking his head, and Eliza thought she might have a reprieve. "We don't want to muddy our message. The gala . . ." he began.

"It won't muddy our message. It will *strengthen* it. We won't *give* the award this year. But we'll announce it for next year. We'll be recognizing education scholarship, and we'll give the award at the annual gala starting next year. *This* year, we can work on cultivating relationships with faculty and invite one of them to speak. It will be okay if they're not well known more broadly, because we'll be billing it as the launch of the award."

What are the odds? Eliza had been counting on work being a distraction from the tumult in her family life, and now the two had collided. She felt sick to her stomach and truly could have cried. How much more was the universe going to pile on her?

Patrice's voice pulled her out of her thoughts. "I'm not sure I'm seeing your vision."

"Look. NOY funds programs to support students. But how do we choose what to support? Shouldn't we be making those choices in accordance with the latest research? It can be a differentiator for us in terms of getting donor dollars. And by focusing on the universities here and bringing in faculty to speak, we'll probably get more people to come to the gala, even if they're just at the base ticket level."

Eliza couldn't fault her logic. One of NOY's problems had always been its scattered focus. But the last thing she wanted was to get involved with the education faculty at NYU. She forced herself to find her voice.

"Vanessa, don't you think time is really short to do this now? Why don't we wait until we get past the gala and then . . ."

"No, no, no. This is exactly the time. I've had several of our board members talking to me for a while about forming these partnerships. I don't think we can put them off."

Ah. Eliza was willing to bet they were the board members who were responsible for keeping the lights on.

They continued to speak for the next hour about logistics and timelines. Eliza scribbled notes and tried to push thoughts of Ross Sawyer and his research out of her mind, but they kept bubbling up. How many professors of education were there, anyway? How many experts in educational policy? Was Ross one of dozens? Or hundreds? Was it inevitable that they would cross paths now? Was the choice going to be taken out of her hands? She kept having to drag her attention back to her colleagues, whose words felt so much less important than the swirl going on in her head.

"Okay. So I'll take care of Teachers College," Vanessa was saying. "The board can connect me there quite well, and quickly."

"I'm happy to reach out to CUNY," Eliza jumped in, writing CUNY in large letters on her pad.

"I don't think that makes sense," Davin interrupted. "I went to CUNY. And I want to have some of these preliminary conversations so I'll get an idea for how to build a story for the press around it."

"Agreed," Vanessa replied before Eliza could respond. "Eliza, you take NYU. Patrice, I'd like you to look into other area schools that we should potentially reach out to."

"I could do that research," Eliza interjected. "With everything else I have to do for the gala, maybe Patrice should handle NYU."

"Fine by me," replied Patrice agreeably.

"Okay. Done. We have a plan, people." Vanessa pushed her seat away from her desk and stood. "Let's get to work."

Back at her desk, Eliza swiveled in her non-ergonomic desk chair and gazed at the family photo leaning up against the African violet. How strange was it that both she and Ross worked in education, in their own ways? Could there be something in their DNA? A shared desire to help children?

Maybe this was a good sign. Ross's students weren't big fans, but the fact that his chosen career was all about kids—wouldn't he be happy to learn that he had a child he didn't know about?

Eliza tried to imagine getting a phone call from someone claiming to be her child. She rolled her eyes. No chance a woman could have a child without knowing it . . . What if Jack had gotten such a call? She really didn't want to think about him having sex. It was bad enough that she now had to face her mom having sex. That imagery was disturbing enough. Not that she was trying to picture the actual baby-making. But what had Laura looked like at that reunion? Had she dressed up in anticipation of seeing Ross again? She had a toddler at home—it must have been a rare weekend away.

The Laura she knew didn't wear much makeup. What had she seen when she looked in the mirror that night? Eliza wasn't far from her ten-year reunion herself. She'd seen some chatter about it on Facebook and had pondered going—if they actually managed to get it organized. Her last years of high school were a matter of survival. Getting through each day. She knew everyone thought of her as "the girl with the dead mother." The only way she was going to a reunion would be as a completely different person. One who was put together—who wore clothes that fit properly and wasn't prone to panic attacks and bursting into tears at inopportune moments.

The Laura she'd seen in the yearbook looked happy and well adjusted. Was she missing those days when she went to her reunion? Wanting to relive who she was? Or had it all been an act—the armor so many teens wore? She'd never know. Unless perhaps she talked to Ross.

CHAPTER TWELVE

Eliza hadn't set out to work for NOY. Her goal upon graduating from college was to move to Manhattan with Mo so she wouldn't have to go "home" to live with Jack and Carol. That house hadn't felt like home since the day the U-Haul had arrived with Carol's belongings. Carol had started to keep the primary bedroom door shut, but when it was open, Eliza hated catching a glimpse of her stepmother's perfume on the bureau. That bedroom was also the first room they redid— replacing the pencil-post bed Eliza had loved with one with a carved headboard. Laura's clothing was boxed up and donated; Eliza rescued a few sweaters that still smelled faintly of her mother—the lavender sachets she kept in her drawers and the fruity bodywash she'd liked.

There was no question in Eliza's mind that she wasn't going back to that house. She spent a lot of time in the career-counseling office senior year, looking for a job that would find her sociology degree appealing *and* would pay enough to cover rent.

Jack took her out to breakfast the morning after graduation, a rare occasion that it was just the two of them. If Eliza hadn't been so hungover, she would have felt downright jubilant that Carol had stayed back at the hotel. As it was, she felt low-level joy. They sat opposite each other at a diner she was more used to visiting late at night with friends. The scuffed Formica tables looked shabbier in the daylight. She'd always thought the vinyl booths were black, but they turned out to be burgundy.

She sipped her hot tea while they waited for their breakfast—scrambled eggs on toast for her, a western omelet for him.

Jack cleared his throat, and she looked at him. His polo shirt was white with blue stripes and a blue collar. His beefy arms were freckled from the sun. "I'm proud of you, Eliza," he said.

What she heard was *I can't believe you managed to pull yourself together and get through college.* It must have shown in the twist of her mouth.

"Seriously, I mean it. Life dealt you a crappy hand, and you pulled through." He looked away, gazing in the direction of the dessert case full of elephant ears and danish that Carol never let him eat.

She nodded, biting her lip. It wasn't the first time she'd thought of her mom that weekend. Wishing she were there.

His eyes returned to her face. "Mom would be proud."

She felt the familiar burn of rising tears, and he reached across the table to pat her hand awkwardly. They hadn't quite figured out how to touch each other after Laura died.

He cleared his throat again. "Anyway. You've got your whole life ahead of you now. I was waiting until today to tell you . . ."

There was only a tiny pause, but it was long enough for Eliza to decide that he was sick, too. That he was dying. That she was about to lose another parent. Or something else. That Carol was pregnant. Could she be pregnant? She'd been thirty-eight when she married Jack. So she was forty-three now. Definitely possible . . .

"Mom wanted to make sure you'd be taken care of. As much as she could," he continued.

Eliza wrinkled her brow and tried to reset her brain. This wasn't about illness. Or a half sibling.

"She set up a trust for her life-insurance proceeds and some other investments she'd inherited from her uncle. One for you and one for Scott, to be available to you when you finished school. I asked Scott not to tell you. I didn't want it to affect whatever decisions you made. But it's yours now."

"Oh." The single short word was all she could force out. Without even knowing the amount, she wanted to give it back in exchange for having Laura sitting next to her in the booth—her cool hand brushing the loose strands of Eliza's hair behind her ear. But that wasn't how life worked. No exchanges, no returns. Not even if what you got was defective.

The amount in the estate was substantial. Well, substantial to an until-five-minutes-before broke college student. Certainly not something she could live on for the rest of her days. But enough that she could think a little differently about where she could live and what jobs she could pursue.

So when she came across the job listing for Nourish Our Youth, she didn't automatically scroll past at the sight of the low starting salary. Laura had been passionate about Eliza's and Scott's education—regularly attending school-board meetings and volunteering for a local organization that raised money to fund programs and projects not covered in the school budget. During her interviews with Vanessa and Johanna—the then director of development—Eliza kept thinking about how excited Laura would be about NOY's mission.

Now, given what she'd learned about her biological father and his work in education, she had to wonder if there was a connection. Had they shared this passion? Did Laura's interest stem from Ross's? Or the other way around? Could her mom have been trying to expose her to some of her "real" father's interests?

Her head hurt thinking about it. It was like playing a game of three-dimensional chess with invisible pieces. She sighed, staring out Grinders' window, her cup of tea slightly too hot to drink.

"Hey. How are you doing?" Josh tapped her on her shoulder, and she turned.

"Okay. Are you getting something?"

"Yeah—wanted to see if I could order for you, but it looks like you already did." He nodded at her bright blue, oversize mug before heading to the counter.

Josh had texted her on Thursday to tell her that he'd learned a bit about Ross. She was dying to have him just send her the information, but he suggested they meet over the weekend. He had a deal closing at work and needed to get past that.

Eliza *might* have left several discarded outfits on her bed that morning before settling on skinny jeans ripped at the knees and an oversize sweater. Looking down at herself, she thought she had probably erred a little too far in the "I'm not dressing up for you and I don't care how you think I look" direction.

Josh returned to the table, pulling off his barn jacket before sitting down. His sweater this time was chunky gray wool. It didn't look as soft to the touch as last time. He cocked his head at her. "You look tired."

Thanks. Thanks a lot. She had the sudden, unwelcome thought that Josh was checking up on her at Scott's behest. Even though she'd told Josh not to tell Scott that they were in touch. Another question to add to the three-dimensional chessboard.

"E?"

Josh's steady gaze on her made her uncomfortable. Like her carefully constructed walls had transformed to glass. "I'm okay," she repeated.

"I can't even imagine what you're going through."

She picked up her tea to take a sip even though it was still steaming. No one ever knew what to say to grieving people, and she never knew what to say back. She had spent so much time as a puddle of emotions after Laura died, and she wanted to think she was stronger now. To mean it when she said she was okay. Besides, she knew what would happen if she said she *wasn't*. That automatic sympathetic gaze nearly killed her. But it was hard to lie to Josh, who was looking at her so earnestly. So kindly. With such lovely eyes. She mentally shook herself.

"Anyway, we're not here to talk about how I'm doing." She aimed for flippancy but wasn't sure she quite hit the mark.

"We can, though. If you want." He waited a moment before turning to pull some pages out of the inside pocket of his jacket. "So, I didn't find out a whole lot, but I can tell you Ross was married once, and then divorced." He slid the pages across to her, which appeared to be printouts from some sort of records system.

"How did you get this stuff?" she asked as her eyes jumped around the pages.

"Eh, don't ask too many questions about that. But it's all public record."

She looked down again. Ross had married a woman named Hannah Briggs two years after Eliza was born. So at least he wasn't married at the reunion. They filed for divorce nearly six years later.

"What about kids?"

"No records of any."

She realized the irony of that statement. There was no

public record of herself as Ross's child. Her birth certificate named Jack Levinger as her father. For all she knew, she had dozens of half siblings running around.

"He lives in the city," Josh continued. "Not far from me, actually, in the West Village. His address is on the last page."

Eliza's hands were shaking slightly, and she clenched them into fists in her lap. She suddenly became aware of the noises in the coffee shop—the clatter of mugs, the hiss of the espresso machine. As if she were in a tunnel where everything was magnified. She sucked in air through her nose. This feeling was all too familiar, though she hadn't experienced it in years.

"E?"

She wasn't going to have a panic attack. Not here. Not now. She took another deep breath and pressed her hands against her thighs until she could feel them through the spreading numbness. "I'm okay," she murmured. Was that the third time she'd said that to Josh in the past ten minutes? Was this veering into "The lady doth protest too much" territory?

"This probably makes it feel real," he suggested gently.

She swallowed. "Yeah, I think you're right. I mean, now I could write him a letter. Or send him an email. Or show up at his door."

"You could. But I think you need to consider what a shock this is going to be to him."

She snorted. "Um . . . yeah, I can relate."

"Seriously. I've been thinking about this. You have no idea how he'll react. And you're probably already feeling . . ."

Please don't say fragile.

". . . I mean, you're still raw from your dad's death. If he's not receptive . . . I don't want this to cause you any more pain."

She looked at him. "What would you do if you suddenly found out you had a child out there?" The question was out of her mouth before she could stop it, and she felt her cheeks flush at the idea of Josh fathering a child.

His eyes widened. "Wow. Yikes. It would be so hard to wrap my head around. I mean—obviously any kid of mine would have to be still young. It's not like I could have an adult kid running around. But I'd probably be a little pissed. Maybe a lot pissed. Not at the kid—but at the mom for having kept it a secret. I wouldn't want to think anyone I'd . . . I mean, that anyone I'd *been* with wouldn't tell me I'd gotten her pregnant."

Eliza nodded slowly and pushed away the image of Josh *being* with this imaginary woman. "I guess it was pretty lousy of my mom." She fiddled with the empty sugar packet sitting on the table next to her mug and realized that this was the part of this crazy situation that she'd been trying not to acknowledge.

Josh sighed heavily. "She was in a tough spot. Maybe an impossible spot."

"Yeah, 'cause she cheated on my dad." She aimed to say it lightly, but the words were heavy on her tongue. On her heart.

"Look. You don't know what was going on with them . . ."

"I know. And I'll never know." She blinked rapidly as her eyes filled, and Josh reached out to touch her arm.

"Hey—I know that there's nothing I can say that will make this any better. But if you want to talk about it . . ."

"Thanks." But she couldn't help wondering why he was here. After so many years of nothing but small talk on the random occasions they'd seen one another. "Did Scott ask you to check up on me?"

His eyes widened again. "No—why would you think that?"

She shrugged. "I know he worries about me. And with everything going on—maybe he doesn't really want to deal with me right now."

Josh pushed his hand through his hair. "I can't imagine that's how he feels."

Eliza took a sip of her tea, which was now not quite hot enough. She'd missed the sweet spot, so to speak. "So, did you get that deal done or whatever you were working on?" She was anxious to get them both onto less emotional territory.

"Yeah, it closed yesterday. Thank God. A little breathing room."

"So, what exactly do you do?"

"General corporate law. But lately I've been involved in a bunch of mergers and acquisitions."

"Do you like it?"

He laughed. "Sometimes. And it's paying off my loans. Not sure I want to do the 'big law' thing forever, but for now it's okay. How about you? What foundation do you work for again?"

"Nourish Our Youth. We support disadvantaged kids. Historically, we've been a kind of jack-of-all-trades—dealing with food insecurity, homelessness, all that—but now we're mainly focused on education. It's pretty crazy that there's this overlap between my job and Ross's work in education research. My boss actually wants us to start dealing with education faculty at local universities."

Josh raised his eyebrows.

"I know, right? Anyway. But I'm just keeping my head down and focusing on the annual gala, which I'm responsible for this year. First time it's all my responsibility."

"Wow, E, that's amazing!"

"Maybe. Stressful, definitely."

"When is it?"

"December. Not great timing with all the holiday festivities. I'd like to try to move it for next year, but I'm stuck with it for now."

"So are you mostly doing event planning, then, or . . . ?"

She wondered if he was really interested. "Well, all of that—coordinating with the venue and all the vendors, staying on top of the RSVPs, swag bags, name tags—but also trying to cultivate bigger donations. Like corporate sponsorships for the program."

Josh ran his finger along the rim of his cup. His nails were neat and clean. Why was she looking at his fingernails? "You know, my firm has a school-law practice. I wonder if they'd be interested in getting a sponsorship. Or buying a table. We're always supporting different nonprofits."

Eliza shook her head. "Oh, you don't have to do that. You've done enough for me already." She gestured toward the print-outs with Ross's information on them.

"It's no big deal. I'll just mention it to one of my colleagues. Former office mate of mine is in that practice. So, what do you do when you're not planning galas?"

Eliza tried to think about what her day-to-day life had been like before Jack died. Before this bomb was dropped on her. She remembered this feeling from when Laura died. The weird, elastic quality of time. How everything got a little blurry around the edges.

"Oh, you know. I hang out with Mo. She tries to get me to go to yoga with her. I try not to go. I run in the park. Travel when I can. Watch too much TV."

He grinned. "You must be sad *One Tree Hill* went off the air."

She put her palm over her face. "Oh my God. Don't remind me how obsessed I was with that show. Wait!" She removed her hand. "How do you know it's off the air? Unless you were watching it, too!"

"Oh yeah—you got me. Secret *One Tree Hill* lover over here." He laughed and tapped himself on the chest. "Not."

"Too late! I know your deep, dark secret. But don't worry, my lips are sealed." She pinched her thumb and forefinger together and ran them across her mouth, zipping it up.

"Ha ha. No one would believe you. They all know it was

only ever *Everwood* for me." Josh winked at her so fast she almost missed it.

"Seriously, though, it's embarrassing to think about the stuff we used to be into as kids, right? The other day I bought some Froot Loops. I used to *beg* my mom for them. *So* nasty!"

"Hey! They're still my favorite breakfast cereal!" Josh grinned, and Eliza hated the little quiver she felt in response to it. Then Josh's smile faded as his eyes strayed over her shoulder. She turned to see Carter behind her, his finger to his lips, apparently trying to keep Josh from alerting her to his presence.

"Damn! You caught me!" Carter grinned, his even teeth offsetting his perfect cheekbones, his dark hair flopping in his eyes. He bent to kiss her, the familiar scent of his soap—a cross between wintergreen and eucalyptus—filling her nose. She quickly angled her face away so his lips just brushed her cheek. "I was hoping I might find you here!" He put his hand on her shoulder and squeezed.

Eliza cringed a little under his hand as she thought of the last time the three of them were in a room together. The scene of her drunken meltdown. She cleared her throat and glanced between them. "I don't know if you remember each other. Josh. Carter."

Josh nodded and reached for his jacket. "I'll get out of your way," he said as he rose from his chair and indicated to Carter that he could take it.

"No, you don't have to go," Eliza said immediately, wishing that she'd chosen a coffeehouse other than her usual haunt to meet him in.

"No, I should go anyway. I've got tons of laundry to catch up on after the last couple of weeks on this deal. And some sleep, too."

Eliza stood as Josh pulled on his jacket before picking up his empty mug. "Oh. Okay. Well—thank you. I really appreciate your help." She wanted to add, *And by the way, this isn't what it looks like.* But wasn't it? And why did she care what Josh thought?

"Hey, anytime. Promise me you won't do anything right away? Give it some more thought."

She nodded, and Josh squeezed her hand as Carter slid into the vacated seat. After she watched him go, she sat down again in her own chair.

"Babe! You've been blowing me off!" Carter grinned at her again, his expression taking any potential sting out of his words. That grin used to set off a chemical reaction, but all she was aware of now was the sensation of Josh squeezing her hand.

"I know. It's been a really bad time." *You may recall, my father recently dropped dead.*

"Babe." He reached across the table, and she consciously extended her left hand, not the right one that had recently been in Josh's. "I can take your mind off things . . ." He ran his thumb over her knuckles and winked at her. It was like being in a *Seinfeld*-esque bizarro world. Just a moment earlier, Josh had sat in that same chair and winked at her. But while Josh's wink had been cute, Carter's was making her queasy. She pulled her hand away, and his eyebrows drew together.

"Come on. What's up?"

"Look. Carter. I just can't do this right now." Was she really going to push this gorgeous man who put no demands on her out of her life? *Appears so.*

Carter's easy smile faded. "Hey. I'm not an idiot. I know you just lost your dad. But that doesn't mean this"—he gestured between them—"has to stop. We're just having fun. And you probably need that more than ever right now."

Not a bad argument. But the thought of him touching her left her cold.

"I don't think so, Carter. It's just too much for me."

"*I'm* too much for you?" He winked again.

Ew. Why had she spent so much time sleeping with this guy?

"I just can't. I'm sorry." She picked up the coffee stirrer Josh had left behind and folded it in two before dropping it into her own empty mug.

Carter stared at her for a moment before shrugging. "Message received."

They both stood, and Carter wrapped his arms around her as she stood awkwardly holding the mug. "Text me if you change your mind," he whispered, his breath warm on her ear.

For a brief moment, she reconsidered. *Why not invite him home? What's wrong with one for the road?* But then she pulled away. *I don't think that's enough anymore.*

CHAPTER THIRTEEN

"So no more Carter?" Mo jabbed at the ice in her diet soda with her straw. They'd met for dinner after work, at a hectic midtown eatery full of dark wood and clattering cutlery. Eliza suspected it was her friend's way of trying to make sure she ate—and that she did more than go to work and curl up on her couch under a blanket.

"No more Carter," Eliza confirmed, lining up her salad fork neatly next to her dinner fork. "How was your date?"

"Really nice, actually."

Eliza could tell that Mo was trying not to smile but failing miserably.

"That's great!" It had been a while since Mo had met someone she liked. "What's his name?"

"Nik. Actually, Nikhil. All these years of me refusing to meet the Indian boys my parents wanted to set me up with—if this ends up going anywhere, they'll be beside themselves."

"Maybe parents do know best." Though they came from her own lips, the words hit Eliza like a club.

She never knew how she'd feel day to day or minute to minute. When Laura died, the grief had been crushing and all-consuming. It was different with Jack. He had been a much less significant presence in her life. They spoke so rarely, and the distance between them often felt unbridgeable. Yet knowing he was out there versus being gone was proving hard to cope with.

Mo reached out and touched her arm, and Eliza's eyes filled. She fluttered her hands at her own face. "No, I'm okay. Let's just move on."

The harried server, her hair coming loose from its ponytail, appeared with a caesar salad with grilled chicken for Mo and a squash soup for Eliza. "Are you all set for now? Do you need anything else?" she asked almost as an afterthought as she turned away from the table.

"We're fine," Mo said to her retreating back before neatly spearing a stack of lettuce and shaved parmesan on her fork. "How are you feeling about kicking Carter to the curb? Hey— that could be the name of a sitcom. Or a band. *Kicking Carter to the Curb.*"

Eliza snorted. "A really bad band, maybe. I'm fine. I mean— he was easy. No pressure, no expectations." *No support, no real intimacy.* "But with everything else going on, it was just one more thing to juggle."

Mo nodded as she popped a crouton into her mouth. "And it goes without saying that you deserve better. Oh. Wait. I think I just said it. Oops." Mo grinned. "Though I will say, once I finally got to see him, I understood the appeal. He's pretty fine."

"Yes. That he is." But when her brain went to conjure an image of Carter, it produced one of Josh instead. She blew on the soup steaming in her spoon. "Changing subjects, though." She sipped the soup while Mo looked at her expectantly. "You will *not* believe the latest at work."

"Vanessa walked in on Davin and Amber screwing on her desk?"

"Oh my God. Ew! Now that's what I'm going to see every time I walk into Vanessa's office."

Mo shrugged. "Sorry!" But her impish grin didn't look apologetic.

"*Anyway* . . . so Vanessa decided to create an award for education research that she wants to announce at the gala." Eliza gave Mo the highlights, ending with the plan to connect with universities.

"Education faculty?" Mo asked flatly.

"Exactly. Education faculty. She tried to assign me to do outreach to NYU."

Mo put her fork down and reached for her Diet Coke, taking a long swallow. "Tried to assign you?" she asked.

"I traded with Patrice."

"Huh." Mo looked thoughtful as she ate a bite of chicken. "What?"

"Just thinking. Maybe you shouldn't have traded. It would have been the perfect way for you to meet Professor Sawyer without having to tell him who you are. Scope him out."

"Sounds like a bad movie." Eliza reached for a piece of French bread from the basket between them.

Mo shrugged. "I don't know. I don't think it's a terrible idea."

Eliza raised her eyebrows. "Well, I suppose I could sneak into the back of one of his classes." She laughed.

"You laugh—but why not?" Mo's eyes sparkled.

Eliza couldn't believe her sensible friend was making these markedly *not* sensible suggestions. "Why not? Because I think someone who is clearly not a college student would stand out like a sore thumb skulking around a classroom!"

Mo wrinkled her nose. "You could totally pass for a college student. Put on a sweatshirt and no one would be the wiser. And in a lecture hall, who would notice? Aren't those NYU classes all huge?"

Eliza shook her head. "How would I know?"

"I can see it now. You'll ask all sorts of clever questions and . . ."

"Oh, so now not only am I sneaking in but I'm making a spectacle of myself? You're not actually suggesting this, are you?" Eliza had gotten caught up in the silliness for a moment, but then it hit her—did Mo not get what this was like for her? That this really wasn't a slapstick comedy? It was her *life*.

A few hours later, as Eliza walked home from the subway, she thought about Mo's idea. She had firmly changed the subject, unused to the harsh feelings bubbling up inside her. At least, unused to them directed at Mo. Now she reminded herself that Mo loved her and had always looked out for her. Maybe she shouldn't rule out her idea entirely. The prospect of having the opportunity to get to know Ross in a "safe" setting—without him knowing who she really was—had some appeal.

She could also see the wisdom of Josh's and Aunt Claude's advice that she not rush into anything. As it was, she could feel the tectonic plates shifting beneath her. Her life had been a series of earthquakes and aftershocks ever since Laura was first diagnosed. Was that everyone's life? Did the whole world feel this constant sense of uncertainty and imbalance? Or was it just her? It was what made staying in bed so enticing—when she was secure on her mattress under the covers, she was a little less afraid that she'd crash against the jagged rocks.

The wind picked up as she reached her front door, and she hurried inside, pulling her keys out of her purse. Locating her silver mailbox key, she fitted it into the lock and opened the small door. ConEd bill, credit card bill, Macy's coupons . . . and a peach postcard from the US Postal Service. *We have item/s for you which we could not deliver. Signature required.* Odd. Item sent by C. Levinger. Carol. Why was Carol sending her a letter? And one that required a signature?

CHAPTER FOURTEEN

Eliza awakened, covered in sweat. Had she just screamed out loud? *It's okay. It was just a dream.*

She'd been in her childhood bedroom, alone, but could hear voices downstairs. She knew everyone was waiting for her, but she couldn't find the right clothes. Every time she tried to put a shirt on, it was inside out or upside down. Her pants were too tight, or so loose they wouldn't stay up and she couldn't find a belt. Her sense of panic rose as she struggled to find a pair of socks that matched. And then a shadow loomed over her. She turned, and outside the window was a figure. Even though she was on the second floor and no one could be there, somehow, someone was. And they were coming in. And she had tried to scream, but nothing came out of her mouth . . .

She gulped in air and looked around her living room. She must have fallen asleep on the couch. She groped for her phone. It was just after five in the morning. *What day is it?* Thursday. It was Thursday. She had a day of work to get through before she went to Scott and Maren's for dinner.

She'd followed the instructions on the note from the post office to arrange for redelivery of Carol's letter, and it had been waiting for her when she arrived home from work the evening before.

> Dear Eliza:
>
> I am writing to you as executor of Jack Levinger's estate.

She was immediately struck by the fact that Carol had not written "your father." And her reasoning soon became clear.

> You are named as a beneficiary in Jack's will. However, as the will explicitly states "my daughter Eliza Levinger," please consider this legal notice that I will be contesting this portion of the will, in light of the new information that you are not, in fact, his biological issue.

"His biological issue"? What was she, some kind of waste by-product? And the word "please"? It was like a mugger jumping out at you from an alley and saying *Excuse me, but would you mind giving me your wallet, please?*

She scanned the rest of the document. Apparently Jack had intended for his estate—excluding the house, which went directly to Carol—to be divided in thirds among Carol, Scott, and Eliza.

She was dumbfounded. Even for her stepmother, this was a new low. Shaking herself out of the numbness that had descended, she called Scott. He answered immediately.

"You got the letter from Carol," he said, his tone matter-of-fact.

"Did you know she was doing this?"

"No. I just got a letter myself, telling me I'm a beneficiary and informing me that she would be contesting your inheritance."

Eliza's eyes stung. Hearing Scott say the words out loud was even more crushing than reading them in black and white, and it had nothing to do with money. It was the feeling that her existence as a member of the family was being erased. Carol had never wanted her around, and now she was excising her entirely, with surgical precision.

"Eliza?"

She realized Scott had been talking but she hadn't heard him through the buzzing in her ears. "I'm here."

"Are you okay?"

She heard the edge of panic in his voice and visualized him putting on his coat, telling Maren he had to go see her right away. That he was afraid of what she might do. She wasn't going to cause anyone that kind of worry. Not again.

"I'm fine." She choked out the words in as normal a voice as she could manage.

He clearly hadn't believed her but let it go when she promised to come for dinner the following night. Now she looked at her phone again. Five minutes had passed since she'd looked at it the first time. She lay back down again on the couch, still unsettled by her nightmare.

Her apartment looked different in half darkness. She'd bought it soon after she started working for NOY—using a chunk of the money her mom left her. When she realized how much she'd be spending on rent, buying seemed a sensible alternative. And she knew, even before she saw it, that this particular unit would be her home. Apartment 507. Laura's birthday had been May 7. She had just turned forty-five a week before she died.

Eliza had baked her a cake. The same Hershey's chocolate cake Laura used to make for her. Laura managed a smile and a couple of bites. Eliza forced herself to finish the small piece she'd cut for herself. Jack and Scott must have been there, too, but in her memory she could only see herself and Laura, choking down cake at the world's worst birthday party ever.

She clicked on the TV. On the screen, a commercial for an antidepressant was playing out. *Of course it is.* Eliza had neither the energy nor the desire to change the channel, and she snuggled deeper into the sofa cushions. As the commercial ended, it gave way to an episode of *Monk*. Laura had loved this gentle, bloodless, funny mystery show. It felt like a sign.

Despite her better judgment, which struggled to keep its head above water, she emailed Vanessa to let her know that she wasn't going to make it into the office today.

It was remarkably exhausting doing nothing. Eliza's limbs felt heavy when she finally dragged herself off the sofa to shower and get dressed for dinner with Scott and Maren. If she hadn't spilled tea on her sweatshirt, she might have trekked downtown in that and the leggings she was wearing, but once she was under the hot steamy water she felt marginally better.

A little while later, she was back at her brother's apartment building, having stopped at the bodega on the corner for a box of chocolate-covered biscuits. As she rang the doorbell, she envisioned Josh on the other side of the door, as he'd been the last time she came.

"Hey, E." And, lo and behold, there stood Josh. Again.

"What, do you live here now?"

He laughed. "Nope. But I've been invited for dinner."

Would have been nice if someone told me. She tried to remember what clothes she'd dragged on after her shower. *Why does it matter?*

"Eliza!" Maren came down the hall toward her, her green silk blouse setting off her red curls, and enveloped her in a hug. "I can't believe Carol's doing this to you."

"Yeah, well, I can." But the truth was, no matter how bad the friction between them had been, she couldn't quite believe it either. Was Carol really so mercenary? So vindictive? "Anyway, I brought cookies."

Maren took the box. "I'm broiling lamb chops. Do you want something to drink?"

"What have you got?" She trailed after Maren into the kitchen.

"Water. OJ. I have a bottle of white open . . ."

"Sounds great."

Maren turned to look at her, and Eliza realized her answer had been spectacularly unclear.

"Wine. I mean, wine sounds great. I'll get it." She retrieved a glass from the cabinet and poured—resisting the urge to fill it right to the rim.

"You think that's a good idea?" Scott observed her from the kitchen door, inclining his head toward her glass.

With all that she was dealing with, her brother's words felt like a slap. "Don't start," she snapped back, even as her eyes filled with tears. She'd never felt more alone. Was her brother going to side with Carol? Was the fact that they were only half siblings going to change how he looked at her, too? She swiped quickly at her eyes and took a gulp of wine.

"Okay, guys. Out of the kitchen. Way too much crowding going on here." Maren shooed them away. "And no fighting."

Eliza followed her brother and Josh into the living room and sat in the corner of the couch, curling her body in on itself. A little voice inside her head commented on her defensive posture. Scott cleared his throat as he lowered himself into one of the armchairs. "I asked Josh to come. Figured he could give us some legal perspective."

She glanced at Josh in time to see him raising his hands. "Whoa. Like I said—trusts and estates isn't my area. But I talked to one of my colleagues." He sat, too, in the other armchair, as Maren came into the room with a glass of wine for herself.

"Could we please not jump straight in?" she asked, and then turned to Eliza as she sat on the couch herself. "How are you doing?"

She shrugged. "You know. It all sucks." She didn't want to start crying, so she decided to go with nonchalance. Although that was the last thing she felt.

Maren looked at her more closely. "Did you go to work today?"

Is it that obvious? The faded jeans were probably the give-away. "Um. I worked from home."

Maren raised her eyebrows, and Eliza caught the quick glance she shot at Scott. Maren and Scott had met in college, and Eliza had always assumed that her sister-in-law was fully up to speed on her coping skills—or lack thereof—at least through Scott's lens. "Nice that they're flexible like that. But it's probably easier to get more done in the office, right?"

"Well, you know, sometimes it's good to just have peace and quiet." Eliza hoped she wouldn't have to spin out this imaginary work-from-home scenario much longer.

"I wish work-from-home was a thing at my job," Josh commented. "Not exactly law-firm culture."

They chatted while Maren went in and out of the kitchen to manage the lamb, and Eliza joined her to help, draining the noodles she'd made as a side dish. It wasn't until they were halfway through the meal that Scott brought them back around to the letters they'd received.

"So, we should talk about the will," he began.

"Have you talked to Carol?" Eliza asked.

He shook his head. "Not yet. I wanted to talk to you first. And"—he nodded toward Josh—"consult an attorney."

"I just can't believe she's doing this." Eliza shook her head. "I mean. Dad just died, and . . ." She trailed off.

Scott's face was impassive. "But isn't that the whole point? He wasn't *your* dad."

"*Scott!*" Maren hissed. "As far as *he* knew, he *was* Eliza's dad. Isn't that the point?"

Josh interjected. "Legally, it probably is. According to my colleague—if Jack believed Eliza to be his daughter and left her a bequest based on that fact, it's likely the will will stand. But it's a bit of a tricky legal puzzle given that the will reads 'my daughter Eliza' rather than simply naming her."

Amazing how such careful legal language could obscure all of Eliza's emotions.

"So what am I supposed to do?" Eliza addressed her plate, unable to look anyone in the eyes.

Scott spoke. "Well, you could just let it go. Is it worth the fight, Eliza?"

She looked up at her brother, not entirely believing what she was hearing. "*Is it worth the fight?* Dad *wanted* me to have whatever he left me."

"Are you sure that's what he would have wanted if he knew the truth?"

"*Scott!*" Maren exclaimed again.

He lifted his hands in surrender. "Hey, just asking the question. Josh, what's likely to happen if Carol's challenge succeeds?"

"Well, again, this is all hypothetical and . . ."

"Yeah, yeah, not your area. I get it."

"I suspect that the court would split what would have gone to Eliza between you and Carol."

Is that what this is about? Is Scott just being greedy?

"So maybe one option would be to just accept it. And I'll give Eliza what comes to me." He turned to her. "So you'd get half of what you would have gotten, and we could avoid all this."

No, it's conflict avoidance. "But, Scott, it's wrong! It's not what Dad would have wanted. It's not about the money."

"Then what *is* it about, Eliza? I mean, you and Dad barely talked. Is it worth a fight?"

Her face got hot. "Yes! Carol can't just erase me!"

"Come on, Lize. Are you being fair? It's not like you ever gave Carol a fair shake. Maybe she's just doing what she truly thinks Dad would have wanted."

She wanted to smack him, and pressed her hands together in her lap. "Well, maybe this shows that I was right about who she is. I mean—who *does* this? Until three weeks ago, I thought Dad was my dad. He raised me. And now he's dead—and instead of letting me grieve *and* deal with this crazy new information—she's taking me to court!" Despite trying to remain calm, she heard her voice become shriller and shriller as she spoke. "And now my brother is taking her side. And yeah, maybe I'm only your *half* sister now, but that's still more blood than you share with Carol."

"Jesus, Eliza. Calm down. I'm not taking anyone's side."

"Bullshit." She drained her wineglass, even as she knew it probably wasn't the best choice—if for no other reason than that everyone's eyes were on her.

"Look, I don't think this is getting us anywhere," Maren said gently. "Scott, if Eliza wants to fight this, it's up to her."

Scott looked at his wife. "No matter what it drags us all through?"

Eliza was genuinely puzzled. "What's it going to 'drag us through'?"

Her brother pushed his chair back from the table and stood. "I don't know. I just don't need all this shit. Do whatever you want." And he left the room.

Eliza looked at Maren, whose forehead wrinkled. "He's having a really hard time," Maren said in a low voice.

CHAPTER FIFTEEN

That weekend, Eliza was back on the Metro-North train, en route to Aunt Claude's. She hadn't stayed much longer at Scott and Maren's after her brother's outburst. She and Josh had walked to the subway together, and Josh had given her his colleague's business card and promised to ask around for a lawyer who would better suit her budget.

They didn't talk much as they walked. Eliza couldn't help feeling that Josh was more distant than he'd been before. More closed off. Meanwhile, she kept turning Scott's behavior over and over in her head. He'd always been the strong one. She said as much to Josh as they parted.

"Maybe he's not as strong as he wants you to think he is," he replied.

When she got home, she called Aunt Claude, who was appropriately indignant upon hearing what was going on.

"Ugh. I never liked that woman."

You and me both.

"Anyway," Claude continued. "I was going to call you tonight. I finally had time to dig around for old photos. I found a box of your mom's stuff that must have been at Grandma and Grandpa's house. I forgot that I took it when they moved. Looks like it's stuff from before she went to college. Mostly school papers, but there are some personal things, too. I was going to go through it and then thought you might want to take a look first."

So now Eliza sat on the train, trying to focus on the book she was reading. She'd picked up the latest Lisa Jewell thriller at Grand Central, hoping it would keep her engaged and not surprise her with something that would tear her heart out. She had quite enough of that in real life.

Outside the train station in Tarrytown, the air felt colder and cleaner than what she'd left behind in Manhattan. Aunt Claude was waiting outside in her Volvo sedan, and Eliza slipped into the front seat.

"Hey, love." Claude reached over and squeezed her hand. "I'm sorry it's been so long since I've seen you. I feel terrible."

"It's fine. I know you're busy." Aunt Claude was an interior designer who focused on large commercial projects and often traveled all over upstate New York. Sometimes beyond.

"I tried to check in on Scott, but I haven't heard back." Claude's smooth pageboy swung like a shampoo commercial as she looked over her shoulder to back out of the parking space.

"Yeah, well."

Her aunt glanced at her. "What's going on with you two?"

Eliza explained what had happened over dinner, and Aunt Claude sighed. "Scott's a peacemaker. He wants everything to go smoothly and everyone to be okay. But I think he forgets that sometimes it can't."

Claude expertly parallel parked in front of a tavern that had been a favorite of theirs for years. "Thought we'd get lunch before we head back to the house."

A few minutes later they were seated in a booth at a rustic wooden table, scanning the oversize menus.

"Ooh—do you want to split the breaded mozzarella for an appetizer?" Aunt Claude asked.

"I'm not that hungry, but if you want it, I'll have a bite." Eliza had a feeling that Claude would get more food into her at this meal than she'd eaten all week. They placed their orders, and within minutes, the server was back with a plateful of golden, crispy goodness.

As Eliza spooned marinara sauce onto her plate, she told her aunt about her research. "So, Ross Sawyer is a professor at NYU now."

"Huh. Interesting. What does he teach?"

"Education—funny coincidence, right?"

Claude swallowed the bite of fried cheese in her mouth. "Yeah. I would have thought maybe political science. He was always all about social justice. Poverty. Racism. Making the world a better place."

Eliza thought about NOY's mission. "Well, that can be what education is about, too. Giving kids a better start in life."

"True." Claude looked thoughtful.

"What?"

Her aunt put her fork down. "I'm worried about you, Liza."

Would there ever come a time when people weren't worried about her?

"I'm afraid you're avoiding dealing with your dad's— Jack's—death by focusing on Ross. Why don't you put this aside? You didn't even know he existed until a few weeks ago. He's not going anywhere."

Eliza's jaw tightened. "And how do you know that? In my experience, parents don't exactly stick around."

"Oh, Lize."

She shrugged, trying to chase away Claude's sympathetic gaze. "Although—what are the chances of all *three* of them dropping dead?"

Her attempt at gallows humor failed spectacularly as

Claude's eyebrows drew closer together. "Liza. Are you okay?"

"No. No, I am *not* okay. But I am getting up every day and getting dressed and doing what I need to do." *Pretty much.* She knew she sounded petulant, and she didn't mean to take it out on Aunt Claude. But sometimes she just couldn't control the anger. The anger about everything she'd lost. She forced a small smile. "Can we just change the subject?"

Claude opened her mouth and closed it again. "Sure. So. Let's see . . . Nora has a new boyfriend."

Eliza listened to her aunt go on about her kids and her latest work project—an open-plan office that wanted to go back to walls and doors—and managed to eat a quarter of the club sandwich she'd ordered.

A little while later, they were at Aunt Claude's house, a Craftsman-style bungalow with a generous front porch. As Claude unlocked the door, the sounds of frantic scratching came from the other side.

"I guess Millie hasn't calmed down," Eliza remarked.

Claude looked over her shoulder and smiled. "Never," she said. As soon as she began to open the door, a small black nose appeared in the crack. "Come on, Millie, inside."

Millie, a curly-haired mini doodle, leaped up at her and then, noticing Eliza, scrambled over the tile floor to her, too. Eliza crouched down to let her lick her hands and face. "Yes, Millie, I missed you, too!"

Claude looked down at them, her hands on her hips. "Maybe that's what you need, Liza. A dog."

Eliza glanced up. "In Manhattan? I don't think so. But maybe I do need to come visit Millie more." She grabbed the squirming dog and cuddled her.

"Looks like our baby girl is happy to see you."

"Hi, Uncle Mitch." Eliza rose at the sound of his voice, and he enveloped her in a hug.

"How you hanging in, kiddo?" He patted her on the back before releasing her.

"You know." She shrugged.

"You're welcome here whenever you want," he said, rubbing a hand across his stubbled cheek.

"Were you napping?" Aunt Claude rose on tiptoe to give him a quick kiss.

He chuckled. "Is there a better way to spend a Saturday afternoon?"

Eliza loved the ease of her aunt and uncle's relationship, at least what she saw of it. They always seemed so relaxed and casually affectionate.

Claude put her hand on Eliza's shoulder. "Why don't I make us some tea?" She turned to Mitch. "You want some, Sleeping Beauty?"

"No thanks. The caffeine might keep me awake."

The large kitchen was bright and white, and Claude filled the shiny yellow enamel teapot with water. "The box I found is in the dining room, if you want to take a look."

With Millie at her heels, Eliza headed that way, quickly spotting the carton in the corner next to the buffet cabinet. She dragged it away from the wall and sat down on the area rug, its abstract pattern a muddle of deep blues and greens.

It felt strange to sift through things that had belonged to her mother and that she'd never seen before. She opened the box and peered inside. Mostly stacks of paper. Rifling through, she found neatly typed and carefully handwritten term papers, the staples holding them together slightly rusty with age.

"I've got your tea." Claude set the mug down on the table near Eliza's head.

Eliza looked up from a title page that read *"The Genius of Madame Marie Curie."* "How come you never gave me this stuff before?"

Claude pulled out the nearest chair from under the table

and sat. "I honestly forgot about it. When Grandma and Grandpa sold the house, they found this box in the attic. It was so soon after your mom died, and you . . . well, you know what a hard time you were having. We weren't sure it would be a good idea to give it to you, so I put it in my attic. And as time went on, it completely slipped my mind."

"*We* weren't sure?"

"Your dad and me."

Eliza wasn't surprised. Jack had often resisted talking about Laura. At the time, she thought he didn't care as much as she did—and when he got together with Carol, she was surer of that than ever. But maybe it was more complicated than that.

She'd gone through a period where she felt compelled to go through family photo albums over and over again, poring over images of them at Disney World, at school concerts, in front of the Christmas tree at Rockefeller Center—an annual tradition after which they'd go home and light their Hanukkah menorah. She knew what would happen whenever she opened those albums and almost welcomed the hot tears that rolled down her cheeks.

Jack came upon her observing this ritual a few months after her mom's death. The next day, he taught Scott how to repair the hole he'd subsequently punched in the drywall in the bedroom he had shared with Laura.

Now Eliza lifted the stacks of school papers out of the box. Underneath, she found an autograph book scrawled with the childish signatures of her mom's friends. On the first page, Laura had carefully printed FOURTH GRADE. Beneath that were drawings. Some crayon and splatter paint, but a few more sophisticated sketches. Based on the dates Laura had penciled in the corners, it looked like they were from high school art classes. Eliza held them up for Claude.

"Oh, wow! I'd forgotten what a good artist Laura was." Her

aunt reached for them and paged through the sheets. Then she handed one back to Eliza. "This is Ross."

She took the page, still unable to process that this man she'd never met was her biological father. She studied the three-quarter profile, sketched in charcoal, recognizing the thick, unruly hair and intense gaze from the yearbook photograph. His eyes, as drawn by Laura, were even more like her own. Gently running her fingertip over the contours of his face, she wondered if her mother had ever done a sketch like this of Jack.

Further down in the box was a manila envelope, its flap clasped shut. Easing her fingernail under the clasps, she bent them upward to release the flap. Inside were photographs.

Eliza uncrossed her legs and moved up to the table to take a sip of her tea while she removed the contents of the envelope. So this was where Laura had put all the photos of her and Ross. She spread them out on the table. There was Laura in a pale yellow floor-length prom dress. It was held up by spaghetti straps, and its skirt cascaded in soft tiers that made Eliza think of a wedding cake. Next to her, Ross wore a powder blue, very seventies tuxedo. In another photo, Laura wore a bright red bikini held together by wooden rings on her hips and between her breasts. She was sitting on Ross's lap. They looked so comfortable with each other—it was almost hard to tell where Laura's limbs ended and Ross's began. Eliza tried to remember if Laura and Jack had had that easy way with each other. They must have. *Right?*

She paged through the photos slowly, feeling like she was looking at images of a stranger. It was clearly her mother. And yet not her mother. Did Laura look as much like a stranger in her wedding photos with Jack? Eliza didn't know that woman, either, but had always accepted her as the person who gave birth to her.

Aunt Claude pointed to one of the photographs. "There's me."

Sure enough, it was. Claude with her hair parted in the middle and feathered back, wearing a pair of patchwork bell-bottoms and a snug white T-shirt. She was sitting on a bench with Laura and Ross.

"That was at Rye Playland. Your mom hated roller coasters, but I loved them. Ross took me on the Dragon Coaster three times that day."

"When was this?"

"Right around when they graduated from high school. I can't remember exactly."

"Did you guys spend a lot of time together?"

"Not a lot." She smiled. "I was the annoying little sister. But sometimes."

Eliza replaced the photos neatly in the envelope and bent down to lift out what remained in the box. Birthday and Valentine's cards from Ross. A small box containing a dried corsage. Its shriveled petals made her think of Miss Havisham and her decaying wedding finery. Also in the box was a tiny key. Perhaps a pendant? And all the way at the bottom of the carton, an old-fashioned diary. It had a patchwork design on the cover, and a clasp with a tiny keyhole.

"Did she write in this?" Eliza asked, showing the diary to her aunt.

Claude shrugged. "Beats me. Is it locked?"

Eliza tried to open it. "Seems like it." And then she went back to the corsage box. Sure enough, the tiny key fit the tiny lock. Flipping it open, she recognized Laura's handwriting, written in blue ballpoint ink. Rifling through, she saw that more pages were blank than were written on, and the dates were widely spaced apart. Laura clearly hadn't journaled every day. Or even every week. She closed the diary again.

"Not sure how I feel about reading this," she said.

CHAPTER SIXTEEN

Eliza's ride back to the city went by in a blur. If asked, she wouldn't have been able to describe how she ended up back in her apartment.

She'd never seriously considered keeping a diary when she was a teenager. She was given one as a gift once—pale pink with the words *MY DIARY* embossed on the front in gold—but never knew how to begin. The pages were so pristine with nothing written in them; it seemed like she should have something important, something remarkable, or at the very least something interesting to say before marring the creamy paper.

She tended to see her life as marked by a bright before-and-after line. Before Laura's diagnosis. After her diagnosis. In the before times, life was just—life. School. Convincing her mom to buy her Ugg boots. Going out for ice cream with friends. None of it seemed worth memorializing. In the after times, everything continued, but with a low-level, staticky buzz of fear and anxiety underlying everything. No matter how much Laura told her that she was going to be okay, Eliza never believed her. Even in the beginning, when Laura may well have believed it herself, Eliza was sure she was going to lose her. And that was definitely not something she wanted to write about. So the pages of that diary remained blank, and somewhere along the way, she added it to a pile of stuff for donation.

Now that she had Laura's journal, it gave new weight to the whole "keeping a diary" question. On the one hand, maybe it would be nice to have those memories recorded. On the other—would she want someone to read her most private thoughts after she was dead? As she tucked Laura's diary into the drawer of her bedside table, next to a box of condoms and some hair ties, she tried to tell herself that a dead person couldn't mind having someone read their secrets. After all, wasn't their biggest problem being dead? In comparison to that, who cared if the world knew who you had a crush on or if you cheated on a math test? But at the same time, she couldn't bring herself to look inside. At least not yet.

After firmly closing the drawer, she went to find her laptop. She'd been delinquent lately on social media. She just didn't have the stomach for everyone's carefully curated happiness. Even her own post about Jack's death—including a photo of him holding her as a baby, along with a photo from Scott's wedding of Jack, Scott, Maren, and Eliza—felt so disingenuous. As if they were this happy, uncomplicated family, dealing with purely uncomplicated grief.

Opening the laptop, she checked her personal email and then scrolled through Facebook and Instagram. She typed "Ross Sawyer" into the Facebook search bar again, but, unsurprisingly, her Ross Sawyer still didn't have a profile. Then she went to Google and searched "Ross Sawyer NYU," not sure what she was looking for. Both literally and figuratively.

The more she thought about her dinner conversation with Mo, the more annoyed she had become—even though she'd tried to talk herself out of what felt like unreasonable anger. She loved her friend's sense of humor—and counted on her ability to pull her out of dark places. But this was uncharted territory, and it didn't seem like Mo got what she was feeling. How unmoored she was—in a way she had never been before. The idea that she should sneak into her biological dad's classroom was appalling. And terrifying. How could Mo not see that?

She mindlessly scrolled the search results on the screen, barely seeing them. And then something caught her eye. Glenside School Speaker Series: An Evening with Dr. Ross Sawyer. She clicked. *"Social and Emotional Learning: A New Approach to the Achievement Gap."* But what popped out at her, as if it were written in bold letters, was "Open to the public." She looked back up at the top to see the date. It was just over a week away. Monday evening.

Tucking this piece of information away in her brain, she had just closed her laptop when a text came in on her phone. She picked it up, expecting it to be the daily check-in from Mo. They hadn't talked since their dinner. Mo was busy at work and had seen Nik a few more times. And Eliza wasn't sure what to say to her, anyway. Ross and Jack were always at the forefront of her mind, and for the first time in their long friendship, she was dealing with something she wasn't sure she wanted to talk about.

But the text was, surprisingly, from Maren.

> **Hey, Eliza. Wanted to check in on you. Can we get together? Just the two of us?**

Huh. That was unusual. Actually, unprecedented, discounting their bridesmaid-dress shopping, but even then it wasn't just the two of them—Maren's mom and a couple of her friends were there, too.

Eliza texted back.

Is everything ok?

As she watched the three dots appear and reappear, she felt the familiar knot in her belly. Was Maren wanting to meet up alone with her because Scott didn't want anything to do with her? Was there (more) bad news? Finally words appeared.

Yes. I just think it would be a good idea.

Eliza sat in a small booth sipping an autumn-themed cocktail. She couldn't remember what was in it but was loving the cinnamon sugar crusted on the rim of the glass. She was a little early for her "date" with Maren and scrolled through her phone while she was waiting.

The bar was in midtown, and most of the other patrons were in groups of two or three, grabbing an after-work drink, or so it seemed. Their voices melded into a low hum that intermingled with the music coming from the speakers in the ceiling. Gradually the strains of a melody disentangled themselves, and she recognized the Nickelback song. It had been a while since she'd heard it, but in another phase of her life, it was one of her favorites.

It was eleven years earlier that she'd been sitting on a bench adjacent to the high school turf, listening to that song on her iPod when Josh pulled one of her earbuds out of her ear.

"Whatcha listening to?" he'd asked, plopping down beside her on the bench.

She had been lost in thought, and it took her a minute to replay his question in her head before she could figure out the answer. "Nickelback."

He'd stuck the earbud in his own ear. "Cool. I have this album." They listened as "How You Remind Me" wound down, and Eliza clicked the stop button. "You waiting for someone?" Josh had asked.

She shook her head. "Nope."

"Then what? It's not a bus stop."

Why was she sitting here? Because she wasn't quite ready to go home, but how could she explain that? It was fall of her sophomore year, and after having had a reasonably good summer, Laura's numbers weren't where her doctors wanted them to be, and she'd started a new treatment that was exhausting her. Or maybe it was the cancer that was exhausting her. It was hard to tell.

All Eliza knew was that, as much as she wanted to spend every minute with her mom, sometimes she just couldn't bear to go home. Sometimes she needed to take some time to brace herself first. She glanced at her watch. School had let out a half hour before, and she hadn't made it any farther than this bench.

"Just hanging out," she replied, finally.

"Well, it's a nice day for it." Josh gestured at the clear blue sky and the autumn-hued trees. A light breeze swirled the falling leaves as they dropped toward the ground. On the turf, the football players were jogging out for practice, suited up in their gear. "Or was that the view you were waiting for?" Josh asked, cocking his head toward the team.

"Hardly." Football players were definitely not on her radar.

Josh slid back to make himself more comfortable. Apparently he was staying for a while. Strange. He spent a lot of time at the Levinger house, but they'd never exchanged more than a sentence or two. "Have you heard the new Nickelback album?" he asked.

She shook her head.

"It's pretty good. They're saying 'Far Away' is going to be the breakout single, but I like 'Photograph.' I can lend it to you if you want."

"You still buy the old-school CDs?"

"Yeah. I load them into my iPod"—he pointed at hers for reference—"but I like to have the discs. Who else do you listen to?"

"Oh—I don't know. Lots of stuff: 3 Doors Down. Coldplay. Green Day." She spun the dial on her iPod, looking at the list of songs. Until recently, her playlists had been mostly pop and electronic dance music—but it turned out that, even with the volume turned up, they didn't protect her from the sounds of Laura being sick from chemo. Cranking up "Yellow," "Boulevard of Broken Dreams," and similar songs did.

Josh peered over her shoulder at the crawl of song titles. "Do you know Jason Mraz?"

"I don't think so."

"I'll lend you his new album, too. Came out this summer."

Somehow, they had whiled away an hour sitting on that bench, talking mostly about music. Josh never asked how things were going with her mom. He probably knew from Scott where things stood. Or he didn't. Eliza had just appreciated being able to sit on a bench with a boy and pretend that life was normal again. Even if just for an hour.

Now, in a darkened bar in New York City, the Nickelback song gave way to something more modern, and Maren walked up to the table, unwrapping her scarf from her neck.

"So sorry! Were you waiting long?"

Eliza looked at her drink, which was still two-thirds full. "Not long at all. Don't worry about it."

Maren placed her structured leather bag on the seat opposite Eliza. "I'm just going to get a drink. Can I get you anything?"

"I'm good."

Her sister-in-law returned a few minutes later with something tall and icy, and slid into the booth. "So how was your day?"

There was some meaningless chitchat as Eliza wondered when Maren would get to the point.

"You're probably wondering why I wanted to meet," she finally said, pushing her hair out of her eyes. "The thing is, I can't even imagine what you're going through. I know it's got to be really hard. I mean, not just Jack's death, but then to get this other news." She paused and sighed before continuing. "But, well, Scott's having a hard time, too."

Eliza nodded.

"I know you know that. But I don't think you know how hard it is for him. He's been the one everybody has leaned on. And I know he wants to be there for everyone. But he can't be. Not always."

Eliza had a feeling that "everybody" equaled "Eliza," and she felt a mixture of guilt and anger. Shouldn't Scott be the one to tell her this? But before she could say as much, Maren continued.

"He wouldn't want me to tell you this, but we've been trying to get pregnant. Not for long—but losing Jack now, and knowing he'll never get to meet his grandchildren . . . it's just a lot. I don't think he has it in him to referee between you and Carol."

Eliza had worn her hair in a braid over one shoulder, and she twisted the end of it. "Did he say that?"

Maren shook her head. "He wouldn't. But I'm worried about him."

The end of Eliza's braid was cutting off the circulation in the finger it was wrapped around. She knew it wasn't fair for Scott to always have to be the sane one. The peacemaker, as Aunt Claude had called him. The inside of her mouth felt dry. "Did he ask you to talk to me?"

She shook her head. "He doesn't know I'm here. He wouldn't want me to be."

Eliza struggled to understand what her sister-in-law was

telling her. Hadn't Maren sounded like she was on her side just a few days before? "So are you saying I shouldn't fight Carol? That I should just do what Scott suggested?"

"That has to be your choice." Maren scrunched up her mouth. "And I totally understand why you'd want to fight her. You *were* Jack's daughter, in every way that mattered. Carol can't take that away from you. I just . . . I'm just worried about Scott taking on too much. He's already stretched so thin, you know, emotionally."

Eliza's stomach clenched. Her relationship with Scott had been lopsided for a long time. He was the strong one. She was the mess. It was an integral part of the family story. And she knew that he was suffering loss, too. He had been closer to Jack, after all. But what about her loss? Not to mention her loss of identity. She didn't want to need support—she wanted to stand on her own two feet but truly didn't know if she could.

She let go of her braid and swung it behind her. "Look, I don't know what you want me to do. Or not do."

"I guess I'm asking you to leave Scott out of it."

Eliza tried to tamp down the anger—and hurt—she felt rising inside her. "Don't you think he'd want to know? I mean, I *am* his sister. And Carol is his stepmom."

Maren pressed her lips together, and Eliza watched the color leach out of them. "I know that. Obviously. But somebody has to look out for Scott."

Did Maren think that Scott needed protection from his own sister? But she had a feeling that this was an argument she wouldn't win—and wasn't sure she even had the energy to try—so she gave a small nod of acknowledgment.

Maren continued. "Look. I'm not saying we're not there for you. We are. But I just . . ." She blinked rapidly, and Eliza recognized it well as a strategy to hold back tears. "I mean . . ."

Eliza felt her anger begin to deflate. She wasn't the only one in pain here. She reached across to touch Maren's hand, splayed on the table, her diamond solitaire and matching wedding band winking even in the dim light. "I got it. I hear you."

Maren gave her a watery smile. "Thanks, Eliza. I knew I could count on you."

Biting the inside of her lip, Eliza wondered what exactly she'd agreed to—and whether it was all going to backfire spectacularly.

CHAPTER SEVENTEEN

Eliza threw herself into work. She followed up with every contact she'd ever made, trying to get their support for the gala; went for another tour of the venue, a beautiful event space that had once been the first floor of a department store not far from Central Park; and chased down items for the silent auction. She also made an appointment with the lawyer Josh recommended. Vicky Muhlfelder was a friend of his from law school who had gone into practice with her dad in Brooklyn. They specialized in wills and estates, and Josh assured her that their rates would be much more reasonable than his own firm's.

Through it all, Eliza tried to forget that Ross was scheduled to speak at a public event. She knew that Patrice had contacted several faculty at NYU but hadn't yet heard back from anyone. Meanwhile, Eliza had spoken with a professor at a small college on Long Island who was very excited about NOY's work and the new award, but Vanessa wanted to hold off on making a commitment. Clearly she was hoping for a bigger, brighter star.

On Monday evening, after work, Eliza found herself exiting the subway a couple of blocks from Glenside School. The truth was, no matter how much she denied it, she had known she'd go to Ross's talk from the minute she saw it was happening. She'd thought about asking Mo to come with her, but if her friend was going to suggest that they wear disguises or spy on him after the event—even if it was just a joke—she thought she might snap.

Glenside was housed in a brownstone on a quiet street on the Upper West Side. It was one of the city's oldest independent schools, known for educational innovation. In fact, one of NOY's board members sat on the Glenside board as well. It really was a painfully small world.

She took a deep breath before ascending the stone steps in front of the building. The heavy front door stuck a little, and she pulled hard, envisioning herself tumbling back down the steps with the effort.

Suddenly the door eased, and Eliza realized someone was helping from the other side. "So sorry! This door is terrible!" The first thing she noticed about the owner of the voice was her voluminous caftan. Eliza had to force her eyes up to the woman's face, which was kind and gently creased.

"Are you here for the talk?" she asked.

Eliza nodded.

"You just made it. They're about to get started."

Eliza glanced at her watch. She'd meant to be a few minutes earlier. She'd been afraid of being too early and stuck making small talk as the room filled up, but she also didn't want to draw attention to herself by coming in late.

"Don't worry, you're not late," the woman said, as if reading her mind. "It's just down this hall in the little theater." She gestured toward the back of the building.

The *little* theater? How small was this room going to be? Eliza felt her body go cold, and if it weren't for the fact that this pleasant woman would think she was crazy, she'd have run back out the way she came. "Thanks very much," she said instead, and forced her feet to move toward the theater rather than back to the street.

The hallway was lined with paneling, and the tile was a prewar herringbone design. She could almost hear the echoes of the children's feet that had run, walked, and trudged up and down this corridor over the years. All too soon, she got to the double doors marked with a small brass plate reading *Florence Bixby Theater*. She was tempted to pause and Google "Florence Bixby" on her phone. Anything to delay entering. She glanced over her shoulder and saw Caftan Lady nodding and smiling at her.

"Just go on in," she mouthed.

If only it were that easy. She opened the door, which creaked gently. As she stepped inside, she was relieved to see that the little theater wasn't so little. At a quick glance, she would guess it seated more than one hundred people. About half the seats were filled, and a woman wearing dark dress pants and a red scoop-neck sweater stood at the podium on the stage, speaking into the mike. A man sat beside and a little behind her, looking comfortable in his own skin in the folding metal chair, one leg crossed over the other, his foot bouncing. *He had trouble sitting still,* Aunt Claude had said. Apparently that was still the case.

Eliza quietly headed toward the right side of the theater and took the aisle seat in the back row. The seats were old and wooden and, she discovered, creaked when folded down. A couple of her nearest neighbors glanced her way as she mouthed an apology and slid into the seat. Clearly, though, the sound didn't carry that far, as the woman onstage kept speaking. Some platitudes welcoming everyone and talking about the theme of this year's speaker series. But Eliza's eyes were glued on Ross. *Her father.*

He was dressed as if he'd gone to a costume shop for a "professor outfit." He wore a blazer—she couldn't tell at this distance if it was tweed or corduroy—over a dark blue button-down shirt, paired with jeans. Not a wash that anyone could call cool or fashionable. Just ordinary blue jeans. Loafers on his feet, including the one that continued to bounce.

Applause echoed around the room, and Eliza joined in without thinking. The speaker must have introduced Ross, because now he stood, shook her hand, and approached the podium. His mouth was moving, but Eliza couldn't hear him over the smattering of applause that continued. She resisted the urge to shush the crowd, and they quieted down.

"Thank you. Thanks so much. I'm truly delighted to be here to speak to you tonight. I've long admired the work done here at Glenside, and there's no question in my mind that we are at a crisis point in American education." Ross's voice was a little husky, the kind of voice that sounded like it was used to shouting. As he continued to speak, Eliza looked around the room and saw heads nodding and a few people taking notes.

She tried to imagine how Laura would see him, up at that podium. Would she be proud? Would her pulse quicken? Or would she feel shame? A living reminder of her betrayal of her marriage. Of the enormous secret she felt forced to keep for sixteen years.

Toward the end, Laura was often too tired to speak. She'd whisper to Eliza, generally sweet memories. The hopscotch boards she'd drawn in the driveway for Eliza to play in. The clapping games she'd taught her. *Miss Mary Mack, Mack, Mack; All dressed in black, black, black.* Finger games they'd played. "Where Is Thumb Man?" Eliza had tried to smile but was so very angry. Unless Thumb Man could cure Laura's cancer, who the fuck cared where he was?

Sometimes, Laura whispered about Eliza's future. The happiness she hoped for her. Now, in the same room for the first time with this man her mother had loved, she could hear her mother's voice. *Don't compromise, Eliza. Not when it comes to*

who you share your life with. You'll have to compromise enough
to keep a relationship going. That's what a good relationship
is. Give and take. But if you make a life with someone—make
sure you're not compromising on who that is. Life is too short to
settle for less than the right person.

Was Laura trying to tell her something? Had she settled
for Jack? Did she always regret not being with Ross? Or would
she have been compromising if she'd stayed with Ross—and
was that night at the reunion just a disastrous mistake?

Ross's voice rose. "We have seen time and again that pro-
gramming and curricula designed to boost social and emotional learning of young children are directly correlated to
stronger academic performance. And those improvements
are shown year over year in subsequent assessments. This is
where we need to focus our efforts." As his gestures became
broader and his expression more animated, Eliza found herself
thinking of Jack, who was always so calm. Even when he was
angry—about Scott's tennis coach, whom he rarely saw eye to
eye with, or about grades they brought home that were less
than he expected—he rarely raised his voice. In fact, he'd get
quieter, more still.

Eliza tried to focus on what Ross was saying but kept getting caught up in the cadence of his voice, the planes of his
face, the increasing wildness of his hair as he moved around.
Now that she saw him in person, could she see any of herself
in him? At this distance, it was hard to tell. Then, before she
knew it, the woman who had introduced him rose to join him
at the podium.

"Thank you so very much, Professor Sawyer. That was *fas-
cinating.* I'm sure we have quite a few questions in the audience. We'll do some Q and A before we break for coffee and
dessert."

"Ah, so I'm going to be standing between everyone and
cake. You're making this tough for me!" Ross grinned widely.

She patted his arm. "Oh, now, I think we education policy wonks are going to be much more excited by what you have to say than by some Entenmann's."

Are they flirting? Eliza missed the first question because she was so focused on what was happening onstage. She could have sworn the moderator's scoop neck was lower now.

Okay, I'm going crazy. So what if she's showing too much cleavage? As far as I know, Ross is single. And my mother is dead. And she was married to Jack.

Several people in the audience asked questions about metrics for social and emotional growth, and Eliza tried to put all the complicated relationship dynamics out of her head. After all, she reminded herself, these topics clearly connected to NOY's work. All these people were potential donors. With her director-of-development hat on, she knew she should ask a question herself, one that would reference Nourish Our Youth. But with *I'm your secret daughter* blaring in her ears, she knew that there was no way that her brain could force her hand into the air.

Red Scoop Neck was now encouraging everyone to give Professor Sawyer a round of applause, and Eliza once again joined in automatically. "Please join us in the lounge for coffee and dessert. I'm sure Professor Sawyer would be happy to continue the conversation there." She smiled at him. *Coquettishly?*

The room filled with the sounds of people standing and gathering their bags and the creaking of the old wooden seats. Eliza picked up her tote and moved quickly toward the exit, planning to slip down the hall to the main doors. The last thing she wanted was to be close to Ross.

But when she got to the exit, Caftan Lady was there, blocking her path. "Just this way," she said, pointing toward the right.

Of course, Eliza could have said, "I'm sorry, but I can't stay," and Caftan Lady surely would have stepped aside. But somehow, her lips didn't form the words, and she just smiled and followed directions mutely.

The lounge was a cozy space with dark wood paneling and a large marble fireplace flanked by two overstuffed burgundy sofas. A fire was crackling in the grate, and a table in the middle of the room held two large urns, one neatly labeled *coffee* and the other *hot water*. A coffee cake and a large danish, pre-sliced, sat beside the urns. Red Scoop Neck wasn't kidding when she said there was Entenmann's.

The room was warm, especially since Eliza had already put on her coat in preparation for leaving. She thought about taking it off but liked the idea of being able to make a quick escape. She pulled her bag closer as she moved deeper into the room, which was filling up fast. Most people made a beeline for the refreshments, so Eliza veered toward the far wall, on which hung a series of framed photographs. She smiled as she peered at the groups of children pictured—apparently each year's collection of Glenside School students.

Why am I still here? She knew she should leave; nothing good could come of her staying. But there was something keeping her in that room. A desire to see him up close? Or at least closer than he'd been onstage? Her pulse raced, and she strained to detect Ross's voice over the others'.

But as she thought about coming face to face with him, her pulse pounded and the need to get out of the room overwhelmed her. She quickly turned from the photo she'd been looking at, her heart feeling like it was going to burst out of her chest. And as she stepped toward the door, her eyes on her feet, she walked smack into a man in a blazer. It turned out to be made of corduroy.

CHAPTER EIGHTEEN

It took a moment for Eliza to register the hot coffee that spilled on her sleeve and dripped onto her hand. But she immediately recognized the voice that spoke to her. The same voice that had been projecting from the stage.

"So sorry! But you really should watch where you're going," Ross exclaimed.

Her eyes remained fixed on the spreading coffee stain. "It's all right. It was my fault." She was about to turn away when Caftan Lady reappeared.

"Oh dear! Let's get you some napkins."

With Caftan Lady's hand under her elbow, she was steered toward the refreshment table.

"Here you go, dear." Caftan Lady swabbed at the stain with navy blue paper napkins embossed with the Glenside School logo in gold. *You know it's an expensive private school when they have their own napkins.*

Ross had followed them. "I guess I'll get myself a fresh cup of coffee. Would you like one?"

Eliza forced herself to drag her eyes up to his face and

could feel her pulse pounding in her throat. "No thanks, I'm fine. I was going to head out."

Caftan Lady interrupted. "Let me just get some water. I don't want the stain to set."

"Oh, but . . ." Eliza turned toward her, but she was gone.

"Force of nature that woman is, I think." Ross took a sip of his coffee. Absently, Eliza noted that he'd taken it black, as Laura had. Jack used to pile his with sugar. *Until Carol.* "So, what brought you to the talk tonight?"

"Oh. Um." She paused. How the hell had she gotten herself into this ridiculous situation? Stupid Mo and her stupid suggestions. Stupid Eliza for thinking this would be a good idea.

He smirked. "So clearly you had absolutely nothing better to do and wandered in off the street?"

She laughed nervously. "Well." *Just stick with the truth. Or at least as close to it as you can get.* "I work with Nourish Our Youth. We're a nonprofit—our mission is to support disadvantaged students, and we're interested in educational policy and research . . ."

"Say no more. You work for a nonprofit. You needed the free food." Ross pointed at the coffee cake. "Don't let me interrupt your dinner."

Really? Was that a joke? She couldn't tell if he was trying to be cute or if she was being dismissed. Either way, now she was pissed off. Anger was an easier emotion to deal with than panic.

"Well, actually, we're looking to make grants, but if you don't need research funding, I can move on." She hitched the strap of her bag higher on her shoulder and started to turn away.

He barked out a laugh and looked at her appraisingly. "Yeah, I deserved that. Good for you. What's your name? I'm Ross. But you probably know that."

She swallowed. *Would her last name ring any bells?* Did he

know Laura's married name? Presumably it had been twenty-seven years since they'd seen each other. "I'm Eliza. Levinger." She didn't see a flicker of recognition. As she watched for it, she noticed the lines creased around his eyes. It was the same face she'd seen in the prom and yearbook photos—but his skin showed the years that had passed.

Caftan Lady reappeared with a sheaf of damp paper towels. "Here you go, dear. Let me know if you need more."

"I'm sure this will be fine." Eliza took them from her and dabbed at her sleeve. How soon could she make her escape?

"So, Eliza Levinger. Tell me more about Nourish Our Youth."

She looked up; Ross was now standing with his arms crossed, a bemused expression on his face. Eyes so like her own were trained on her. It was eerie.

She struggled to push her brain into work mode. "We've been around since 1962 . . ."

"Well, *you* haven't been around since 1962. Probably more like—what? 1992?"

Hilarious. Who is *this asshole? Oh, right. He's my father.* "Something like that. Anyway, historically, NOY has . . ."

"Noy? What's a Noy?"

She sighed. "Nourish Our Youth," she repeated, carefully enunciating the words to emphasize their initial letters. "NOY is our acronym."

"Gotcha." Ross picked up a piece of coffee cake and took a large bite.

Eliza didn't want to tell him that he'd sprinkled powdered sugar all down the front of his shirt.

"Go on." He gestured with the hand holding the cake, scattering more powdered sugar and crumbs onto the rug.

Eliza stepped back to avoid the spray, noticing that a small older woman was hovering nearby, trying to get Ross's attention. *If only she'd try harder.* "Right. Well, *Nourish Our Youth* was founded to help pull children out of poverty. In the past we dealt with a whole bunch of issues like homelessness and food insecurity, but now we're mostly focused on education. So we make grants to schools and teachers, but we're looking to get more involved in funding education research."

Ross popped the last bite of coffee cake into his mouth. "Sounds a little scattered," he remarked around the mouthful of cake.

He's not wrong. "We're evolving."

"So, tell me . . ." But Ross couldn't complete his sentence before Red Scoop Neck appeared, much more effectively intervening than the poor gray-haired lady who'd been waiting so patiently.

"Ross. Excuse me. But there are a few people I'd like you to meet." She put her hand on his arm and then turned to Eliza. "You don't mind, do you?"

She shook her head numbly.

"Sorry," Ross said apologetically over his shoulder. "I'll find you later. I want to hear more about *NOY.*" He emphasized the acronym like it was incredibly amusing.

Eliza watched Red Scoop Neck steer him to a cluster of three people—two women and a man—who greeted him with wide smiles.

"I'll find you later," he'd said. Not if she could help it.

CHAPTER NINETEEN

The first time Eliza had a full-blown panic attack was at Laura's graveside. Just thinking about that horrible, steamy afternoon brought back the terrifying sensation. The feeling that her heart was pounding out of her chest. The pins and needles in her hands and feet. The conviction that she truly couldn't breathe.

It had happened when Scott attempted to hand her the shovel. The shovel she was meant to use to deposit dirt on top of Laura's casket. Eliza had felt anxiety before. Who hadn't? She got especially stressed before tests, and it had gotten worse since she started high school. Which, of course, coincided with Laura's diagnosis. Eliza had always wanted to do well in school. But with so much more important stuff for everyone to be concerned about, she didn't want anyone to waste energy worrying about her grades.

She'd gotten into the habit of going to the girls' bathroom before tests to run her wrists under the cold water—the soothing technique Laura had taught her. She didn't know if it was the cold water or the fact that it made her feel like her mom was there with her, but the practice slowed her heart and helped her breathe again.

But there was no faucet in the cemetery. The shovel slipped out of her hands, and she had no choice but to drop to her knees on the ground, gasping for breath. She had made a spectacle of herself. Made the moment about her when it should have been about Laura. About their family. But in that moment, she truly thought she was going to die, right there, at her mother's grave. Aunt Claude crouched down beside her, rubbing her back and then somehow getting her to the car. She'd caught a glimpse of Jack, staring into the distance, his back to her, but everyone else was a hazy, undulating blur.

Later that evening, after Claude and the neighbors had cleaned up from the shiva, Eliza found her dad in the den, sitting in his recliner. But he wasn't reclined; he was perched on the edge of the seat, his head in his hands.

"I'm sorry about today, Dad," she'd said.

He didn't reply, and she thought he hadn't heard her.

"Dad? I'm sorry about what happened at the cemetery."

He didn't lift his head but waved one hand at her. "It's okay, Eliza. We're just lucky I didn't pass out, too." His voice was choked and watery, and the sound made Eliza's knees weak. She'd wanted to run to the nearest cold-water tap, but her feet were rooted in place. In the end, she sank to the floor, tears streaming down her face, while Jack remained like a statue, his head still in his hands. After what felt like hours but might have only been minutes, Scott had found her there and led her up to her room.

At some point, the fear of panic attacks became almost as bad as the attacks themselves. It was that fear that kept her in bed so many days in the months that followed. The thought of having a panic attack at school was unbearable. It was bad enough being the girl whose mother was dead. She didn't want to be the girl who freaked out in the chemistry lab. Or in gym class. Or in the cafeteria.

Now, as Eliza practically ran down the steps of the Glenside School, it felt like she was running from more than Ross Sawyer. She was running from a return of the panic attacks that paralyzed her. That turned her into someone everyone worried about. As she walked rapidly to Columbus Avenue, she had trouble catching her breath. *I'm just walking too fast. This is not a panic attack.* She slowed and took a deep breath. Or, rather, attempted a deep breath. She tried again. Better.

She headed up to get the crosstown bus at Eighty-First Street. It was fully dark, but the streets were still full of people—the beauty of the city. Couples, singles, and groups, heading home, going to dinner, talking loudly on their phones to invisible people.

Once on the bus, seated sideways between an older man in a three-piece suit and a young guy in ripped jeans whose dreadlocks were peeking out from beneath a bandanna, she rewound the evening in her mind, consciously modulating her breathing.

She'd come away from that interaction not liking Ross very much. With a hint of why his students referred to him as pompous. No question he had an edge.

But was she going to judge him based on a five-minute interaction? Was she looking for a reason to dismiss him? To decide not to pursue this further? It would certainly make life a lot easier. She could go back to mourning Jack as the only dad she had. It would make Scott—and therefore Maren—happy. Aunt Claude would have nothing to worry about.

Was that what Laura would want? Did it matter what she would want? Eliza had spent so much of her life wondering what her absent mother would think. Imagining her at her college graduation. Envisioning how proud she would have been when Eliza was promoted to development director. Wondering if she would have liked Maren. Some part of Eliza consistently lived outside herself, observing her life—her choices, her triumphs, her mistakes.

Unlike her friends, Eliza had never had a challenging relationship with her mother. She hadn't fought with her about what she should wear or how late she could stay out. The cancer had made those battles irrelevant. Perhaps, had they had those tussles, she would have broken away from the *What would Mom think?* that hovered over her like a specter.

Before she knew it, the bus reached Third Avenue, and she disembarked, pausing for a moment to decide if she should head home or pick up something to eat. She tried to remember what was in her fridge and, failing, stopped at the bodega on her corner. Even at this hour, the extensive salad bar was well stocked, and she piled a random assortment of three-bean salad, hard-boiled eggs, and olives into a container. She had just paid for her "dinner" when her cell phone rang. She glanced at the screen. Mo.

Her friend's voice sang out of the speaker. "Hey, stranger!"

Eliza readjusted herself to hold the phone to her ear as she headed toward her apartment. "What's up? How's Nik?" Her mind raced, wondering if she should tell her about meeting Ross. She tried to imagine her friend's reaction. Based on their prior conversations about him, Mo was likely to make light of it—or, alternatively, go "mama bear" protective. Neither response would make Eliza happy. On the other hand, she wasn't in the habit of keeping secrets from her best friend. And she had to tell *someone.*

Meanwhile, Mo giggled. Not a sound she usually made. "Good. We had a sleepover last night."

This was big. Mo did not enter sleepover territory lightly. "Wow! And?"

"Let's just say it was a *very* pleasant evening. And not much sleep was had."

Eliza smiled. "Good for you!"

"But how are you? I feel like we haven't talked for ages. Not since you got that awful letter from Carol."

Wow, it has been a while.

"Hang on, I'm letting myself into my building." Eliza juggled her bag and the phone so she could check her mail—an exercise that had taken on much more gravity since that registered letter had come. But so far, no further missives from Carol. "Okay, I'm back."

"So have you heard from her again?"

"Not yet. But I'm meeting with a lawyer next week."

"Good idea. When? Do you want me to come with?"

"That's okay. I know you're busy. You know. With your new *man*." Eliza drew out the word *man* so Mo would know she was teasing.

"Ha! Sisters before misters. You know that."

Now in her apartment, Eliza put down her bag, took off her coat, and found a fork so she could dig into her meal, such as it was. "I do know that. But I'll be fine. Thanks for offering."

"Wait, is Scott going with you?"

Eliza swallowed a mouthful of vinegary kidney beans. "No. Wow. So much to catch you up on." She filled Mo in on her conversation with Maren.

"Wait, seriously? Where does she get off? He's your *brother.*"

Eliza was trying hard not to feel the same way. "Yeah, but he's grieving, too. And this is my problem, not his."

"Okay, I don't really buy that."

Eliza sighed. She loved having Mo in her corner—and her friend wasn't wrong—but she couldn't afford to get riled up about this. She couldn't help but think that if forced to take sides, Scott would choose Maren. After all, she was his wife.

But sharing that very real fear of abandonment was just too much to say out loud. She could barely even whisper it to herself.

"What can I say? There's only so much I can freak out about right now." She aimed for airiness in her tone, willing Mo to drop it.

"All right. We can stick a pin in this one and come back to it."

Eliza closed her takeout container and put it in the fridge, still mostly full. "Actually, I have much bigger news. I met Ross Sawyer tonight."

"Wait, what?" Mo screeched. "How did that happen? Tell me *everything*."

Eliza explained how she'd come across the public talk and how she'd planned to just watch and sneak out—but that it hadn't turned out that way.

"Oh my God! I can't believe you met him. What was he like?"

"Honestly, he was a little obnoxious." Eliza had been pacing around her apartment and now stopped to stare out her window. If she stood at the right angle, she could see a sliver of the city between two other buildings.

"See! It was a good idea for you to check him out first."

But that wasn't what she wanted Mo to say. She wanted her to tell her she shouldn't judge so quickly. That there could still be a relationship worth building. But that wouldn't be in her friend's protective nature.

"Well, I don't know that it's fair for me to judge based on just a few minutes."

"True. So why don't you follow up with him? Set up a meeting to talk about NOY."

"And not tell him who I am? That doesn't feel right."

"But once you tell him, there's no going back."

Eliza was silent.

"Anyway," Mo continued, "there's no rush on this, right? Just take some time."

But that was the part Mo didn't understand. Life had proved itself to be unexpectedly and frighteningly short. And the knowledge that Eliza had a father out there—someone who had been intimately connected with her mother and had a long history with her—was weighing heavily on her. It wasn't something she could just set aside.

"I don't know. Now that I've met him—I'm kind of freaked out. How am I going to explain any of this? He's going to think I was stalking him."

"Who cares what he thinks? He's a stranger."

"But he's my *father.*"

"Just by DNA."

Mo said it as if DNA were nothing. And maybe it wasn't everything. But it was *something.*

"Eliza. Look. He's not going anywhere. A few weeks ago, you didn't even know he existed. You have this crazy situation with Carol to deal with, and your dad—the only dad you ever knew—just died. You have to work through that grief. That's going to take time."

She knew Mo meant well. She *knew* that. So she bit her tongue rather than tell her that her grief wasn't going any-where. That her grief over Laura still sat with her as a nearly constant companion—it didn't talk to her all the time like it used to, but it was still there. A calcification in her heart.

Eliza closed the window shade, hiding the city from view. "Yeah, I see what you're saying." She sighed. "I think I need a long, hot shower."

"Oh, that sounds so nice. You do that. But let's get together over the weekend. Foot rubs?"

"You're on." She clicked the off button on the phone and

set it down on the arm of the sofa before heading into the bathroom. She turned on the hot water and stripped off her clothes, feeling incredibly lonely.

Ever since they'd met, Mo had always *gotten* her. She instinctively knew how to help her feel better. But now it felt like they weren't quite aligned. Maybe her situation had become so unique, so bizarre, that no one could help her anymore.

CHAPTER TWENTY

The subway rattled beneath the East River as Eliza rode to the lawyer's office in Brooklyn. She emerged at the Borough Hall station and looked around to get her bearings. Brooklyn wasn't her usual stomping grounds, but this part of it looked a lot like Manhattan. The street was crowded with people, cars, and city buses, and food carts dotted the corners. She found her way to the building she needed, despite its extensive scaffolding, and entered the main doors.

A security guard sat behind a desk, turning the pages of a newspaper, not sparing her a glance. She likewise ignored him and headed straight for a wall directory displaying hundreds of listings. Scanning, she confirmed the suite number for Morris, Muhlfelder and Gleason, and rode the elevator to the seventh floor.

The law firm's name was engraved on a small plaque on a door halfway down the hall. She took a deep breath before turning the handle; this would be the first time she'd ever met with a lawyer.

As she entered, the receptionist—an older woman with short metal gray hair—looked up.

"I'm here to see Vicky Muhlfelder," Eliza said.

The receptionist nodded and picked up the old-school corded phone on her desk. "Please have a seat while you're waiting."

Obediently, Eliza sat and looked around the small space. It reminded her of a dentist's office, minus the brochures about tooth-whitening services. An innocuous seascape hung on the wall, and a couple of business magazines lay on the end table. Before she had a chance to even consider picking one up and leafing through it, a woman appeared in the open doorway. She wore charcoal pants and a tailored white shirt. A gold link necklace sat in the hollow of her throat, and her dark hair was worn in a sleek, inverted bob. It was the kind of haircut Eliza was impressed that anyone had the discipline to maintain. Her own long hair was so easily braided or wound into a bun that she didn't have to worry about regular cuts.

The woman stuck out her hand. "Eliza? I'm Vicky."

Eliza rose from her seat to shake the proffered hand. "Nice to meet you."

"Well, probably not that nice, considering the circumstances, but I'm used to it in my line of work." Vicky smiled. "Let's go to my office."

Beyond the reception area, a tiled hallway snaked past a warren of minuscule offices. Eliza followed Vicky into one with a small window and a large desk piled with file folders, haphazardly stacked. It was the kind of space Eliza would never be able to focus in. It needed a good clear-out and—as she noted the stain on the carpet near the door—perhaps a scrubbing as well.

"Sorry for the mess. It's hard to stay on top of all the paper sometimes." Vicky pointed to the seat across from her as she sat behind the desk. "I guess I shouldn't say that out loud. But don't worry, I haven't missed a filing yet."

Vicky grinned, and Eliza smiled weakly in return. This was

certainly not the kind of law office she was used to seeing on TV, all shiny and neat. But the lawyers in those offices probably charged a lot more than Morris, Muhlfelder and Gleason.

Vicky clasped her hands together. "So. Tell me how I can help you."

Eliza opened her mouth, but Vicky spoke again before she could continue.

"Josh filled me in a bit. I'm so sorry, by the way, for the loss of your father."

Eliza nodded.

"But don't assume I know anything. Start from the beginning."

Eliza opened her mouth again and hesitated, wondering if it was her turn now. After a moment of silence, she determined it was.

"So, like Josh told you, my father—well, Jack Levinger, the man I always thought was my father—passed away last month. Unexpectedly. My mom died ten years ago. And it turns out that my biological father was someone else." She felt like she was reciting the plot of a soap opera rather than discussing her own life.

Vicky pulled a legal pad toward her—somehow unearthing it from the mess around her—and picked up a pen. "And how did you find out that you have a different biological father?"

Eliza explained about the letter, taking a copy of it out of her purse and passing it to Vicky.

"And have you met this man?"

"Um, it's complicated."

"Eliza. I can't help you unless you are completely honest with me. We'll only run into trouble if you keep secrets."

Perhaps someone should have told Laura that twenty-seven years ago.

"I never heard of him before this, but now I've Googled and discovered he's a professor at NYU. I went to an event the other night that he was at. We spoke for a minute, but that was it. I didn't tell him anything."

"That's fine. I just want to have the whole picture. And you're sure that you didn't have this information until *after* Jack died?"

"Correct."

Vicky scribbled on her pad. "How many siblings do you have?"

"Just one. My brother, Scott."

"And I presume your stepmother isn't challenging his inheritance?"

Eliza shook her head.

Vicky looked up from her note-taking. "And how long was Jack married to—what's your stepmother's name?"

"Carol. They got married about nine years ago."

"And Carol is the executrix of the will? Have you seen the will?"

"I haven't seen it, but she says she's the executrix. And she sent me this letter." She passed the document across the desk, and Vicky scanned it, making additional notes on her pad.

"Okay. So. Let me give you a crash course in estate law." She put down her pen. "Actually, first, can I get you anything? Water? Coffee? Tea?"

Eliza felt like she had whiplash. "No, I'm fine."

"Are you sure? I'm going to get water."

"Okay, water, then."

While Vicky was gone, Eliza looked around the small office. The walls were painted a pale peach, and the industrial carpet was navy, which made the visible stain that much stranger—and more alarming. Diplomas and bar admittances hung on the walls, and a sad fern sat on the windowsill. It wasn't the cheeriest of spaces. But, then again, this wasn't the cheeriest of subjects.

Vicky returned with bottled water for them. "I know, it's

terrible for the environment. Sorry about that." She sat back down. "By the way—I bet you have amazing hair hidden in that bun."

What? Who is this person? Eliza reminded herself that Josh had recommended her. *She must know what she's doing.* She smiled weakly at the compliment.

After a long swig of water, Vicky began again. "Anyway. The purpose of a will is to ensure that the deceased person's property is distributed according to their wishes. It's the job of the executor—or executrix in this case—to file the will with the probate court and notify the heirs.

"There are specific reasons under which a will can be contested. The claim can be made that the person wasn't of 'sound mind' when they made the will. You hear that a lot in the movies. A claim can be based on 'undue influence' or 'duress'—saying that a beneficiary unfairly influenced the making of the will in their favor. And then there's fraud—if the will was based on someone having lied."

Eliza nodded, and Vicky paused to take another swallow of her water.

"So, if you knew that Jack wasn't your biological father but continued to let him believe he was, Carol could legitimately claim there was fraud."

"But I didn't know! I just got this letter! My aunt can confirm . . ."

Vicky put up her hand to stop her. "Understood. I'm just trying to give you the big picture. So far, however, it doesn't look like your stepmother has filed to contest the will with the court."

"Then what's this letter?"

"Just that. A letter. What's interesting is that the court gives a lot of leeway to executors. There's an expectation that they'll complete the probate paperwork accurately, and unless the court catches a discrepancy in terms of the named heirs, an executor can simply leave out a beneficiary."

Eliza shifted forward in her seat. "What? That's crazy!"

Vicky shrugged. "The courts are overloaded. Stuff happens. I suspect that your stepmother sent you the letter since you'd be expecting to be named in the will. But what she's essentially saying is *I don't think you're entitled to inherit.*"

"But how can she do that? It's not what my dad would have wanted."

"Well, there's the crux of the issue. We need to file what's called an order to show cause, asking her to demonstrate *why* you're not entitled. Let me ask you another way. Was Jack the only father you ever knew?"

Eliza nodded.

"And is his name on your birth certificate?"

"I assume so. Yes. It must be. I got a passport a few years ago and I needed to use my birth certificate. I'm sure I would have noticed if his name wasn't there."

"And your legal last name is Levinger, same as his?"

"Yes."

"Good, good. I need to do a bit more research, but if the information you're telling me is accurate, I definitely think you're entitled to inherit under the terms of the will as written. If Jack raised you, and always believed you to be his daughter, and is treating you in the will the same way as your brother, this new information shouldn't be relevant." Vicky paused and looked up at the ceiling. "Case law ensures that adopted children have the same inheritance rights as biological children. Interesting that in this situation you're actually neither biological nor adopted . . ." She trailed off as she gazed at the acoustic tiles.

Eliza felt a knot in her stomach. "So what does that mean?"

Her voice seemed to remind Vicky that she was there, and the lawyer readjusted her gaze. "Just an interesting legal puzzle. It really isn't relevant."

This consultation was feeling more like an amusement-park ride every minute. Just when she thought it was over, there was a sudden turn or drop. It wasn't doing Eliza's stomach any good.

Vicky tapped her forefinger on the legal pad, which was now covered with ink.

"And what about your brother? Where does he stand in all of this?"

Another sudden drop. "Not sure. He's not keen on fighting with Carol. He actually suggested we go along with this, and when my share gets divided between her and him, he'd just give me the half he gets."

Vicky started shaking her head as Eliza spoke. "I don't think you need to give in to her like that. *And* I think an agreement like that has the potential to screw up your relationship with your brother. You don't know how often people make promises to share and then somehow 'forget' that they did, or want to renegotiate."

"I don't think Scott would do that to me." *Or would he?* Everything felt so tenuous now.

"Well, it's up to you. But I still think you have a right to what your dad left to you, in full."

Eliza suddenly realized she had forgotten the most important thing. "It's not about the money . . ."

Vicky raised her perfectly arched eyebrows.

"Really. It's about what's fair. And about the fact that I don't want Carol to just write me out of the family."

Nodding, Vicky picked up her pen again. "Well, all the courts care about is the law. So. Here's my advice. We need to obtain a copy of the will as filed with the court so I can take a closer look at the language. Assuming it's what we're expecting, I'll file an order to show cause."

The wheels in Eliza's brain were just catching up to where Vicky was. "Wait, so we have to go to court, where Carol will testify that my mom cheated on my dad?"

"Well, yes. But then we'll be arguing that it's not relevant to the relationship that you and Jack had and shouldn't have any bearing on your inheritance."

Eliza tried to envision herself in that courtroom. Giving Carol an opportunity to testify in open court about what Laura had done. Maybe even talk about the—minimal at best, volatile at worst—relationship Eliza had had with Jack. Those images swirled in her head as Vicky talked to her about fees and timelines. The image of Carol's smug face using the words "affair" and "cheating." And her entering into evidence a neat record of the dates on which Eliza had visited her father. She could see them on a color-coded calendar, dwindling to fewer and fewer as time wore on, and her breath caught. *And this is the situation your mom got you into,* a small voice whispered in her ear as Vicky walked her out to the reception area. Eliza quickly shoved that voice back into its hiding place.

Vicky smiled at her. "It was very nice meeting you. Again, sorry for your loss. Why don't you think about all of this and then let me know if you'd like to proceed?"

"I'll do that."

"And say hi to Josh for me. How do you know him again?"

Eliza blinked, shaking the courtroom drama out of her head. "He's my brother's best friend from growing up."

"Ah. Makes sense. He's a good guy. He dated my law school housemate for a while." Vicky paused and looked at the ceiling again. "Before that, he was with a girl in my study group. Or maybe it was the other way around. Anyway, that's neither here nor there."

"No, I guess not." Eliza smiled thinly. She'd certainly had her own share of male companionship. Not at all surprising that Josh kept busy, too. She'd just prefer not to think about it.

CHAPTER TWENTY-ONE

Whenever Eliza went to Mo's favorite yoga studio, she understood why her friend loved it there. It was located in the West Village, not far from Mo's apartment, on the second floor above a wine store and a clothing shop that specialized in batik and gauzy cotton prints. The space had shiny hardwood floors, high ceilings, and large windows. Mo liked their early classes best, when the shafts of morning light dappled the floor.

But it was already dark outside when Eliza met Mo there following her appointment with Vicky. Mo was convinced she would need some "centering" after that meeting, and since the Village was sort of on her way from Brooklyn to the Upper East Side—depending on which subway line she took—Eliza agreed.

In the small changing room, Eliza pulled her T-shirt and yoga pants out of her bag and stripped off the skinny black pants and cotton sweater she'd been wearing. After she filled her water bottle at the sink, she paused in front of the mirror to unwind her hair from its loose bun and twist it up again more tightly. Cascading hair and downward-facing dog didn't go well together.

In the studio, Mo was already sitting cross-legged on her yoga mat, stretching her back in exaggerated good posture. An empty mat sat next to her. "Saved you a spot," she said, smiling. Whenever Eliza agreed to come to yoga, Mo was convinced that this would be the time that converted her to a devotee of the practice.

Eliza sank down beside her and folded her legs into their own crisscross-applesauce position. Meanwhile, Mo stretched her own legs in front of her, then brought one knee up and twisted her body around it to face Eliza. "So, how did it go?"

"Okay, I guess. She thinks I'm probably entitled to inherit."

Mo made a face. "Well, of course you are!"

Eliza stretched her neck from side to side. Apparently, the need to stretch was contagious. "The lawyer is going to do some research, but most likely we have to file some sort of order to get Carol to 'show cause' that I'm not entitled. Then there would have to be a hearing."

Mo nodded. "Sounds simple enough."

Eliza opened her mouth, but before she could respond, the yoga teacher assumed her spot at the front of the class. The woman wore a loose tank top over a sports bra and tie-dyed yoga pants. From the neck down, she could have passed for a much younger woman—fit, slim, and muscular. But her face bore deep lines, and her skin looked like it had spent many years in the sun. Her nearly white hair was wound up on top of her head, much like Eliza's.

"Welcome," she said softly, immediately quieting the chatter in the room. Eliza glanced around; there were a dozen people of varying ages seated on their mats, mostly women. "Let's begin in lotus. Sitting bones deep into your mats. Hands on your knees. Eyes closed."

Eliza obediently assumed the position and followed the teacher's instructions to take deep breaths, hold them, and slowly release. They joined together in a simultaneous "Om" before extending their legs in front of them for some seated forward folds. Eliza couldn't help but notice that her toenails needed a pedicure. This was why she found it hard to commit to yoga. She knew she was supposed to release all other thoughts and be at one with her breath. Yet, there were her chipped toenails. As they moved into a series of warrior poses, her mind wandered back to her meeting with Vicky. The more she tried not to think about it, the more present it was.

She wanted to talk to Scott about the conversation but was afraid to. Bringing him into it was exactly what Maren had asked her not to do. And she worried about Scott's reaction. She wasn't at all sure she could count on him taking her side in this, especially if it meant airing the family's dirty laundry in public.

A sheen of sweat cooled on her skin as she lay on her back in Savasana. Tinkling music played in the background, overlaid on top of what sounded like rushing water. If only she could turn her brain off, it would be very soothing.

Before she knew it, they were sitting in lotus again, joining in another "Om" to end the class. Eliza pressed her hands together, first at her forehead and then in front of her heart, as instructed, wishing this had been as centering as Mo had promised. At least her muscles were limber.

"Wasn't that great?" Mo was wiping her own neck with a towel.

"Definitely."

Mo rolled her eyes. "You could try saying it with a bit more conviction, Lize."

"Look. I try. I find it hard to get out of my head." Eliza stood to wipe down her mat.

"Well, maybe if you did it more than once every full moon." Mo stood, too, and put her hand out for Eliza's mat.

"I know, I know."

Mo returned Eliza's mat to the stack at the back; her own

was in a mat bag slung over her shoulder. They were walking down the stairs when Mo returned to their earlier conversation. "So, tell me more about what the lawyer said."

Eliza tried to remember the particulars, but the part she kept getting hung up on was the bit about inviting Carol to testify about Laura's infidelity.

Mo was puzzled. "So who cares? It was all those years ago. Your mom won't know. And neither will your dad. And it's not like this is the trial of the century. It won't be headline news in the *Post*."

Eliza and Mo stood on the sidewalk, groups of people parting on either side of them as they made their ways to their destinations. "I know," Eliza said. "It's just—I can barely wrap my own head around it. Do I really want to open up this can of worms?"

"Eliza! You didn't open it. Carol did. You have to fight for what's right. No matter what your mom did, Jack was your dad. And he wouldn't want Carol to try to take that away from you."

But there it was. Maybe that was what was underneath it all. A part of Eliza—the emotional, anxious part that found it hard to listen to reason and rationality—wondered if Jack would feel exactly as Carol was suggesting he might. "But what if . . ."

"No what-ifs. There isn't even a decision to be made here."

But Mo's view was unclouded by the emotions that tied Eliza in knots. And she wasn't sure it was so simple.

Mo had invited Eliza back to her apartment, but she'd declined. She needed some space to think, and rather than go straight down into the subway and change trains in midtown, she headed east to pick up the Lexington Avenue line, which would take her directly home. Josh lived somewhere in this neighborhood, but she didn't know where.

Back in high school, Josh had stayed true to his word that

he'd lend her the latest Jason Mraz and Nickelback CDs. In return, she shared Radiohead and the Killers with him. Josh was at the Levinger house a lot, even though Laura's illness had caused their home to be less of a hangout. Scott, Josh, and one or two other guys shot hoops in the driveway or played video games in the family room. When Eliza and Josh found themselves in the kitchen at the same time, they somehow got into long conversations, Josh in the doorway and Eliza leaning back against the counter, very conscious of the angles of her body.

It started with music but segued into TV shows, and school subjects, and which teachers they'd both had, and which ones Josh advised her to avoid like the plague. And Josh talked about college applications and what he thought he wanted—a school with a contained campus in or near an urban area. Somehow they just connected and never ran out of things to say.

Scott looked at them strangely whenever he came upon these tête-à-têtes. After he'd drag Josh back outside or to the sectional sofa, Eliza would return to Laura's side. With the constant hum of fear about Laura's condition clogging her brain, she didn't have a lot of room for the crushes her friends were constantly falling in and out of. But, without her realizing it, Josh had carved out a little corner for himself. And late at night, or while she was walking home from school, she enjoyed her visits to that little corner.

Now, as she walked across town, she found Josh in her thoughts again, wondering about those women Vicky had mentioned. The girl Josh had taken to the prom was beautiful. Although it was only a week after Laura died, Scott had gone anyway—Jack said there was no need for him to stay home, and, besides, he had a date to consider. In that era before Facebook and even the first iPhone, Eliza never saw photos from the festivities, but somehow she still had an image in her mind of Josh in his tux, his arm around the lovely girl with dark brown hair who was in Eliza's gym class.

There had been a time when Eliza imagined it might be her on Josh's arm—before she realized that she'd been misinterpreting his kindness toward her. That wasn't a mistake she planned to make again. Nonetheless, when she finally got home that evening, she shot him a quick text to let him know she'd met with Vicky and to thank him for the referral. He replied immediately.

> Great. Glad you could get in to see her so quickly. Do you have a plan?

> Maybe. There's some stuff I need to think about.

> Really? I thought it would be pretty straightforward.

You and Mo both.

> Legally, I guess it is. But I'm not sure what I want to do.

There was a pause, and the three dots came and went a few times. Then:

> Do you want to talk?

Excellent question.

> Sure.

Her phone rang immediately. "That was fast," she said.

"Well, no time like the present. What did you think of Vicky?"

"She seems nice. Maybe a little . . ."

"Quirky?"

Eliza laughed. "Perfect word for it."

Josh laughed as well. "But she's a good egg, and she knows her stuff. So what did she say?"

She lay back on the sofa, her legs dangling over the end and her hair coming loose from its bun, as she once again explained the legal strategy Vicky had recommended. One would think that this afternoon hadn't been the first time she'd ever heard the phrase "order to show cause."

"It sounds reasonably simple. What's the issue?"

Eliza twisted a loose strand of her hair and exhaled a long breath. "I guess I just don't like the idea of having people talking about my mom cheating on my dad. And I don't think Scott is going to like it either."

"First, Scott is a separate issue. This is your inheritance, and you're the one who has to decide what to do." Eliza pictured him sitting straighter, putting on his attorney hat, so to speak. "And as far as people talking about your mom—why does that bother you?"

"Because she's my mom. And she made a mistake, and . . ." She trailed off.

"Does that mistake make her any less of a good mom?"

"No, I guess not. Though . . ."

"Though what?"

Eliza's throat clogged. "I just wish she hadn't put me in this situation. Things with my dad and me were hard enough, and now there's this."

"E. Listen. Whatever your relationship was with your dad is what it was. Whether you were his biological child or not, he's the dad who raised you. And he loved you, and you loved him. Carol is messing around because that's the kind of person she is."

She sat up as her nose clogged and she had to sniffle.

"Maybe. But maybe she's right. Maybe my dad would have looked at me differently if he'd known. Maybe . . ."

He cut her off. "I find that really hard to believe. I know things were rough with you guys. You went through a lot. More than you should have had to. But you were his *child*. In all the ways that matter."

Eliza nodded, but she couldn't find the words to speak.

"E—are you there? Are you okay?"

She managed to make a little squeaky noise.

"Are you crying?"

Ugh. This was so not how she wanted this conversation to go. Or any conversation. She hated this part of herself.

As if he could read her mind, Josh continued. "Look, you're dealing with so much right now. Of course you're sad. And confused. And discombobulated. You're an incredibly strong person just to keep on going. I've always thought so."

Eliza snorted.

"Seriously. I know you don't see yourself that way. But you are. Always have been."

She wiped at her eyes. "I think your memory is faulty."

"Being emotional and being weak aren't the same thing."

"Yeah, well, they can feel like they are."

"Even so. They're not."

She swung her legs to the floor and sat up. A part of her was tempted to just stay on the phone all night to hear his voice—which made hanging up all the more important. "I should go. I haven't eaten anything yet."

"Okay. Go eat. And call anytime."

She clicked end and set her phone down on the coffee table. She was tempted to just lie down on the sofa again, but Josh's description of her as strong floated in her mind. *Strong people manage to get off their butts and eat dinner.* So she did.

CHAPTER TWENTY-TWO

Eliza dropped a tea bag into her mug and filled it with hot water from the red tap on the office cooler, hoping that the boost of caffeine would wake her up a little. She'd slept even worse than what had become her usual, tossing and turning as snippets of her conversations with Vicky, Mo, and Josh swirled in her brain. She gave up before her alarm went off and flipped through the channels on TV, finding another episode of *Monk*.

It was so nice, but so unrealistic, that Adrian Monk's late wife visited him in his dreams, sitting on the edge of his bed as a beautiful, ghostly apparition. For months, if not years, after Laura died, whenever Eliza dreamed of her, she was deathly ill, as she'd been during those last months. Skeletally thin and weak, her hair wispy on her scalp. So far, she hadn't dreamed of Jack at all.

Tea in hand, she returned to her desk and the spreadsheet she'd been putting together. When it came to work systems, her modus operandi was to consider what her disorganized predecessor would have done, and then do the opposite. As a result, RSVPs for the gala immediately went into this document, which would later generate name tags, a check-in list, and seating charts. Scrambling the day before to put those things together was an experience she did not want to replicate.

Vanessa stepped into her office. "Eliza. Just thought I'd check on you," she said, lowering herself into one of the chairs. "How are you doing?"

Eliza turned away from her screen. "Fine," she said cautiously, surprised that her boss would visit purely out of compassion.

Vanessa crossed one leg over the other and pushed her dark hair behind her ear before clasping her hands around her knee. "I know you have a lot on your plate, with your father's death. I want to make sure you're okay."

"I'm okay, Vanessa." *Whatever okay means.*

"I'm glad to hear it. I think the best thing to do is to throw yourself into other things. Distract yourself."

Had Vanessa ever lost anyone close to her? If she had, she'd surely know that distraction simply wasn't always possible, but Eliza nodded all the same.

"I know you've missed a couple of days and had to leave early yesterday. Totally understandable. But you know we're heading into crunch time." Vanessa raised her eyebrows as if to say, *So I hope you won't need to take any other time off.*

There we go. Now this little visit is making a lot more sense.

"Don't worry, Vanessa. I don't anticipate any other issues. And, of course, if I need to take any time off, I'll make up the work. I'm on top of it all."

"Excellent."

The intercom buzzed on Eliza's desk phone, and she pressed the button to answer.

Amber's voice responded. "Eliza? You have Professor Sawyer from NYU on the line."

Eliza's body heard this news before her brain, and her heart began to pound.

"NYU?" Vanessa asked. "I thought Patrice was handling NYU."

Eliza pressed her lips together as she tried to gather herself. "Oh. Um. I went to a talk the other night just out of personal interest, and I met Professor Sawyer." A moment ago, she'd been counting the seconds until Vanessa would leave her office. But now she wanted nothing more than for her to stay and continue to question her dedication to the job. "I'll have Amber take a message so we can keep talking."

"Oh no, no. You take this. I don't think Patrice has had much luck connecting there."

Eliza nodded numbly. "Okay, I'll be right there, Amber." She waited, expecting Vanessa to leave the room, but apparently that was not her boss's plan. When she couldn't put it off any longer, she picked up the receiver, feeling it slip in her sweaty hand.

How had he found her? *Why* had he found her? For one insane moment, she thought he'd learned the truth. That he knew he was her father. She took a deep breath. *Eliza Sharon Levinger. He has no way of knowing you're his daughter.* Of course, that also meant she was about to have a second conversation with him under false pretenses. Great way to build a relationship. She desperately tried to produce enough saliva to swallow.

"This is Eliza," she said, acutely aware of Vanessa's eyes on her.

"Eliza. So glad I found you."

How in the world was she meant to respond to *that*? Fortunately, he spared her overstretched brain cells from figuring it out as he continued to speak.

"I looked for you the other night after I was pulled away, but you must have gone. Can't say I blame you. But you did mention your organization's grant-making, and as I'm sure you know, that makes any perennially underfunded professor's ears perk up. And I have to commend you on your use of the acronym. I'm quite sure I would have completely forgotten the name of your foundation, but NOY stuck in my head, so with the help of one of my grad students I found you."

"Great," she said weakly.

"I spent a few minutes on your website. I can definitely see alignment between my department's current work and NOY's mission." He emphasized *NOY* in such a way that she could tell he still found the acronym oddly amusing, despite acknowledging that it had served him well. "Bottom line, of course, I'm interested in seeing how we might benefit each other. Which, of course, comes down to those grants you mentioned. So what can you tell me about that?"

Eliza hated being on the spot in front of Vanessa, especially when her words were at risk of being short-circuited by her knowledge of who Ross really was. "Well, historically we've invested in educational programs in local and regional communities. But we're working on launching an award for education policy research. We're looking for guidance on how to do that, who to partner with, and what it will look like. Some possibilities are grants to the winners, and/or partnering with faculty—who will receive stipends in return for peer review." Vanessa was nodding, so Eliza concluded that, although she could barely hear herself speak over the buzzing in her brain, she was at least making sense. "I understand that my colleague Patrice Foster has reached out to some of your colleagues. I'm not sure of the status on that, but I can easily connect you . . ." Vanessa had begun frantically waving at her. "I'm sorry. Can you hold for just one moment?"

She covered the mouthpiece of the phone as she clicked the hold button. Nonetheless, Vanessa whispered as if she might be overheard.

"You've already made this connection. Stick with this. Set up a meeting with him."

Shit. Shit, shit, shit, shit, shit.

She took a deep breath as surreptitiously as possible and took Ross off hold. "Sorry about that," she began.

Ross interrupted before she could continue. "Maybe what makes sense is for me to gather a couple of my colleagues to talk with you about their current research—we've got some great data sets we've pulled together over the past few years, especially in the early grades, that we've been mining. And we can take it from there."

"That sounds great." *Just slightly better than falling down an elevator shaft.*

"Why don't you give me your email address and I'll loop back with you."

"Perfect." She rattled off the information as Vanessa smiled widely.

CHAPTER TWENTY-THREE

Eliza's new obsession with *Monk* was doing nothing to distract her from her self-flagellation, induced by the foolish decision to attend Ross's talk at the Glenside School. She was now in precisely the situation that Mo's ridiculous suggestions would have led her to. And she had no one to blame but herself.

When she'd told her friend about her unavoidable upcoming meeting with Ross and his colleagues, Mo had been both horrified and, Eliza thought, almost gleeful. "I wish I could be there! I can see why you're stressing, but, look, you're getting a chance to get to know him a bit without having to take that big step. And you're seeing him in his natural habitat—who he really is."

His natural habitat. As if she were Jane Goodall and Ross were a chimpanzee.

She switched off the TV in frustration and looked at the time. If she went to bed now, she absolutely wouldn't fall asleep. Ross had managed to pull together a meeting much sooner than Eliza would have expected—and certainly sooner than she would have hoped. Mo's perspective had been that the short time frame meant less opportunity for

Eliza to stress out. But it was also less time for some intervening incident to occur—like an alien spaceship abducting all the NYU faculty.

In desperate need of distraction, she remembered Laura's diary. She still wasn't sure how she felt about reading it—it felt like such a violation of her mother's privacy, and, even more so, she wasn't sure she wanted to know any more of her mother's secrets. But she found herself retrieving it from her bedside table.

She sank down onto the fluffy white throw rug next to her bed and held the diary in her lap. She ran her fingertips over the words *MY DIARY* and felt the weight of the small book. Both figuratively and literally. She was about to open it but then paused to get her emergency bottle of white wine. She didn't believe in drinking alone but decided that she'd be having a drink with Laura. Something she'd never been able to do with her while she was alive. Glass in hand, she returned to her bedroom rug, and after toasting the air and taking a sip, she carefully set the wine on the floor beside her.

Okay. No more stalling. She hadn't relocked the diary, so she opened it to the first page. The date indicated that Laura was seventeen when she started writing.

Dear Diary,

Is that how you're supposed to start one of these things? Claudie gave this to me as a birthday gift a couple years ago, and I completely forgot I had it. I think she was hoping I'd write my secrets in it, and then she'd be able to read them. Joke's on her—I don't have any secrets! Or at least not any good ones. But I just found it again and figured, why not try to use it?

Well, that "no secrets" thing certainly hadn't stuck.

> *So, we've got another month of school to go. I cannot WAIT for summer to come. And then just ONE MORE YEAR of high school!*

It was so strange reading Laura's teenage voice. Turning the pages, she learned how much her mom had hated her physics teacher, and that she desperately coveted a red-yellow-and-blue swimsuit Christie Brinkley had worn in some magazine. And then finally, she found the word she'd been looking for: *Ross.*

> *I don't think I've written anything about Ross yet. I don't want to be one of those girls who's always saying "my boyfriend this and my boyfriend that." But we just had our six-month anniversary. He took me out to Arturo's and gave me this gorgeous bracelet. I wish Mom and Dad could understand how I feel about him. I know they don't like him—they think he's not respectful or something. But he's the smartest boy I know and he really wants to make the world a better place. I told Mom that he isn't sure he wants to go straight to college—he'd rather find a way to make a real difference. She said "he can make a difference once he has a degree." I wanted to scream.*

Eliza pressed her lips together. She never got to have fights like this with Laura—she'd been gone before Eliza had the chance to date anyone at all, let alone someone her mom didn't like. She was quite sure Jack wouldn't have thought much of the boys and men she'd been with, but she hadn't given him the chance to get to know them. For the first time, she wondered if she would have picked the same partners if her mom had still been around.

Laura was not a regular diarist. There were big gaps between entries, and when she did write, it was often remarkably uninteresting. Eliza began flipping through, looking for Ross's name. She found it again on a page dated midway through their senior year.

> Ross's parents are going away this weekend. He wants me to lie and say that I'm staying at Janine's and stay with him instead. You have no idea how much I want to. Two whole days just him and me! But the truth is—I'm not ready to have sex. We've done lots of stuff but . . . I just don't know. I'm scared, I guess. Kathy did it with Mark and basically right afterward he dumped her. And she said it wasn't even that great. I know it's different with Ross, but . . . AUGGHH!! I don't know what's wrong with me. I know he's getting frustrated, even if he doesn't say so. But what if I get pregnant?

Eliza's heart was pounding as she slammed the book shut. She didn't want to know about Laura's sex life. She threw the diary back into her drawer and forced herself to take a deep breath. But she felt like screaming. *It wasn't supposed to be like this.* Her mom's high school boyfriend shouldn't be relevant to her. None of this should be.

She brushed her teeth so hard that her gums bled and climbed into bed, hoping that the wine would help usher in sleep, but she couldn't force her eyes to stay shut. Had Laura decided to sleep with Ross? And how ironic was it that she was scared of getting pregnant? *Maybe she should have thought of that ten years later.* But then again, if she had, Eliza wouldn't be here. For the first time, she realized that perhaps she should be grateful for how things transpired. But somehow, that thought made her angrier than ever.

The taxicab halted at the curb, and Patrice paid the fare. Eliza slid across the dark green vinyl seat and followed her out of the car. She was enormously grateful that Vanessa had decided the two of them should go together to this meeting. Her plan was to let Patrice do as much of the talking as possible, while she would do her level best to fade into the woodwork.

They let themselves in through the glass front doors, and a receptionist directed them to a lounge where Ross sat, wearing professorial garb that resembled the outfit he'd worn at the Glenside School event. This time, it was mocha-colored corduroy pants and a cream V-neck sweater. He hunched over his smartphone, thumbs flying.

"Dr. Sawyer?" He'd introduced himself to Eliza as Ross, but she felt awkward calling him by his first name. Or, indeed, anything at all.

Ross stood and slipped his phone into his pocket before sticking out his hand to shake. "Eliza. And you must be . . . ?"

"This is my colleague, Patrice Foster."

"Appreciate you both coming downtown. My colleagues will meet us in one of the seminar rooms to chat. I'm glad we were able to get this set up before Barbara heads out of town. She's on sabbatical this semester, so she's not in the city much."

Eliza and Patrice followed a half step behind Ross as he

guided them to the elevator. They rode up several floors and made their way down a hallway to a small classroom with an oval wooden table surrounded by uncomfortable-looking aluminum swivel chairs. Three women and another man sat at the table, an array of folders, cardboard coffee cups, and reusable water bottles surrounding them.

"Everyone—meet Eliza and Patrice from Nourish Our Youth." Ross pointed to each of his colleagues in turn. "Barbara Sylvester. Ian Glass. Julia Spencer-Marks. Kristen Johnson." There were smiles and handshakes and an offer of water or coffee, and then everyone found seats around the table. Eliza found herself next to Barbara, a petite brunette who was probably Ross's age. A chunky, brightly colored necklace adorned her simple dress, and Eliza wondered if she had a child who had made it for her.

"Thanks so much for inviting us," Patrice said, smiling and taking a journal and pen out of her bag.

Kristen—or was it Julia?—smiled broadly back. "We're so interested in hearing about your work. Ross tells us that you're focused on education policy?"

Eliza found it hard to keep herself in the moment as her brain spun with the knowledge that she was sitting at a table with her biological father.

Patrice turned to her. "Eliza, do you want to—"

Eliza quickly cut her off. "No, Patrice, why don't you do the honors?"

While Patrice talked about the history of NOY and the research award they were looking to launch, Eliza watched Ross. He continuously clicked his ballpoint pen open and closed and swiveled his chair from side to side. Though he appeared distracted, somehow she could tell that he was listening intently. As soon as Patrice paused, he jumped in to invite everyone to talk a bit about their current research. While Julia—or was it Kristen?—described her work on puzzle-based math-teaching techniques, Ross pushed his seat back from the table and began pacing.

"Oh, don't mind him," Barbara remarked. "Ross can't sit still. I'm amazed he stayed in that chair as long as he did." They all laughed, and Eliza couldn't help but think back to Claude's description of the fidgety teenage boy Laura had dated. Apparently, some things didn't change.

They all continued to talk, interrupting each other to clarify points and ask questions, and Patrice asked them for thoughts on structuring a review panel for the NOY award. Eliza tried to force herself to engage with the conversation, but she found her eyes following Ross instead. There was such an intensity about him as he offered his very definite opinions on the right—and wrong—way to go about establishing an award. She couldn't help but smile to herself when Barbara kindly but firmly cut him off to ensure everyone's voice was heard.

"This is terrific," Patrice interjected as she scrawled in her journal.

Ross stood across from her, his hands on the back of an empty chair. "So. What are the next steps?"

Eliza didn't hear Patrice's response. Instead, she was brought up short by hearing those same words echo in her head, but in Jack's voice. That was exactly the phrase he used when she or Scott went to him with a problem. Poor performance on a test? Broken bicycle chain? Jack never told them what to do—he'd turn it around on them. *What do you think you need to do? What are the next steps?* And they couldn't leave the room until they'd outlined at least three actions they needed to take to solve the problem.

She pushed her seat away from the table, and it was only when heads turned in her direction that she realized she'd stood. "Oh, sorry. Can someone let me know where I can find the restroom?"

Julia—or Kristen—pointed her in the right direction, and

she swiftly headed down the hallway. The ladies' room was a standard, institutional space with square tile and pale green stalls. She went straight to the sink to run the cold water over her wrists.

Was she betraying Jack by even being in that room with Ross? By seeking Ross out, was she just compounding what Laura had done to him twenty-seven years ago?

She looked at herself in the mirror and wanted to touch up her lipstick but realized she'd left her handbag behind. What was she doing here? Mo would probably want her to slip personal questions into the conversation. *So, Ross, you must make your kids' teachers crazy since you have all this educational knowledge. Oh, you don't have children? That's so interesting. Did you ever wish you had any?*

She sighed. She couldn't put off returning to the seminar room any longer. She shut off the tap and realized that the cuffs of her blouse were now spattered with water. She unbuttoned them and carefully rolled them up, aware as she did it that she was just delaying the inevitable.

An animated conversation was happening when she got back, and she slipped into her seat.

"I'm really excited about this," Patrice exclaimed. "Of course, we have to talk to our colleagues." She nodded at Eliza as if she hadn't been sitting there, mute, for nearly the entire meeting. "But I think these are some great ideas."

Eliza absently wondered what those ideas were.

And then everyone was standing up and shaking hands again, and Eliza found herself holding the folders that had been on the table. Apparently they contained printouts of journal articles and abstracts describing current research.

"I'm going to run to the ladies' before we go," Patrice said as they moved toward the door.

"I'm going that way myself," Kristen/Julia replied.

Barbara put a small hand, decorated with a variety of silver rings, on Eliza's arm. "Just wonderful to meet you. Can't wait to get this off the ground." Eliza smiled back at her, wishing that Ross's personality were more like his warm colleague's. She watched her new acquaintance's retreating back, and then, suddenly, she was in the hallway alone with Ross.

He leaned against the wall, apparently intending to keep her company until Patrice returned. "So, how long have you been with NOY?"

"A little more than four years. Since I graduated from college."

"Is your degree in education?"

"No. Sociology." Was this how she normally made small talk? She seemed to have forgotten how.

He cocked his head. "But I guess it's held your interest. These days, four years is an eternity when it comes to jobs."

"I've learned a lot, and my responsibilities have grown." Why did her words sound so awkward and stilted? Did they sound that way to Ross as well? She could hear Mo like a devil on her shoulder. *Ask him something about himself! This is your chance!*

"So. Um. How about you? Have you always been in academia?"

"Oh, I bounced around a bit. Took a gap year partway through college. When I went back, I changed my major to education. Thought I might teach high school. Actually, I did teach high school for a couple of years before I decided to go back for my doctorate. I do better when I don't have to be in daily contact with other humans."

"You seem to do okay." She gestured at the room where they'd gathered.

He laughed. "Yeah, in small doses. I don't have a lot of patience for people."

Somehow that didn't surprise her. Eliza wrinkled her brow. "But don't you teach now?"

"Yeah, but there's a big difference between teaching high school and teaching at the college level. At least in terms of hours in the classroom." He pulled his pen out of his pocket and began clicking it rhythmically. "Sorry. Bad habit."

"You should get one of those fidget spinner things."

"You're probably right."

"We gave them out at last year's gala in the swag bags. I bet we have some left over. I'll have to send you one."

"Or just give it to me at our next meeting. Sounds like we'll be working together."

Does it? She realized she really hadn't been listening.

Patrice came back down the hall at that moment. "Ready to go?" she asked before turning to Ross. "Again, really nice meeting you. I'm looking forward to our collaboration."

"Likewise. Especially now that fidget spinners are on offer."

Patrice looked puzzled.

"Eliza can explain. Do you know how to find your way out?"

"I think we're good."

And then finally they were back in the elevator, Patrice going on and on about how successful the meeting had been and Eliza wondering if perhaps it was time for her to look for a new job.

CHAPTER TWENTY-FOUR

The next day, the NOY team was all aflutter. Vanessa was thrilled with the prospect of partnering with the NYU faculty on the new award. Everything else came to a screeching halt as they were all roped in to working on a proposal for the board. The strategy was complicated, but the crux of it was that NOY would help support NYU research, and, in return, the NYU faculty would be part of the peer-review process for the award. Through their connections in academic circles, they would also put together a presentation for the gala on some of the most cutting-edge work currently being done in the field.

As far as Eliza was concerned, this couldn't have turned out worse if she had scripted it. Ross would likely be deeply involved in this presentation, and as the gala was her baby, there'd be no avoiding him. How long could she let this go on before telling him who she really was? Did she *want* to tell him who she really was? If only this had happened a month earlier, Ross Sawyer would only be a slightly pompous professor she now had to work with. If only Jack hadn't died.

If only. She looked at the family photo still propped up against her wilting African violet and was overcome with a desperate sense of loss. Loss of her mother, her father, and everything she'd ever believed about their family unit.

The therapist she'd seen shortly after Carol came onto the scene talked a lot about Eliza's anger at her mother, but Eliza didn't buy it. Sure, mothers weren't supposed to abandon their children. Not when they were nowhere near done growing up. But it wasn't like it was Laura's choice to leave. So it wasn't fair for Eliza to be angry at her. The therapist had peered at her, tapping her pencil against her lips, but Eliza just stared back. This woman Carol had recommended she talk to wasn't going to tell her how she was feeling. *What kind of daughter would be mad at her mother for dying?*

Now, though, she was finding it harder and harder to deny that something that felt alarmingly close to anger was simmering in her blood. She didn't know if it was because her mom had cheated on her dad, or because she had kept it secret, or because she had decided to reveal it after all . . .

She looked at the handful of fidget spinners she'd pulled out of her desk drawer that morning. They bore the NOY logo on one side and the logo of the educational-toy company that had provided them on the other. She wanted to hurl them against the wall.

At that moment, her phone lit up with a text. It was Mo, confirming their drink for that evening. *Ugh.* All she wanted to do was go home and curl up on the couch with her good friend *Monk.* But not only was she meeting Nik for the first time, she then had to celebrate Scott's birthday.

She hadn't seen Maren or Scott since her sister-in-law's edict about keeping Scott out of the debacle with Carol. When Maren had invited her to join their group of friends at a bar, Eliza was sorely tempted to ask why she wanted her to come.

I'm sure he'd like you there, Maren had written.

Why? So I can remind him how fucked up our family is?

* * *

When Eliza arrived at the bar Mo had selected, it was surprisingly quiet, despite it being Friday evening. It was decorated in the style of a traditional Irish pub, with a heavy oak bar, behind which were displayed rows and rows of whiskey, alongside a blackboard listing all the beers and ciders on tap. Old-school Tiffany-style lamps hung from the hammered-tin ceiling, and the redheaded, fair-skinned bartender looked like he was straight from central casting.

Mo waved at her from a high-top table near the back and jumped off her seat to give her a hug. "Eliza, this is Nik. Nik, this is Eliza."

Eliza extricated herself from the hug and turned to the attractive man who had risen from his own seat. She noted the thick dark hair and well-cut suit.

"Eliza. So nice to meet you. I feel like I know you already." He bent to touch his cheek to hers, and she caught a whiff of not-unpleasant aftershave.

"So good to meet you, too."

"I was just going to get some drinks. What can I get you?"

Eliza thought about her day and the evening ahead of her and wondered if she could order a scotch and make it a triple. She'd never actually done that, but it might be fun to try. But she restrained herself. "I'll have a Magners."

"Ooh, me, too!" Mo reached out and squeezed Nik's arm before he walked away.

Eliza slipped off her jacket and hung it on the back of the chair before sitting.

Mo's eyes sparkled. "So what do you think?"

"Well, based on thirty seconds in his presence, I'm not getting any warning flags."

"I know, I know. You just met him. I'm just excited."

"Really? I hadn't noticed." Eliza smiled to soften her deadpan delivery.

Nik returned, impressively holding three pint glasses and

managing to set them down on the table with only a little sloshing.

"Sláinte!" he exclaimed as he lifted his own drink for them to toast. They all clinked and sipped.

"So, Nik, tell me about yourself," Eliza asked, putting her glass down.

He smiled widely. His teeth were very straight. "Wow. Tall order. Let's see. I live in Battery Park City. I work in finance. I went to college in Boston . . ."

He went on, and Eliza asked questions where appropriate. And Mo jumped in to fill in blanks. They already had some well-coordinated couple-speak going.

"And you? I know you and Mo go way back. I bet you could tell me some stories!"

Eliza lifted her glass. "I'd need to get more of this in me if I'm going to give away any of her secrets."

He grinned. "Fair enough."

Mo smacked Eliza playfully. "Girl code. No matter how much you drink, you don't spill your girlfriend's secrets." She took a sip of her own cider. "So, anything new with Ross?"

Eliza glanced at Nik, who looked openly curious. Apparently, girl code didn't apply to Mo telling her new boyfriend about Eliza's family drama. With a sinking feeling, she described the meeting the day before in as few words as possible.

Mo's eyes widened. "Wow. That's wild!"

Wild. That was one word for it, but not the one Eliza would have chosen.

"So what are you going to do next?"

Both Mo and Nik seemed mesmerized. All they needed was some popcorn.

"I don't know. It's actually getting really complicated and stressful." Eliza drank deeply from her glass.

"I can only imagine." Mo touched her arm, but somehow

Eliza drew no comfort from it. She wanted to talk to her friend about how she was really feeling—not only about Ross but about Scott—but this wasn't the time or place. And while she didn't begrudge Mo being in the throes of her new romance, she wasn't sure when that time or place might be at this point. She decided to change the subject instead.

"Anyway. What do you guys have planned for the rest of the evening?"

"One of Nik's friends plays in a band. We're going out to Brooklyn to hear them."

"Cool. What kind of music?"

Nik tried to describe it, and Mo laughed at him, and before she knew it, it was time for Eliza to head to her next stop for the evening.

"We have to do dinner next time," Mo said, giving her a hug.

"Definitely."

Nik kissed her on the cheek. "It was great meeting you."

"You, too."

But as she walked away from them, she felt drained. It had taken everything she had to converse like a normal person, and now she was going to have to do it all over again, at another bar across town.

CHAPTER TWENTY-FIVE

The Kips Bay venue where Maren had summoned her for Scott's birthday was much more crowded than the Irish pub she'd just left. Eliza wove her way through swarms of people to find the back room where she'd been told to go. She slipped past the small sign that read *Private Party* and immediately spotted her sister-in-law. Red hair was useful that way. Maren was holding what looked like a martini and laughing with the man and woman standing with her.

Scott wasn't far from them, a beer in his hand. He appeared to be in a more serious conversation with some people who looked vaguely familiar. She made her way over to him and caught his eye. He didn't seem surprised to see her; nor did he seem overly delighted.

She leaned in to give him a half hug. "Happy birthday, Scott."

"Thanks, Liza."

"I know it's probably a pretty sucky one."

"You could say that again," he replied, and took a long swallow of his drink. "You can get yourself a drink; Maren ordered apps for everyone." He waved toward the bar, and Eliza felt she'd been summarily dismissed.

Obediently, she headed in the direction that Scott had indicated, her eyes sweeping the room for any familiar faces. She felt a jolt when she saw Josh. He was sitting at a high-top table, his head tilted to listen to a sleek, well-pressed woman who kept touching his arm as she spoke. She wondered if anyone would notice if she just slipped out and went home. Or, more importantly, if anyone would care.

Instead, she caught the bartender's eye and ordered a chardonnay. As she sipped it, she couldn't keep her eyes from wandering over to Josh, still seemingly engrossed in whatever his companion was telling him.

At some point during Josh's senior year of high school, his parents had gotten a new car and given him their old Toyota Camry. It wasn't sexy, but it had wheels and an engine, and that was really all that mattered. Eliza typically walked home; Scott didn't have a car and usually stayed late at school anyway. If it wasn't tennis season, there always seemed to be some sort of club meeting or activity that kept him from going home straightaway.

The first day that Josh had pulled up alongside her as she walked and offered her a ride, she'd initially said no.

"I'm practically home already," she objected, shifting her backpack higher up on her shoulder.

"Look at you, you're like a Sherpa with that thing. Just get in."

So she did. And it became a routine. Sometimes it was just a quick ride with Eliza immediately hopping out of the car. Other times, they sat side by side in the bucket seats and talked for a while. She discovered that Josh could do spot-on imitations of nearly everyone at school—from the principal with his honking laugh to the lunchroom lady who so strictly apportioned the pasta that you'd think there was a global ziti shortage.

And she discovered that she hadn't lost her sense of humor, despite all that was going on with Laura. Not only could he make her laugh until the tears rolled down her cheeks, but her random thoughts, which she normally kept to herself, made him guffaw. Like her observation one afternoon that Madonna's "Open Your Heart" seemed like it was about a stalker.

"I mean, come on. Is that supposed to be romantic? How would you like it if someone said they were going to force you to love them?"

Josh laughed. "Well, I suppose it would depend on who it was."

"Right. Even if it was someone you liked—you'd probably change your mind and decide she was crazy!"

No matter how long they sat and talked, it wasn't long enough for Eliza. She had come to look forward to that part of her day more than anything else. It was the buffer between school and Laura, who was getting weaker all the time. But even when she wanted to stay longer on that vinyl seat, she was always sure to go inside before Scott came home. She and Josh never talked about him, but they both seemed to sense that their friendship was something they should keep to themselves.

Now, Eliza twirled the stem of her wineglass and watched Scott shift from one cluster of friends to another. Quite a few of the faces were at least somewhat familiar—from parties over the years, their wedding, or the shiva. *The shiva.* Thinking about the fact that many of these people had been present for her outburst made her even less inclined to try to make small talk. Unsurprisingly, she had only the blurriest memory of who had been there—except, of course, for Carol's nephew

Adam, who didn't seem to be at the bar this evening. Perhaps he wasn't invited. It would be nice to believe that Scott and Maren had deleted him from their list out of respect for her, given what Adam had started. But she suspected it was just as likely that he simply hadn't yet arrived.

She felt a hand on her arm and turned. It was Josh.

He smiled at her, and she wondered where his lady friend had gotten to. "Hey, I was hoping you'd be here," he said. "How are you doing?"

"You know. One foot in front of the other."

"Sometimes that's all you can do." He glanced at her wineglass. "Can I get you another?"

"No, I'm good for now." Just what she didn't need—to end up making another scene in front of Scott's friends.

Josh caught the bartender's attention to order another beer. Just one, Eliza noted.

He turned back to her. "No Chester?"

She rolled her eyes at him. "Carter. No. We're not together anymore."

He looked surprised. "But the other day at the coffee place . . ."

She cut him off. "Nope," she said firmly.

"I'm really sorry, Eliza. This is such a rough time for you, and then to have a relationship end, too . . ."

He clearly didn't have a very accurate picture of what she and Carter had. Did he think she'd been dumped? She shook her head. "It's all fine. It ran its course. That's it." Her eyes scanned the room for Josh's friend. Maybe she'd gone to the ladies' room. "Who's your friend?" It was out of her mouth before she could stop it.

His eyebrows drew together. "My friend?"

She wanted to kick herself. Hard. "The woman you were talking to." She inclined her head in the direction of where they'd been sitting. "Thought you were together."

He shook his head. "Nope. Just met her. Her name is Shaina or Shonna or something. Tough to hear in here."

With how close your heads were to each other, it's hard to imagine you missed a word she said.

"She works with Maren, I think," he added before taking a swallow from his beer.

Of course she does. Why did that irritate her so much? Eliza found herself draining her wineglass.

Josh chuckled and pointed at her glass. "Now can I get you another?"

"Sure, why not?"

When she had her fresh glass of chardonnay in hand, Josh shifted her a bit away from the bar to make room for the people crowding behind them. They ended up in a corner a few steps from the swarm.

He bent toward her. "I don't want to be nosy if you don't want to talk about it, but anything new on the whole 'new birth father' front?"

Eliza was surprised his phrasing didn't irk her—but somehow, it didn't. It was just the degree of lightness about the subject she needed. And, she couldn't help but notice, it felt so different from Mo's question.

"A lot, actually." She told him about her meeting with Ross and that they were likely going to have an ongoing working relationship.

"Yikes. What a mess."

"Right. Here I am stuck working with him and pretending we have no connection."

"What are you going to do?"

She shrugged. "I don't know. On the one hand I feel like I should just come clean now, because the more time that goes by, the harder it will get."

"But you don't know if you're ready."

It was like he could read her mind. "Exactly."

Josh picked at the label on his beer bottle with his thumbnail. "Do you have any sense of what he's like?"

"Not really. Honestly, he seems a little obnoxious. But it's hard to tell. We've spent so little time together, and it's been in work settings."

"And you're probably analyzing everything about him much more than you would any random stranger."

She hadn't thought about that. "You're right. So maybe I'm seeing stuff that isn't there." She put down her wineglass and covered her face with her hands. "This is such a mess," she said from behind her self-created shield.

He gently pulled her hands away from her face and pushed back the strands of hair that had escaped from her braid and gotten caught in her fingers. His skin was warm. "Whatever happens, it will be okay. You're in an impossible situation. No one is going to be able to tell you what to do, but you have people who care about you and support you—and will, no matter what."

Eliza's breath caught, and it took her a minute to remind herself that whatever this looked like, it was just big-brotherly. She slipped her hands out of his and forced herself to meet his eyes.

"That's a nice idea, but not exactly true."

His forehead wrinkled. "What do you mean? You've got Scott and Maren. And your friend—her name's Mo, right?"

"Yeah, well, Scott and Maren don't really want to deal with this. Or me. You saw how Scott was the other day. I'm sure he won't be happy to hear that I'm hiring a lawyer." Until that moment, she hadn't been sure that was what she was going to do, but she realized, as she said it, that it was the only avenue she could take and live with herself.

Josh's gaze traveled over her shoulder and she followed it, alighting on her brother. "He'll get over it," he said, returning his eyes to her. "Like I said to you the other day, he doesn't always know what's best."

"Maybe—but he certainly thinks he does." She lifted her glass to her mouth and found that it was empty. "And as far as Mo goes—she's great. She's always been great. But lately, I don't know . . . she doesn't seem to get what I'm going through."

He ran his hand through his hair. "It's a lot for anyone to understand. Hell, I don't understand it either. But if she listens to you and is there for you, that's good, right?"

She nodded.

"Have you eaten? There's some snacks and stuff." He pointed toward the other side of the room.

She looked down at her empty glass. "Yeah, probably a good idea. I haven't been eating much."

"I can tell." His eyes swept down her, and she felt acutely uncomfortable. She didn't know how much weight she'd lost but had started to think of herself as "bones and boobs." *Had his eyes lingered on the latter? No, of course not.*

As they made their way toward the food, Scott intercepted them. "Hey, what have you guys had your heads together about?" He looked from one to the other, and though he wore a smile, it didn't reach his eyes.

Josh grinned. "Oh, I was just telling Eliza about some of your other birthday celebrations. She was trying to guess at which one you got the most shit-faced."

"Very funny," Scott replied, barely amused, and Eliza smiled to herself. Then Scott changed the subject. "Hey, I saw you talking to Shira earlier . . ."

Josh glanced at Eliza, and she spoke before he could reply to her brother. "I'm getting something to eat," she said, sidling away through the crowd to find the decimated charcuterie boards. The last thing she needed to hear was how hot Josh thought Shira was.

CHAPTER TWENTY-SIX

Eliza didn't stay long at the birthday party after she ate a few cornichons and some spicy salami. Some guy introduced himself to her as Ken and thought it was a good line to point out that her long blond hair meant she could be Barbie—*Seriously?* That pathetic come-on pushed her over the edge, which admittedly she'd been standing pretty close to already. She gave Scott and Maren hugs and told them she was out, but not before they invited her to a Friendsgiving at their place.

She'd been trying to avoid thoughts of Thanksgiving, even though it was bearing down like a hurricane. Hurricane Tom the Turkey. Laura had loved Thanksgiving and always made lots of classically uncool sides—like green-bean casserole and canned cranberry sauce. Carol was all about catering. The food was always delicious, but prepared by strangers. The meal became the perfect embodiment of how life had changed. The switch from homey and low-key but full of love to superficially gorgeous and elaborate but, at best, cold.

Not surprisingly, Carol hadn't extended an invitation to her for this year, and she didn't know what communication she'd had with Scott about the holiday, but Scott and Maren

had decided to host a Friendsgiving dinner the Tuesday evening beforehand and go to Maren's parents' place for the day
itself. "We didn't think you'd want to drive all the way to
Vermont," Maren had said.

Or you don't want to be stuck in a car with me for six hours.

As she rode up the elevator to the law offices of Morris,
Muhlfelder and Gleason, she wondered if she'd be disinvited
once they knew that she was officially fighting Carol's interpretation of Jack's will. She'd told Vanessa that she had a dentist's appointment and would be in late. She didn't want to
talk about her family situation with her coworkers, and if she
were lucky, she'd miss at least part of the meeting scheduled
for that morning with NOY board members, Ross, and several
of his NYU colleagues. The less time she spent in his presence
the better. She bit her lip at that thought, which had ruled her
when it came to her relationship with Jack. Now that she had
no time left with the father who'd raised her, she realized perhaps that had been a mistake.

When she opened the office door, the first thing she saw
was a large bouquet of flowers in shades of yellow, orange, and
red on the receptionist's desk. Eliza was probably the only person in the world who didn't smile at the sight of a bouquet.
They always reminded her of the ones that were constantly
coming to the house while Laura was sick.

The same receptionist with steel gray hair stood to greet
her. Someone must have told her that she was now going to
be a paying client. "Come on back," she said. "I'll take you to
Vicky. I'm Pam."

"Nice to meet you," she replied as she followed her down
the hall.

When Vicky rose from her desk, Eliza could see that today
she was wearing a cream twinset with navy pants, the same
gold link chain around her neck. She was like a walking adver-
tisement for Ann Taylor.

"Come in, sit down," Vicky urged, and Eliza obeyed. "Thanks so much for coming back in. I know we can do a lot by PDF and email, but I like to get original signatures to start, and thought it would be good to meet again in person."

Eliza nodded. Vicky had already told her this by phone when she'd called to say she was ready to sign on the dotted line. Vicky had also told her what it would cost, and Eliza had a check in her purse. She hoped that the legal fees would be outweighed by her portion of Jack's estate, but even if they weren't, she couldn't let Carol get away with this.

"So. After you called me the other day, I went ahead and got the probate documents that were filed with the court, along with your father's will. Your stepmother didn't name you as a beneficiary on the paperwork, but, as she told you, the will leaves one-third of his estate, excluding the house, to you."

Eliza opened her mouth to squawk, but Vicky cut her off.

"I know. It's bullshit. And the probate court should have caught the discrepancy. But welcome to my world." She waved her hand around her small, crowded office. "It's stuff like this that keeps me in these fabulous digs. Speaking of—did you have trouble with the elevator?"

Eliza shook her head.

"Glad to hear it. They've been super wonky lately. I'd take the stairs if we weren't on the seventh floor. Anyway. 'What's next, Vicky?' That's what you're thinking, right?"

This time, Eliza nodded.

"So, I write up the order to show cause. We file it with the court, and a copy goes to your stepmother. Cheryl, right?"

Eliza sucked in her breath. "Carol."

"Sorry, sorry. Don't worry, I'll get it right in the paperwork. Always do! Well, almost always, anyway. Ha! Kidding."

It's like watching a one-woman show. "How long will the process take?"

"Well, it won't take me long at all to write it. After I file, we should get a relatively quick hearing date from the judge . . ." Vicky was making a note on a yellow legal pad.

Eliza's pulse quickened. "I wanted to ask you about that. Does there have to be a hearing?"

Vicky put down her pen and looked at her. "Yes. Unless Carol folds right away. Which she could do. But I wouldn't count on it. A woman who does this isn't going to just back off, in my experience."

Eliza wondered if her face was as white as it felt.

"Look. This is pretty routine stuff. One thing I need to know from you—do you want to challenge her as executor? Or just limit the order to restoring you as a beneficiary? You could go either way."

Eliza bit the inside of her lip. She wished she had someone with her to squeeze her hand. The image of Josh appeared to her, unbidden. She quickly switched him out for Mo. "I'm sorry. Can I get some water?"

"Sure, sure. Be right back."

While Vicky was gone, she was tempted to put her head between her knees but didn't think that would make a very good impression on her lawyer—her lawyer! How had she become a person who had a lawyer? She had to at least *seem* like someone who would do well in court. So instead she attempted some deep, steadying breaths.

"Here you go." Vicky handed her a bottle of water, and Eliza took it gratefully, unscrewing the cap and taking a long swallow.

"I know. This is tough stuff," Vicky said, sitting back down at her desk. "Where were we? Oh, right—are we challenging her as executor?"

Eliza swallowed. "I don't think so. That's what my dad wanted. And that's what this is about—restoring what he would have wanted."

Vicky nodded. "Good, good. So I'll get this done and keep you posted."

"Thanks." It occurred to her that she had probably said only a few dozen words since she'd arrived.

"I'll walk you out."

And then they were heading back down the scuffed linoleum-tiled floor of the hallway toward the reception area.

"Aren't those flowers gorgeous?" Vicky exclaimed as they arrived.

"Gorgeous," Eliza echoed faintly.

Vicky extended her hand, and Eliza shook it. "Hang in there. I'll be in touch to let you know when I've filed the order."

Eliza headed out in a daze and, a few minutes later, was back in the elevator. As the doors shut, she glanced at the time. The meeting hadn't taken anywhere near as long as she'd hoped. Perhaps she could dawdle on her way to the subway. She was considering her options when there was a creaking noise and the elevator suddenly stopped moving.

She waited a moment for either the door to open at another floor or the downward motion to resume. Neither happened. Did people really get stuck in elevators? Somehow it seemed like something that only happened in movies when ninja-types clambered around and messed with the pulleys. How far up was she, anyway? In other words, how far would she plunge if she were to end up in free fall?

Stop it. This elevator had last been inspected earlier this year. At least that was what the photocopied form covered in plexiglass told her. She pressed the alarm button and immediately covered her ears as a shrieking noise started. Then, almost as quickly, the shrieking stopped and there was a disembodied voice asking her if there was a problem.

"Yes! I'm stuck in the elevator."

"Hold, please."

Hold, please? Where was she supposed to go?

A few minutes passed. Then the voice returned. "All right. We've got someone checking into it."

Eliza set her bag on the floor and wondered if she should sit down. It didn't look particularly clean, but who knew how long she'd be here. Oh, screw it. At least she was wearing black pants.

She pulled out her phone and texted Amber.

> Hey Amber. Could you tell Vanessa
> I'm stuck in an elevator? Not sure
> when I'll be in.

Rereading it, she couldn't help thinking that it sounded like a "dog ate my homework" excuse. A few moments later she got Amber's response.

> Yikes! I've told her. How's your
> tooth?

Oh, right. She was at "the dentist."

> It was just a checkup.

> Well that's good at least. Anyone in
> the elevator with you? What a great
> meet-cute! 💏

> I think it's probably been done. And,
> no, I'm alone.

> Bummer.

She tried to look on the bright side; maybe she'd end up missing the whole meeting, kicking the can down the road on her next interaction with Ross. And she had her phone, so she could scroll mindlessly through social media.

She was watching cute puppy videos and reconsidering what she'd told Aunt Claude—that she couldn't have a dog in the city—when the Yorkie desperately trying to hop up onto a couch was interrupted by an incoming text. It was Josh.

> Hey, E. Just wanted to give you a heads-up.

What, that you're bringing a date to Friendsgiving?

> I told my colleague in the school law practice about your gala. He and his group decided to buy a table!

Okay, why had her mind gone in that other direction?
That's great! Thanks! she responded. **Nice to get good news while I'm stuck in an elevator.**

> What?!? Where are you?

> Your friend Vicky's building in Brooklyn.

> Are you ok? Are you alone?

> Yes and yes. It's actually quite peaceful here.

She looked at the faux-wood paneling and the honeycomb fluorescent lighting. Perhaps *peaceful* was a bit of an overstatement.

> Are they working on getting it fixed?

> No. I thought I'd just hide out here
> for a while. ☹ Yes, they're working
> on it.

The three dots danced for a moment. Then:

> So would you rather be stuck in an
> elevator for a day, or a sewer for an
> hour?

She laughed. She'd forgotten their endless games of Would You Rather. Would you rather fail all your classes and have to repeat a grade, or be in a coma for a year? Would you rather run naked down the school hallway, or give a speech in front of the whole student body in your underwear?

> I'd take the elevator. At least it
> doesn't smell in here.

> Ok, what if your boss was in the ele-
> vator with you?

> Ooh. Good question. Probably I'd
> pick the sewer then. Vanessa's not a
> bad sort, but to have to make small
> talk with her for the whole day . . .
> How about you? Same choice.

> Sewer. No question about it. (Insert
> joke about lawyers and sewer rats
> here.)

They lobbed a few other unpalatable choices at each other before Josh had to jump off to go to a meeting, and Eliza went back to her puppy videos. Finally, there was a creak and a lurch, and the elevator started moving again. She rose to her feet, brushing off her pants, and was standing ready when the doors finally opened, revealing the lobby. She expected an elevator mechanic or a building super or someone to be standing there, but no. Only the same bored security guard sitting at his usual post. She glanced again at the time and didn't rush walking to the subway.

CHAPTER TWENTY-SEVEN

Her timing wasn't quite perfect. When Eliza arrived at NOY—having missed one train because she chose not to run down the stairs to catch it—the reception area was filled with board members, staff, and NYU faculty glad-handing and congratulating one another on a good plan. She wondered if she could sneak back out without being noticed, but eagle-eyed Vanessa spotted her.

"Eliza! You made it!" her boss exclaimed loudly, causing multiple heads to swivel in her direction.

She smiled weakly. "Yep. Just barely." And then she pulled herself together, pasting on her high-wattage smile for the board members.

There was so much cross talk, she felt like a buoy bobbing in not-very-calm seas, and everyone made it sound as if they'd achieved peace in the Middle East. She felt guilty for being a bit disappointed that this collaboration hadn't crashed on the rocks of bureaucracy, as so often happened.

She made her way through the group, smiling and murmuring platitudes, hoping to avoid Ross. But then there he was, large as life.

"Eliza! I hear you had quite the adventure this morning."

"I don't know if getting stuck in an elevator constitutes an adventure," she replied.

"Well, I suppose it's all relative. What usually spices up your life?"

Is he flirting with me? She felt her skin crawl.

"Oh, you know, encouraging donors to make big contributions."

He smiled knowingly.

Ew. That was *not* what she meant.

He clapped his hands together. "Almost forgot! You promised me some fidget spinners."

Safer ground. "You're right. And I pulled some out. They're in my office. I'll just get them."

She turned to walk away, hoping her backside wasn't covered in elevator grime.

"I'll come with you."

Great.

He followed her to her office, where she quickly went to her desk to get the gadgets she'd tucked into a drawer after she realized she was playing with them too much. Meanwhile, Ross walked around the small space as if doing a military inspection.

He paused by her file cabinet. "I think your plant needs watering."

"Probably." She shut the drawer, spinners in hand.

"What's this?" His voice was strange, and she looked up. He was holding the family photo from Scott's bar mitzvah.

Suddenly her heart was racing, and her hands went cold. She tried to speak, but her mouth was dry. She cleared her throat and tried again. "Just a photo from my brother's bar mitzvah. A long time ago." Could she possibly pretend her mother just looked remarkably like his ex-girlfriend? They said everyone had a body double. Or, as Mo liked to say, an evil twin.

He looked from the photo to her and back again. Then he pointed at Laura. "What's your mom's name?"

She swallowed again. "Laura Levinger."

"Levinger." He stared at the photo and then off into the distance before looking back at her. "Was her maiden name Saperstein?"

Eliza's ears were on delayed playback, and it took her a moment to hear the question. She nodded slowly, knowing what he was going to say next. Her thoughts were whirling. Could she pretend this was all a shocking surprise? One of those "what a small world!" moments? Like bumping into someone you knew from home when you were traveling abroad, or discovering that your new neighbor was your college roommate's cousin?

But if she did that, she'd be slamming the door on ever revealing the truth. Ross was looking at her, waiting for her answer.

She nodded slowly. "Yes, Saperstein was her maiden name."

He started to shake his head. "You're not going to believe this, but she and I dated in high school."

Eliza felt like she was going to throw up. How had she ended up having to have this conversation here, in her office, with her boss steps away? And all her coworkers?

"Actually, I know," she said.

"Wait. What?" He rubbed his chin like he was trying to erase a stain. "You *know*? Did your mom talk about me?"

"Not exactly."

"Then how do you know?" His voice rose a little, and Eliza glanced nervously at her office door.

"Can we go somewhere else to talk about this? Get a cup of coffee?" At that moment, she would have gladly drunk the most bitter cup of coffee rather than have this conversation. Especially here, where Vanessa could walk in at any moment.

He took a small step forward, forcing Eliza to step back. "Talk about what? What is this? What's going on here?"

"Please," she pleaded, touching his arm, which he pulled back immediately. "Let's get a cup of coffee."

He narrowed his eyes at her, clearly on the fence. "Fine. Lead the way." He motioned with his hand for her to go ahead of him, but despite the surface solicitousness of the gesture, to Eliza it felt hostile.

Foolishly, it wasn't until they were through the doorway that Eliza realized they'd have to pass by whoever was left in the reception area, and they'd need to have some explanation for their abrupt departure. Most everyone was still there, chatting. Eliza ducked over to Amber, sitting at her desk. "I need to run out for a minute to Duane Reade." And she looked at her meaningfully.

Amber immediately caught on, but unfortunately reached for her purse. "Wait, I'm sure I have something . . ."

"No, no, I'm just going to run downstairs."

Amber looked puzzled but shrugged, and Eliza tossed a "Be right back" to a startled-looking Vanessa. *Great.* Now she could plan on having another difficult conversation after this one.

Ross was right behind her as they headed to the elevator and stepped inside. Eliza pressed the button for the lobby, and the shiny doors slid shut. She was looking straight ahead, but when she realized that meant she could see Ross in the reflection, she dropped her eyes. What were the chances that this elevator would get stuck, too? A choking sound burst out of her as she stifled the hysterical giggles that started to rise up at that thought. She covered the noise with a cough but felt Ross turn to look at her anyway.

Once downstairs, he again gestured for her to lead the way. Why was he being so quiet? What was going on in his head?

They walked briskly to the chain café at the corner. It had a French-sounding name, but she and Mo liked to laugh about the fact that it was actually headquartered in Omaha.

"What can I get you?" were the first words out of Ross's mouth since they'd left her office.

"Just a cup of tea. Any kind. It doesn't matter." *Nice, Eliza. Be easy and accommodating before you turn his life upside down. And yours.*

CHAPTER TWENTY-EIGHT

Ross found Eliza at the table she'd snagged in the corner of the café. He set her cardboard cup down in front of her, steam escaping through the small slit in the plastic lid, and pulled out the chair opposite to sit.

"Okay. Talk," he said, without preamble.

Eliza put her freezing hands around the warm cup. How was she supposed to begin? Despite all the space Ross had occupied in her brain, she'd never actually thought about what she'd say in this moment. How she'd explain. She took a deep breath. "So, my dad died a couple months ago." Had it really only been two months?

"I'm sorry to hear that," he said, in a tone that sounded like *Yes, and . . . ?*

"You probably know that my mom died ten years ago." *Oh my God. What if he didn't know?*

He closed his eyes and sucked air in through his nose. "Yes, I did know that. I went to her funeral."

That was news. "I didn't know that. It was a really hard time for me." *Way to state the obvious.*

"I didn't talk to anyone, really. Just wanted to be there."

Eliza nodded. She opened her mouth to go on with her story but was surprised when he continued to speak.

"I'd heard she was sick and wanted to come see her, but I didn't think I'd be welcome."

She blinked at him. This was new information, too. She automatically raised her cup to her lips but realized she wouldn't be able to swallow and put it back down. "So," she continued, trying to find her place again in this uncharted territory. "After my dad died, my aunt Claude, my mom's sister . . ."

He was watching her intently and nodded in recognition of Claude's name.

Eliza continued. ". . . gave me a letter my mom had written me. In it, she said . . ." She swallowed, imagining this must be what it would feel like in the moment before a skydiver jumped out of a plane. Especially if they weren't confident that their parachute would open. "She said that you're my father."

She could see as the words entered his ears and made their way through the nerve endings to his brain, and the moment at which he deciphered what they meant. He looked like he'd been punched.

"I'm sorry, your father?" He shifted in his seat.

"She said that at your reunion . . ."

"Yes, I know what happened at the reunion," he said impatiently, covering his face with his hands for a moment and then slowly drawing them apart like curtains. Seeing his features again, Eliza knew for sure what it meant when people described faces appearing "like thunder." And then he opened his mouth.

"I'm sorry, but what the fuck? I got her pregnant and she never told me? How the hell does she even know it was me?"

Eliza's eyes stung, and part of her wanted to just walk out and never look back. What was he mad at her for? She wasn't the one who'd kept the secret. She wasn't the one who'd cheated on her husband. She stopped just short of the thought that came next—the one that blamed Laura for all of this.

"I don't know what to say. This was news to me, too." She swiped at her eyes, frustrated with herself for crying in front of this angry stranger who happened to share her DNA.

Ross suddenly stood up, and she thought he was going to leave. But when he stalked away, he left his jacket on his chair. She watched him scrub at his thick hair with his hand as he stared, probably unseeingly, at the menu board above the counter. And then he swiveled and returned to his seat.

He huffed out a long breath. "Wow. This is a lot to take in."

She widened her eyes. "Um, yeah," she said, trying to indicate through her intonation that she wasn't exactly an uninvolved bystander here.

Ross drummed his fingers on the table. "Right. Of course. Look. I don't even know what to say. All this time . . . And otherwise, she never mentioned me?"

Eliza shook her head. "Not a word."

"And when's your birthday?"

She sighed. "March nineteenth."

"And our reunion was in June, so that's . . ." He looked at the ceiling as his fingers moved, clearly counting.

She felt a flash of annoyance. "You really think she didn't do the math?"

He focused on her again. "Look. I don't know what you expect from me. You drop this on me out of the blue—you can't expect me to accept it like that." He snapped his fingers.

"I don't expect anything at all. Don't worry," she retorted. *How did Mom ever feel anything for this guy?*

"And besides," he continued as if she hadn't spoken, "am I supposed to believe this is all some sort of weird coincidence? You show up at my talk and tell me about NOY and now all of a sudden we're working together?" Not surprisingly, he pronounced *NOY* with something bordering on disgust.

She clenched her fists and tried to steady her breathing. "The first time I ever heard your name was two months ago. Obviously, I tried to find out who you were, and, yes, I did figure out that you teach at NYU. When I saw that you were giving a public lecture, I decided to go. Just to see. Obviously, this hasn't been easy for me to accept either. I didn't plan to talk to you—if you'll recall, we literally crashed into each other. It's completely unrelated that NOY was looking to work with education faculty. Believe me, it was the last thing I wanted to happen. I wanted more time to absorb all of this and figure out how best to handle it. But it all got taken out of my hands." She picked up the cup of tea and managed to take a sip, needing to focus on something else, if even for a moment.

He nodded slowly. "I can't imagine Laura thought I'd take this well. Why did Claudia only give you the letter now?"

"That's what my mom wanted. She said to do it after my dad died."

There was a long silence before Ross spoke again. "Look. I'm gonna need some time. Interpersonal relations aren't my strength under the best of circumstances—and these are hardly the best of circumstances. I know we're going to have to deal with each other for this collaboration project. But I can't . . ." He stopped abruptly.

"Got it." She stood and picked up her mostly undrunk tea. "Have your people call my people," she said roughly, over the clog in her throat.

"Wait. Eliza . . ."

She paused, but he didn't have anything else to say. So she walked out of the fake French café and remembered to stop at Duane Reade for a box of tampons she didn't need before going back to the office.

The rest of the afternoon at work was a nightmare. Eliza made up a story about bumping into an old college friend at the pharmacy to explain why it took so long for her to return with her feminine hygiene products. And then she had to sit through Vanessa, Patrice, and Davin bringing her up to speed on the plans moving forward. Davin was going to write a press release about NOY's collaboration with these esteemed education scholars, and Eliza was going to use that content to update the gala attendees about the exciting presentations that were going to be happening in place of the promised keynote speaker.

The whole time, all she could think about was having to watch Ross in the spotlight at what she had come to think of as *her* gala, knowing what a jerk he was.

On the other hand, she argued with herself, what should she have expected? Surely she didn't think he would have just embraced her, delighted to learn that he had a twenty-six-year-old daughter he never knew about? A dream come true! *Not.*

She left for home as early as she possibly could, given that she had come in so late. She wished that her lie about the dentist had been more elaborate. If she were recovering from a root canal, it would have been easier to duck out.

She went straight from her front door to her bedside table, still in her coat. *Do not pass Go, do not collect two hundred dollars.* Yanking open the drawer, she pulled out the diary. She needed to see what else Laura had written about Ross.

As she'd noticed the first time, there were big gaps between Laura's entries. She wrote a few times as she was preparing to leave for college—including some very dull paragraphs about a new quilt and her phone conversation with her assigned roommate. Finally she found Ross's name again.

> Everyone keeps saying I should break up with Ross before we leave for school. That I'll be missing out and that it won't last anyway. And it kills me that we're

going to be so far apart, but I love him. I truly think he's THE ONE. And he keeps saying that he doesn't know how long he'll last in college anyway, so maybe he'll be able to come to the West Coast. Not that I want him to drop out of school, obviously. I don't know. It's just so hard. And meanwhile he keeps saying we should have sex before we leave. And I want to. I really do. But I'm so scared of getting pregnant. I know I'm being ridiculous. That's what condoms are for, like he says. And I definitely worry that if we DON'T do it, he'll just sleep with some random girl at Hampshire. But that's not a reason to do it. But the other thing is—I feel like if we do it, it's going to be even harder for me to be away from him. Does that make sense?

It was so bizarre. Laura was younger than Eliza when she wrote these words, and yet the Laura she knew, of course, was an adult. A mother. Someone who definitely would *not* have sounded like this. Meanwhile, she had to keep pretending to herself that the writer of this diary was *not* her mother. In Eliza's fantasy world, in which her mother was still alive, she would have been the cool mom. The one who would have helped her decide among birth-control methods. Who she could have confided in, no matter what. That was the beauty of a fantasy mom. She could be perfect.

The next entries were about college. Not much about Ross, except that they talked on the phone. And then there was his name again, in January of their freshman year.

I don't even know why I'm writing about this. It's not like I want to remember this forever. But I don't even know who to talk to. Ross and I broke up. Nobody ever thought it would last, so they're all just saying, "oh well." But that's not how I feel. I don't know if I'll ever love anyone again like I love him. But he says we want different things. And maybe he's right. I don't know. I want a family. I mean, I want a career, too, but I want to have a life like I had growing up. And Ross is talking about joining the Peace Corps. Backpacking around the world. He doesn't even know if he ever wants kids! I keep telling him that we should just give it time. That we can work it out. But he said it's not fair to me. That he's a bad boyfriend. What does that even mean? I asked him if he cheated on me, and he said no, but maybe he did. Maybe it's because we didn't go all the way. And now we never will.

I guess you were wrong there, Mom. Eliza skimmed the rest of the entry, in which Laura expressed over and over again how devastated she was. It was so hard to square her mom's words with the man Eliza had spent time with earlier that day. How could Laura be so sad over the loss of *him*? And it sounded like, even back then, he was displaying some of the qualities he'd shown off to Eliza in living color.

She turned the pages and found that Laura expressed the same feelings on several separate occasions before she stopped writing entirely. Nothing about meeting Jack, or anything else for that matter.

So that's that, she thought as she closed the book. There would be no other words or thoughts from Laura. *And that's all she wrote. Literally.*

Realizing she was still wearing her coat, she rose from her bed and headed to the closet to hang it up. She poked gently around the edges of her emotions. She felt . . . numb.

Fishing her phone out of her purse, she texted Mo a brief **Hey, you around?** message. Almost immediately her friend responded.

At Nik's. You ok?

No, she wasn't okay. But what could Mo do to fix it?

👍 **Just checking in.**

She put her phone in her pocket and, absentmindedly, started to sort the laundry from her hamper to keep her hands busy. She'd gotten used to not relying on anyone. People had a tendency to disappear. Better to not depend on anyone but yourself. It was probably why she always picked the wrong men. If she picked the right ones, she might be inclined to actually count on them to be there for her. In her experience, that never worked out.

But right now, being alone was making her feel . . . hollow. She knew she should probably reach out to Scott. It didn't feel right that she hadn't told him about her legal plans. And now that she'd actually met Ross and told him the truth . . . how could she not tell Scott? But Maren's words echoed in her mind. *Scott can't be there for everyone.* How could she dump this burden on him?

She left the laundry piled on the floor of her bedroom and went to the fridge, where she opened the door and stared inside before shutting it again. Then she pulled her phone out of her pocket and scrolled through her contacts. Somehow, she'd known this was what she was going to do, and she'd just been delaying.

> **Hey.**

Josh responded immediately.

> **Hey.**

She paused and then typed again.

> **I told Ross the truth today. It was pretty bad.**

> **Oh, E. Where are you?**

> **I'm home.**

> **Give me your address. I'm coming over.**

CHAPTER TWENTY-NINE

It was March of Eliza's sophomore year in high school when Jack had called her and Scott into the living room to talk. Eliza had immediately gone cold and started to shake. She glanced at Scott, whose face was impassive. He was holding himself so tightly, she could barely see that he was breathing—and then she noticed the tic of the vein in his jaw.

Laura had been on the couch, her skinny legs tucked under her, her birdlike arms wrapped around her middle. She was always chilly these days, with no fat on her for insulation. Jack sat beside her and put his large hand over her tiny ones. It almost looked like that alone could break her.

"We met with your mom's care team today," Jack had begun. "The new treatment isn't working as they'd hoped. We always knew it was a long shot."

Eliza looked at Laura, who was glassy-eyed.

"So what are they going to do next?" Eliza asked, her eyes bouncing from one parent to the other when neither replied. The only sound was the noise Scott made in his throat.

Finally, Jack sighed. "There's nothing else to do."

"What do you mean, there's nothing else to do?" Eliza's

voice rose. "There's got to be something else." But even as she said the words, she knew they weren't true, and tears were already rolling down her face.

Laura reached out a hand to her, her icy fingers gripping Eliza's with more strength than they looked capable of. "I've fought as hard as I can fight. I'm so tired."

Eliza pulled her hand away. "What do you mean you're tired? Are you giving up? Can't you keep trying with the new treatment?" Her voice was shrill.

Laura blinked slowly before replying. "Liza. Scott. If I thought there was an iota of hope that it would work, I'd keep going. But there's been no change. And I want whatever time I have left to be about being with you. Not about more doctors' visits. Or about more treatments that make me feel worse and don't do a thing to stop the damn cancer."

Jack nodded. "This hasn't been an easy decision. But it's the right thing. The doctors agree, too."

Eliza was suddenly filled with rage. "The doctors! What do the doctors know? They're supposed to be able to *help* people! Not make them sicker!"

"Enough, Eliza." Jack's voice was unyielding.

She jumped up, unable to sit still. "But how can we . . ."

Scott stood beside her. "Liza. Enough." He took her elbow and nearly dragged her from the room, pulling her upstairs and into her bedroom. He shut the door behind them and sat her down on the bed.

"Liza. You have to stop."

"But, Scott . . ." She looked up at him, and realized the tears in her own eyes were mirrored in his. All the fight went out of her, and she just cried.

That was the day she'd learned that things don't always just "work out." That doing everything the right way doesn't mean anything. The day she learned to bottle it all up. Keep it inside so it didn't spill over and hurt other people. And the day she had learned that needing anyone was a recipe for inexorable pain.

Now, as she waited for Josh to arrive, she couldn't help but think about those weeks she'd tried so hard to . . . not forget, exactly, but to not dwell on. Ross said he'd wanted to come visit Laura when she was sick. What if he had? Would Laura have told her who he was?

The buzzer interrupted her thoughts, and she pressed the button to release the downstairs door to let Josh in. She glanced around her apartment, realizing she'd done nothing to straighten it up, and down at herself, still in the V-neck maroon sweater and black pants she'd been wearing when she sat on the elevator floor that morning. *How was that only this morning?*

She opened the front door in time to see Josh coming down the hall from the elevator. His eyes were on his phone, but he looked up as he got closer. "Hey, E. How are you doing?"

She shrugged and stepped back so he could enter, wondering if he'd hug her. She wasn't sure if she wanted him to or not. When he didn't, she figured it was for the best. Better not to blur those lines.

"Can I get you anything? I don't know what I have." She opened the refrigerator door again. The shelves didn't contain anything new since she'd looked a half hour earlier. She could feel Josh standing behind her, and he rested his hand on her shoulder.

"I'm fine. Come sit down."

She curled up in one corner of the sofa; he sat in the opposite corner. For a moment they were silent, and she picked up the end of her braid and pulled the hair tie off, absently unweaving and reweaving the strands of hair.

"E? What's going on in your head? What happened?"

Her eyes filled, and she blinked rapidly to stop the tears from leaking out. "It was awful."

She explained how Ross had seen the family photo and she'd been forced into telling him the whole story. "He was so *angry.*"

Josh's face looked almost as thunderous as Ross's had. "What a prick. I mean, I get that this was a big shock for him. But he shouldn't take it out on you."

A small part of Eliza couldn't help but feel something warm and fuzzy at Josh's anger on her behalf. "I don't know what I expected." She paused and continued to undo her braid, combing her fingers through her long, tangled hair. "I've had two months to get used to this idea—it came out of nowhere for him. But I guess part of me thought he might be at least a *little* happy. I mean, presumably he cared about my mom, at least once upon a time."

Josh shifted a little closer to her. "You can't take it personally. You're right, he wasn't expecting this when he woke up this morning. And, to be fair, it *has* been a long time since he was with your mom."

Eliza managed a half smile. "Are you saying I'm old?"

"You know that's not what I mean."

"I know." She paused. She hadn't told anyone about reading Laura's diary. Not even Aunt Claude, who was the only person who knew it existed. "My aunt found my mom's diary from back when they were together."

Josh's eyebrows reached toward his hairline. "Wow."

"I know, right? I feel bad reading it—obviously she never expected anyone to see it."

"Don't beat yourself up like that. She's the one who got you into this . . ." His voice trailed off.

"This mess. You can say it. You're right. Anyway, it turns out they never slept together back then."

"How long were they together?"

"I'm not totally sure. My mom wasn't much of a diary

writer. But they were together a couple years in high school. He dumped her over holiday break their freshman year of college."

"Do you know why?"

"He said he was a 'bad boyfriend,' whatever that means. That they wanted different things in life."

Josh cocked his head to one side. "Wanting different things doesn't make him a bad boyfriend."

"What do I know? They were kids. Eighteen years old. How does anyone know what they want in life at that age? I don't know what I want *now*." She shook out her hair and wound it up on top of her head, securing it with a hair tie. His eyes followed her movements. "I'm sorry. I play with my hair way too much."

He laughed. "Hey, if I had that much hair, I'd probably play with it, too." He rubbed his hand across his face. "You know, I actually could use something to drink."

She started to rise, and he stopped her.

"I'm sure I can find my way. Do you want something?"

"Maybe just some water. There's a pitcher in the fridge."

He went into her little kitchen and easily found a couple of tall glasses in a cabinet. It was so weird, after all these years, to see him making himself comfortable in her apartment. She reminded herself not to get used to it.

She took the glass he offered her upon his return and had a long swallow. Then she pulled her legs out from under her and swung her feet up onto the couch. He sat back in his corner and drank from his own glass before putting it down on the coffee table.

"So what now?" he asked. "I mean, with Ross?"

She sighed. "I don't know. I think the ball's in his court. We're going to have to work together, either way." She updated him regarding the gala and their ongoing collaboration.

"Maybe he just needs some time to adjust."

"Maybe." But she knew what Laura had written in her diary. The part she hadn't shared—that Ross wasn't sure he ever wanted kids. True, he'd been a teenager when he said that. And it wasn't like she was a kid anymore. She rotated her ankles and arched her back. It felt like every stress of the day had lodged itself in her muscles. In muscles she hadn't even known she had.

"And what about Scott? Have you told him what's going on?"

She shook her head. "Maren basically told me to leave him out of it."

Surprise crossed his face. "Really?"

"Yeah. She was really talking about the situation with Carol and the will—but she made it pretty clear that he doesn't want to deal with my problems right now. Or can't deal with them. And I get it. He's grieving and can't be expected to take care of me all the time." The words stung as she said them.

Josh picked up one of her feet and gently began to rub it, seemingly absentmindedly. "That doesn't sound right. I don't think he'd want you to shut him out."

She was distracted by the foot massage. *Is this weird?* She looked at him, but he appeared lost in thought, gazing at the opposite wall, so she pulled herself back to the conversation. "Well, that's what Maren said. And I know I haven't exactly been easy."

"Stop being so hard on yourself, E. You've been through a lot." He paused his foot rub. "And when it comes to your relationships with people, you have to decide for yourself what's right. If you want to talk to Scott, talk to him. Let him tell you to leave him out of it, if that's what he wants."

"I guess." But even as she said it, she doubted she'd be calling Scott anytime soon. Other than his birthday, the last time they'd spoken he'd stood up and left the dining room table to get away from the conversation. Josh's thumbs felt good on the instep of her foot, and her eyes fluttered closed. She was just so tired, and she could probably just put her head back and fall asleep. As her mind floated, she wondered what his touch would feel like if it moved up her calf, to that sensitive spot behind her knee, and then . . . Her eyes popped open and she pulled her foot away from him, feeling a blush rising up her face. "That tickles!"

"Oh, sorry. Didn't mean to." Josh shifted back into the far corner of the sofa.

Didn't mean to. Exactly. As she'd suspected.

"It's fine. No worries." She folded her legs beneath her again. "I really appreciate you coming over. It's good to have someone to talk to." Her voice sounded stiff and formal.

He looked at her for a long moment. "Of course. Anytime."

CHAPTER THIRTY

Firm hands massaged Eliza's scalp, and she had to suppress a moan. Maybe this hadn't been such a bad idea of Mo's after all.

She'd filled her friend in on the latest, and soon thereafter Mo sent her two messages. The first invited her out to dinner with Nik and some other friends (I'm not taking no for an answer), and the second was a gift certificate for a blowout at a posh salon.

Eliza immediately called her. "You do realize that asking someone to blow out my hair is cruel and unusual punishment," she said as soon as Mo picked up the phone. "They'll all be fighting *not* to do my hair."

"Please. Just think of the satisfaction they'll have turning it into glossy golden sheets! You'll look like a shampoo commercial. And the package includes an extra head massage. Who couldn't use an extra head massage now and then?"

So now she sat in an unusually comfortable shampoo chair, her head in the sink, while someone she'd never met before today lathered her thick hair and made her feel better than she had in weeks.

Too soon, she had a towel wrapped around her head and

was being escorted to one of the paisley-printed swivel chairs lined up in front of a mirrored wall.

"I'm Daniela," said the technician who was waiting for her. Daniela's own jet black hair was swept up in a tight ballerina bun, and her makeup looked like it had been done by a professional artist. She unwound the towel from Eliza's head. "Oh my. You have a lot of hair, girl!"

Eliza caught Daniela's eyes in the mirror. "Sorry about that."

"Oh, no apologies necessary! I love a good head of hair. I'd have nearly as much as you if I took mine down." She pointed at her bun. "And it's a lot easier to blow dry someone else's than your own, let me tell you."

"I'm sure. I usually just let mine air dry."

Daniela spritzed something on her head—"detangler"—and used a wide-tooth comb. Even this felt like pampering. "So, are you getting ready for something special?"

Eliza spoke from behind her closed eyes. "Not really. My friend gave me a gift card. She was trying to cheer me up."

"And what do you need to be cheered up from?"

"My dad passed away earlier this fall." That was certainly the easiest response.

"Oh, I'm so sorry. He must have been young. How's your mom doing?"

Eliza opened her eyes. "She actually died ten years ago, when I was a teenager."

The combing stopped, and Daniela put her hands on Eliza's shoulders, looking at her in the mirror. "You poor girl! No wonder you need pampering."

Eliza gave her a half smile. "And you don't know the half of it."

"No?" Daniela put her comb down on the little rolling stand beside her and picked up what looked like clothespins, expertly winding the top layers of Eliza's hair out of the way.

Why not share? She'd never see this woman again. "I found out on the day of my dad's funeral that my mom slept with her high school boyfriend at their reunion, and that guy is actually my father."

Daniela's eyes widened, and Eliza continued.

"*And* my stepmother is challenging the will since my dad wasn't my biological father."

"Are you serious?" Daniela's face was the picture of indignance.

"Unfortunately, yes."

"I'm amazed you're even here. I'd be at the bar myself. Tequila, and keep it coming." Daniela turned on her blow-dryer and got to work.

Eliza closed her eyes again. Despite the murmur of voices throughout the salon, it felt like they were in a cozy cocoon. "And I found my real dad. He's here in the city."

"Oh my God!"

"Yeah, and he doesn't want anything to do with me."

"Why would you say that? Is he married? Was he cheating on his wife with your mom?"

Eliza started to shake her head before realizing that Daniela's ministrations made the movement impossible. "Nope," she said instead, and then found herself sharing the other details she knew—Laura's letter to her and the revelations in the diary—along with the part about having to work with Ross.

"Were you and your dad close? I mean, the dad you grew up with?"

"Not really. I was super close with my mom, so when he got remarried . . . it was really hard."

"And now you're probably rethinking how you saw your mom," Daniela said matter-of-factly as she readjusted the pins in Eliza's hair.

Am I? "You mean because she cheated?"

"Well, that, but also the way she told you about it. And when. I mean, your dad just died, and instead of being able to focus on grieving him, you've got this other mess. I'd be mad, but maybe that's just me. I tend to shoot first, ask questions later."

Daniela laughed, but Eliza bit her lip. She hadn't thought about it that way. It actually was a pretty shitty thing for Laura to do. Her instructions to Aunt Claude guaranteed that Eliza would get this letter immediately after Jack's death.

She allowed her head to be moved from side to side as Daniela pulled the round brush through her hair. She always drew back from the fire whenever her fingertips got close to the idea that Laura wasn't perfect. That she could have done something wrong. Or hurtful. It had always been easier to direct all her anger at Jack and imagine how much better life would be if Laura were alive. But maybe that wasn't doing her any favors.

Daniela changed the subject to chat about Eliza's hair— Had it always been long? What products did she use? She'd swiveled the chair as she worked, but when she'd turned off the dryer and run a final comb through, she turned Eliza back to face the mirror. "Ta-da! What do you think?"

Eliza barely recognized herself. Her hair, which was always in a bun or a braid, hung around her like curtains of golden silk. She reached up to touch it, hardly believing it was the same stuff that had been attached to her head that morning.

"You look gorgeous, girl! I mean, you already looked gorgeous when you came in, but you're a knockout!" Daniela's grin in the mirror was wide.

"Wow. I didn't know my hair could be this smooth."

"Or this pretty, right?"

Eliza shook her head slowly. She might have become a blow-dry convert. The therapy was just the side benefit.

* * *

The restaurant Mo had selected was Mediterranean, with rustic decor. Rough-hewn stone walls gave the space a cave-like feel, and canvases displaying scenes of turquoise water, white-washed buildings, and window boxes overflowing with bougainvillea were hung strategically throughout. Eliza told the hostess that she was there for the Mohini Bansal party and was led toward the back.

As soon as she saw Mo and Nik, she wanted to turn back around. She'd been anticipating a group, but they were seated at a table for four, along with a dark-haired man she could see only from the back. She couldn't believe Mo would set her up without warning. But before she could flee, Mo spotted her and jumped up from her seat.

"Oh my gosh! You look gorgeous! I see you already got the blowout!"

Eliza returned Mo's hug, her annoyance slightly abated by the compliment. She'd resisted the urge to tie her hair back, figuring Daniela's hard work deserved to be shown off. The hair had also deserved a nice outfit, so she was wearing a cream silk tank and a short navy skirt with tights and tall boots. As she took her coat off, she realized that it would appear she'd dressed up for this man she hadn't actually known was coming.

Nik reached across the cluster of water glasses on the table to shake her hand. "Nice seeing you again, Eliza. This is my friend Griffin."

Griffin smiled at her. "Nice to meet you." He was cute, with dark curly hair and blue eyes that were nicely set off by the blue in his plaid shirt.

"Likewise. Sorry—I just need to run to the ladies' for a minute." She looked pointedly at Mo, who had just started to sit down again.

Mo popped back up. "I'll join you."

It turned out that the ladies' room was a single, but Eliza

pulled her friend inside with her anyway and slid the latch shut.

Mo backed up against the small sink. "Are you going to kill me?"

"I might."

"Seriously, I wasn't planning a setup. This other couple that Nik is friends with were supposed to come, but she got food poisoning. And Heather and Kaity from work bailed at the last minute."

Eliza crossed her arms and stared at her.

"Really! I swear!" Mo made a crisscross in front of her heart. "Anyway, you're here now, and we can just have a nice time. I'm sure you can use a distraction from everything that's going on. And why should you waste that fabulous blowout?"

She could never stay mad at Mo for long. "Fine. Get out. I really do need to pee."

"As long as you promise you won't sneak out the back door."

"I left my coat at the table, so no chance of that. Poor planning on my part."

"Ha ha."

After Mo left, she blinked at herself in the mirror. Her lipstick could use a touch-up, but she didn't want to give Mo anything to gloat about.

The bottom line was, while she would have appreciated a heads-up, it was likely she would have bailed if she'd had one. And maybe this was exactly what she needed. She wasn't missing Carter, but what was wrong with a little male companionship? And maybe Griffin could take her mind off Josh. Any fantasies her heart might have begun to spin about *him*, in violation of her better judgment, were a waste of time.

So, soon she was sitting at the table and letting Nik pour her a glass of wine.

Griffin turned to her. "You're a college friend of Mo's?"

She nodded, putting down her glass. "Guilty as charged. How about you? How do you know each other?" She gestured between Griffin and Nik.

"We actually went to high school together in New Jersey."

"Cool."

Over shared hummus and tzatziki with pita, the four talked about work and food and Mo's obsession with *Stranger Things*.

Griffin passed Eliza the shared side of lemon potatoes. "What's everyone doing for Thanksgiving?" he asked.

Eliza glanced at Mo and Nik, wondering if this was potentially awkward, given how new they were.

"Not sure yet," Mo said. "My parents want me to come down to Maryland, but it's such a terrible time of year to travel."

Nik nodded. "My family is in California. Definitely not flying out there."

In other words, Mo is thinking she'd like to spend the holiday with Nik, but isn't sure about bringing him home to meet the parents.

Eliza passed the potatoes along to Mo. "I'll probably go to my aunt's."

"Scott and Maren, too?" Mo asked.

She shook her head. "No, they're going to Maren's family in Vermont. But they're having a Friendsgiving that Tuesday night, so we'll still have a meal together."

"That's good." Mo turned to Griffin. "Scott's Eliza's brother. They just lost their dad."

"I'm so sorry to hear that." The standard look of sympathy came across Griffin's face, and Eliza realized how much she'd been enjoying the brief respite from anything related to Jack's death and the fallout it engendered.

"Thanks." Eliza took another swallow of wine, draining her glass.

"How's everything with you and Scott?" Mo asked then.

Why does she think I'd want to talk about this in front of someone I've just met? She shrugged. "Dunno," she said, realizing she sounded a bit like a belligerent teenager, before putting a forkful of grilled chicken into her mouth.

Griffin picked up the wine bottle. "Looks like we're empty. Should we order another?"

A while later, they'd drained their second bottle of wine and shared two portions of baklava. When the check came, Nik and Griffin insisted on splitting it, making Eliza feel extremely awkward—though the wine was helping dull some of her discomfort.

As they put on their coats and made their way to the exit, Mo whispered in her ear. "So what do you think? Nice guy, right?"

Eliza concentrated on not stumbling in her high-heeled boots. "I guess."

She was surprised Griffin wasn't more of a draw. Nice-looking, well spoken, employed—he could be a good diversion. But then they were out on the sidewalk, all together again.

"This was fun," Nik said. "We should do this again."

"Definitely." Griffin aimed a warm smile toward Eliza, and she tried to enjoy returning it.

Mo put her hand on Nik's arm. "We're gonna head home, but if you guys want to go for another drink or something . . . ?"

Could Mo be any more obvious if she tried?

Eliza squeezed her friend's free arm. "I totally would, but it's been a really long week, and my bed is calling."

Griffin laughed. "I totally get that. Sometimes I don't even go out on Friday nights anymore. It's just too hard. I need Friday night to recover so I have the energy to go out on Saturday. But which way are you going?"

"Uptown. Upper East."

"Oh, too bad. I'm in Hell's Kitchen. I would have suggested we share a cab."

Eliza noticed that Mo and Nik had started to—unsubtly—move away from them.

"Are you guys leaving without saying good night?" she called out.

"No, no, no!"

And there was some hugging and cheek-kissing, and Eliza managed to scoot away without Griffin asking for her number. Partly because she wasn't sure she wanted to give it, and partly because there was a chance that, if he did suggest they share a cab after all, she might have said yes.

CHAPTER THIRTY-ONE

Life at NOY was more hectic than ever. The countdown to the gala had begun, and with the late change to the program, it was all hands on deck. Board members were in and out of the office—which was a mixed blessing. Organizing RSVPs and making an initial pass at table arrangements were helpful; proposing menu changes—or just gossiping over coffee—was not.

Eliza was in the midst of following up with the vendors and sponsors who were contributing to the swag bags when yet another email notification popped up on her screen. She wished she could be one of those people who turned off notifications to avoid distraction, but she lived in fear of missing something important. She clicked over to her email.

It was from Ross.

Dear Eliza:

I've been thinking a lot since our conversation. Truthfully, I've been thinking of nothing else, which has made me useless as fuck to my students.

When can we meet? I'm free this evening if that
works for you.

—Ross

"When can we meet?" Not *Can we meet?* Or *I'd like to
meet.* But *when.* She started to compose a response but then
abruptly pushed her chair away from her desk. Why should
she jump just because he asked her to?

She took herself to the staff kitchen to make a cup of tea.
She couldn't decide if she was surprised to hear from him
or not. She'd tried not to have any expectations, given his
reaction—and even did her best to convince herself that if they
never spoke of the situation again, it might be for the best.

Why did it matter that he'd been biologically necessary to
her existence? In the grand scheme of things, did that have any
real relevance? She'd said as much to Aunt Claude when she'd
called her.

"Only you can answer that, love," Claude had replied.

"I mean, Dad's gone now—and you know how rocky things
were with us, anyway. I know it's ridiculous to have some kind
of fantasy that Ross will be a new 'dad' to me. He's a complete
stranger."

Her aunt's voice was gentle. "Your head can know something that your heart doesn't, though."

"I suppose. And I guess . . . there's just so much mystery
about all of this. It's hard not to want to know more about,
well, about how I came to be. Who I am."

"Who you are is Eliza Levinger. The person you've always
been." Aunt Claude paused. "The word 'mystery' is interesting,
though. Is this about Ross? Or is it about your mom and who
she really was?"

Maybe Aunt Claude was right. The letter had enabled
Laura to speak to Eliza again, ten years after her death. Despite

the havoc it had wreaked, on some level, it was a gift. And now Ross was potentially another one—someone who had known Laura, intimately. Who could tell Eliza new stories. Give her new insights.

She strolled back to her office, her mug of tea in hand. *Might as well get this over with.*

Dear Ross:

Tonight works. Midtown is best for me.

—Eliza

His response was almost immediate, proposing a bar near Grand Central Station. Apparently, this was a conversation requiring alcoholic lubrication.

Ross's venue of choice was surprisingly kitschy. It was library-themed, with book-lined walls and pen-and-ink drawings. When Eliza arrived, he was already seated at a high-top table for two. In front of him were an iPad in a sleek leather case, a glass of water, and a scotch on the rocks. He looked up as Eliza approached.

She put her handbag on the table. "Hey," she said, unwinding the scarf from around her neck.

"Hey."

After draping her coat and scarf on the back of the empty chair, she sat, extremely conscious of her posture and not sure what to do with her hands. A server, clad all in black, appeared before either of them could say anything else.

"Can I get you something?" she asked, cheerfully oblivious to the cloud of awkwardness.

Eliza glanced at Ross's drink. For some reason, she wanted to match his liquor level, but given the circumstances, she decided it was a bad idea. "Just a glass of chardonnay."

"I'll have another scotch rocks," said Ross.

"Gotcha."

The server made quick work of the drinks and soon returned with them. Ross lifted his in a toast, and Eliza clinked glasses, despite not knowing what they were toasting. Fatherhood? Family reunions?

He took a sip of his scotch and placed it back on the table, running the tip of his finger through the condensation on the surface. "First things first. I owe you an apology," he said, lifting his eyes to her. "I shouldn't have bitten your head off. But I was truly shocked. The idea that I'm your father . . . I still can't wrap my head around it."

Eliza realized her jaw was clenched, and she tried to release it. "Me, neither."

His mouth curved into a small smile. "Well, there's something we have in common."

"My mom said we have the same eyes." *Ugh.* She hadn't meant to share something that personal so soon. But maybe on some level she was hoping he'd do the same?

He peered at her. "Maybe we do. I've never been good at seeing resemblances. Laura used to say I might as well have face blindness—that thing where you can't remember what people look like—but that was just because I didn't pay much attention to putting names to faces."

Of course, Laura had had plenty of conversations Eliza wasn't privy to, and a whole life before her birth, but she couldn't get over how strange it was to hear this man talking about her. Especially with the degree of intimacy his tone suggested. It wasn't the words, she realized, but the softness in his eyes as he spoke of her.

He swirled the ice in his glass, watching it as if mesmerized. "So Laura really never mentioned me?" he asked, without looking at her.

Eliza paused before answering, truly trying to reach

into the recesses of her memory. Maybe there was a drawer, jammed shut, that she could pry open? But she could recall nothing Laura had ever said about her romantic life before Jack. Maybe, had she lived to see her daughter start dating, she would have shared some nuggets—but given the secret of Eliza's parentage, she probably would have trod very carefully. Eliza shook her head. "Not that I can remember."

He looked up from the vortex in his glass. "Did they have a good marriage? Laura and Jack?"

Her eyebrows drew together. That was not a question she was expecting. "What does that have to do with anything?"

"Really? I would think it would be obvious."

"Because she cheated?" She tried to keep the annoyance out of her voice. "Look, I don't know anything about that. At all. And the last two years they had together, she was dying. Before that, I was in middle school. What could I know about their marriage?"

He snorted. "I think kids know a lot more than we give them credit for."

"Is that what you wanted to talk about? My parents' relationship?"

Ross sighed. "I don't know. I'm at a bit of a loss."

"You're the one who reached out to me," she reminded him. This time the sharpness in her tone was evident.

He took another sip of scotch, as if to fortify himself. "You're right. Okay. Look, this isn't easy for me. Your mom . . ." He paused, looking at the ceiling for a moment. "She was the one who got away."

"But *you* broke up with *her*!"

His eyes narrowed. "You said she didn't talk about me!"

When would she learn to think before speaking? "She had a diary. My aunt Claude just found it recently." She hurried on as he opened his mouth. "She didn't write in it much. But she *did* say that. You dumped her."

"And she's right. I did. Because I was young and stupid. We were long-distance. I felt like I was missing out on things. I believe they call it 'sowing one's oats.' And Laura was so sure about what she wanted. Husband, family, white picket fence. That wasn't me. At least, it wasn't me then. Probably isn't me now, to be fair. I wanted to travel the world. Lead protests. Set things on fire. Figuratively speaking, I mean." He smiled at her, but Eliza didn't smile back.

He continued. "Anyway, when I saw her at the reunion, it was like no time had passed. I knew she was married and had a kid—but she was the same girl. Woman. Just more beautiful. More sure of herself. Less likely to put up with my shit.

"She didn't say much about Jack, but it sounded like things weren't great. And, well, we ended up in my hotel room. Funny, because I wasn't even going to book one. I thought I'd just drive back to the city after the party, but at the last minute I figured I might as well spend the night. I wonder if we hadn't already had a room—if we'd have had to stop and check in somewhere . . ."

Eliza wondered, too. She tried to picture the scene. Laura at twenty-eight, with a toddler at home, deciding to go to her ex-boyfriend's hotel room. It didn't feel real. And yet it was. Here she sat, living proof.

Ross took another sip, the ice clinking in his glass. "I thought it might be the start of something. But Laura was clear, she wasn't leaving Jack." He looked at Eliza. "She didn't tell me she was pregnant. I heard through the grapevine that she'd had another kid. You." *As if that clarification was necessary.* "I'll be honest. I was crushed. But it was my own fault. I knew that. I got married myself not long after. In retrospect, probably for all the wrong reasons—knowing that Laura was lost to me for good. It didn't last. Partly because I didn't want kids."

Eliza raised her eyebrows. *So nothing's changed.*

"I'd always been pretty anti kid. For all the 'save the world' reasons—overpopulation, blah, blah, blah. But I think I also knew Hannah—my ex—and I weren't cut out for the long haul."

The server appeared at the table, startling them both. "Can I get y'all anything else?" She picked up Ross's two empty glasses and put them on her tray. Eliza still had a swallow of wine left in hers.

"I think we're fine," Ross said, glancing at Eliza, who nodded.

"All righty, then. Wave at me if you change your minds."

Ross cleared his throat after she'd walked away. "So," he said.

"So," Eliza echoed.

"I wanted to meet today to tell you where I'm coming from. Why I reacted the way I did."

She searched his face, looking for some clue as to what was coming next. Somehow, she had the sense that it wouldn't be good. But what would *good* be anyway?

"The thing is—I don't know what you want from me. If anything. But I do feel pretty confident that I can't give it. To be fair, I haven't ever been very good at giving women what they want. And to be honest, I'm not in a good place with all of this. I know it's not your fault, but the idea that Laura didn't tell me that I'm a father . . . ? It's not sitting well with me. I'm gonna need some time to . . ."

Eliza cut him off. When had this become the Ross Sawyer show? As far as she could tell, she was the only one here who had done nothing wrong. Unless being born was a crime. "Look. I'm not asking you for anything. I thought you deserved to know. And, of course, I was curious about you. But that's it." She wished that what she was saying were true. After all, she had no parents left. On some level, hadn't she hoped Ross would embrace her? Be happy to learn of her existence? That they'd build a relationship? Of course it wouldn't happen overnight, but given that they had both loved Laura, couldn't that be a bond?

She stood abruptly. She wasn't going to let him control this any longer.

"Eliza, wait. I'm not saying . . ."

She interrupted again. "I'm sorry. But I just lost my dad. Life for me is pretty shitty right now. I'm not going to listen to your problems on top of that. *You* decided to bang a married woman. That had nothing to do with me." *Of course, that married woman was equally responsible,* a voice whispered in her head. The same woman who decided to keep this huge secret—and reveal it at perhaps the worst possible time. Eliza had tried so hard to keep the door closed and locked on her anger at Laura, but it was in danger of being broken down. If she spent any more time with Ross, it was likely all her efforts would come to naught. "I know we're going to have to deal with each other because of the gala and the award, but don't feel you owe me anything else. You don't."

She swung her handbag off the back of the chair so fast that it collided with the wineglass on the table, knocking it to the floor, where it splintered into dozens of pieces. Ignoring it, she headed for the door so she'd be outside before she started to cry.

CHAPTER THIRTY-TWO

The first day Josh didn't show up to drive her home from school, Eliza didn't think much of it. She figured he'd forgotten to mention having a conflict, or maybe he had to stay late at school.

The next day, she was mildly annoyed. She'd come to count on the rides—and, even more so, the conversation.

The third day, she was mad. But underneath the anger, she was hurt. Did their daily visits not mean anything to him? How could he not have the decency to at least tell her their routine was no more?

Even worse, the rides had stopped very soon after Laura and Jack announced that Laura was no longer seeking treatment. That there were no other options.

None of Scott's friends were coming around at that point, so other than glimpses in the halls at school, Josh had disappeared completely. And then Laura died, and she saw him at the funeral with his parents and some other friends of Scott's and their families. When they came for shiva, he gave her an awkward hello at some point before Eliza disappeared upstairs, refusing to come down again.

When Eliza thought back on it, she still felt some of the same hurt. Whatever was in Josh's head, for Eliza, it was rejection, pure and simple. And Josh hadn't even had the decency to discuss it with her. (Even Berger on *Sex and the City* left Carrie a Post-it note.) The experience certainly hadn't done anything to dissuade her from her growing belief that no one could be counted on to stick around.

She couldn't help reflecting on this as she rode the elevator up to Scott and Maren's for their Friendsgiving celebration, just a day after her sit-down with Ross. She'd gone straight home afterward and reread everything Laura had written about him in her diary. It was like mourning someone she never really had in her life. It shouldn't have been that painful. But it was, excruciatingly so.

Before leaving work a half hour earlier, she'd gone to the bathroom with her full makeup kit. To explain the puffiness around her eyes that remained after hours of crying, she'd told her colleagues that she had had a reaction to a new face cream. She could still see evidence of it even now, but figured that, with a new spackling on of foundation, eyeliner, and eyeshadow, no one would notice.

When Scott opened the apartment door, she immediately handed him the chocolate ganache cake from Zabar's. "Dessert, as instructed," she said.

"Excellent choice. Come in." Scott stepped back to allow her to enter and then gave her his usual half hug.

"So who else is coming?" she asked as she took off her coat to hang on the hooks near the front door.

"Let's see. Our neighbors Thad and Jeremy, Maren's friend Olivia and her fiancé, Luke, her other friend Rhiannon, and, of course, Josh."

So I guess Rhiannon is the potential setup for Josh? Maybe she should have invited Griffin from the other night. They could have a whole fake-dating trope going on.

Apparently, she was the last to arrive. Everyone was perched on the couch and chairs in the living room with glasses of wine or bottles of beer, chatting. The only one not sitting was Maren, who had just set down a platter of nibbles. "Please eat!" she said before turning to Eliza to give her a hug. Eliza pretended to be happy to see her. They'd always gotten along fine, and she knew Maren was only looking out for Scott, but she still felt a pulse of anger at the sight of her.

"Everyone," Maren said then, "this is Scott's sister, Eliza." She pointed to everyone in turn to introduce them. Eliza noted that Rhiannon, who wore glasses and a sweet smile, was sitting nowhere near Josh.

Josh slid over on the couch. "E, come sit."

She squeezed in beside him, and he bumped his shoulder against hers. "How's it going? You look . . . tired?"

So much for the magic of makeup. "Yeah, stuff's been really busy at work."

Olivia, who was sitting nearest to her in an adjacent armchair, leaned toward her. "So, Eliza, what do you do?"

"I work for a nonprofit that focuses on education for disadvantaged students."

"Oh wow, how wonderful. That's a much better answer than mine." She laughed.

"What's yours?"

"I do marketing for a pharmaceutical company. I get to write all that small print. *May cause headaches, brain tumor, uncontrollable bleeding, and death.*"

Eliza laughed. "I'm sure there's more to it than that."

Olivia shrugged. "Maybe a little."

The conversation ebbed and flowed around work, Thanksgiving plans, and what everyone had been streaming lately on Netflix. Then, during a pause, the man who'd been introduced as Thad suddenly exclaimed, "Oh! How could I have forgotten to ask you, Eliza—have you learned more about your biological father?"

All eyes turned to her, and she felt her face go hot. No mystery as to whether Thad had been at the infamous shiva. But before she could even begin to get her brain on board with answering, Thad's partner, Jeremy, smacked him. "Jesus, Thad!" Then Jeremy turned to Eliza. "Please ignore him. He was raised by wolves."

"Hey!" Thad objected. "I thought you *liked* my mother."

The group laughed, but Eliza noticed Maren's eyes on Scott, and Scott's eyes on her. While everyone was engrossed in Thad and Jeremy's clearly frequently repeated story about the first time Jeremy met Thad's parents, Josh murmured to her, "How *are* things going with Ross?"

"Yeah, not good. But I can't talk about it here." She anxiously glanced at Scott and Maren, but they weren't looking their way.

"I'm so sorry, E. Is that why you look so wiped?"

She raised her eyebrows. "Not sure how I should feel about you constantly telling me how terrible I look."

He shook his head. "You never look terrible. But seriously, you can call me anytime."

She nodded. But it was not her MO to trust that kind of statement.

Across the room, Maren stood. "Is everyone ready for dinner?"

There was a chorus of affirmative responses, and they all made their way to the dining table to find seats. Eliza and Olivia helped Maren bring in the food—turkey, of course, and a raft of sides: stuffing, green beans, sweet potatoes, some sort of corn casserole, brussels sprouts, and bread rolls—while Scott and Josh refreshed drinks.

Maren had just sat down—after Rhiannon and Olivia

yelled at her to stop fussing—when she smacked herself in the forehead. "Oh my gosh. I totally forgot the salad."

Eliza stood. "I'll get it." She couldn't imagine where on the table it would fit, but whatever.

"Thanks, Eliza. It's in the fridge."

She made her way around the table and toward the kitchen door. As she approached, she could hear Josh and Scott talking. As she reached the doorway, Scott was just pulling his phone out of his pocket. "I'm sending you Shira's contact information right now."

Before Josh could respond, he saw Eliza, and what she read as a guilty expression crossed his face.

"Don't mind me," she said, heading straight for the fridge. "Just here to get the salad." She easily found the large serving bowl covered with cling wrap and placed it on the counter. "Scott, do you know where the tongs are?"

Her brother found them in a drawer. "I'll bring them in, with these." He held up two bottles of wine.

She was dropping the cling wrap in the trash when Josh touched her shoulder. "E—I know this isn't the place or time to talk, but why don't we get together?"

"Oh, no need for that. It's a crazy time for everyone." And she picked up the salad and left the kitchen.

During dinner, she was seated between Rhiannon and Luke, and she and Rhiannon ended up in a long conversation about travel and all the places on their bucket lists that they wanted to visit. Josh kept glancing over at her, but she kept her eyes on Rhiannon, or on her own plate. She was also distracted by Scott, who was constantly looking at his phone. Maybe there were other women whose contact information Josh needed.

Finally, Scott stood and went over to Maren at the opposite end of the table. Eliza strained to hear without being obvious in her eavesdropping.

"Carol keeps calling me. I'd better call her back, just in case it's an emergency. I'll be right back."

Eliza's stomach sank, turning her meal into stone, and she put down her fork. Vicky had told her that Carol would be receiving notice of the order to show cause very soon. Perhaps even before the holiday. Eliza began to suspect—more than suspect—that it had landed.

She took a large swig from her wineglass and looked around the table. Thad would probably enjoy the fireworks that might ensue upon Scott's return. Unless, maybe, there was another reason for the call. Perhaps she just urgently wanted to wish him a happy Thanksgiving two days early. Or maybe she'd had an accident and was in the hospital. Or . . .

It was a while before Scott came back, and Maren took the opportunity to start clearing the table, with everyone's help. "Who wants coffee?" she asked, counting the hands that were going up.

"Do you have tea?" Josh asked.

"Sure—do you want to see what kind?"

"It's for Eliza."

Maren's eyebrows drew together, and she glanced between them.

Eliza stood. "I can fix my own. No worries, Maren. Not sure I even want any." She added that last remark simply to be contrary. Why did Josh think he knew what she wanted? She picked up her plate and brought it to the kitchen sink to rinse it before putting it in the dishwasher. Then she found the tea bags and used the fancy hot-water dispenser in the fridge. Why cut off her nose to spite her face—or, rather, cut off her tea bag to spite her palate?

She had just sat back down when Rhiannon came to the table with the cake Eliza had brought. "Oh my God, this is the absolute best!" she exclaimed. She set it down beside the pumpkin pie, and Jeremy followed with the apple pie in one hand and a handful of forks in the other.

"So much for my diet," Thad moaned. "I'll take a slab of each, please."

There was a clatter of coffee cups and dessert plates as everyone descended on the sweets as if they hadn't already stuffed themselves with dinner.

Olivia slid the server under the apple pie she was slicing. "Eliza?" she offered.

"No thanks. I actually have this weird aversion to baked apples."

"It's true. It's one of my sister's many eccentricities," Scott quipped, returning to the table. Eliza glanced at him to try to read his expression, but his face was closed. He did, however, appear to be avoiding her gaze.

The chatter over dessert was more subdued. Everyone was in a bit of a food coma. Eliza, however, was on edge, wondering about Scott's call with Carol. She was finding it hard to concentrate on Luke and Olivia talking about their honeymoon plans. As soon as they paused, she pushed herself back from the table.

"I don't want to break up the party, but I have an early start tomorrow. I'm going to head out," she said, standing up.

Scott looked directly at her for the first time since his phone call. "Actually, I need to talk to you about something. Can you wait?"

Maren's eyes bounced between them like Ping-Pong balls.

"I guess." She looked at her watch. "It *is* late, though."

Apparently reading the rising tension level in the room, Olivia and Luke rose. "We should head out, too. Thank you so much for dinner. It was amazing."

And then everyone else was getting up, rubbing over-stuffed bellies, and hugging Maren and Scott. Eliza brought her now-empty mug to the sink and eyed the half-full wine bottles. *Probably not the best idea to switch back.*

Josh sidled up to her at the sink. "Are you hiding out?" he asked.

She looked around. "I don't think I can fit into one of the cabinets."

"Do you know what Scott wants to talk to you about?"

She swallowed. "I have a bad feeling it's about Carol and my legal action."

"Do you want me to stay?"

The truth was, she did. But as she pictured the last time Josh had been in the kitchen, when Scott had given him Shira's number, she knew that it was precisely because she wanted him to stay that she needed him to leave.

"No. You should go."

He touched her arm. "Are you sure?"

She hated how right his fingertips felt on her skin, and she pulled back. "Yeah. Don't worry about me."

Josh flinched at the clipped sound of her tone. "Okay. Got it," he said, his hands raised in apology.

As he backed up a step, Eliza saw Scott in the doorway over his shoulder. "Everything okay in here?" he asked.

"All good," she said, hating the pang she felt as she turned away from Josh. "What do you want to talk about?"

CHAPTER THIRTY-THREE

Sitting in an armchair in the living room, opposite Scott and Maren side by side on the couch, Eliza almost wished she hadn't kicked Josh out. But she knew relying on him wasn't a good idea either. Maren was biting her lip, twisting her hands together. *What is* she *so anxious about?*

Scott leaned forward. "This really takes the cake, Eliza. You took legal action against Carol without telling me?"

Eliza glanced at Maren. What was she supposed to do now? Tell Scott she was just obeying his wife's instructions? "I . . . I didn't want to bother you." *How lame did* that *sound?*

He looked it her incredulously. "You're kidding me, right? You didn't want to *bother* me?"

"Well, I know it's not what you wanted me to do . . . the last time we talked . . ." She trailed off. Her eyes darted to Maren. Was she just going to let her dangle here?

Scott ran his hand across his face. "Jesus, Eliza. I'm still your brother. You should have told me. If for no other reason than that I'm a beneficiary, too. Not to mention, it would have been nice for me to know the facts when Carol called me screaming."

Eliza felt anger rising. "She called *you* screaming? First of all, she should have called me. I'm the one who filed the order. Second of all—what right does she have to be mad? She's the one who started this fight. What did she think, I was just going to roll over and play dead?"

"Come on, you had to know this was going to explode. It's so like you, to just act and not think about the fallout."

"Hey, that's not fair. The only reason I didn't come to you first . . ." She stopped abruptly.

Scott raised his eyebrows. "The only reason was . . . ?"

Maren took a deep breath. "It was because of me."

He turned to gaze at his wife. "What are you talking about?"

"I told Eliza that she needed to handle this on her own." Eliza watched the emotions crossing Scott's face as Maren spoke. "You've been having a hard time. I didn't want you to feel like you had to manage this whole situation." Maren's eyes shone with tears. "I guess maybe I made it worse."

Scott looked back and forth between the two women, seeming utterly flabbergasted. "I don't even know what to say. To either one of you." He stood. "I need a drink."

Maren put her head in her hands after he left for the kitchen. "I was just trying to help," she said, without looking up.

Eliza almost felt sorry for her. *Almost.* "I'll go talk to him."

Scott stared out the kitchen window into the darkness, drinking his beer.

"Beer after liquor, never been sicker?" Eliza said from behind him, just able to make out his reflection in the glass.

He snorted. "Is that what they say? Well, I just had wine before, so maybe I'm okay."

She paused, recalling Aunt Claude describing Scott as the peacemaker. Had they swapped roles when she wasn't paying attention? "I don't think Maren was entirely wrong," she offered.

"Oh yeah? What do you mean?" he asked, still facing away from her.

"I had to figure it all out on my own. And I managed it. Well, I'm still in the middle of it, but still, I'm managing. I don't think I've been a total fuckup."

He sighed. "Why would you be a total fuckup, Eliza?"

"Isn't that what I usually am? Look what happened to me when Mom died. I totally fell apart."

He swiveled his head to look at her. "And then you put yourself back together again. You don't give yourself enough credit."

Now she snorted. "Yeah, well, just five minutes ago you said that I act and don't think about the fallout. Hardly an endorsement of my ability to handle things."

He sighed. "You're emotional. It's just how you are. That's all I meant. And I was hurt. Hurt you didn't talk to me. I didn't know what Maren had told you."

"We're quite the pair, aren't we?"

He turned and shrugged. "Yeah, but we're all we have left."

She felt a lump rise in her throat and tears burning her eyes. "That's not true. You have Maren."

He shoved his hands into his pockets. "You could have someone, too. You never let anyone get close to you."

"Yeah, well, I haven't had the best luck counting on people."

He tilted his head as he looked at her. "Maybe that's because you go out of your way to date bozos."

She shoved him. "Hey—they're not all that bad."

"How would I know? You almost never introduce me to any of them."

Eliza suddenly felt exhausted. She slid onto the floor and wrapped her arms around her knees. Scott sat, too, his legs extended in front of him. He nudged her with his foot. "By the way, what was happening with you and Josh?"

Her pulse fluttered. "What are you talking about?"

"When I came into the kitchen before. Something was going on with you guys."

She shook her head and hoped she looked convincing. "He was just offering to stick around. Like we're friends or something."

He cocked his head. "Why do you sound so pissed off?"

"Do I? I don't know. He hasn't exactly been the most reliable person, in my experience."

Scott extended the beer bottle toward her. "Want some?"

"Why?" she asked suspiciously.

"Just thought you might want a drink."

She narrowed her eyes at him. "You encouraging me to drink isn't exactly normal behavior."

He sighed. "Yeah, well. I need to tell you something."

Her stomach dropped. What was it lately with people needing to reveal their secrets? She waited, trying to slow her breathing and reminding herself that whatever he was about to tell her couldn't possibly be as dramatic as her father not being her father.

Scott kept his eyes trained on the beer bottle, avoiding her gaze. "Back in high school. I told Josh to leave you alone."

She didn't know what she'd been expecting, but didn't think that was it. She blinked and then squinted at him. "You did *what*?" Her voice sounded shrill to her own ears.

"It was right after Mom stopped treatment. You guys thought I didn't know he was driving you home every day, but I'm not an idiot. I was worried about you. Everything was such a disaster, and I thought the last thing you needed was him messing around with you."

She suddenly stood, enjoying towering over him. "Messing around with me?" Her voice was dangerously low.

He looked up at her. "You're my little sister. I was trying to take care of you. I don't know. I thought I was doing the right thing. I told him I needed to look out for you."

"Oh my God." She shook her head. "I can't believe this." She struggled to make the puzzle pieces fit together with this new information. Josh hadn't just blown her off. He'd been listening to his best friend. His best friend whose mother was dying. And Scott had told him it was for her own good. She opened the fridge and took out a beer, waggling the bottle at him. "I think I need a whole fresh one for this."

Popping the top and taking a long swig, she wandered out of the kitchen, her thoughts swirling. She found Maren back at the dining table, sitting in the detritus of the dessert course. Her sister-in-law looked up at her. "I think I owe you an apology."

The coincidence was remarkable. Scott had decided to interfere in her relationship with Josh, allegedly for her own good, and then ten years later, Maren stepped into Scott's relationship with Eliza, allegedly for Scott's own good. She didn't know quite what to make of the parallel, but somehow, it seemed significant.

Scott appeared behind her, and she looked between the two. "How about moving forward we keep out of each other's relationships?" she suggested.

Maren looked puzzled but nodded.

Eliza took a deep breath. "And as long as we're putting everything on the table, I should tell you that I've met Ross. And I've told him he's my biological dad."

A muscle ticced in Scott's jaw and Eliza waited for the explosion, but it didn't come. He simply raised his eyebrows, inviting her to continue.

She opened her mouth, but as she tried to form the words that would describe Ross's reaction, a wave of emotion clogged her throat.

Scott put a hand on her arm. "Eliza?"

She took a gasping breath and hugged her arms around herself.

Her brother's grip tightened. "What is it? What happened? Are you okay?"

Nodding, she managed to choke out, "Yeah." She sank into one of the dining room chairs, and Scott followed suit.

"I guess it didn't go well?" he said after a moment.

Eliza bit her lip and shook her head. "It was awful." She tried to remember what she'd told Scott and Maren already and realized that she had to start from the very beginning, about NOY and Ross's talk at the Glenside School and the gala. Just coming up with the words was exhausting, and she was conscious of their eyes on her as she filled them in.

"So when he saw the photo and recognized Mom . . . he was so *angry*. I guess he thought I'd been playing some kind of game with him. I've tried to understand it from his side. I really have. Obviously this was a huge shock. But there's just no part of him that's at all happy about it. He doesn't want anything to do with me. And as far as Mom goes . . . he's just so pissed at her."

There was a long silence while Eliza stared at the place setting in front of her, lining up the dessert plate, smeared with chocolate, with the edge of the table.

Scott cleared his throat. "Can you blame him, Eliza?"

She looked up at him so quickly, she felt a head rush. "What do you mean?"

"Look. He's probably a creep. Sleeping with a married woman. But how's he supposed to feel, finding out, what, twenty-seven years later, that he has a kid? The more I've thought about what Mom did, telling you like this . . . I mean, it's bullshit. She never should have put you in this position. If she didn't have the guts to tell Dad before—to tell you before—she should have kept her damn mouth shut."

Eliza's eyes stung, and she felt her nose clog. "But . . ." she started.

"Eliza. Listen. Mom wasn't perfect . . ."

"I know that," she interrupted quickly.

"Do you?" Scott's voice was sharp, and Maren glanced at him. He softened his tone. "Mom was human. She made mistakes. Obviously some pretty big ones. I still love her. I still miss her. Every damn day. But I miss a real person. Not some idealized version of who she was."

Eliza felt anger rising, and she pushed her chair away from the table, standing abruptly. "That's not what I do. I don't idealize her."

"Are you sure about that?"

Was she? She walked away from the table, her arms wrapped around herself again. Her eyes were blurred with tears, and she blinked rapidly, finding herself facing the painting hanging above the sofa. It was an abstract array of oranges, greens, and blues that evoked trees reflected in water. She'd always thought it was just a riot of autumn colors, but now it looked like a forest fire encroaching on the edge of a lake. Funny how different lighting or an angle—or maybe her own mood—had changed the very heart of the landscape.

Scott sidled up beside her. "I had an extra two and a half years with Mom. More time that she wasn't sick. Maybe it gives me a little clearer view of things. Or maybe I'm just more of an asshole. I don't know. But all these years—everything that happened with Dad, and Carol . . . I *got* it, why he moved on. I remember the way he and Mom fought. A lot, for a while. And how hard those two years were when she was sick. And now, I put it together with what we know now about what she did . . . We'll never really know what went on inside their marriage, right? In the end, we all do the best we can, I guess. And sometimes it just sucks."

Eliza looked at her brother, whose eyes were trained on

the painting, too. She didn't want to be angry at Laura. It hurt too much to have those feelings toward her mom. But she'd had them toward Jack. For years and years. And now he was gone, too.

CHAPTER THIRTY-FOUR

"What do you think?" Eliza turned in front of the mirror, looking at herself in the black crepe fabric.

Mo wrinkled her nose from where she stood, leaning against the wall, arms crossed, one knee bent, her foot flat against the wall. "Blah," she said.

"You do realize this is for a *work* event? Not New Year's Eve?"

"What is it they say—dress for the job you want, not the job you have?"

Eliza thought about some of the sparkly numbers Mo had been showing her as they browsed. "I have a feeling you think I want the job of a *Price Is Right* spokesmodel."

"Ha ha. Next dress, please." Mo waggled her fingers, shooing her away.

Eliza went back into the dressing room and reached for the next hanger. This would be dress number six. She had originally planned to simply go with the same dress she'd worn to the gala the year before, but then Mo reminded her that there would be a photographer, suggesting that a new outfit was advisable.

She truly hadn't been sure when she'd find time to go shopping. Life at NOY had become completely insane. Launching an award and changing speakers on such short notice were things she hoped never to have to do again. Everyone had an ever-growing to-do list, and Vanessa's master to-do list was the ring to rule them all, as Tolkien might say. On top of all the obvious items, there were SignUpGeniuses so board members and volunteers could staff the check-in table; a Google sheet listing any mobile number anyone could possibly need the night of the event—from the caterer to Amber's cousin who could be counted on to carry heavy things; and a shared document tracking every item they had to bring to the venue.

The table assignments were an ongoing puzzle, and Eliza had startled when she saw Josh Abrams pop up on the RSVP list. Then she remembered that Josh's firm had bought a table. She'd been feeling awkward and guilty ever since Scott had told her the truth about what had happened back in high school, and had texted Josh to apologize for her curtness the night of the Friendsgiving. He'd texted back a **Don't worry about it** message, but nothing more. Whatever had happened ten years earlier, clearly they were both in different places now. She kept checking the guest list for anyone named Shira.

In the middle of it all, she and Scott made plans to meet Carol on neutral territory—the food court at the Westchester mall. It felt good that she and her brother were on the same team—and as teammates, rather than as coach and towel girl. After the big "coming clean," as she'd begun to think of it, they had spent a long time talking. But the part of the conversation that kept replaying in her head was what Scott had said as they'd ridden the elevator downstairs together to make sure she got a cab.

"I'm so pissed that Mom did this to you." He'd said the words so matter-of-factly, seemingly okay with being angry at Laura. She knew she loved their mom. And it was a revelation that he could hold that love and that anger at the same time, so easily.

"Yeah, I'm pretty pissed at her, too," she replied, surprising herself. Maybe if Laura had come clean earlier, Eliza could have actually had a relationship with Ross. But more than that—she was pissed that Laura was gone. Yes, it was irrational, but it was real. And now that she'd admitted it, she'd felt some of that anger—so long kept tightly bound and hidden—begin to ebb.

Now, in the cramped dressing room, she slid dark blue satin charmeuse fabric over her head. She had had doubts about this dress when Mo picked it up, but looking in the mirror, she realized that her friend was onto something. The gown was sleeveless, which was a plus when you never knew what you might be called upon to do—such as adjusting wires to get tech to work correctly. It had a high neck, so no cleavage issues, and the top was blousy and then cinched into ruching at the waist. The skirt was short, so easy to move in, but not so short that she'd have to worry about inadvertently flashing anyone.

She stepped out of the dressing room, and Mo looked up from her phone.

"Wow, girl. You look hot!"

Eliza twirled in front of the mirror.

"That is *the* dress. No need to try on anything else."

"You think?"

"Definitely. Do you have the right shoes?"

"I have silver strappy sandals—they're heels, but pretty comfortable."

Mo nodded approvingly. "Perfect! And now we have time for tea!"

After Eliza put her regular clothes back on and paid for the dress, they found their way to a quiet café nearby, where Eliza was able to give her garment bag a chair of its own.

Mo dipped her tea bag in and out of her mug with one hand and slid the plate bearing a croissant toward Eliza. "You have to eat some of this. It's way too big for one."

Eliza obediently tore off a corner and popped it into her mouth.

"So," Mo continued. "You're seeing Carol this weekend?"

Eliza nodded, still chewing.

"You know, I was thinking. You could kill two birds with one stone. Maybe you should try to set Ross up with Carol. It would give Carol something to distract her, and maybe it would loosen Ross up."

The croissant suddenly felt like lead in Eliza's esophagus. "Wait. What?"

Mo ripped a piece of croissant off for herself. "Joking! Obviously!"

Eliza picked up her mug and then set it back down again, hesitating. "I'm actually not in a place where I can joke about that stuff."

Mo peered at her. "You're serious," she said slowly.

Eliza nodded.

Her friend's face fell. "Oh, sweetie, I'm sorry! You know I'm just trying to help . . ."

Eliza reached out to touch Mo's hand. "I know. And I've always counted on you to lighten stuff up for me. But this time . . . it's just a lot."

Mo pressed her lips together. "No, I get it. You should have said something before. Me and my goofing around about this stuff . . ."

Eliza pushed back some loose strands of hair. "It's okay. I'm just having a hard time, and it's tough to see any humor in this right now."

"Oh, totally. Look. I'm a moron. I should have asked what you needed, instead of just blathering on and on."

"Honestly, I don't even know what I need." Eliza put her

cold hands around the mug and tried to pull her mixed-up thoughts together. "It's silly, but I guess I had this fantasy about having a new dad, instead of realizing that Ross Sawyer is a total stranger who owes me nothing."

Mo scooted her chair around the table so she could put her arm around Eliza. "You know," she began, "it's probably easier to focus on the possibilities of a new dad than on the loss of the one you had."

Eliza swallowed around the lump in her throat and found she couldn't speak.

"Oh jeez, now I'm making you cry. I think I'm going to get demoted from best-friend status this way." Mo dug around in her purse. "And I don't even have tissues!"

Eliza laughed. "You're never getting demoted. You've collected too many points over the years for a lack of tissues to knock you off your pedestal."

Mo touched her head to Eliza's. "Seriously, you know I'm here for you. Always, and no matter what."

"I do." She blew her nose into a napkin and held it aloft. "It's not just anyone I'd blow my nose in front of, you know."

"Obviously. And I'm honored to be able to witness it."

Eliza dabbed at her eyes while Mo moved her chair back around to its original position.

"More croissant?" she offered. "If you get any skinnier we're going to have to go back for that dress in a smaller size."

Obediently, Eliza ripped off another piece.

"By the way," Mo continued, "Nik's friend Griffin asked for your number. Can I give it to him?"

She hesitated. "Oh, I don't know . . ."

"No pressure, but he's a nice guy. I've met him a few times, and Nik has known him for years."

Eliza tried to get herself excited about the idea but failed miserably, despite reminding herself, *The best way to get over one man is to get under another one.* "It's just not the right time."

"Fair enough. But tell me if you change your mind."

Back in her apartment, Eliza hung the garment bag in her closet and dug out her silver shoes so they would be readily accessible. Her conversation with Mo had lifted a huge weight she hadn't realized had been dragging her down.

As she settled in to stream the next season of *Monk*, a light bulb went off over her head. Mo's comment about focusing on Ross to avoid thinking about Jack had sounded so familiar. Aunt Claude had said exactly the same thing.

Jack's death had come as such a shock, it didn't feel real. And she and her dad had had such a fractious, distant relationship, she wouldn't have thought his absence would be something she'd feel so acutely. And yet . . . for their small family to have contracted that much more tightly, and for him to no longer be just a phone call away, definitely squeezed her heart. She'd always thought there would be time to get onto better footing with Jack, but the sands in the hourglass had run out.

At Thanksgiving dinner, Aunt Claude, Uncle Mitch, and Eliza's cousins Teddy and Nora had been as warm and kind and fun as ever. Nora was full of stories about her new boyfriend, and Teddy had entertained them with live renditions of his funniest YouTube videos, but as much as she'd tried to avoid thinking about it, Eliza was constantly aware that Jack—who undoubtedly would have made a crack about hoping that Teddy didn't intend to pay off his student loans by doing comedy—wasn't there.

Perhaps Scott was right that she didn't let people get close to her. It wasn't as if she hadn't heard that critique before, particularly from Mo. But trust didn't come easily for her. Maybe it was time to try to change that.

CHAPTER THIRTY-FIVE

Sitting in the passenger seat of Scott's car, Eliza felt mildly nauseous. She didn't know if it was due to the prospect of seeing Carol or her brother's driving. For a generally responsible, cautious person, Scott definitely enjoyed speed when he was behind the wheel. And given that he was a New Yorker whose transportation was usually managed by a subway engineer or taxi driver, it was hard to feel secure as he bobbed and weaved.

Eliza grabbed at the door as they changed lanes. "You know, it's okay if we're late."

Scott glanced at her, and she cringed at the sight of his eyes leaving the road. "We're fine. Don't be such a baby."

She closed her own eyes to see if blindness made it better. It didn't, especially not when a horn suddenly blared nearby.

As they pulled into the parking garage, she sighed with relief. Scott lowered his window to snag a parking ticket from the machine and then rolled forward in search of a spot.

"Do we really have to do this?" Eliza asked, her stomach's lurching increasing. Apparently, it hadn't been Scott's driving.

"Hey, you're the one who wants to challenge her

interpretation of the will." Scott glanced in his rearview mirror as he paused to choose which way to turn.

Eliza waited until he made his choice and found a parking space. She didn't respond until he'd shifted the car into park. "Scott. I need to know you're with me on this. You're not some neutral arbiter. You're my brother."

He nodded. "I am. I'm with you. I'd be lying if I said there isn't a part of me that wants it all to just go away. But you're right. This isn't what Dad would have wanted. I mean, I'm still pissed about the whole situation, and no doubt Dad would have been, too. But you were his daughter in every way that counted. I can't take my anger at Mom out on you."

That was the part that Eliza was still struggling with: anger at Laura. It was so much easier to be angry at Ross. At Carol. Even at Jack, for dying without giving any advance warning. Laura had always been sacrosanct in Eliza's mind, but her halo was definitely getting tarnished of late.

They found their way to the elevator and rode it to the top floor of the Westchester. Eliza had grown up coming here. This was where her mom had taken her to get her ears pierced when she was ten. This was where she and her friends were first allowed to go on an excursion alone, no adults humiliating them by their very presence. This was where she and Aunt Claude had shopped for the dress she wore to Laura's funeral. But now that she was so used to Manhattan, the indoor shopping mecca felt alien.

Scott looked up from his phone, where he'd been texting Carol. "She's here already. At a table near Melt Shop."

Eliza suddenly stopped, feeling lightheaded.

"Liza? You okay?"

She took a deep breath. "Yeah. Just not looking forward to this."

Scott draped his arm around her, and she appreciated the

weight of it. The realness of his presence. "You're gonna be fine."

Vicky hadn't been thrilled about this plan. She didn't think meeting "outside the presence of legal counsel" was advisable, but, at the same time, she acknowledged that rules were sometimes hard to follow when it came to family disputes. Eliza spotted Carol almost immediately when the food court came into view. Her posture was perfect, and she wore a maroon sweater that looked like it could have been custom-made for her. No matter what Eliza was wearing, her stepmother always made her feel like she'd just rolled out of bed in her pajamas.

A coffee container sat in front of Carol on the table. "Can we get something to drink first?" Eliza asked, stopping again.

"I don't think they serve alcohol here."

"Ha ha."

She let Scott talk her into a chocolate shake at Melt Shop and immediately got brain freeze as she took her first sip. *Terrific.*

Remaining a step behind him, she followed Scott to Carol's table, where her stepmother greeted them with a chilly smile.

"How was your drive?" Carol asked, as if this were a normal day, instead of the potential start of World War III.

Scott fielded the question. "Fine, not much traffic," he said, while Eliza pulled out a chair to sit. Scott followed.

Carol tapped her manicured nails on the white marble tabletop. "There's probably not much need for small talk," she said before taking a sip of her coffee. "Obviously, Eliza, I got your lawyer's communiqué."

Communiqué? Are we in Victorian England?

Carol continued. "I gather you're questioning my interpretation of Jack's will."

No shit, Sherlock. Scott put his hand on Eliza's in warning, clearly reading her mind. She dialed herself back. "Yes, I'm questioning it. Dad believed I was his daughter. And we were father and daughter in every way that counted. I can't imagine you truly think he'd want you to disinherit me."

"Oh, I don't know about that." Carol's voice was light as she swirled the coffee in the cardboard cup. "It's not as if you and Jack were close. He was very hurt by that, you know."

Eliza flushed with anger. "*He* was hurt? News flash—so was I. And I was the kid who'd lost her mom." So much for keeping herself dialed back.

Scott scooted forward in his seat. "Look, I don't think trying to measure who was more hurt is productive here."

Carol put her cup down on the table again. "As executor, it's my role to ensure that Jack's wishes are carried out. Nothing more. Clearly, I have new information he didn't have, and it's my responsibility to consider how that information would have influenced his choices."

Eliza took a deep breath. She was seething. She hated that Carol was holding herself up as the person who knew Jack best—but if she were honest, perhaps at least part of her anger stemmed from the kernel of truth in her stepmother's claim. No one could legitimately argue that she and Jack had been close—but didn't a lot of parents and children have complicated relationships? She tried to step back and focus on what Vicky had said instead.

"My lawyer tells me that you're not going to win this battle. Overturning a will isn't easy. And you're admitting that Dad didn't know he wasn't my biological father. So as far as he was concerned when he wrote the will, I *was* his daughter."

"Maybe so. But do you really want to put us in a position where we have to make your mother's affair a matter of public record?"

So that was her trump card. It wasn't surprising. Carol knew how much Eliza venerated Laura. So many of her snide remarks over the years—always out of earshot of Jack—had been aimed at knocking Eliza's mom down a few notches.

Eliza gritted her teeth. "If I have to make it public, I will. It's what's *right*, Carol. I know you don't like me. You never liked me. But that's not reason to . . ."

Carol held up her hand. "Hold on there. I don't dislike you. I didn't come into this relationship—this marriage—hating you. I know that's what you think. But it's not true."

Eliza raised her eyebrows in disbelief.

Carol dropped her hand again. "Scott. Would you give us some time alone?"

Scott looked at Eliza. "I don't know . . ." he began.

Carol rolled her eyes. "I'm not going to beat her. You can watch us to make sure I don't try anything funny." She gave a quirky little smile to show that she was attempting humor.

"Liza?" Scott cocked his head.

The last thing Eliza wanted was for her brother to get up and leave. She suspected it would be the last thing Vicky would want, too. But wasn't she supposed to be working on her self-reliance? She nodded. "It's fine."

Scott hesitated and then rose. "I'll just be over there." He pointed vaguely in the direction of the children's play area before heading that way, Eliza watching him go.

Carol cleared her throat. "You may not know this, but I always wanted children."

Eliza turned back to look at her.

"I actually thought Jack and I would have our own. We talked about it, but to be fair, he never made any promises. I knew going in that it might not happen."

Eliza nodded, wondering where this was going.

"But things were so hard with you. And yes, I know, it was totally understandable. You'd lost your mother. But I thought I could help—I didn't expect you to just shut me out. And then

I thought maybe a baby would bring life back into the house." She stopped, looking up at the ceiling for a moment. "In the end, obviously I didn't know how to connect with you. I don't think you wanted to connect with me."

Carol looked directly at her, and Eliza couldn't deny it. *I was sixteen years old when you moved in, and my mother had just died!*

"And, well, Jack couldn't see how we could bring another child into the family. It would have been too much, he said." Carol took another sip of her coffee before playing her last card. "Maybe, if he'd known you weren't really his, his answer would have been different."

Ah.

Eliza managed to rein in her snort. "Seriously, Carol? Is that what you think?"

Suddenly, and to Eliza's shock, her stepmother's face crumpled, and she covered it with her hands, her shoulders shaking.

"Carol?" Eliza reached out and touched her arm. Where had her ice-queen stepmother gone?

Carol didn't respond, but she didn't move her arm away either. After a few moments, she pulled herself together, dabbing at her face with a napkin. "I miss him, Eliza," she said simply. "And I have nothing left. I'm alone. I don't know how I got here, but here I am. And when Adam told me about your mother's revelation—I don't know—it just hit me so hard. How different things might have been if Jack had known the truth."

Would they have been? If Jack had known he wasn't Eliza's father, would he and Carol have had a baby? She tried to play this out in her head. But what she kept banging up against was the fundamental truth that she suddenly realized she'd known all along. Jack loved her. No matter what. No matter how hard things were with them. No matter what the DNA said. He was her dad and he loved her. And she loved him. Despite everything.

Her eyes filled with tears, and she struggled to speak around the clog in her throat. "I loved him, too, Carol. Whatever was wrong in our relationship, he was my dad and I was his daughter. And I've lost the chance to ever make things better with him. Don't you think that crushes me? I can't change what my mom did—it's a reality I have to deal with. But it's not my fault, or Dad's fault. It just *is*. And if you want to keep fighting with me, you can, but I'm not giving up. Maybe if you let it go, we can figure out where you and I can go from here. But if you don't, well, obviously there's nothing we can salvage. It's up to you."

Eliza's face was wet, and she swiped at it ineffectually. This was the stuff dreams were made of—crying at the food court. It could be the title of a book.

They sat silently for a few moments. A sniffly, tearstained standoff. Or maybe a truce. Eliza couldn't tell.

Carol rummaged around in her purse, extracting sunglasses and car keys. Eliza recognized the engraved Tiffany's tag on the keys: cLj—Carol Jordana Levinger. "I'll look into re-filing the probate paperwork," she said quietly.

"Thanks," Eliza replied, feeling ridiculous for expressing gratitude to her stepmother for doing what she should have done in the first place—but she could hear Jack's voice in her head asking her to do just that.

And that was it. No apology. No further conversation. Maybe this was a new start for them. If this were the bestselling novel *Crying in the Food Court*, for sure it would be. But given that it was real life, it probably wasn't.

CHAPTER THIRTY-SIX

The event space looked fantastic. The decor was black and gold—sparkly, but sophisticated. The programs and signage were printed in an art-deco-style font, and the centerpieces on the tables were collections of faux ostrich feathers. The volunteer decoration committee had done a bang-up job, and Eliza was grateful it hadn't been up to her to figure out how to execute a roaring-twenties theme without it looking completely kitschy.

She walked through the space wearing her trusty Converse, waiting until the last minute to put on her silver heels, checking off items on her clipboard. As she looked around, she felt a swell of pride at seeing how all their hard work had come together. Waitstaff were setting the tables, and Davin was with the tech people, getting the microphones and projectors in order.

In the front room, volunteers under Bridget's direction were buzzing around the check-in table and the silent-auction display. Propped up on easels were images of beautiful vacation homes in Aspen and Kiawah Island—a week at each donated by two different board members.

When Eliza and Scott were kids, the Levingers rented a house for a week every summer on Long Beach Island on the New Jersey shore. They always stayed in the same Beach Haven neighborhood, in walking distance to the beach and to the cluster of restaurants, the amusement park, and the mini-golf courses.

Since meeting with Carol, Eliza had been thinking a lot about the past. The good times, before Laura got sick. How she used to ride on Jack's shoulders everywhere. How they played cutthroat games of gin rummy. And she remembered the silences when her parents weren't speaking to each other. The time that doors slammed and Jack got into his car and roared away, while she cried and Scott climbed onto a kitchen chair so he could reach the ice cream on the top shelf of the freezer. He served her a huge bowl of mint chocolate chip.

The memories weighed on her, but they were also comforting. For a long time, she'd cast Laura as the heroine and Jack as the villain in their family drama, but it was so much more complicated than that. She was realizing, finally, that recognizing that was a critical part of dealing with all the loss.

Vanessa appeared, wearing a sleek black dress that hugged the curves and angles of her body. "This looks terrific, Eliza. Any problems I should know about?"

Eliza shook her head. "Looks like everything is under control. We lost one volunteer who was supposed to be at check-in, but we should be fine—I can always jump in if necessary." She looked down at her clipboard. "Otherwise, I think we're all good."

"And I presume you didn't forget your shoes?" Vanessa looked down at Eliza's sneakers.

"No—I've got them, don't worry."

Vanessa glanced at her watch. "T minus thirty minutes. I'm going to check on the podium and the tech."

"Great." Eliza didn't think it was necessary to mention that she'd just done that and it was all fine. Better for Vanessa to have been the last one to inspect it if something were to go wrong. Instead, she found her bag containing her shoes and slipped them on before heading to the ladies' room to touch up her makeup. She'd treated herself to another visit with hair magician Daniela, who this time created some waves around her face while the rest of her locks remained sleek and straight.

She'd been surprised that Daniela remembered the story about her father not being her father and the issues with the will. On the other hand, it wasn't the kind of tale you heard every day. It was painful telling Daniela that Ross didn't want to have anything to do with her, but she knew she'd be okay with it. She had enough to deal with without worrying about building a relationship with him. Fortunately, in terms of the gala, Vanessa and Patrice had taken over communications with the faculty, and she hadn't seen him even once. Tonight would be the first time since they'd met at the bar, and she planned to give him a cool nod and move on. Nothing more was needed.

She emerged from the ladies' room gala-ready. Staff circulated with platters of full champagne flutes, and she was dying to grab one but resisted. Instead, she went over to the check-in table to give another smile to the volunteers. They were going to have a hectic next little bit as people began to arrive, and she wanted to be on hand for any glitches.

Soon enough, people began to wander in. She greeted the bigger donors she recognized until Vanessa appeared and clearly wanted to take over that task. As Eliza hung back, she saw Ross arrive with his colleagues Ian and Barbara. Barbara, whose warmth had made such an impression on her at the meeting at NYU, wore a big smile, clearly delighted to be there. Ross's own face was much more reserved as his eyes scanned the room. She longed to walk over and coolly offer him her hand in welcome, but as he headed her way, she panicked. Instead, she turned to the nearest person waiting to check in.

"Hi! Welcome. So delighted you could make it."

The woman smiled back. She looked a little older than Eliza, had brown wavy hair, and was wearing a unique but beautiful orange dress. "Thanks. My boss was supposed to come, but she got sick—dangers of being around preschoolers I guess—so I hope it's okay that I'm using her ticket. I sent an email earlier, but I'm not sure anyone would have seen it. I mean, I'm sure you were busy setting all this up." She waved her hand around to take in the room.

"Oh, right, I did get your message. Apologies for not getting back to you. I'm Eliza Levinger. Remind me of your name?"

"Callie Dressler. I'm here in place of Judith Preston."

"Callie, hi! The correction should be made on the guest list, but let's just double-check."

In her peripheral vision, she saw Ross take a champagne flute as he joined the line of guests, and she steered Callie to the other end of the table to get her settled in.

The cocktail hour quickly got into full swing, and Eliza worked the room in between fielding questions from co-workers and volunteers. *This guest doesn't have a table assignment—what do I do? If people want to bid in the silent auction, do they have to put their credit card number into the app or can they pay later?* A board member who hadn't RSVPed necessitated a quick conference with her liaison at the venue, and a squeezed-in place setting was added at one of the tables near the podium. She had just finished resolving that situation when she felt a hand on her shoulder. *What now?*

But when she turned, it was Josh. She'd almost forgotten he was coming. Or at least that was what she told herself.

"E. You look amazing." His voice was quiet as his eyes took her in. "Not sure I've ever seen you with your hair down." He was in a dark blue suit, white dress shirt, and no tie. Eliza had never been a big fan of men in suits, but she thought she might have to change her mind.

She touched her hair self-consciously. "Blowouts. They're my new crack."

"Well, if crack makes you look that good, it can't be all bad."

Eliza smiled and felt her cheeks flush, and she cleared her throat. "I owe you a proper apology. That night at Scott's—I was rude."

"It's okay. You've been going through a lot."

She looked down at her silver sandals. "Still. You've been nothing but kind to me." *Kind. Like a good friend.* She raised her eyes again. "So, are you here with people from work?"

He glanced around. "Not sure they've made it yet. But I'm sure you have work to do yourself."

She took in the room; everyone seemed comfortable and taken care of. "No crises right now. Did you see the silent auction? Come look."

They made their way through the clusters of people. In addition to the vacations, there were spa treatments, autographed sports memorabilia, meals from personal chefs, collections of gift cards, and—arranged by Mo—a just-released Swishtech-brand smartwatch.

"Wow—you must rake it in at this thing," Josh remarked, peering at the opening bid on a baseball signed by Derek Jeter.

"That's the goal." Eliza missed the days when people wrote their bids on clipboards; now it was all done via an app—which, of course, got a cut of the take.

Josh turned to her. "So, this probably isn't the place to talk—but how are you doing?"

Eliza's eyes darted around to see who was nearby. Ross was at the far side of the room with Vanessa, who appeared to be hanging on his every word. "Do you want the good news or the bad news first?"

He lifted his eyebrows. "I'll take the good news."

"Carol's dropping her challenge of the will."

His face broke into a smile. "E! That's terrific! How did that happen?"

She gave him the broad brushstrokes of the sit-down they'd had. "I don't know if it was that she came to her senses or the unlikelihood that she'd win in the end." She shrugged.

"Probably both. But I'm glad for you. One less headache. But what's the bad news?"

She glanced at Ross again. "I met with Ross. He doesn't want to have a relationship with me." Concern crossed Josh's face, and she hurried to continue. "But the truth is, that's okay. Three months ago, I didn't know he existed. I *had* a father. And even if things with us weren't ideal . . ." She trailed off as her eyes filled. Josh put a hand on her shoulder, and she blinked rapidly. "Don't be nice to me—then I really won't be able to stop myself from crying."

He removed his hand. "Gotcha. Should I be obnoxious instead?"

She laughed. "I don't know if that's necessary. But you could take lessons from Ross in that department. That's him over there, actually. The guy with the blond hair, next to the woman in the green dress. The other woman, in black, is my boss." She tilted her head in that direction, and Josh turned.

"Yeah," he said, swiveling back. "Definitely looks like a creep."

She laughed again, louder this time, and then saw Amber approaching. She was wearing a flowy maxi dress in rich tones of burgundy and dark green—so utterly Amber.

"Eliza—sorry to interrupt, but should we be starting to move people into dinner?" she asked.

Glancing at her watch, she nodded. "Sorry, Josh—duty calls."

"No worries. Go do your thing. I'll find my colleagues. One of them is a Rangers fan—maybe I can get him to bid on that hockey stick."

Eliza and Amber corralled Bridget as well and gently began nudging everyone into the banquet room, which was soon filled with the sounds of chairs being moved away from tables and the clatter of butter knives as people immediately fell upon the bread rolls as if they hadn't eaten in weeks. Eliza had made sure to have an afternoon snack, since she knew from experience that it was unlikely she'd be able to sit down for her meal.

Vanessa made her way to the podium at the front of the room and, with difficulty, got everyone's attention. Eliza hovered to the side, awaiting her only speaking role of the evening. She took deep breaths and reminded herself that compared to burying two parents, discovering that her biological father was not the man she always thought he was, and filing legal documents opposing her stepmother, saying some innocuous words to a couple hundred people in various states of inebriation was pretty much a nothingburger.

"Thank you, everyone, for joining us this evening. I feel like it was just yesterday that we were here together last year—time truly does fly." Polite laughter met Vanessa's words as she went on to outline some of NOY's highlights of the past year. "Later this evening, we'll have an exciting announcement, and will be hearing from some of the country's leading education-policy scholars. In the meantime, I'd like to invite our director of development, Eliza Levinger, to say a few words."

Just don't trip, she warned herself as she climbed the few steps to the small stage. Vanessa gave her a performative hug, and Eliza took her place at the podium. She looked out over the room and forced a smile. Some faces were turned to her; others were engaged in whispered conversations with neighbors. She knew that as speakers on the program went, she wasn't one of the most interesting. Betraying her, her eyes skated over to the NYU table. Ross was deeply engaged with his phone. How could he not even look up at her? She swallowed and wished there were a glass of water nearby. She shifted her gaze and somehow found Josh, who gave her a warm smile.

"Good evening. And, again, thank you for coming. This is such an important event for Nourish Our Youth. Without your help, we couldn't possibly do even a fraction of the good work Vanessa was just telling you about." She glanced at her notes so she could get the figures right as she shared what they had already raised that night. "But there are still opportunities to give. The silent auction will be open for bidding until 10:00 p.m. If you have any questions, come find me. And thank you again."

There was a polite smattering of applause as she passed the mike back to Vanessa.

"Nice job," Amber whispered as Eliza took her seat beside her. The rest of the NOY staff were scattered around the room, and Eliza did her best to get down at least a few forkfuls of the weedy salad that had been put in front of her.

The salad was whisked away and replaced by a "duet" of steak and salmon. Next to her Amber had the vegetarian meal—pasta primavera. And then Vanessa was back up at the podium, introducing the president of their board of directors—a small but remarkably loud woman in a tailored red suit—who announced the Nourish Our Youth Award for Education Scholarship, followed by Ross, Ian, and Barbara, who each spoke about the importance of educational research.

Ross was in his element, loving having a roomful of people all turned his way. Eliza thought it might be a good time to check on the silent auction and any belated check-in-desk activity, and rose. As she turned toward the back of the room, Ross momentarily stuttered but quickly found his place again.

As expected, everything was under control, and she took some time scrolling through the auction app, pleased that nearly every item had been bid on and several were hotly contested. It was going to be a good night for NOY. The sound of applause rose again from the dining room, and she presumed Ross had finished speaking. Glancing at herself in a nearby mirror, she saw that her lipstick could use a refresh, so she ducked into the ladies' room to take care of that. She breathed a sigh of relief. The evening was more than halfway over. It was homestretch time.

Another moment to adjust her dress, and she was on her way back to her seat. And then there was Ross, right in front of her.

"Eliza."

She stopped, waiting for a crack about her leaving during his speech, but it didn't come.

"Ross," she replied. She tried to think of what she'd say if he weren't her father. If they had no history. "Seems like a successful evening."

He nodded. "Definitely."

So much for small talk.

"Well, I'm going back in." And then she was past him, only realizing as she walked away how much her heart was pounding. She made it back to her seat, and Amber turned toward her.

"You missed . . ." she began, and then stopped. "Are you okay? You look pale."

Eliza pressed her hands against her cheeks. "I'm fine."

Amber looked unconvinced. "Okay. Well, you missed Barbara. She is *really* funny. You should get her to tell you this story about when she was a research assistant and . . ."

Eliza wasn't listening, but she nodded as if she were. She was concentrating on the roaring in her ears and trying to calm her breathing. And then a server came around with dessert—something dark and chocolaty, with raspberries. Eliza had finalized the menu only a few days earlier, but she couldn't remember what it was.

Amber immediately picked up her fork. "This looks amazing!" she exclaimed, digging in.

Taking a small sliver of her own, Eliza turned to her seatmate on the other side—a former board member wearing dozens of bangles with whom she'd chatted earlier in the evening—to ask her opinion of the speeches. Anything to get herself back into the groove of director of development at a gala rather than rejected daughter.

Bangles was in the middle of describing the first NOY gala she'd attended when Davin appeared, looking a bit like he'd run a marathon. He'd actually wrangled a number of press people to attend, so was likely out of breath from pitching them stories. "Eliza. Amber. We're going to be grabbing some photos. Can you join us over by the silent-auction table?"

Terrific. She'd forgotten the posed photos. At least she'd touched up her lipstick. Maybe she could convince herself it would serve as a protective force field.

She put her napkin on the table. "Excuse us," she said to Bangles, and followed Amber out of the room. The photographer was already there, snapping photos of the board president, Vanessa, Ross, Ian, and Barbara, while Bridget hovered nearby.

From her spot in the center of the lineup, Vanessa waved. "Great. You're here. I'd like to get some shots of staff only, staff and the board, and then everyone all together." The usual shuffling and reshuffling ensued as people were asked to angle themselves this way and that, move backward half a step, lower their chins, put their hands into their pockets, take their hands out of their pockets . . .

As the photographer moved them around once again, now into a group that included the faculty, Eliza found herself standing next to Barbara, who was oddly squirmy.

"I'm sorry," she said as she bumped her elbow into Eliza. "I don't know what's wrong with me." She rubbed at her neck, and Eliza looked at her more closely. What were those blotches?

"You're awfully red," Eliza said, pointing at the other woman's upper chest, which was bare in her square-necked dress.

Barbara stopped scratching and looked down at herself. "Am I? I'm *crazy* itchy."

The photographer interjected loudly. "Can you all look this way, please?"

Barbara managed to stand still, but as soon as the camera was no longer pointed at them, she went to work again on her neck.

"Could you be having a reaction to something?" Eliza asked.

"I don't know. But I'm not feeling right." She took a wheezy breath.

Eliza touched her arm. "Let's go sit down."

She guided her to one of the chairs where the check-in volunteers had been stationed. "Bridget, could you get her some water?" she called as she pulled over a second chair so she could sit beside her.

Barbara touched her own lips. "My mouth feels funny."

By then, Patrice and Davin had wandered over, Patrice looking troubled. "Can you breathe okay?" she asked. "My wife recently discovered she's allergic to bee stings. Her lips and tongue swelled . . ." She glanced at Eliza and added more quietly, "It wasn't good."

Bridget returned with a glass of water, but by then no one was paying attention to her.

"I don't think I have any allergies," Barbara said, her breath sounding shallow. Patrice pinched her own mouth with her thumb and forefinger. The same thing she did when she was studying budget figures that didn't add up. Eliza's eyes darted over the people hovering around them. Everyone was so close. No wonder Barbara was having trouble breathing. She wished they'd move back and was about to say just that when Patrice bent down to peer more closely at Barbara.

Patrice quickly stood back up. "Does anyone have an EpiPen?" she asked, catching Davin's eye. "Are there any doctors here?"

Eliza fumbled around with the skirt of her dress. No pockets. She knew that. What was wrong with her? But the bottom line was that she didn't have her phone—it was in her purse back at the table. "Maybe someone should call 911," she heard herself say in an oddly high-pitched voice.

CHAPTER THIRTY-SEVEN

"Do you think I need to do damage control with the press people who were here?" Davin asked, but no one answered him.

As soon as 911 had been called and Vanessa had announced from the podium that a doctor was needed, the whole scene became a case study in rubbernecking. It turned out that there were two doctors in the house, both of whom agreed that Barbara was experiencing an anaphylactic reaction, and fortunately one of the guests had an EpiPen in her pretty silver purse.

Eliza did her best to get the extraneous people moved away from the scene, but somehow more and more began streaming out of the dining room. Some headed out, but others hovered, as if their presence could somehow be helpful. The arrival of the EMTs helped clear the area, and pretty quickly, they carried Barbara out, with Ross, Ian, and Vanessa following.

Amber rubbed her own arms as if she were chilly. "Wow. Not at all how I expected this evening to end."

"Well, at least she should be okay," Patrice replied, putting her arm around Amber to give her a little squeeze and then reaching out to squeeze Bridget's hand as well.

Vanessa reappeared. "They're en route. Ross rode along in

the ambulance. Ian is trying to get in touch with Barbara's husband, but everything should be fine." She paused and looked
around at her team and the various guests who were still
milling about. "This has been a long night, folks. Best thing
we can do now is to head home. We can deal with notifying
the auction winners tomorrow. Doesn't feel quite right to do it
now." She pasted on a smile and turned to the nearest guests to
begin to nudge them out.

Eliza felt a bit shell-shocked but went through the motions
of thank-yous and good-nights before heading back into the
dining room in search of her purse. She found Josh sitting at
her table, and he looked up at her.

"Hey. I figured I should stay out of the way, but I wanted to
stick around. See if you're all right."

She put her hands on the back of the chair she'd been sitting in. "It was all so strange. One minute she was fine and
then she was having trouble breathing."

"Scary stuff. What do you need to do now?"

She shrugged and then sat. "We're going to wrap up the
auction stuff tomorrow. I guess I'll see if we can store everything here overnight." But she didn't move.

"E? You okay?" He shifted to face her, his knees almost
touching hers.

She looked up from her hands, which she'd been studying.
"I barely know her. And she's going to be fine. I just feel—I
don't know—shaky."

He squeezed her knee. "Stay here. Let me get you something to drink." And then he was gone, and Eliza gazed around
the ballroom, where servers were moving about, efficiently
clearing the tables. She wasn't sure how much time had passed
when Josh returned with a glass of ice water.

"Here you go. I talked to your coworker—Patrice, I think?
There are a bunch of volunteers out there packing stuff up, and
Patrice made arrangements to keep it here until tomorrow."

Eliza took a sip of water. "I should be out there. This is my job."

"It's okay. It's being taken care of."

She didn't have the energy to argue with him, or even to wonder why he was hanging around with her, so she just drank again, the ice clinking in the glass.

Josh ran a hand through his hair. "Whenever you're ready, we can go. How about I take you for a drink? Or dessert?"

She thought about it. All she really wanted was to go home. And to get some air. Where were they again? They were just under twenty blocks to her apartment. And a couple of avenues. "I wouldn't mind just walking home."

He looked down at her feet. "In those heels?"

"I changed when I got here. I have other shoes."

"Well, then. It's a plan."

A little while later, after Eliza had gathered her things and confirmed with Patrice that everything was, in fact, taken care of, she was back in her Converse, and she and Josh stepped outside. The air was brisk—it was, after all, December.

"Are you sure you're not too cold?" he asked.

"My coat is warm. And the air feels good. You don't have to walk with me."

"I could use the exercise."

So they fell into step beside each other. It was past ten—closer to eleven, in fact—but they were far from alone. New York didn't get the "city that never sleeps" nickname for nothing.

Eliza sucked in a breath of chilly air. She still felt . . . off. Like something was nagging at her that she couldn't put her finger on. "I don't know why I feel so shaken up. I barely know Barbara. And she's going to be fine."

He raised his eyebrows. "You've been through a lot the last few months. I'm not surprised being so close to a medical emergency would affect you."

She nodded. "I never thought about what actually happened when my dad died. I mean, calling 911 and all that . . ." *What must that have been like for Carol?* Had they tried to bring him back? Or was it far too late? Her heart squeezed at the thought.

"I'm so sorry, E."

She shrugged. "What are you going to do, right?"

He bumped his shoulder against hers, and they continued walking in silence for a bit. When they stopped at a red light at Sixty-Third Street, he spoke again.

"By the way, the event came off really well. You did an amazing job."

She smiled. The program felt like it was ages ago. Strange how time could be so elastic.

"Thanks. I can't imagine you had much fun, though."

"Why would you say that? It was all good, and it probably doesn't hurt my career to spend some time with partners from the firm. Besides, who doesn't love a roaring-twenties theme?"

She laughed. "At least they didn't make us wear flapper dresses and do the Charleston."

"That certainly would have been different. Who chooses those themes anyway?"

"The board votes. You wouldn't believe some of the things people propose."

"Like . . . ? You can't leave me hanging like that."

She reached back into her memory, before her life had been turned upside down. "Let's see. Somebody wanted to do a seventies thing. But they couldn't figure out how to execute it other than lots of disco balls and lava lamps."

"I could imagine a lot worse. I thought you were going to say something like World War II. The whole place could be decorated like a bunker."

She laughed. "How about nuclear winter? That could be fun."

"Well, it *is* the holiday season—what's more cheerful than that?"

They stopped again at a traffic light, an Italian restaurant facing them at the far corner. "They have the absolute best lasagna," Eliza noted, pointing.

"That's quite an endorsement, especially considering the competition all over this city."

They continued on, chatting about food, and then suddenly, they were at Eliza's building. *Should I invite him up?* She didn't really want him to go, but she knew he was just being kind, and she didn't want him to think she'd gotten the wrong end of the stick.

She shifted her bag on her shoulder. "How are you getting home?"

He looked around, as if there might be a limousine waiting. "I'll probably get a cab."

Might as well bite the bullet. "You wanna come up for a minute first?"

He studied her face for a moment before answering. "Sure."

She led the way and was soon unlocking the door to her apartment. "You want something to drink?" she asked, stepping inside. She had a sudden inspiration. "I can make hot chocolate."

"What kind of good American would I be if I turned down hot chocolate?"

A few minutes later, barefoot and wearing her cocktail dress, she was heating milk on the stove and then adding it to cocoa powder in two mugs. Automatically, she brought it over to the couch. Josh was still standing, facing her bookcase, where he'd been commenting on her collection. "I really should read more," he said, turning to join her. "I always end up reading the same authors I already know. I'm sure I'm missing good stuff."

Eliza blew gently on her drink. "Who do you like to read?"

Josh sat and picked up his mug. "This smells great. Hmm. Ken Follett. Jon Krakauer."

"You should try *The Girl with the Dragon Tattoo*. Oh—and he's very different, but Matt Haig."

"Cool." He sipped his hot chocolate.

"Is it okay?" She nodded toward his drink.

He grinned. "It's chocolate. How can it be bad?"

They drank for a bit in silence. "Are you feeling better?" he asked.

She poked gently at her psyche. "I think so. I haven't been getting much sleep for a while, which doesn't help either."

He set the mug down on the coffee table and turned to her. "You need to take care of yourself."

His forehead was creased in concern, and Eliza had trouble tearing away from his steady gaze. His eyes were a rich chocolate brown, his hair curled just a tiny bit over his collar. She was starting to forget why she needed to keep her distance. That he was just her brother's friend. Self-consciously, she pushed her hair behind her ears. She wasn't used to it being loose, and she reached back and pulled it over her shoulder. His eyes followed her movements.

She blinked. "So, have you connected with Shira?"

It seemed to take him a moment to focus on the question. "Who?"

"Shira. Maren's friend. I saw Scott give you her number at Friendsgiving." She potentially sounded like a weird stalker, but she had to get this back onto safer ground for her own good.

One corner of his mouth curled up. "Oh. I'd forgotten her name. Yeah, he was trying to get me to call her. But I'm not interested. In her."

Oh. *Oh.* Maybe the reason she'd been having trouble convincing herself about what was going on here was that she'd actually been wrong about what was going on. That what she had been afraid to hope for was actually the reality. As her mind spun and her pulse quickened, she moistened her lips, an action he seemed to find very interesting.

And then suddenly the chorus of "Boulevard of Broken Dreams" blared. Her ringtone. They both startled. Who was calling at nearly midnight?

CHAPTER THIRTY-EIGHT

It took a moment for Eliza to stand and get her phone from her purse on the kitchen table. The number was unfamiliar; she looked again at the time. A phone call this late from an unfamiliar number? Josh came to stand beside her as she said hello, hesitantly.

"Eliza?"

She couldn't place the voice. "Yes?"

"Oh. I didn't think you'd pick up this late. I was going to leave a message. It's Ross."

Her eyes widened, and Josh raised his eyebrows questioningly. "Ross," she mouthed to him. Into the phone, she simply said, "Oh."

Ross cleared his throat, which sounded unreasonably loud through the phone's speaker.

She suddenly remembered Barbara. "Wait. Is Barbara . . . ?" She felt Josh's hand on her shoulder. Her bare shoulder.

"Oh. No. Barbara's fine. It was an allergic reaction to something, but it's been managed. They'll keep her overnight to be safe, but all good."

"Okay . . ."

"No. I, uh, I was calling because I've been sitting here at the hospital for the past two hours, thinking. Well, first in the ambulance. Then in the hospital." He paused. Based on what she'd seen of him, he didn't seem like someone who was typically at such a loss for words. He cleared his throat again, and she moved the phone away from her ear a bit. "I was hoping we could talk."

Her heart was pounding in her ears now, but not in the same way it had been a moment before. "I guess so. When?"

"Tomorrow? I don't have classes to teach. So anytime."

Vanessa had made noises about the day after the gala being an "optional" workday, but now they were going to have to deal with wrapping up the auction. "Midafternoon?" she suggested.

"Same place as last time?"

Sure. Because that went so well. "Okay."

She continued to stare at her phone after they'd confirmed a time and she'd clicked the phone off.

"What was that about?" Josh asked.

"Beats me." She looked up at him, and he seemed to read the question in her eyes.

"Look," he said gently. "It's late. You said you haven't been sleeping. I think I should go. Unless you want to talk about that." He pointed at the phone.

No, she didn't want to talk about Ross. She felt deeply, deeply exhausted. And just a little bit crushed. "No, you're right. I should sleep."

He picked up his jacket from where he'd dropped it on a kitchen chair and pulled it on. Then he touched her nose with one finger. "Good night, E." And he was gone. Just like that.

The idea might have been that she'd get some sleep, but after staring at the ceiling for an indeterminate amount of time and flip-flopping like a trout on the deck of a boat, Eliza gave up in favor of more *Monk*. She managed to drop off watching one of the detective's "here's what happened" explanations and squeezed in a couple of hours of shut-eye before she had to get dressed for work. Staring at her closet with unseeing eyes for a while, she finally decided that the Friday after the gala didn't require her usual level of professionalism. So she left her apartment in a pair of distressed skinny jeans and a loose sweater over a tank top.

Why did Ross want to meet? And why now? And what had his call interrupted between her and Josh? He'd ditched out so quickly afterward, she couldn't help but think she'd misread the situation.

Everyone at work was clearly fried after the pedal-to-the-metal speed they'd been operating at for the past few weeks, and they were moving as if through molasses. Davin and Bridget went back to the venue to collect everything that had been left there overnight, and they were gone for an inordinate amount of time. There were calls and emails to be fielded from auction winners who wanted to know how to get their prizes, and others who had not been tracking their bids on the app who needed to be notified. The goal was to get as many people as possible to come to the NOY office to collect their winnings, but in a few cases—especially with bigger donors and board members—Vanessa decreed that deliveries were to be made.

Eliza ended up responsible for bringing the autographed Rangers hockey stick and Giants football helmet to a board member's West Village loft, so she texted Ross to change the location of their meeting. The more she thought about it, the more opposed she was to sitting with him again in that same library-themed bar. And though she didn't want to admit to him that she knew he lived in the Village, she figured it was reasonable to suggest that they meet near NYU instead.

It was emblematic of New York that no one even glanced at her on the subway carrying a hockey stick and football helmet. She rode down to the Christopher Street Station and found her way to the board member's building before heading over to the coffee shop Ross had suggested. It was unseasonably warm for December, and she walked slowly, pondering. Was it significant in some way that Ross hadn't chosen a bar this time?

Her destination proved to be a café that could have come straight out of a movie set. A large, glass-fronted wooden case showcased pastries, and the counter was white marble. The small round tables were also marble topped, and the chairs were wooden with curlicued backs. Once again, Ross was already there when she arrived, eating a slice of cheesecake, a coffee cup on the table in front of him. Clearly stress didn't affect his appetite the way it did hers—or he wasn't feeling the same anxiety she was. She ordered a cup of tea and joined him.

"I've been coming to this place for at least twenty years," he offered, gesturing at their surroundings with his cup. "It sucks in the summer when it's crawling with tourists, but it's great in the winter."

Eliza nodded. *What does that have to do with anything?*

As if he could read her mind, he smirked. "Sorry. Not sure where to start."

She waited, resisting the instinct to try to put him at ease.

He drummed briefly on the table with both hands, as if it were a set of bongos. "So," he began. "I've been trying to avoid thinking about you, and this"—he gestured between them—"but I haven't been very successful. And last night, the thing with Barbara . . . It just hit me what a kick in the head life can be.

"I fucked things up royally with your mother. After what happened at our reunion, I was delusional enough to think that we were going to make things right. That she'd leave your dad."

Eliza flinched. Scott had been a toddler then. Could Laura really have entertained the idea of ending the marriage?

Ross shook his head. "I doubt that was ever even in her

mind. But I was pissed anyway when she cut me off. Pissed and hurt. So for you to come to me with this news . . ."

She shifted in her seat. Was she going to have to sit through the same speech again in different words? And "this news"? He couldn't even say that he was her father? "I got all this the last time. I don't need to hear it again," she said sharply, readying herself to rise and wishing she'd gotten her tea to go.

Ross put out his hand. "No, no. Please. I got off on the wrong foot. As usual, as lots of people would probably say."

She relaxed her back but remained on alert for any signs that she should bolt.

"Let me start over." He paused and took a deep breath. "We only get one time through this life. At least as far as we know. And if we're potentially only one allergic reaction away from shuffling off this mortal coil, I don't want to lose the chance to get to know you. I mean, it's sort of amazing to think about the fact that this young woman sitting here"—he gestured toward her—"wouldn't exist without me. I want to learn more about her. That is, about you."

Without realizing it, she'd clenched her fists, and her fingernails were digging into her palms.

"So, what do you think?" Ross asked.

What did she think? She had whiplash from his about-face. Who was to say he wouldn't change his mind again next week? Or next year? Did she want to put herself in a situation where she could get dumped—again—by her own biological father?

"I don't know," she said quietly.

He chuckled. "I get it. You're wondering if you can trust this jerk sitting across from you. I'd like to say you can. That I wouldn't be here if I wasn't sure about building some sort of relationship with you. But all I can promise is that I fully intend to try. Self-sabotage is definitely part of my MO, though . . . so it's fair that you're wary."

She studied him—his cocky smile, his eyes that so closely resembled hers. And thought she could see something else there. Fear, maybe? Fear that she'd say no? Fear that he'd screw this up? Fear of death? Who knew?

"What would this even look like?" she asked.

"You got me. But we're intelligent people—I mean, you *do* have half my DNA, and Laura was always smarter than me; I told her so all the time. We'd figure it out."

She could tell that he was turning on whatever charm he had. Counting on his sense of humor to win her over. She stalled, taking a sip of her tea. Her instinct was to run, as fast as she could possibly go. But she reined herself in. "I need to think about it."

His eyebrows drew together, and she forced herself to elaborate. Exposing herself—figuratively, that was—had never come easy to her.

"I've been numb the last few months, but now it's hit me that my dad is gone. And that I miss him. And I was really . . . hurt . . . by what you said last time. I need some time."

He winced a bit but nodded. "That's fair. I knew you were smart." He smiled, his eyes crinkling, and she could tell that that, too, was a go-to move for him. When she didn't respond, he shrugged. "So the ball's in your court now, I guess."

"I guess it is."

He'd finished his cheesecake and his coffee, so he picked up the plate and cup. "I'm gonna go. And I hope I hear from you. Seriously."

She watched him leave his items on the counter and smile at the barista, feeling her intestines relax a bit. Now what? The obvious choice was to head home and try to get some sleep, but the idea of being alone in her apartment wasn't very appealing. She slowly finished her tea and went outside, heading north on Bleecker Street.

Because it was Mo's neighborhood, she knew it reasonably

well, and wandered in and out of shops, browsing. Her feet took her to Chelsea Market, where she spent an inordinate amount of time in the aisles of Artists & Fleas wondering if she could make a living crafting handbags or jewelry, and then feeling impelled to support those making a go of it by buying herself a hand-hammered bangle and a purse with all sorts of cleverly concealed zippers and pockets. She was putting her wallet away when she realized she hadn't checked her phone in a while. There was a text from Josh, **just checking in** and telling her that he was hoping to get out of the office early if she was around. What did that mean?

She looked at the time. Somehow, she'd whiled away the afternoon. For the heck of it, she Googled Joshua Abrams and "New York" and found his address. Not far from where she'd met Ross. If she lied to herself, it was on the way back to the subway. It was doubtful he was even there yet. But that was where she headed, anyway.

CHAPTER THIRTY-NINE

Josh's building was a narrow brownstone with a stained-wood front door about five steps up from the pavement. The sun had fully set—she hated these short days—and a very tall man walking a dachshund passed her as she stood there, pretending to look at something on her phone.

What's the worst that can happen? She walked up the steps and found the button labeled *Abrams*, expecting no answer. But then came Josh's disembodied voice. "Yes?"

For a second, she forgot how to speak. "It's Eliza."

"Come on up. Second floor." The front door buzzed as it unlocked.

She went inside and climbed the stairs. There were two doors on the landing. One was open, and Josh stood there, wearing a button-down shirt open at the collar, khaki pants, and socks. "This is a surprise," he said.

"I was in the neighborhood."

He raised his eyebrows and stepped back to allow her into his railroad-style apartment. A small kitchen was to the left, and straight ahead was a living room, where a midcentury-modern sofa faced a TV mounted on the exposed brick wall.

Beyond that, she could see the bedroom through French doors, obviously installed so the windowless living room would get some light.

Josh scooped up the newspapers scattered on his coffee table and an empty mug. "I wasn't expecting anyone."

"No, it's fine. Obviously. I was down this way to deliver some silent-auction items to the winning bidder. I don't know if your colleague bid on the hockey stick, but he didn't win. You wouldn't believe what one of our board members paid for it." She was babbling.

Turning from the sink, where he'd deposited the mug, Josh opened the fridge. "You want anything?" He lifted a bottle of Blue Moon and waggled it at her.

"Sure."

He grabbed a second one, along with the opener from a drawer, and deftly popped the two tops. "Glasses?"

"Bottle is fine."

He handed one to her and clinked the necks together. "Cheers. Come sit."

With him at one end of the sofa and her at the other, they each took long swallows of beer. Josh put his bottle down on the coffee table. "So. Did you see Ross?"

She picked at the label on her bottle with her thumbnail. "Yeah. That's the other reason I was down this way."

"Do you want to talk about it?"

She sighed. "He says he wants us to get to know each other."

He leaned forward, his elbows on his knees. "And how do you feel about that?"

She laughed ruefully. "Isn't that the million-dollar question? I mean, I thought that's what I wanted. You know— insta-dad! But now, I'm not sure."

"What changed your mind?"

"Another excellent question. I guess . . . I had a dad. I mean, I knew that, but I think I was using Ross to avoid focusing on my dad dying. That's what Mo and my aunt said—and I think they were right."

He nodded. "But that doesn't mean you can't see if there's a relationship worth building with Ross."

"Maybe." She took another long swallow of beer and went back to picking at the label, this time with her index finger.

"Eliza."

She looked up. He didn't usually use her full name.

"Why are you really here?"

She felt her heart stutter. "What do you mean?"

He shifted closer and reached for the bottle, taking it out of her hands and placing it on the table next to his. His knees were near hers, his eyes steady on her face.

"Um. I don't know. I . . ." Her voice trailed off.

He waited. There was a tiny freckle next to his left eye. Had it always been there? She'd noticed it last night, too. *Last night . . .*

She began again. "Last night, I thought . . ."

"You thought . . . ?" he asked gently, but she'd lost her words somewhere in the pools of his eyes. He lifted his hand to her face, brushing back the strands that had come loose from her braid. Her eyes closed as he moved toward her, and she felt his lips on hers. How many years had she been waiting for this? And it was perfect. Firm but gentle, his hand sliding down to her neck to pull her closer and deepen the kiss.

He drew back. "Is that what you thought?"

She nodded dumbly.

"Yeah. That's what I was thinking, too. For a very, very long time."

And then she was kissing him again, their mouths parting, his tongue finding hers. Why had they waited so long to do this? He tasted of beer and himself as he experimented with lighter and deeper kisses, his tongue making her shiver as it ran across her bottom lip. When she felt like she couldn't breathe anymore and her skin was burning up, she drew back to pull her sweater over her head.

His eyes dropped from her face to her chest, and he ran his finger along the edge of her tank top, across the swells of her breasts. Then he reached for her braid. "May I?" he asked, showing her the elastic band at the end of it.

She nodded again, and he pulled it off, pushing his hands through her hair, loosening it so it cascaded around her. "Even silkier than I thought it would be," he whispered wonderingly before his mouth returned to hers, his hands still tangling in her hair.

Eliza moved closer, climbing into his lap, and he groaned as she settled into the hardness in his khakis. She broke their kiss to start to unbutton his shirt, but then his hands came up to hers, stilling them. She looked at him questioningly.

"I want you to understand something," he said hoarsely, shifting beneath her.

The blood roared in her ears as she waited for him to continue.

"This isn't just about this." He gestured between them. "This isn't what I want from you."

She raised her eyebrows, and he smiled. "Well, of course I want this," he clarified. "But I want a lot more. I want to make you eggs for breakfast. I want to keep you company when you can't sleep. I want you to take me book shopping. I want you to be my plus-one at parties."

What he was saying should have terrified her. But somehow, it didn't. She grinned. "You want to hold my hair back when I'm throwing up?"

"Definitely. That would be my favorite thing." His fingertips returned to the tops of her breasts, and his eyes grew hazy again. "As long as we're clear."

"Clear," she said, and then carefully she lifted herself off him, though she really didn't want to break contact. He watched her with a puzzled look on his face, but then she took his hand and led him into the bedroom.

Somewhere in the back of her mind she noted that his bed was made, a navy-and-dark-green-plaid comforter neatly pulled up to the pillows, which wore navy pillowcases. *Impressive.* She climbed onto the bed and knelt in the center before pulling off her tank top.

"Jesus," Josh whispered as he joined her on the bed, his lips on her neck and then moving downward as he pushed down the cups of her bra. She heard herself gasp as he figured out exactly how to touch her. And then the rest of their clothes were coming off, and his hands and lips—and hers—were everywhere.

She could barely breathe as he fumbled in his bedside-table drawer for a condom that he quickly sheathed himself in. And then he was inside her.

"Oh my God, Eliza. You feel so good." His voice was husky and she couldn't articulate anything in return as he began to move, and she shifted her hips in rhythm with him. He bent to kiss her again and then rolled onto his back, pulling her with him.

She moaned as she resettled herself, and he looked up at her. "You are so beautiful," he whispered, his hands on her hips.

She'd barely begun to move again before the pleasure became almost unbearable. "I'm close," she breathed.

"Then come," he said, and she did, with him following immediately after.

Eliza collapsed on top of him, and he brought his arms around her, rolling them back over again. Then he lifted his head to look at her and bent to kiss her eyelids, her nose, her lips. "I'll be right back."

She watched him walk away to dispose of the condom, unable to avoid admiring his ass, before closing her eyes and letting her arm fall across her face. Her skin was covered in a sheen of sweat, and her heart was just beginning to slow. He returned a moment later and curled himself around her, pulling the covers up over them.

"That was worth waiting for," he whispered into her ear.

"Have you been waiting long?"

He lifted his head and looked at her. "You know I have."

"Actually, I didn't. I didn't know until the night of the Friendsgiving that Scott had told you to leave me alone."

He clapped his hand onto his forehead. "I never should have listened to him."

"It's okay." But she felt the familiar sensation of hot tears in her eyes.

"Oh, E." Josh wiped at the tears that leaked out with his thumbs. "I'm sorry you got hurt. That I hurt you. It kills me that I just . . . disappeared . . . on you the way I did."

She took a shuddery breath. "We were kids. And if we'd gotten together then—it never would have worked. I was a mess." She sighed. "I've been a mess for a long time."

He shook his head. "You've been human. You've been in pain. And I wanted to be sure I wasn't taking advantage of that."

Her mouth curved into a wry smile. "No chance of that. I've become really good at running away."

He smoothed her hair away from her face. "Are you ready to stop running now?"

"Yeah. I am." And she meant it.

CHAPTER FORTY

Josh put a plate of perfect scrambled eggs onto the table in front of Eliza, who wore a soft gray T-shirt he'd lent her, her hair up in a messy bun. "I told you I wanted to make you breakfast," he said, dropping a kiss on her head.

The night before, they'd ordered Thai food, after which they ended up back in bed. The second time was, amazingly, even better than the first. Afterward, for the first time in a long time, Eliza fell into a deep sleep.

He sat opposite her at the tiny bistro table with his own plate of eggs.

"These are delicious!" she exclaimed, savoring the flavor.

"Don't get your expectations too high. They're just about the only thing I know how to cook. And sorry I don't have any tea for you. I'll have to pick some up."

There was a time that a man offering to buy tea bags to keep in his apartment for her would have sent her running, but she loved the idea of Josh studying all the options on the shelves at the nearest bodega and then selecting a few for her to sample.

"So, I was thinking," he started. "About Ross. Are you afraid that you'd be betraying your dad by getting to know him?"

She swallowed the bite of eggy goodness in her mouth. "Maybe, in part." She paused. "I think I'm also scared of getting hurt. Him changing his mind again. It's tough for me to believe people are going to stick around."

He reached across and rubbed his thumb across her knuckles. "The people who are worth having in your life will stay."

She turned her hand to squeeze his. "I like that."

"Maybe I should embroider it on a pillow."

She laughed. "Your next career if this lawyering thing doesn't work out."

"Yeah, well, first I'd need to learn how to sew."

"We could work on that today, if you'd like."

He stood, picking up their empty plates and forks and depositing them in the sink. Then he pulled her out of her chair. "Our day is already completely booked," he said, tilting her chin up and capturing her lips with his own.

Scott groaned. "I'm not sure how I'm going to get used to this," he said, but the corners of his mouth threatened to turn up.

Eliza and Josh had just approached the table where Scott and Maren were seated. A basket of rustic bread was already there, and Scott had a beer in front of him. Maren was drinking . . . lemonade? Scott rose to hug Eliza and then punched Josh in the arm. "You know what that's for, man, right?"

"Yeah, yeah." Josh rolled his eyes, and he and Eliza took off their jackets before sitting opposite Scott and Maren. It was Friday night, and it had been just about two weeks since Josh had first cooked scrambled eggs for Eliza, and Eliza suspected she'd already spent more time with him than she had with Carter over the two months or so that they'd been "together."

Or, indeed, with anyone else. She occasionally got heart palpitations at the thought of it—but mostly Josh caused her heart to race for all the right reasons.

Maren grinned. "Well, I think you guys make a cute couple. It's about time."

About time that Eliza was with someone Maren approved of? Or that she and Josh got together? Eliza decided not to ask.

They perused the menu, where so many things sounded delicious. Eliza's grief-blunted appetite had begun to return, and a few of her lost pounds had come back. Once they'd ordered a feast that not long before would have turned her stomach, they fell into easy chatter. "What are you doing this weekend?" Maren asked, spreading butter on a slab of sourdough.

"We're going to lunch with Ross," Eliza said, looking nervously at Scott. Her brother didn't look happy, but he nodded. She decided not to share the thought that kept popping into her head—that she'd known her new boyfriend much, much longer than she'd known her "father."

"How's that going?" Maren asked.

"Okay, I think. We're taking it slow. Just getting to know each other. It's weird, and yet not weird, if that makes sense."

"Oh yeah, it makes perfect sense." Scott rolled his eyes.

"Maren—would you mind smacking your husband for me?" Eliza smiled to show that she was kidding . . . sort of.

Maren exchanged glances with Scott, and they seemed to share a telepathic communication. Finally, Scott spoke. "Well, I'm sure she'd be happy to, but then she'd be smacking the father of her child."

"Oh my gosh!" Eliza exclaimed.

"Congratulations! That's fantastic," Josh chimed in.

Maren wore an ear-to-ear grin, and Scott's smile was nearly as wide.

Eliza couldn't have imagined being more excited. "Wow! Tell us *everything*!"

Scott tapped his fingers on the table and gave her a sly look. "Well, you see, when a man and a woman *really* love each other . . ."

She stuck out her tongue at him. "Ha ha. Very funny. I mean, when are you due? Are you going to find out if it's a girl or a boy?"

As Maren and Scott answered her questions, Eliza couldn't help thinking about Scott's comment. Obviously, not all babies grew out of love. Some grew out of one-night stands. And some grew out of something in between. She truly wasn't sure what was going to happen with her and Ross, but that was okay. And she wasn't sure what was going to happen with her and Josh, but for now, she was happier than she'd ever been.

She'd never stop missing Laura. Or Jack. And she and Carol were unlikely ever to be any more than acquaintances who had once loved—in very different ways, of course—the same man. But she no longer thought that Laura was perfect, or that Jack was irredeemably flawed. And whatever scars her parents had left her with weren't going to keep her from risking her heart. Not anymore.

Beside her, Josh reached for her hand under the table. She let him take it and held on tight.

ACKNOWLEDGMENTS

When I started writing *Dear Eliza*, my own mom was still alive. When I picked it back up again after a pause, she'd passed away. While Eliza's story is nothing like my own, there is a universality in the pain of grief, and working through Eliza's with her became part of my own journey.

And now for the thank-yous!

First and foremost, thank you to my readers. You have no idea how meaningful it is to know that people as nearby as New Jersey and as far away as Australia have read and loved my debut novel, *Typecast*. Without readers, there would be no books—so, from the bottom of my heart, thank you.

I've been thrilled to get to know fellow authors who are really such a wonderful, supportive, and kind group of people. In particular, it has been a joy to connect with Angela Terry, Lisa Roe, Liz Alterman, Amy Impellizzeri, Nora Zelevansky, Colleen Oakley, Elyssa Friedland, Annie Cathryn, Abbi Waxman, Steven Rowley, Laura Hankin, Jane Rosen, and Judith Natelli McLaughlin.

I also want to thank my Writer's Circle friends—Vinessa Anthony, Michelle Cameron, Debra Feldman, Kim Harwanko, Niv Miyasato, Suzanne Moyers, and Elizabeth Schlossberg—for their feedback each week. Thank you also to my wonderful editor, Sarah Branham Velez—even though you told me I've "graduated," I will always appreciate your insights!

I'm grateful to my friend Stacey Sacks, who connected me

with Cara Bradshaw and Corina Borg so they could give me an inside scoop on working in the nonprofit world—thank you to Cara and Corina! And Naim Bulbulia gave this non-lawyer a crash course in inheritance law. Any errors are my own, not his!

Thank you to my *Dear Eliza* beta readers, Bonnie Lafazan and Christine Krahling. Your close reading and careful commentary were invaluable.

I'm delighted to be back with the terrific team at Girl Friday/Flashpoint—Christina Henry de Tessan, Emilie Sandoz-Voyer, Kristin Duran, Georgie Hockett, Laura Dailey, Karen Upson, and the rest of their wonderful crew.

I also want to thank everyone who supported *Typecast* by posting reviews, inviting me to their book clubs, buying multiple copies for friends and family, and/or sharing the book on social media. This list is far from exhaustive—and apologies to those I missed—but thank you especially to Kathy Abbott, Linda Alberts, Carol Angle, Jennifer Battista, Georgi Becker, Janice Berliner, Heidi Block, Sandy and Jonathan Bloom, Esther Bloustein, Sharon Brody, David Burd, Lisa Campbell, Suzanne Campbell, Cyndi Coe, Melanie Cohn, Celia Colbert, Lacey Cotter, Janell DeGennaro, Carolyn and Brian Dempsey, Mary Dickey, Stacy Donck, Darcy Draeger, Renata Estupiñan, Janet Fiorentino, Marjorie Fox, Heidi Francus, Lara Freidenfelds, Diane Gallo, Heather Gittleman, Nancy Gorman, Nicole Greene, Amanda and Steve Greenblatt, Diann Groff, Gretchen Harders, Susan Haines, Meredith Hendra, Reha Kamdar, Galit Kierkut, Joanne Klapper, Margy Klaw, Karyn Kloumann, Judi Knott, Janice Kovach, Anita Kuan, Natalie Leighton, Ulrika Lerner, Brett Levine, Sandy Louro, Lisa Mandelblatt, Beth Manes, Doreen Markowitz, Carolyn McGhee, Sarah Meiring, Audrey Napchen, Holly Rizzuto Palker, Donna Patel, Nora Radest, Marianne Rampulla, Nancy Jo Rettig, Tina Rosen, Emily Seamone, Hazel Siegel, Judi Sills, Nancy Simon, Ian

Singer, Sheila Srere, Terri Tauber, Meghan Terry, Gwen Thompson, Claire Toth, Jen Velez, Audrey Wallock, Sharon Wesoky, Melanie Wilson, Rania Yi, Mat Zucker, Rachel Zucker, and Mimi Zukoff. And thank you to all the bookstagrammers, book bloggers, and reviewers who had such lovely things to say about my debut novel. I hope you'll enjoy *Dear Eliza*!

Finally, to Bablu, Ravi, and Kieran—I love you more than you could ever know. And I promise that I'm not keeping any earth-shattering secrets from you.

ABOUT THE AUTHOR

© Maricel Stoveken Photography

Andrea J. Stein is the award-winning author of *Typecast* and a lifetime lover of books. Born in Brooklyn, she was raised in New Jersey before attending a small, quirky liberal arts college and a large, preppy university, both in New York State. A book publicist by profession, she lives with her husband and sons in suburban New Jersey.

Andrea spends an inordinate amount of time taking pretty photos of books. Things that make her happy include strong tea, turtles, sunshine, sheep, and the ocean. For more information, go to andreajstein.com and follow her on Instagram at @books.turning.brains_ajstein.

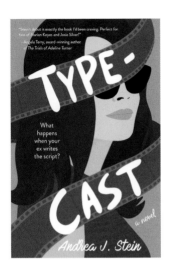

ALSO BY ANDREA J. STEIN

TYPECAST

"Insightful and bighearted and oh-so-deliciously page-turning, *Typecast* is like a road trip with friends, complete with detours and surprises and wildly satisfying moments. A perfect next read for fans of Camille Pagán and Kristy Woodson Harvey, Stein's *Typecast* is a don't-miss debut!"

—Amy Impellizzeri, award-winning author of *I Know How This Ends* and *In Her Defense*

"With patience and realism, Andrea J. Stein explores the complexities of first love, family dynamics, and adulting. A relatable journey fraught with growing pains, *Typecast* reminds us that in order to truly evolve—and find new, lasting love—we must first accept the past and ourselves."

—Nora Zelevansky, author of *Competitive Grieving*

Callie Dressler thought she'd put her past where it belonged—behind her. But when her ex-boyfriend brings their breakup to the big screen, she can no longer deny that their history has been looming over her all along.

At thirty-one, Callie Dressler is finally comfortable in her own skin. She loves her job as a preschool teacher, and although living in her vacant childhood home isn't necessarily what dreams are made of, the space is something she never could have afforded if she'd stayed in New York City. She knows her well-ordered life will be upended when her type A, pregnant sister, Nina; adorable four-year-old niece; and workaholic brother-in-law move in, but how could she say no when they needed a place to crash during their remodel? As Nina pointed out, it's still their *parents'* house, even if their mom and dad have relocated.

As if adjusting to this new living situation isn't enough, the universe sends Callie another wrinkle: her college boyfriend—who Callie dumped ten years earlier for reasons known only to her—has a film coming out, and the screenplay is based on their real-life breakup. While the movie consumes her thoughts, Callie can't help wondering if Nina and her friends are right that she hasn't moved on. When a complication with Nina's pregnancy brings Callie in close contact with Nina's smart and funny architect, Callie realizes she'd better figure out whether she wants to open the door to the past—or risk missing out on her future.

CHAPTER ONE

Before

When I woke up, my arm was asleep. It was neither surprising nor unusual, considering Ethan and I were snug against each other in the twin-size dorm room bed. It would be the last morning we'd wake up together on this thin mattress sagging in the center, tilting us toward each other more than strictly necessary in the narrow space.

I opened my eyes and took inventory of the institutional square I'd worked hard to turn into a home. The framed *Spellbound* poster I splurged on for Ethan's twenty-first birthday hung across from the bed. Other movie posters—*Marathon Man* and *Jaws*—decorated the other walls, and the huge bulletin board for which I had painstakingly chosen fabric was a collage of photos—mostly of Ethan and me—flyers for rallies, on-campus plays, and concerts I meant to attend but never did; takeout menus; birthday cards; and hastily scribbled notes so heartfelt they became keepsakes. A gauzy piece of batik-printed fabric draped the window, hiding the plain white window shade. Two blond wood dressers stood side by side near the closet with its accordion door, the trio of them housing our clothes—Ethan's jeans, plaid shirts, and white T-shirts, and my random assortment of hoodies, loose sweaters, flippy skirts, tights, and a handful of body-hugging scoop-neck tops that I wore occasionally because Ethan liked them. I preferred my "girls"—bigger than oranges but not quite grapefruits—to be a little less conspicuous.

Ethan and I moved in together at the beginning of junior year. Well, kind of. The truth was we each had a single room across the hall from one another. This one we used as our bedroom. The other, as our study. That's where our two desks lived, along with a mini fridge and the other twin bed—which we'd tried to move into this room to create a king, but gave up on when we discovered we'd never be able to open the closet. Besides, we didn't mind having to sleep so close together. A few of my sketches and paintings hung on the walls of the study. A few were from a drawing class I took, and a couple I did on my own, when I realized how much I enjoyed trying to capture images on the page—Ethan's profile when he was studying, his brow furrowed; my favorite tree near the library entrance with its gnarled roots and twisted branches.

This room with this boy had been my home for two straight years, and we'd been together for nearly all four years of college. But yesterday we graduated, and today we were moving out. I was going back to Brook Hill, New Jersey, and Ethan was returning to the suburbs of Chicago. Soon he'd drive out to San Francisco and get us an apartment. The plan was for me to meet him there in September, after spending the summer temping, reconnecting with my parents, and visiting my older sister, Nina, in Manhattan—if she could tear herself away from her office in one of the city's ubiquitous glass towers.

I felt Ethan stir behind me; his hand, which had been resting on my hip, slipped down onto my belly and then slid up toward my breasts. I didn't think our bodies could get any closer, but instinctively, my lower half pushed back toward his as he caressed me exactly the way he knew I liked. I turned toward him, and he pulled my T-shirt over my head.

Afterward, we lay naked and spent. Ethan pushed my hair off my forehead. I'd conducted an unfortunate experiment with bangs a few months prior—they were finally growing out and were at that awkward stage.

"Wow," he whispered. "How am I going to live without that for the next three months?"

I smiled and reached for his hand. "There's always this," I said, giving it a squeeze.

"Ha, ha. As if it's the same." He grinned, his eyes crinkling, but then his face turned serious. "Come on, Callie, spend the summer with me. You can still go home and see your folks first. And then fly out to Chicago so we can drive to California and start our life together." He ran a finger down the side of my face, along my neck, and past my collarbone. "Just think of all the fun we can have on the road."

I giggled. "I'm sure we could," I said, brushing my own hand across the junction between his thighs. But then I looked into his blue eyes, their sandy lashes visible without the barrier of his glasses, and something clenched deep inside me. I swallowed. "But you know I need to spend some time at home. I *want* to spend some time at home. I've barely been there since I left for Welford. Besides, you know what my mom would be like if I changed my plans. She can't stop talking about having her baby back, even if it's just for the summer. If I'm moving all the way across the country from her and my dad, the least I can do is be with them for a while before I go."

Ethan sighed. "Fine—but don't forget, you're *my* baby, too. And come September, you're *all* mine."